DISPOSABLE PEOPLE

A Novel Inspired by True Events

Ezekel Alan

Disposable People

This is a work of fiction. All of the characters, names, incidents, organizations, and dialogue in this novel are either the products of the author's imagination or used fictitiously.

Printed in the United States of America

First Printing, 2012

ISBN-13: 978-1467922739

ISBN-10: 1467922730

FT
Pbk

Dedication

In memory of my mom, dad, sister, dog, and a few of the rest that did not make it out.

"Is it nothing to you, all ye that pass by?" –
The Bible. Lamentations 1:12

"Our past is like our shadow - though it is behind us, it follows." –
Diary of K. Lovelace, June 2009

"If everything written in this diary is true, it would probably mean that I am mad. And the little man sitting at the end of the Ganga spliff hanging from my lips tells me that I am not. If I cannot believe him, then who can I believe? Who can I have faith in?" –
Diary of K. Lovelace, circa 1984

Splinters of Memories

Dedication

Acknowledgements

CHAPTER I

2.15 a.m. - Private Property

My parents often locked me out of the house from I was four years old. This was back in the 1970s when 'house' was a fancy and deceitful way of labeling the one-room structure which I lived in with them and my older brother. My sisters weren't yet born, but my mama and papa were making constant efforts to remedy this.

Whenever they argued, attempted home-based childbirth with an untrained midwife, or just had a random urge for sexual activity, they locked me and my brother out. My brother, Martin, didn't seem to mind as much as I did. It sickened me.

"You don't have nothing better to worry 'bout?" was his way of dismissing my misery.

The windows of our house were made of regular float-glass; they weren't stained or reflective. Whenever the curtains weren't properly drawn, which was always, I could see right through to the dramatic acts of the arguments, the staging for the still-born births, and the performances that ensued when sexual urges are acted on. I remember the shouts and the sounds - the humps, the "push!", the panting, the threats, the encouragements, the "never again!", the "almost there!", the exclamations announcing various forms of arrival, the sympathies.

When they first started locking me out, I was too young to go to school. All the kids in the neighborhood in which we lived, and which the Member of Parliament for the area once slightingly referred to as a 'Depression', went to school at about six years old. This was because no adult thought we could learn anything in school before that age. Rural Jamaica was not like Japan, where kids have tutors before they have teeth.

When they locked me out I had little to do. I didn't want to have to play with marbles, throw rubber bands, or look for John Crow beads to decorate my carton box cars. So I stood there, outside, waiting, even when it rained. Of course, I could have found shelter in anyone's house, on Aunt Martha's veranda, or even under a tree. There were trees like the willow tree, the big guinep tree, and, in my own backyard, the common mango tree under which a wide dry circle appeared after a heavy downpour. Sometimes when it rained we would stand under those trees with our pockets full of marbles chatting about what game we'd play next, now that the ground was wet and wormy.

But when I was locked out, I didn't go under the trees. I stood beside our house, in the rain, getting soaked, smelling the wet earth. The rain tasted bitter as it ran down my lips. Years later I realized that it was the mixture of rain, tears and resentment that I tasted. Standing there swallowing my polluted spit I felt its poison corroding my stomach, and my insides burned. Then I felt like I was living inside another body, and that this was not my life. I was trapped inside someone else's corpse. That person had come for its body and I wanted to give it back to him, but the real me inside had no place to go just yet. My time had not yet come. So we both stood there, waiting.

My neighbor Billy saw me standing in the rain one day. "Kenny, you can borrow my cap," he said, in one of his customary, ill-timed acts of kindness. He didn't know I had completely lost my head and had nothing to put a cap on.

Billy the kind, age nine

I felt I had a right to be inside my house, and so I always stood there, loitering. I never went far, always wanted them to know I was there. Waiting. Perhaps because of this, no matter what I eventually did or which games I sometimes gave into playing, I could always hear them. The sounds. The creaking springs of the mattress. The thump of the bed against the shiny, red, wooden floors that I often had to go down on my knees with a coconut husk brush to clean. Those beautifully shined, wooden floors that would have looked modern and middle-class if the square yardage was larger and if one or two of us kids didn't have to sometimes sleep on them.

I longed for my own - my own room, to be at my own desk, surrounded by schoolbooks with my own name written in them, wearing a headset connected to my own radio and studying under my own desk lamp. Most of all I wanted a house of no sounds, no secrets, no strange people, no arguments. A house in which we – just my papa, mama, me and my brother - could all live normal, wonderful lives. 'Our' house, with rooms for each of us and a fridge well-stocked with food and a bunch of grapes that I could eat every day after school.

Perhaps it was at the beginning of 1979, just after I turned eight, that I began, gradually and painfully, to learn more about our true condition and what was and wasn't, 'ours'. The first thing I learnt, on a walk around the neighborhood one day with my brother and older cousins Wayne and Brian, was that even the one-room structure that we lived in was never truly 'our' house, because it was never our land. I had, many times before, seen the signs indicating 'private property', but on that day I asked Wayne what it meant.

I learnt that our property wasn't private. Wayne explained to me that we – every last one of us - were all squatters on someone else's land. It was a *rich* man's land.

That same day I learnt a lot about the rich and how they lived because, as it turned out, my other cousin, Brian, was an expert on that subject. [Wayne, Brian, Garnett, Tommy, Cudjoe, and Billy were the boys I was closest to while growing up.] One of the first things he did was to explain to me the difference between a man who 'has' money and a man who 'is' money. A man who 'has' money was often the kind that boastfully went into an expensive store and said, "I want that, that, that, that...and, let me see...that!" This kind was normally regarded as a 'hurry come up', newly rich, pretentious person. While respected, they were viewed quite differently from the other kind of men whose wealth had richly stewed for generations, and who were more powerful and established. Whenever this kind of man was seen there would be a flurry of people scrambling to spread the news. "Joe, you see that man sitting in the car over there? That man *is* money!"

In the late 1970s the rich man on whose land we squatted, was considered to *be* money. I never saw him, but a few years later he sent his emissaries to reclaim some land, demolishing two of my aunts' houses, a number of childhood memories and my paper-thin sense of security, all to build a small shopping complex. Thenceforth we lived with the brutally tangible fear that 'our' house, that wasn't ours, could be next.

Back in the seventies, our house was all part of a huge family compound. At first there was one temperamental standpipe in the yard, and one illegal electric connection. Little by little though, and through undisclosed means, a few pioneering relatives rigged their own individual electric connections, which they shared with others. Some built additions onto their houses, some put zinc or wooden fences around their yards, and some sub-let. Wayne told me, however, that no one ever had a title to their piece of land, and that not one single one of these houses was worth more than three quarter cup of dirt.

After this, I started to think more about all the things we shared in that communal yard. As kids we were often sent to aunts and uncles' houses to borrow or lend different items, such as sugar, ice, cornmeal, mackerel, eggs, money, Vaseline, cooking oil, chicken and coffee. I realized that we shared everything, including each other. One of my cousins moved in with us in the mid-1980s, after his parents migrated, joined later by a stray boy my mama found in the market.

It was also during the late seventies that I learnt, through more window-peeping, that, despite the wedding ceremonies and promises to 'take him or her and have no one else', neither the legal nor the common-law spouses in our yard, were 'private property'. When the alert came from a cousin to "hurry and come look!" we would go to the side of someone's house and take turns raising our heads to the window. Brian, giggling, normally made gestures with his hands or mouth, parodying what he saw. I, however, never giggled when I saw the pitch-black, hairy ass of a man who was not my uncle, humping vigorously between the wide-spread legs of my uncle's wife; violating his private property.

"Lord Jesus! Lord Jesus! Have mercy! Have mercy!"

"Bomboclaat! Bomboclaat!"

"Yes! Yes! Fuck it! Fuck it!"

"Raasclaat! Raasclaat! Spread it! Spread it!"[1]

More thumps against the wall; more scrapes against the floor; the guttural repeated phrases. The sounds hurt my ears, as if nails were being hammered in. At times like those I wished I could stop time with the sharp hydraulic brakes of my anger, so I could go and stab the intruder in his back. Something monstrous was taking seed inside of me. However, the elephant may be big but sometimes its feet are tied, and so time passed.

Often, when this man was finished with my aunt, he found me outside, staring at him. Sometimes he smiled, revealing a set of teeth that a cosmetic dentist looking for a challenge would die for. He often tried to rub my head or to give me money to go and buy myself a popsicle. I never let him touch me, and I never took his money.

Brian, on the other hand, lived for such days, and did take his money. He hunted excitement to fill the vacuum inside his head, and on those occasions when he found some, he'd be in pig's heaven. Then he'd constantly replay the scenes for us for days after, until the emptiness returned and something new was needed to fill it. Anytime you saw him it would be the same, "Kenny, you remember...?" followed by

---

1   Raasclaat, bomboclaat, pussyclaat, etc. are all extreme forms of Jamaican expletives and are used with equal fervor during moments of excitement, happiness, or anger.

his left thumb and index finger making the shape of a circle that his right index finger would jab into repeatedly.

Sometimes the adults put their mattresses out to sun. Brian would call us over to show us the many stains. These were often second-hand mattresses inherited from someone else or obtained from the Salvation Army. There were stains of various shapes, sizes, and colors. It would challenge even a modern-day CSI team to have traced every person who humped on those mattresses.

If there was a discount for being dumb, Brian would probably get everything free. At sixteen years old, he still held firm to the belief that Lefty the alphabet salesman on Sesame Street ("Pssst, hey buddy, over here... [Opens coat]... you want an 'O' to buy?") was really preparing kids for drugs. His sense of humor had also not gotten beyond "Hey Kenny, you know what is funnier than 23? Hehehe... 24! Hehehe." He still farted and tensed his body and face as though he was trying to follow through, and then laughed. It was just his level of humor.

When once he begged me for a piece of my mango, it took me less than two minutes to convince him that what he really needed was the love of Jesus Christ. It settled the issue, and I finished my mango, which was one of the things I least liked to share in the world, along with my house, my aunt and, while we are at it... my mama.

The fury I felt the first time my mama closed the door in my face to 'speak' with a gentleman who wasn't my papa, with the curtains carefully drawn, fuelled the anger I'd felt a week previously on finding out that she was in the habit of not telling me the truth.

"If you touch yuself, you going to go blind," she had told me the week before. I was about nine years old.

I asked Wayne about it the same day and he shed some light on this bit of fact, in his own unique manner, "You a jackass? You believe everything people tell you?"

I touched myself that day, and while I feared for a moment that my mama may have been right, I persevered through to the deliciously sweet end, with my vision fully intact. A lot would change thereafter. The newly acquired knowledge that ethics was a foreign language that few people spoke turned out to be very enlightening.

About two years later Wayne also clarified that it also wasn't true that if I didn't ejaculate often and release my 'oil' it would harden in my back and eventually paralyze me. In many ways, Wayne was like my own personal encyclopedia.

Anyway, I also had to acknowledge that even my dog was everyone's dog. He roamed from one house to another to be fed scraps of food, disappearing for an entire day, straying from one yard to the next, before coming back at about 6 p.m. to offer his jaundiced opinion on whatever tidbits survived from our own dinner menu for him to nibble on.

This reminds me of something else.

When I was in the Congo last week, I dropped by an animal shelter to look at a dog, though since I don't live there, I never intended to take him home. I told them I was thinking of adopting one. I saw two cute little mixed-breeds that they said were only six months old.

"They're sisters, the two of them. That one is the shy one," I was informed. But she came to me when I stretched out my hands to her. She came into my arms, and looked at me with tenderness and expectation. "You shouldn't feed her the same food you eat, only dog food. And don't feed her at your table."

I smiled and nodded, but wasn't convinced. These were, again, signs of 'private property' - things I have long stopped believing in. I knew that if I were to ever have another dog, he would live inside the house with me, and my dog would be allowed to have some of my bones.

CHAPTER 2

2.43 a.m. – The Rod of Correction

Sticks and stones
May break your bones,
But words can never hurt -
That's an old time saying;

Now, call a black man a nigger once more,
Tell him his mama is a whore,
And that you've put your finger up his sister's skirt,
Then see if that causes physical pain.

K. Lovelace, June 1999

They said that her pussy was fucked so hard and so often that it was dead and no one would want to fuck it anymore.

Well, it was actually Garnet who said it, and the other boys defended the position. His actual words were:

"Y'all don't see that her pussy get fuck so much that it dead? Y'all idiots? Y'all don't know that pussy only have nine life?"

They said this was the reason no one wanted to fuck my cousin Carmen's pussy anymore. This was a group of teenagers having what, in our yard, would have been considered a scholarly discussion.

Garnet, one of the neighborhood boys who hung around with my cousins, similarly enlightened us to the fact that a coochie was something that could go 'stale' if left inactive for too long and if not frequently 'aired'. He fancied himself to be a 'girl's man'. Also, he'd often passionately claim that his dick was longer than 'six months'. Whenever he made these claims, the other boys, especially the older ones like my brother, laughed and teased him, saying that he was "born beside a pig." Like everyone else, I knew that Garnet loved pork, but I have to confess, I spent the greater part of my childhood laughing at the joke without knowing what it actually meant. What is true, is that Garnet's ego was more brittle than a Chinese-made wine glass, and this teasing frequently led to trouble.

There was not a day that the good Lord gave us, that there wasn't an argument in that yard. The adults mainly rowed over gambling, or politics, which many folks thought was sweeter than pork. People loved politics back then, and would wait until their dogs turned eighteen to try and get them enumerated so that they too could vote Socialist or Labourite. And everyone was illiterate and ignorant, in spite of all the Free Education, JAMAL and other government programs. My grandma was clear on the fact that Acts of Parliament could not undo the Laws of Nature. The poor, she said, will always be with us, and so too, in her words, "the damn illiterates."

Whatever the adults did, we as kids did as well, so we argued a lot too. Often this was over marbles or someone saying something hurtful about your sister or just mentioning your mama in a conversation. Rarely, though, did one of those arguments turn out as badly as this one about my cousin's coochie.

The brawl in our yard required parents and neighbors to grab and haul the group of us hot-tempered boys, still trying to throw punches, apart. At the end of it, eight of us got our asses whipped good and proper by our parents. My brother and I knew we'd get a beating; this was in line with the traditions of rural Jamaica when boys were caught fighting. But we didn't expect the mother of all whippings.

"What you fighting for Martin? Bwoy, don't you hear me talking to you? Oh, so you deaf? Kenny, you deaf too? Well y'all just wait! Y'all just wait and see!" I can't begin to count the number of times I had heard these expressions from my mama. I therefore knew that the waiting was to see what'd happen when papa got home.

At the time mama was suffering her own personal Great Depression, but that's another subject for another time. Suffice to say that on that day she also said that we had gotten onto her "very last nerve!" which I suspected to be at the very back of her head in a remote spot. Because of this, the regular buckled belt was not considered adequate for the crime we had committed. This is how it came to pass in those days of 1982, that she asked my papa to prepare a special Rod of Correction from the branches of the tamarind tree. World without end, it was dreadfully painful! But by the standards of the day, it wasn't child abuse.

Looking back now, I believe it was not only the statement about my cousin itself, which was presented as a matter of *fact*, but the passion and conviction with which it was made and defended which truly reflected the thickness of the fog of darkness and ignorance that blanketed our deep rural community.

CHAPTER 3

3.17 a.m. — Crime Doesn't Pay

I had hesitated a while, Semicolon, but finally I read the letter they sent. It was dated June 16, 2010. I read it in September.

In it, they said that he was now dead. Uncle Bob. Good old Uncle Bob. Finally. Dead and gone. Twenty-seven fucking years late, if anyone were to ask me, but dead. That's what they said.

Isn't it a strange world when the people you most want to see dead turn out to be the ones to live the longest? My grandpa was right, there really ain't no justice in this world. So much for pastor and his sermons, and his false promises. So much for the years I spent in church, listening to him preach that *Crime Doesn't Pay,* that *The Wicked Will Soon Be Wiped Away From the Face of the Earth* and that the Savior will *soon* return. We sure learn our lessons.

I was at college in Kingston in 1988. I had taken one of the buses that ran from Papine to August Town. We all had to pay our fare to a conductress who sat on a seat near to the rear exit. A young man came on the bus and walked past her. She reminded him, "Young man, you need to pay your fare." He reminded her that, according to the Church, "Crime doesn't pay." He added, "Bitch." Then he raised his shirt to confirm to us all that he was, in fact, the Crime whose coming was foretold. He then robbed half of us before jumping off the moving bus and disappearing into some alleyway. I had already stopped going to church, and I would not go back for over twenty years.

Uncle Bob kept on living for those twenty years and more - one of the few to reach a ripe old age. On top of that, he had the luxury of dying peacefully in his sleep. In their letter, they said that he looked "more peaceful and content than a Rasta man smoking weed." I wonder what pastor would have made of that. No cancer. No bullets. No diabetes. No kidney failure. No murder by mob. No Alzheimer's. No maggots eating him. No signs of fucking retribution. Just calm and content. Finished royally fucking us, so he rolls off to sleep, and leaves us to find our own comforts. Just like that.

CHAPTER 4

4.21 a.m. - Belligerent Masturbation

"It seems that I have missed my revolution. I have been running to catch up with it for an awfully long time, but I must stop now, although I have no idea where I am."

K. Lovelace, September 2010

"It doesn't need to be dark, rainy or gloomy outside for us to speak the truth." This was a common expression back when I was a child growing up in rural Jamaica. I generally never took note of it, and for well over seventeen years the expression had completely slipped my mind, until my second wife, herself being Jamaican, scribbled it down as the introduction to the most hurtful note anyone has ever written to me. A picture may be worth a thousand words, but I cannot think of a picture that could capture the 652 words that followed that opening. Anyway, that note wasn't the reason I remembered the expression a couple days ago while sitting in Heathrow Airport. And while I was in fact in London, it also wasn't rainy, gloomy or dark outside.

I had been sitting in the lounge for a while, before I met Secret Agent Piu Piu Piu, who had, secure in her possession, a document full of important secrets that no one else should ever find out about. She was the youngest member of the Secret Service - she could not yet even spell her own name, and was so secret that not even the Service was aware of her existence. She was fighting some really horrible, bad men, and her fearlessness had no limits. "Piu! Piu, piu, piu, piu, piu!" she shot at them.

I had moments like those when I myself was a child; days when there was nothing that my superhuman powers could not conquer. Sometimes I wonder whether my life would have turned out differently if moments like those occupied more of my childhood.

Instead, the truth is, when I was a child, I was often ashamed and afraid – nay, terrified - of many things. No real surprise there – poor, skinny-ass negro in deep, rural Jamaica must have plenty to be ashamed of, and those being the days when a man and his mule were likely to share the same beliefs, a child would often be afraid of even his own shadow.

I was also often unhappy, that is until a Jehovah Witness lady, fearing for my soul, gave me a pamphlet to read. "Ever wonder why you are unhappy on earth? Well, it's because earth is not your home." Wow! Puzzle solved! Enlightenment! After that, I could file away unhappiness and focus squarely on my fears.

What really struck me the other day, is just how deep rooted our fears can be, and how easily a person's childhood terrors can be aroused when, thirty years later, he looks up and sees the thing he feared most in his life, sitting comfortably across from him in an airport lounge thousands of miles from where it was spawned.

Let me explain. When I was ten years old, I made my own secret, Top Ten list of the scariest things in the world. I wrote my final draft in my home-made diary on one of those days when I didn't have any global summits to attend, or people in collapsing buildings to save. I remember agonizing over which terrors should be included and what order they should have. After a week, I was satisfied. The only change I ever made to that list was done about three months after, when I erased what was in the Number 1 spot, and replaced it with the thing that sat across from me at Heathrow.

Nuclear war would have been at the top of the older folks' list of fears in 1980. Almost every day, and especially after the seven o'clock television news, I heard them discussing what Russia or America might do to keep Jamaica in the socialist or capitalist flock; what was already done to Cuba and what the Americans might do to Grenada now that some group of moving jewels had seized power and were reaching out a friendly hand to the Russians. [Much later I recognized the name "New Jewel Movement" in a political science class at college.] The tantalizing question which capped these conversations, centered on which side - the Russians or the Americans, might be evil enough to drop the first nuclear bomb.

But this seemingly inevitable war, that could be the END TO ALL MANKIND, did not make my Top Ten list. It wasn't because I thought of a nuclear war in the same way as I thought of the doomsday messages in cartoons, or that I was too young to appreciate the gravity of war. Even at that age, my mind could form clear images of bombs exploding and ripping people apart, and I was old enough to know that Superman would not appear to save the day. My ever-imaginative mind could also visualize the Russian submarines stealthily crawling along the bottom of the Caribbean Sea, unseen but deadly like serpents in tall grass. I understood these things, and so I listened intently to the talk. I knew the military strategies that the two sides were employing; the names of the main communists, suspected spies and CIA 'operatives' in Jamaica; where some of them had their nests, and what those niggas were trying to do to our country. At ten years old I was very well-informed.

The reason I swallowed these nightly stories, digesting them with the juice from my King Kong popsicles, and later went to sleep with nothing but Tweetie Bird on my mind, was that I never thought I would actually ever see a Russian, a submarine, or a nuclear bomb. This was, simply, too far removed from the realm of what I considered possible.

Instead, the Top Ten list of things that scared the shit out of me, was made up of things that I considered real or highly probable.

For example, taking up the Number 10 spot, was seeing my papa coming home angry. Even under the best of circumstances, the sternness in my papa's eyes was harder to face than a life sentence. On the days when he was angry the sun would take cover behind the clouds, leaving them to darken the day and the personality of everyone in and around our house. My papa was not one of those men who came home with their livers drowning in alcohol and mouths drooling acid rain, so when he was angry it meant that his violence could neither be confused nor excused. And he was in the habit of laying a violent hand to quell the most modest irritation.

The neighbors would see him coming too and busy themselves, pretending to be working harder than Panamanian whores, but all really just curious to see what would happen. I often felt the urge to cry without knowing why, while trying to keep quiet and still inside our house. Waiting for his hurricane to blow away. The only reason this *dread* was not higher on my list was because, order was based on whether there were remedies and protections available. In the case of my papa, I knew that if I behaved my ass and stayed out of sight when he came home angry, then he would likely go to the side of the house with his cigarette or weed and gradually release his rage. This way I would smell smoked anger, but wouldn't have to taste it.

At Number 9 were those large, gray, croaking lizards that always came inside our house, climbing up to the roof and threatening to free fall on me during the night and then slither inside my nose or ears to gain access to my tasty brain. I had few protections against them: I would either try to get a position closer to the middle of the bed with my brother to the wall or, if my brother was being a bitch and pushed me against the wall, then I would try not to sleep at all.

In 8th place, was the three-legged horse that folks had habitually seen pulling a coffin through the village at night. If you were caught alone late at night by that three-legged horse, then it would be your sorry ass that would find itself inside that coffin. I used the simplest form of protection against this: I kept my sorry ass at home late at night.

The reason why no dinner appeared on our table for days in a row, came in at Number 7. I was increasingly afraid of this because I knew it wasn't due to my mother's occasional bouts of forgetfulness. Somehow, by the end of the 1970s, I had a growing suspicion that my family was joining the ranks of 'the poor'. Borrowing more from the neighbors and eating fewer meals, were some of the lesser consequences of becoming poor; being told to swallow your spit for dinner was an example of the more worrying trend of increasing callousness in parent-child conversations. It did not take long before I learnt that it was wiser to "keep your raasclaat mouth shut" than to recommend higher sources of protein than butter to accompany the bread for breakfast.

Upon turning ten, it was also made clear to me that I now needed to join the ranks of the working class that carried buckets to fetch water in the mornings in order for our families to bathe, cook and clean. This involved walking a few miles and past the houses of folks who you didn't want to see you (young girls especially). I went with my bucket on top of my head in the discreetly early hours of the morning, not wanting these folks to know that I was one of 'the poor'.

The realization that we were poor and getting poorer sank in at about the same time as I started noticing the size of my mama's little bundle of cash which she wrapped in a handkerchief and tucked away in her bosom. This was her meager earnings from selling stuff in various markets during the week and on weekends. I wasn't sure why she insisted on concealing her dwindling bundle when it was clearly time to take it openly to the Lord in prayer, and ask for it to be multiplied so she could feed her family. "That's what they did with the five fishes in the Bible," I told her one day. She slapped my ears, hard.

I should say that in those early days I had also started to wonder if

26

mama needed to learn Aramaic, which is the language pastor said that Jesus spoke, to avoid any further misunderstandings in her increasingly frequent but obviously futile communications with the Lord.

I sure wasn't fat in the morning; even less so by evening. 'Skinny' and 'wormy' are only introductory words. The sad thing was that the change in our condition appeared to me not only irrefutable but unstoppable. I had neither remedy nor protection against our poverty. The only reason this did not occupy a higher position is because there were things much more frightening on my list.

Count Dracula terrified me! As kids, we told vampire stories almost every night on someone's veranda. After, I would spend the night watching for bats at my bedroom window and listening for a voice asking for permission to come in. But Dracula was no higher than Number 6 because, at the end of the day, if you had garlic, then you also had Dracula by his balls.

The Blackheart Man was at Number 5 because, though he had fewer powers than Dracula, he was more real. Every now and then, we would hear about a child that was killed in the bushes and had their heart ripped out by the Blackheart Man. As such, we were constantly reminded never to walk through certain bushes alone, and never to take the *short cut* home as he would be waiting there. Yours truly never took the short cut home.

The ghost of an Indian woman, known as *Coolie Duppy*, was the 4th most frightening thing on my list. It was real, because others had seen it. It was also the meanest and most malicious of the evil spirits. Alive, Coolies (Indians) were known for their laziness and for being the worst liars and thieves. Coolie men had no redeeming qualities whatsoever, even though they liked playing cricket. As for the women, their only slightly compensatory qualities for being extremely nasty in their house cleaning habits, were their crotch and their curry. With regards to the crotch, it was a known fact that Coolies had 'white liver', which accounted for their remarkable sexual stamina. This was the reason some black men slept with them. Since there is no point in hiding it now, I should say that in my later days, I took a few samples to my Petri Dish apartment for observation and, more importantly, testing. I noticed no real difference between them and black women, beyond a certain degree of hairiness.

Dead, all the nasty things about Coolies were multiplied a thousand times over. Coolie Duppies were masters of deception - appearing as your grandmother; a real person walking ahead of you in the lane at night when you are anxious for company; or maybe even your dog. They would call your name in a human voice, just so that you would say 'yes' and in so doing invite them to follow you home. Once they came home with you, things would start to go dreadfully wrong… and it was one of the hardest things to get rid of them. Maybe your papa would lose his job, then break his leg, then get sick and meager, and, sooner or later, die.

The Rolling Calf was Number 3. This was no 'calf', but a huge black bull with the fires of hell rolling in its eyes. This evil spirit was rarely seen and always in the very late hours of the night. Once it saw you, from whatever distance, it was impossible for you to outrun it. Immediately your head would begin to swell, your tongue would thicken and fall to the bottom of your mouth, your eyes would bulge, your feet would become heavy and immobilized. Essentially, from what people said, you would soon be unable to move, speak or close your eyes, and would therefore have to watch the unspeakable horrors that this evil thing would then do to you, eating your intestines and all. The thought of it sent shivers down my spine. There were nights when I could swear that there was a Rolling Calf at the back of our house, quietly snorting fire and waiting for my mama to ask me to go outside and get her a drink of water. There were protections, mostly involving things you could do with a piece of old iron, but I always thought it was safer to simply stay inside.

Number 2 was the ghost of a baby, or *Baby Duppy*. Outside of the devil, there was nothing more evil than this Duppy. It would often appear as a real baby on someone's doorstep, but it could also take on the appearance of anything or anyone, to ensnare you. Sometimes you could hear it crying outside at night, waiting for someone to come and take it up and bring it inside.

Whereas the Coolie Duppy lived in your house and brought so much bad luck and evil that someone might eventually die, the Baby Duppy went straight to business. It would jump on your back and start sucking your life juice out of you. Like a malicious ex-wife, a Baby Duppy would suck you dry! You could not dislodge it, no matter how frantically you shook yourself or slammed your body against the wall or the ground. It wouldn't take weeks, but days, before you died. The only remedy against the Baby Duppy was a powerful Obeahman[2]- a witchdoctor, who knew how to prepare a special, potent 'bath' that could dislodge the Duppy quickly, before it could suck you dead.

With the Baby Duppy also came the constant worry about whether someone meant you harm. Perhaps some wicked, nasty, grudgeful, dirty, worthless, vengeful person might go to an Obeahman to ask him to set a Baby Duppy on you. It was best not to leave any form of personal effect (shoes, socks, comb, etc.) outside your house at night, in case one of those niggas found it and brought it to an Obeahman who would hand it on to the Duppy, so that it could find you wherever in the world you went.

This was the Top Nine. The Baby Duppy had once been Number 1, but now I had something more terrifying than all these horrors combined in that spot.

---

2   If you have heard of voodoo, Black magic or Witchcraft then you have heard of Obeah. This is the Jamaican version of the various forms of black magic brought to the Caribbean in the bowels of slave ships from Africa. The person who brought it was the only slave who didn't lose weight on the journey, who wasn't whipped, and who never had one of the white men look him in his eyes as he sat without working throughout the long journey across the sea. I shit thee not, that dude was the Obeahman!

Almost every night in 1980, while the adults talked about elections and war, the older boys took turns telling us stories on someone's veranda. These stories generally left us younger boys shit-scared.

Then, later in the night, mama would invariably ask, "Kenny, go outside and get me a glass of water."

Then I would in turn ask, "Martin, can you follow me to get-" before being cut off by his usual, curt, "Why the raasclaat you can't get it yourself?" And thus I prepared myself mentally for the whipping to come, as my feet became paralysed and planted themselves like a tree on the spot. I always knew that my mean-spirited brother would not follow me, as he knew perfectly well what the combination of mama's request, the dark, and a lack of company would lead to. The nigga relished it when I got whipped.

One night, almost three months after I had made my list, I finally erased the Baby Duppy from the Number 1 spot, after Courtney told us a story that has lived with me ever since. It went something like this:

Once upon a time, there was a man who lived alone with his son and daughter in Sligoville. The man's name was Joseph and his fourteen year old son was called Little Jay. His daughter, Pamela, was five years old. The man had lost his wife two years before, when his donkey fell off a mountainside while carrying her from the market.

One morning Mas Joseph asked Little Jay to go to the market to buy some yam, cassava, peppers and pork for them to cook for dinner later that day. He gave Little Jay some money and a bag of limes and sent him on his way to the market. When he got to the market, Little Jay went to the food stalls and bought the yam and cassava. He then went by Mas Tom's stall and got the pepper. His papa was a good friend of Mas Tom, and Mas Tom would always give them a little extra pepper or maybe some onions or pimento. They traded the limes for the pepper with Mas Tom.

On his way to the meat section of the market, Little Jay saw a woman sitting by herself at a stall, in an area of the market that he had not noticed before. She looked like an old woman, but it was hard to see her clearly or what she was selling. She seemed alone. Little Jay's mama had always told them to be kind to older people, and so he decided to go by her stall and see what she was selling. He was sure that his papa would not be mad at him if he bought something small from the old lady, so that she could have some money to take care of her own kids. Many older folks also liked having a young boy or girl to talk to, and it would probably make her smile if he went and said hello. He was very polite, Little Jay was.

Instead of going to buy the pork, Little Jay went over to where the old lady was sitting with her back to him. He then politely said, "Excuse me, mam, what are you selling?" [I knew at this point that this was not a Jack and the Beanstalk story.]

She started to slowly turn around to face him. It was then that Little Jay noticed the old woman's cloven feet, like a goat's hoofs, sticking out beneath her dress. He started to step back, but it was too late. She turned and raised her head and looked at him with surprise. Then he saw her deep, blue eyes.

For a moment he was paralysed as she spoke to him. Then Little Jay dropped his bag of food and his money and ran without stopping all the way home to his papa. He fell into his papa's arms and started crying and wailing, saying that he was going to die. Mas

Joseph asked him what happened and Little Jay explained that he had just seen the devil and she was going to take his soul. He told his papa about the old lady in the market and how surprised she had looked to see him. He said that once he saw her eyes he knew that she had come for him to take him away, and that he had to get far away from Sligoville. Mas Joseph didn't know what was happening or what to do, but he could see that something terrible had happened to Little Jay and that he was deeply afraid. He told Little Jay to take their donkey and go, as fast as he could, to his grandmother in Trelawny, which was very far away. Little Jay ran outside immediately, without taking anything with him, and jumped onto the donkey. He went straight away to Trelawny.

About an hour after Little Jay left, his papa decided to go to the market to see what had happened and exactly what Little Jay had seen. When he got to the market, he walked around for a long time, looking for an old lady sitting by herself in the market. He was almost about to give up when he finally saw what looked like an old lady in a part of the market he hadn't noticed before.

Mas Joseph went over to the old lady, whose back was turned towards him. "Excuse me, mam, my son came to the market this morning and said he saw an old woman-"

"Yes, I saw Little Jay," the old woman said, before he finished. This made Mas Joseph very worried as he did not know how this woman came to know his son's name. He then said to the old lady, "He told me that you are the devil and that you have come to take his soul. He said that once someone sees your eyes, they will die."

The old woman again said, "Yes, I have come for his soul." Mas

Joseph was now becoming afraid of this mysterious old woman and what she was saying. [Courtney's imitated old woman voice was very chilling.] Before he could say anything else, however, he noticed her feet, which were cloven, like a goat's hoofs, as Little Jay had said. He then started to back away, as he asked her, "But he said that you looked surprised to see him, was that true?"

For the third time the old lady said "Yes." She paused, then went on to say, "I was surprised to see Little Jay here this morning, Mas Joseph, because I was expecting to see you. I was supposed to see Little Jay in Trelawny this evening and take his soul from there."

The old lady then turned and looked at Mas Joseph with her evil, deep-blue eyes.

That story screwed me up for about two months! It was partly the message that our fate follows us wherever we go. It was partly the coldness, cruelty and vileness of an evil that would take a man and his son and leave behind his five year old daughter. But it was also something about an evil that would show no pity to a boy who was attempting to show kindness. It was the chilliness of the imitated voice that Courtney put on to let us know that there are evils in this world that do not mind explaining to us who they are and what they will do to us, knowing there was nothing we could do to stop them. I tried hard to avoid looking down on any woman's feet. I couldn't be made to go to the market (more whippings). I constantly looked behind me wherever I went. I became suspicious of the movements of my own dark shadow. I asked my mama if I could sleep by my grandma, whose house had no glass windows to see anything or anyone through at night.

That was thirty years ago, and the thing I feared most in life was Evil in human form, with deep-blue eyes.

You can put your childhood memories behind you, but, like your shadow, they always follow. Your childhood fears and shames do not need to take a cab to come and visit. Wherever you are, open your closet, choose your shirt for the day, and say hello.

Back to Heathrow Airport, 2011. After the encounter with Agent Piu Piu Piu, I saw a spoilt six or seven year old child fuss and cry herself to sleep at her North American-looking mother's side, a few seats to my right.

The preceding conversation:

"Mom, what happens if the plane starts to crash when we're flying over the ocean?"

"They'd give us a flotation device... I mean a lifejacket or something to use when we're in the water."

"They wouldn't give us a parachute to fly to land?"

"No sweetheart, we would get a lifejacket or something like that."

"But if we're in the water, the sharks will come and eat us Mommy! They'd just let us die like that?"

"No love, no sharks would eat us. We'd be rescued-"

"But why can't they give us parachutes? The sharks will eat us! I don't want them to leave me in the sea so the sharks can eat me!"

Tears, then sobs, then sleep, followed. She was probably returning from vacation, had been to an aquarium and seen a few sharks baring their teeth, or had watched a discovery channel feature on the last leg of their flight.

It was after that, that I saw the Western European-looking woman. She was white and holding a Chinese-looking child. She must have adopted him before the new *too fat, too single, too old, too poor* Chinese adoption policy, that came into effect a few years ago. I spent a little time watching mother and child interact, which was very much in line with Standard Western Operating Procedures: the child laughed, then ran, and the mother smiled, encouraged and tickled, and so on.

As my eyes drifted from them, I noticed a McKinsey label on a folder resting on a laptop in the seat beside the lady. I could tell it wasn't hers. When I looked up, I saw a human form with the deepest blue eyes I had ever seen. I immediately felt the cold sweat run down my neck, and my hands trembled. Something inside me cried out. I am a grown man, I know, but these things have grown with me.

Blue-eyed Ignacio was from Barcelona, Spain. He was a strategy consultant with global management consultancy, McKinsey, and had spent three years in their office in Norway - partly because his mother was Scandinavian. She was the reason for his icy-cold, continental shelf dark, ocean-blue eyes.

He had a copy of the FT - standard reading material for business school graduates, but was engrossed in Simon Winchester's *Krakatau*. He appeared 'decent' and focused.

Though undoubtedly over-worked like all young consultants, Ignacio seemed quite comfortable and relaxed. Perhaps his conscience was clear. Perhaps he had nothing to fear. *He* had no need to wear an amulet to protect him against anything from his past that might still be following him across continents. *He* didn't have childhood memories reclined in seats 12 F and D, requesting blankets and an extra pillow, and waiting for him to come onboard. *He* had no reason to wonder whether someone might come up to him there in the lounge and ask, "Hey, were you the one whose sister used to poo in her chimney while sitting on the veranda and waving to people passing by?" Not him. This man was used to traveling far from home in airplanes, and from an early age. This man never had to drive an imaginary car to school. This man went skiing in the winter, and, in the spring, played in the grass with a dog that he would never secretly hope would forget its way home. Ignacio was comfortable in his skin - the boy Simon and Garfunkel thought was "born at the right time."

I initiated the conversation; part of a tried and proven method of conquering my fears. He was on his way to start a one-year assignment in

Jakarta, Indonesia, where I too was heading.

"You'll probably find yourself a nice Indonesian wife and a couple of kids, if some large, pot-bellied Australian doesn't beat you to it!" I made my best attempt at good-humor. "And a small, well-trained dog that won't bark at Muslims when you take it for a walk." He laughed. I kept my eyes diverted from his, preferring to watch the planes outside touching down, their pilots landing them nice and smooth like a black man saying "hey baby" in a night club.

I wondered whether Ignacio was just a regular two-kids-and-a-dog straight kind of guy, who would wear his wedding ring when he went on business trips to Bangkok. Or, maybe straighter? Maybe the too-straight kind that would go searching for ambiguity after hours in the notorious Block M neighborhood of Jakarta?

I was also thinking that even though the two of us - two consultants, both going to Jakarta, may seem superficially alike, one was feeling like a goat in a woman's womb. A man may win an Olympic gold medal in a blaze of glory, and another may collect one two years later after someone has been disqualified. There are some who will say it is still gold, but I have always known the difference. I know that we are not the same, and that it doesn't make a difference that I understand the subject of dark matter or have traveled to countries that have 95% of the elements of the periodic table in their soil. I am still who I am.

Ignacio looked to be in his late twenties, but spoke with the soft, measured tone of someone older, wiser. He didn't speak of parties or women; didn't mention the latest iPhone or Blackberry; didn't drop a hint about his frequent flyer status or whether a Gold, Platinum or Senator card or cash had gotten him into the lounge. He was well dressed, with his shirt neatly tucked into his pants, and he kept his fingernails short and clean. He had had a recent haircut, wore plain, white shirts and, I imagined, had on his 'Saturday' boxers to match the day.

In our conversation he mentioned God respectfully. Had my

grandma been alive, she would not have spoken to him, because as an older generation of slave descendants her views on color and class were different from ours, but she may have given him one of those tender smiles normally reserved for polite grandkids, or have tried to touch his hand in case he was, in fact, God.

We spent most of the time talking about the Spanish Civil War and what it had done to people – to neighbors, friends, and families. Ignacio's father had told him many stories of Franco's era. We compared notes with what I had heard about Bosnia. I had been there a few years before on a business trip and had taken a tourist tour which included a visit to a cemetery on the hills surrounding the city. Our guide was once a doctoral student in Sarajevo, but after the war, ended up driving a taxi and offering tours as a second job. He was very knowledgeable. His not-so-subtle message in the selection of the cemetery as the location to narrate the history of the war wasn't lost on me – having heard about how the war had begun, all we needed to do was look around and see how it ended. This was part of his perverse punch line.

I told Ignacio what I had learnt from the guide that day, but mostly I listened to his stories of Spain. I believed the stories told to him by his papa were faithfully recounted. I felt his father in him. I had a feeling that his father often called him 'son'.

Ignacio suggested that I watch the film 'Pan's Labyrinth', or 'El Laberinto del Fauno' in Spanish, to learn more about that era. I felt the usual impulse to say that I would look for it on Blockbuster and watch it, but I didn't. As consultants, we know the percentage of time that people actually follow through on their promises - whether to buy a book someone recommended, to give someone a call to "do lunch" next week, or to start saving *soon*. That's the kind of stuff they teach you in Human Psychology and Behavior classes in business school. To Ignacio's recommendation, I simply said, "Interesting."

He mentioned his insomnia. As consultants, we invariably always talk about how much we work, and how little we sleep. Insomnia is an abomination. I told him that mine was back as well. His was, he felt, due to the late nights and frequent travel across different time zones. Melatonin no longer seemed to make a difference. He asked me what I thought was causing mine. I told him I wasn't sure, but that somehow I felt as though a civil war was going on inside me.

"Hehe," he chuckled. "What do you think you're fighting against?"

"You know, I am really not sure... still trying to figure it out." The truth would have taken only two words: my past.

"Like a civil war, huh? My dad once told me that a civil war is like belligerent masturbation..." He chuckled again.

The moment he said it, I understood what he meant - sometimes self-exploration can indeed be painful. Perhaps like writing a memoir I thought.

CHAPTER 5

In the Beginning

Dear Semicolon,

I might as well use all these sleepless nights productively. I do need to tell you my story. It is not about birds and trees and colors and smells, but about people, and what happened to them.

Last night I had another dream. It seems like the pattern may have broken as I dreamt about someone I did not know. Her name was Cheryl. I can't remember her face, but she died in the dream. She may have been a character from Law and Order or CSI, but I can't quite recall.

I dream every night. Normally the same dream stays with me for weeks, sometimes months. I did not tell you this before, Semicolon, but there is a dream that has plagued me, on and off, for the past seven months. An awful dream.

I am alone in my mama's womb, slurping her vitamins and minerals. Then the devil comes to visit me, right there in her womb. He comes in the body of a child and snuggles up beside me, as though we were twins. He has the creased face of a weary old man, but I know who he is, just as certain as he knows who I am. He puffs smoke from a cigar into my face and tells me that he has come to make me an offer. The negotiation is always, fittingly, brief.

"If you want to make it out of here alive and see the world that your so-called creator has made for you, you must promise me one thing: when the time comes you must say one word and one word only, 'No'. You will know when the time has come. Are we agreed?"

Sometimes in my dream I think I see him smile before leaving, but at other times he appears not to complete the effort. Then he vanishes. Without waiting for my answer.

People tell me that there were complications during my birth. They say that I bloody nearly killed my mama. Breech birth, with another one of those untrained midwives, in our old one-room house, far from the hospital in which my mama and papa would both die years later. My mama was bleeding so badly that the *Nigga, it's either gonna be me or you* time was approaching. But then, according to the Old Timers, 'something' happened and my body, mysteriously, turned.

When those dreams started seven months ago, I wondered if they were my forefathers' way of telling me that that 'something' was, in fact, real – that, just over forty years ago, I gave the devil the answer he wanted before he stuck his hands up my mama's womb and turned my head. In any event, my story began under mysterious circumstances, and the Old Timers said that either the hand of God, but more likely that of the devil, was involved.

I was born to Charles and Sonia Lovelace, in a remote, rural village in Clarendon, Jamaica. A small village. A *hateful* fucking place.

They gave me the name Kenneth. Kenneth E.S. Lovelace. Folks generally called me Kenny. They sometimes called me Stephan, which is one of my middle names. This was initially done to confuse the evil spirits that an Obeahman had convinced my parents was following me, when I was about seven or eight. After a while, Kenny and Stephan were used interchangeably. Sometimes in that *hateful* fucking place, folks would also call me Stupid or Jackass, but everyone gets called names at some point in their lives, so I don't hold it against them.

I was born on December 2, 1970. It should have been December 3, from what my mama always said, but it wasn't, and, since then, my life has been filled with what could or should have been.

I didn't become who I am yesterday on an Air France flight. I have always been me. This is the hand I have today.

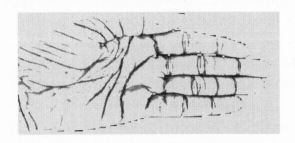

It is the same hand that I was born with. Most folks in the *hateful* village where I grew up use the terminology of gambling to describe the hand I was dealt. They all say it is a 'bad hand.' A hand with these many lines is a sign of a curse. Kids are supposed to be born with three main lines in their hands, forming the outlines of an 'M'. An 'M' for money. Not me.

Also, I have a nose that would be too large for a horse but which could help a rhino win a beauty contest. Courtesy of my iPhone, this is my nose, it has caused me endless grief.

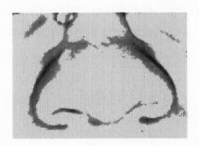

If you happy and you know it clap your hands
If you happy and you know it clap your hands
If you happy and you know it, and you really want to show it
If you happy and you know it clap your hands...

My family? Dead silence from the Church benches. We were a real sad ass family. Darkness described not only our pigmentation, but also our living and mental conditions.

On my side of the big, communal yard there were somewhere between 80 to 90 of us, though at the time it felt like 5 billion. My own immediate family, not counting the dog, accounted for 7: mama, papa, three sisters, a brother and me. Then there were the uncles (4), aunts (5), grandparents (2), cousins, more cousins, even more cousins, then second cousins and even more second cousins. On the other side of the big yard lived another 70 or so people who weren't related to us, including Tommy and his family, who all looked like burnt fries. I never learnt how all these people came together on that squatted land. I suspect it may have had something to do with someone on my side of the family renting out some land to outsiders, and those outsiders gradually bringing in their own relatives, having kids, and multiplying like rabbits. Until there was a multitude of them.

Collectively we owned a large piece of nothing - not one of us had more than dried shit in our behinds. Even those who later made it out and migrated never felt comfortable when they tipped.

The dog was popularly called Damn Dog or Rassclaat Dog, but officially christened Ruffy. He was, somehow, considered to be my dog. That's enough about me.

Now,

> *Eeny, meeny, miny, mo,*
> *catch a rabbit by his toe,*
> *if you ever let him go,*
> *then eeny, meeny, miny, moe: Brian!*

Brian it is then.

CHAPTER 6

He Had Really Nice Hair

In 1983, when I last admired Brian's hair, he was sixteen years old, not fourteen as I had written in my home-made diary. And in that same year, it was me, not him, who had watched my mama give birth to another still-born child. It was me, not him, who had stood there at the float-glass window, thirteen years old, bugle eyes raptly watching my sister come from between my mama's legs. Watching the musical chords wrapped tightly around her neck, body puffed and purple like a Jazz trombonist holding a high, melancholic F. But no sounds came. There was just the one bloodied, stiff hand pointing in the direction my sister's soul had gone.

In 1984, it was Wayne's sister, not Brian's, who had lost her unwashed, fifteen year old virginity, and her way home after that. Virginity, like identity, once lost, was never regained in our neighborhood, and she was no longer considered to be her mama's child. So it was Wayne's sister, Punky, who became another child-mother put out of her mama's house, and who had to quickly learn the secrets of pleasing and keeping a much older, rent-paying, food-buying, partner-abusing, man.

In that same year, it was not Brian's parents, but another couple unrelated to us, and who lived in the oldest, most rundown house on the other side of the yard, whose fecundity marveled me. They had nineteen fucking children and lived in one of the most depressing houses I have ever seen.

"Wayne, I went inside their house!"

"Is lie you telling!"

"I serious as a judge! You want to know what inside their house look like?"

"Tell me!"

"Close your eyes."

"What?"

"Just close your eyes. Tighter! Can you see the darkness?"

"Yes...?"

"That's it!"

Nineteen of them in that one house, the last child a mongoloid that people said was the result of incest. All in all, a wretchedness fossilized and traceable to the mammoth misery of their forefathers. But theirs is another story, not Brian's.

The disturbing memories I have of the pathetic, rusty, decrepit old man playing with a dirty, half-naked female doll every freaking day that the good Lord gave him, are memories of my own senile grandfather, not his.

And while Brian was indeed the type of person that would make butter afraid to spread, the little nigga was never arrested for rape. That was Garnet.

The first time I wrote about what happened to Brian it was in a story I scribbled in my diary. I embellished it quite a bit to make it a more interesting read. This is what really happened:

June 14, 1983. Truth be told, they had indeed beaten him severely that day. But, contrary to my first written account, the reason they had held Brian against the wall and literally beaten the shit out of him, was not for raping a girl. The real reason was the goat. No, he had not raped a goat; he had attempted to steal one. In deep rural Jamaica. Please take a moment to reflect on that, Semicolon. Think: poor country. Think: poor, rural folks whose livelihood is derived from the livestock they own and the produce on their farms. Now think: Brian attempted to steal a goat. A whole goat. An entire goat. A whole, entire fucking goat!

There are things we all knew as kids growing up in rural Jamaica. We knew that cows were not hard to steal; whether by day or night they would come quietly as you led them away. Pigs you generally left alone unless you went with anesthesia; they would squeal so loud even your ancestors would hear. Goats were always a bit tricky, and you could never tell whether they would bleat loudly or be quiet. If you attempted to lift them up, they would surely bleat. Brian tried to lift a tricky goat.

The consequences of his action are not in dispute, given that many of us saw what happened. It was the causes - the reasons why Brian got himself in that situation, that were debated and quarreled about for months and years after that day. People mainly spoke about five or six main causes of the events.

First, everyone was in agreement that Brian's parents were married, catholic-style, to poverty. We also knew that with his family it was not the *poor as a church mouse* decent type of poverty; but more a case of the *never had, doesn't have, never will have even shit in their backside* type. Was this a factor in making Brian a thief? I myself never formed an opinion. It is hard to see the people you play with every day, for who they really are.

Second, they all said that the devil spent more time helping him than other people, though no one was sure exactly what it was about his soul that made it more valuable than the rest of ours. Brian could therefore easily find weed, women and alcohol, and got into trouble as easily as he got into whores. It also seems that because he loved telling lies, and the devil loved listening to them, the two were always chummy, at least according to my grandma. The boy was rotten, right through to the core, they said. The sun had given lots of color to his skin (the boy was jet black!) and vitamin D to his body, but had no gifts for his brain, so the little fucker walked around idly every day, looking for mischief.

Third, on the day the beating took place it was six of us boys who had gone out together to play. Me, my brother Martin, Tommy, Garnet with his big ass ears, Billy and, of course, the half-breed nigga himself, Brian. The product of a Negro and a Coolie. Like we did almost every other day, we had all gone out on our usual three to five mile expedition to the properties of our not-so-close neighbors. And we were busy plundering their mango trees, eating their canes, shooting their birds and calling to their daughters to join us in the cane-fields. We were in the territory of strangers, all of whom were farmers in deep rural Jamaica. This last bit was well noted, and considered a crucial part of the causes. We had gone to the 'private property' of strangers.

Fourth, while everyone acknowledged that as rural kids stealing the fruits of our neighbors' labors was normal, Brian had a reputation which went far beyond the norm. Brian was exceptionally gifted at all forms of stealing, and was known for his great feats. There was nothing that the little nigga could not, and did not, steal. The milk in your coffee? Stupidness! One minute you have your café latte, next minute, BRAP! You are all calcium deficient drinking your black coffee while this nigga's teeth and bones are getting stronger. A fine, luxurious car that exists only in your dreams? BRAP! Gone! Your twelve year old daughter's virginity? BRAP! Gone! When people said that the little nigga was talented, they meant that he was truly talented! Strangers who had gold teeth in their mouths were warned not to smile near the boy. My brother sometimes cautioned me at nights as well to count all my teeth to know how many I had, just in case when I woke up some were stolen.

When most people in our village spent their lives dreaming about winning the lotto, Brian was dreaming about how to rob those who won the lotto. This was simply his role in life.

Now, for the fifth and final part of what brought us to that moment in time: Brian was on his own. Brian had left the rest of us eating our mangoes and whistling at girls, and had said that he would "soon come back." None of us knew exactly how long he had gone, because only my brother had a watch and, in addition to being cheap and plasticky,

Ezekel Alan

it also behaved like a civil servant – if it rained it didn't work, if was too windy it didn't work, and so on. But the hours that had passed since Brian had said that he would *soon* come back didn't mean much to us as kids, because we were all used to hearing our pastors preach about how the Savior would *soon* return, and that hadn't happened. Moreover, this was Jamaica, where time didn't matter shit to us. Some people say that Jamaica is the place that Time forgot, and because we are an arrogant people who can't stomach insults, Jamaica, in pure spite, then chose to forget Time. Nonetheless, some folks faulted us for not having gone to see what Brian was doing for so long. And said that what happened next wouldn't have if we had stayed with him. This is what happened:

Sixteen year old Brian, with not even shit in his backside, but with a mastery of the fine art of thieving, had gone off on his own quietly, and had ventured onto the private property of others. I had seen him leaving, with his early afternoon shadow following reluctantly, like a stray dog with nothing better to do. He had gone off on the private property of strangers, searching for bigger prizes than mangoes. Smooth and sly, scouting and rummaging, scavenging and surveying... until he laid his eyes on that goat. He had bypassed an empty pig sty, had ignored a noisy fowl coop, had passed a donkey praying for water but despairing of relief, and had softly gone up to the tree where the solitary remnant of that family's fortune was tied.

And here is where things got really interesting. Two eyes inside the old wooden house were looking in exactly the direction of the tree, and they saw Brian lay his intentions on that goat. Peekaboo... I see you! Right about then it appeared as though a media frenzy over a celebrity sex scandal, broke out. The alarm and fanaticism! The zeal and determination! The speed! The fury! The persistence! The chase was fast and furious. You would think that with so many of them chasing that one boy, he would have been easier to catch than ringworms, but the little nigga was fast! Through the cane-field, around the back of Mr Joseph's house, past the barking mongrel dog, down the lane, through the church cemetery, through the fields of yams and dasheens, around the old abandoned shed where it was rumored that Stevie the Shotta was lying low after getting out of prison early (but not for good behavior), around the corner - scattering the marbles on the ground where the kids were playing but were now cursing with adult vocabulary, through the tighter-than-Monique's little hole at the Mount Clair school gate, across the school yard, past the school toilets, past the june plum tree which was heavily carved with love verses (TREVOR LUV TRICIA, and probably did too for a few weeks before sampling her coochie, but who knows?), past the little shack that the watchman lived in, then over the school wall... almost. The little nigga might have gotten over the wall and away but, as they say, puss and dog don't have the same luck, and the little nigga got viciously struck by a stone as he climbed the wall. It was enough to throw both him and his fate off balance. So he fell, hard, like Lucifer.

I knew they would catch him - mobs generally caught those they chased, and my grandma had had a dream the night before, which, when deciphered, had sent many people off to the local Dropon (a form of lotto) man to buy a set of numbers which included the sinister 3 and 13. Mostly I knew because I had seen the look on their faces as they chased him. They were more focused and determined than a Somali med student on a US scholarship, and were never going to fail in their pursuit.

Based on where I was perched in a mango tree at the time, I was the first to see those farmers chasing Brian and, consequently, the first to get to the wall where they held him. The reason I remember so clearly, is because on the day in question, I was still only thirteen years old, and there are some things a boy of thirteen should never do, see or hear, no matter how poor he may be. Screw his eleven year old cousin, is certainly one of those things. Watch his wretched mama giving birth to a second fucking still-born child, is certainly another of those things. Watch a group of idle boys set fire to an old, mad woman, is another. But the thing I really want to get to here, is seeing your cousin's eyes as he is held against a wall by a Jamaican mob of rural farmers, who had just sent for their machetes.

There were two things that were universal truths about farmers and their machetes. First, a true rural Jamaican farmer was a person who, no matter how much effort he made, could not speak well enough to be understood by a tourist (can you get "eat it" from "iti"?), and who had <u>at least</u> two machetes - with blades sharper than a ghetto woman's tongue.

Second, machetes were more widely owned than pride, and better kept than dignity. A machete was the Swiss Army Knife of farming tools: the pointy end could be used for digging and planting the fields; the blade could be used for clearing bushes, chopping branches off trees or limbs off people; the face could be used to strike your partner during a domestic dispute; and the blunt side could be used for cracking open dried coconuts (or skulls). Every farmer I ever met loved his machete, and spent hours sharpening it. If ever he had spent as much effort lavishing attention on his wife, the beneficial impacts on the family and community would have been inestimable.

When I got to the wall where they were holding Brian, the machetes were just arriving. The beating was ending, and the real work was beginning: they had begun to chop. It's true to say that Brian's body had already long passed the stage where it could one day return to its Maker with only the normal wear and tear. He had already collected scars like boy-scout badges, and was covered with them. But those were simple scars from normal skirmishes, and none went too deep.

That day, they went deep. Those farmers weren't doing a precise, measured, samurai sword *Kill Bill Volumes 1 and 2* on my cousin. No. Those niggas were carcassing and cadavering my cousin, right there in front of my eyes.

I remember an old man standing at some distance away from the action. He looked like a retired member of the mob, proud to see the continuation of his work. I suspected that his son may have been one of the farmers chopping up my cousin, for he was urging excitedly, like a father would cheer a son at a high school sports event.

I noticed Brian had started shitting himself. Much later I would learn, from my Uncle Bob, that since Brian was a baby, the little nigga would often shit in his diaper and would run away from his mama because he didn't want it changed. Seems he got some peculiar form of comfort from having that warm load on his ass. I doubted, however, that on this occasion he was shitting for comfort, but one never truly knows how the human mind and body work under extreme stress.

With whatever was left of his eyes, Brian saw me standing back from the crowd, and I remember the curious words he screamed,

"Stephan! Stephan!! Help me!!! Please! PLEASE!! Don't let them kill me!!!" And he screamed it with an earnestness which suggested that I might have had the power to stop a Jamaican mob. But Brian must have known, mustn't he? He must have known that at that moment in time, no one at all in this whole fucking world, could have helped. Mustn't he?

I was the first one to get to the scene, and my brother came right behind me. Then, the other kids that we were playing with, came. Garnet stood next to me, on my left. You could see his veins in his neck pulsating beneath a dark yellow spot where some evil spirit had touched him a couple of weeks before, when it crawled into his bed and molested him. He was still coughing and waiting for his grandmother's leaves to cure his illness. And he was spitting in front of everyone; any decency he ever learnt was in school, not at home, for his parents were fucking worthless, as everybody knew. Tommy, who was not as tall, made his way in front of me to get a better view. His sorry, skinny ass was sticking out of the backside of his worn out, old, short khaki pants that hadn't entered a school gate in years. He hadn't put on any weight, as the two back pockets of his pants were still touching. Skinny ass nigga was twitching with some perverse sort of excitement. A few red ants were doing hundred meter sprints in his head. I saw Georgie arrive as well, along with the rest of the gang.

Brian was already dead when they got there, but they still got something to watch as some of the farmers continued to chop. Chop, chop, chop. Some dogs find it hard to stop barking at cars that have long driven away.

Diary entry: Watch him wail. Wail Brian wail. See them chop. Chop, chop, chop. See him bleed. Bleed boy bleed. See them hack. Hack, hack, hack.

Here are three things I just can't do, no matter how hard I try: (1) I cannot spell Nietzsche without looking it up in the dictionary; (2) I cannot prepare Jamaican fried dumplings perfectly, no matter how many times I see others do it; (3) I cannot get this image out of my head: a large group of men swarming my cousin like flies, killing him, and continuing to chop as though they were also trying to get down to his soul.

A little while later, our older family members also came. Brian's papa, Uncle Thomas, came. Said nothing. Just stood there. By then he was well into his *can only make love twice a month* stage of life, but, like a true Jamaican, still wanted it to be with two different women. His mom, Aunt Beverley - Auntie B for short, also came. Not one intelligible word from her either, but her body shook and trembled like a Pentecostal caught by the spirit, before she was taken away by Aunt Josephine and Aunt Frida. Aunt Martha came also, and she led the screaming. She was in her 300th month of pregnancy (growing up I cannot remember a time when she wasn't pregnant), and we all worried for her health as she hit those high-pitched notes. When I looked around I saw that Miss Jacky had come as well. She was not a member of our family, just one of those that lived on the other side of the yard. Like a second-hand car, she always had a used look about her. She lavished more attention on her face, and had more control over her hair, than she did her kids. I remember she spent endless hours at the hairdresser and beauty salon, and took those birth control pills that reduce acne. Anyway, I digress, perhaps because I was distracted by her long, flowing, artificial hair at the time.

Every one of the other older folks also came, except Grandpa, who had something (not someone, for the Old Timer was long past that stage), eating him. [For clarity: cancer had taken over where the girls had left off]. After his second heart attack, he was stuck on his verandah with spit on his chin, hanging down like stalactite. Useless and abandoned like a condemned building, he sat there with his shriveling skin looking like a roll of wet toilet tissue put out to dry.

As the older adults came, tempers began to run as high as the rates of illiteracy, and so the police were called.

Before they arrived, Brian's Uncle Bob - who was also my Uncle Bob, also came. Stood beside me, as usual, for it seemed I was the only person who would tolerate him and his weedy aura. Right then he said the only words anyone would ever hear him say on that day about the events that had transpired,

"Always a thieving little fucker, that bwoy."

The police, normally slow but brutal, like a tropical hurricane, this time came with the force of a rat's fart, and simply stood and watched. The security guard from the church also came – one of those guards people hired so that they had someone to watch: watch him sleep, watch him play cards, watch him listening to the radio, watch him watch the girls walking by. Like the police, he just watched.

The best words to describe what we all watched? "Lord Jesus no! No! No! No! Jesus Christ noooooooooooo! Heavenly father noooooooooooo!" Adults were using the Lord's name in vain and getting away with it. If it had been one of us kids I can't begin to tell you what might have happened to us.

So, there he was that day, my cousin, Brian, dead. Remnants of life oozing out of him like bubbles of methane from month-old cow dung. And right there at my foot is where I saw a piece of his half-breed scalp, with that beautiful curly Coolie hair on it, that I had always coveted.

CHAPTER 7

Cookie

"The mound"

I once met a mountain
which was like my first whore -
promised to make a man of me,
and also left me quite sore.

Excerpt, unfinished poem on cycling, circa 1993

June 12, 1983. Psychologists say that we tend to remember the most traumatic days and events of our lives, and other events that happened at about the same time. This much of what they say seems to be true.

Two days before the slaughter of Brian, I had fucked Cookie, again. Cookie was a young girl back then, still at the age where you would expect young girls to be pure and chaste and have their legs closed tighter than a missionary's mind. But we come to learn that there are differences between young female children from developed and under-developed countries. These differences can, at times, be quite significant, like those between apples and goats. Take the delicate issue of sex, for example – for North Americans, a young girl's coochie is put away like a trust fund that a boy can gain access to when they both turn eighteen or twenty-one, but, in our Depression it was well understood that if a young girl could ride a bicycle, then she was ready to ride a dick.

There were few things that set us apart from the adults. Unlike them we had to use "sir" and "madam" in our conversations. But outside of this, we were adults either by height or by declaration, and could do as adults did. And we fucked a lot, like adults did.

Cookie's real name was Simone, but like most kids she was given a nickname. If I recall well she got the name because as a baby she was round, pudgy and dimpled and reminded someone of a cookie. In my diary I once wrote that her real name should have been Shemoans or, better yet, Shefucks, but I guessed that such names would have gone against the positive expectation that parents have of their kids at birth. I reasoned that babies are born beautiful, and it would be callous and psychotic for parents not to imagine that their lives will be the same.

Growing breasts, wearing bra, but still losing baby teeth, Simone was about eleven years old at the time. Two days before the slaughter, there were five of us boys with her in a corner behind a door in my house. She was lying on top of a crocus bag filled with newspapers. That crocus bag used to be one of my favorite places to hide my newspaper-wrapped mangoes, and wait on them to ripen.

I remember how pink she was that day. I had, of course, given it to her hard a few times before, but never in a group of five. On that day I got the opportunity to stand back and watch as the others took their turn. My brother was in the process of dismounting, and Brian, who was next in line, was being considerate,

"Garnet, go call Wayne so him can come get some."

Garnet thought Brian's timing was off, and made a counter suggestion, "Why the raas you no go call him yuself?"

I was standing back, fretting and sweating while keeping a lookout for any adult that might see us. Simone, however, simply kept on moaning and groaning and, as my brother pulled away, rubbing what I could see was a very pink crotch. My ears had tingled and hurt a bit while I watched her, but by then I was no longer as bothered by the sounds of humping and panting as I had been as a small child.

Simone was another of my cousins. For the next decade or so she offered that pink crotch to us and, more and more, to other men. More and more, these were bigger and older men. Soon enough people started calling her a slut and a whore because once the word got out that she was 'easy', not even sodium benzoate could have helped to preserve her reputation.

Simone was my Aunt Josephine's daughter. Aunt Josephine's house was two houses up from mine, on the right side of the lane. They were eight in their house: Aunt Josephine; Simone's older sister, Carmen; three brothers and two younger sisters. I never really knew Simone's papa, Tall Man, because when she was very young Aunt Josephine had asked him to leave after discovering that he was even less faithful than she had thought. From what I pieced together later, she had at first accepted the fact that for each child he had with her, he had a matching child with another woman somewhere else. But things got out of hand when her own kids became outnumbered, and when those other mothers started sending kids to Aunt Josephine's house to ask Tall Man for 'their' money.

A story can be told about each person that lived in Aunt Josephine's house. I choose to mention briefly only the following: Carmen had had the same reputation as Simone. Some say that she had set an example for her younger sister, because she too had spent years sleeping around with men. People say that it started while she was working at a bar close to the ice factory in our neighborhood. After she started serving men whatever they paid for, it became a habit, like most things we do for twenty-one days or more. Sometimes she would go with them to wherever they took her, sometimes it was in the store room of the bar, and sometimes they came to her at the house in our yard and created excitement for little eyes that peeped through windows.

After a few years the men had stopped coming, and this is where the dispute I mentioned before, started. There were many points of views on why the men stopped visiting. Some of my cousins argued that it was because, after a time, Carmen's weight and her underwear, which both used to be *easy on easy off*, went their separate ways. At least this is how Brian had joked about it. As she got fatter and fatter, fewer men were attracted to her, Brian and others reasoned. Others argued, however, that the real reason the men stopped coming was because a few of them had contracted either gonorrhea or some other STD that itched badly and caused someone's pecker to fall off. After that, they say, her coochie was officially condemned, and there was a proclamation far and wide that nothing good could ever come from it, not even a child, and hence no one should put anything in it. Garnet added, as I mentioned before, that all nine lives of her pussy had been fucked out and it was now dead. This was the line of argument that had led to the brawl.

Whatever the real reason, a couple of things were true. One was that she did, indeed, become quite huge, looking as though she was eating pork skin for breakfast, lunch and dinner every day. The other is that the men did stop coming. She was mostly seen sitting alone on her mama's veranda, day after day. No matter their ages, almost all of my cousins continued to live in their parents' houses all the days of their lives – either, like Carmen, in little, built-on adjoining shacks, or, like Simone, in a confiscated room they turned into their own house. Carmen had five kids of her own, none of whom referred to her as mama. No man of her own, no house of her own, not even a dog. Just a few black and white photographs on her dresser, the preserved memories of an enjoyable beach trip she once went on. In those days I captured her in my diary, alone in her little room at nights. I subjected her to a lifetime of ordinary dreams filled with unspectacular romances, imagining the "Thanks for breakfast, see you later sweetheart" in the morning, the "This food is delicious, honey, how was your day?" at dinner, and the mutually satisfactory encounter ending with a kiss before bed. Not once would she have thought of Rome in my story, for she was just an ordinary person, with simple dreams.

Whether Carmen actually had these ordinary romantic dreams or any thoughts of travel, I have no idea, but what she certainly did do, was embrace religion with a passion normally reserved for politics and sports. She now found her comfort in the bosom of Abraham, like so many others in our Depression.

Another of Simone's siblings, her younger brother, Jimmy, would also bring attention to the family. Many years later, he became closely associated with the worst forms of evil to visit our neighborhood, before being gunned down himself, right at his mama's gate.

But back to Simone. Was she really a whore? No. We will get to whores in a bit but, for the record, Simone wasn't one. At least not by the pure definition that if a whore doesn't fuck, she doesn't eat. For she clearly had free rein at her mama's dining table, plus she also had a trickle of income from her various baby fathers. This flow wasn't as steady or secure as an annuity, but was expected to continue for as long as the kids remained young and, well, alive. So she wasn't a whore. She wasn't your regular, garden variety slut either, as I have explained. She was more like a train that men rode to and from work, in a rural community, at a time when women had no power over men and there was no love lost between men and condoms. Which, in a nutshell, explains why she had many kids.

The first of her litter came out while she was only fourteen years old.

This child was only about ten months old on the day I walked by Simone's place – her little one-bed, one-stove, one-radio, one-window, one-dresser, one-chair room, that was attached to her mama, Aunt Josephine's house. One of the older men she was sleeping with had seen me in the lane and asked me to go and tell her he was waiting. (The fucker didn't even give me fifty cents for my efforts, but money wasn't on my mind that time anyway.) I walked into Simone's room to bring her the message; it wasn't necessary to knock, for certain kinds of politeness could be considered pretentious in poor neighborhoods. She had the baby on the bed, had just finished giving him a bath, and was now in the process of French kissing him, though in those days it was referred to as 'deep throat'. As she turned and saw me at the door, she giggled, then asked me if I wanted "some of this" and proceeded to suck on his little pecker. These were the days when oral sex was just becoming popular, and it seems Simone was practicing her newly acquired skills. I am quite sure she wasn't doing this because of what pastor had said a week before about how "the church advances on its knees." Simone never went to church and would not have been able to make any such mental connections if she had.

I knew it was a serious offer, as it was very natural for people to simply turn up at her door and get *some*. In fact, she often seemed to be begging us to come over for a fuck. You would see her there at her door hopping from foot to foot like someone who has *the runs* and is waiting on the toilet. She had the urge. So I wasn't surprised by the casual invitation, only at how she planned to fit me into her schedule along with the gentleman she'd been rehearsing for. But I had other things on my mind at the moment. I told her that the man was waiting for her, then asked a question that had been building up in me for a long time.

"Simone, why do you let them use you like this?" Partly I asked because she was my cousin, someone who belonged to *us*, our private property, and strangers kept taking her away. Partly because the images in my mind of pitch black, hairy ass men humping between her legs, made my ears hurt. And partly because she now had a child that she left to sleep alone in that room, so that these strangers could use her.

Her reply to my question:

> *Kenny, what you lack is a full and proper grasp of the universe and the way things, at their essence, are. The earth changes but never at its core. We, you and I, need to understand who we are, and the purpose for which we are here. I know who I am, and what I was made for. I suffer not from the existentialist malaise. And because I*

understand my purpose, no one can use me. Also, I know the value of my vagina, for it is, indeed, the most powerful thing that I own. Do not feel sorry for me.

But it came out in one sentence,

"Kenny, yu no kno' seh a jus so me tan?" Translated: "Kenny, don't you know that this is just the way I am?" And would always be. And this one statement, from a fourteen year old girl, has haunted me ever since. For though she giggled it, like she giggled so many other comments, I knew that, like her offer a minute before, this too was genuine. It was her truth.

Hers became a hard life. Simone moved in and out of our village the way men moved in and out of her. She would go to one town to live with her newest baby papa, and return a few months later after the first, or second, or third, beating. But she always came back, and each time she seemed like a different person. Until she no longer seemed like my younger cousin, but like a woman who had earned the right to speak to even our grandparents with the familiarity of an Old Timer.

This girl's shame tree had died, completely. Though she was still a child, all kinds of men visited her, from all over, and it was plain for everyone to see. Tall men, short men, stumpy men, rich men, poor men, black men, Indian men. There was also an elder in the church; as kids, we gossiped that his dick was firmer than his faith. And to round things off, there was also a Chinese man, whom I recall because he owned the bread factory and a few other shops. He was a very short man with naturally short hair, as though the good Lord had never intended to have much of him in the world. It was rumored that he had a sword to protect himself. Apparently didn't think he could rely on either the police or our local brand of black magic, Obeah, to protect him. But we will get to these issues later.

Anyway, Simone was getting a lot of action with these men. So much so that it was rumored that when the dogs in our yard saw how easy

Simone was, and the range of homo sapiens coming to visit her, they too had a conference to decide on how to get some of the action. Funny the way these stories begin. One night at story time, Garnet said he had seen all the dogs gathered in congress earlier that day. My own dog Ruffy, who was no natural leader, was somewhere at the back of the pack. He said they appeared to be in heated conversation on the subject of whether they too had a right to some of that human coochie. The debate came down to two options: (a) a small group of selected and well-spoken dogs would go to the human who was, in any event, behaving like a bitch in heat, and make a case for equal rights and opportunity (a popular expression in the socialist 1970s), and (b) a group of the strongest dogs would grab hold of Simone one day and simply haul her off into the bushes where all the dogs could give it to her. In the end, as far as we know, nothing ever happened to Simone, so it was never clear what the outcome of the congress was. But a couple of us kids, while we jokingly dismissed the story after it was told to us, were kept in quiet suspense for a few days, waiting to see if something was really going to happen. I can only comfort myself now with the thought that there are white people who genuinely believed the world would end in May 2010.

There was no Match.com or E-harmony in those days, so it was very hard to figure out how and where this little girl kept meeting these men. Most peculiar were the rich ones, who would drive and park at the end of our lane, waiting to pick her up and take her places. Sometimes we'd see them in the bars (don't worry about it, in those days it was ok for kids to go to bars to buy things for their parents), laughing out little earthquakes that shook other men around them, including those that didn't get the joke. These men had big cars, big houses, big dicks, big laughs, but small wallets – this latter was certain, for it was clear that Simone was getting very little financially from these encounters and would never be able to retire on her coochie's pension. What she did get, she got rough and in good measure, judging by (a) her duck-like walk when they dropped her off, and (b) the truth universally acknowledged in Jamaica that all women liked it hard and without foreplay.

I also mention Simone in order to introduce the owner of the ice factory, Mr Jackson, or Mr Man, as he was more commonly referred to - a person, I believe, who plays a critical role in many of the memories I have of that *hateful* fucking place, and a part of our grand puzzle. It is not that hard to figure out how he and Simone may have met, because, as kids, we all went to the ice factory at some point and he was always there, in his office. Moreover, he also lived nearby, less than a mile from our Depression, in a big house that was - Ripleys Believe It or Not, complete with gardener, pool boy and helper. So there were any number of opportunities for the two to meet.

Now, what do we know about Mr Man at this point? Mr Man:

Had money, shitloads of it.

Had a swimming ool (he had a sign by his pool that he found amusing, saying *"Notice there is no P in it? We would like to keep it that way."*)

He liked under-aged girls, judging by the one we know of. (This was not an uncommon thing for grown men. Indeed, in our Depression,

"You see how fast that dog run when Tommy hit him with that stone?"

and

"My Lord! You hear how Miss Frida nearly caught her house on fire trying to cook crab?"

and

"You know that little Simone start fucking big man?"

passed as simple, gleeful accounts of everyday ghetto news, and nothing more. But I digress.)

Since he was very short, he was always going to be either overly-bubbly or overly-disagreeable, to compensate. He was overly-disagreeable. He was also the kind of man who would have all toilets flush themselves and also help spare him the indignity of having to wipe his own ass.

On his forty-fifth birthday he cut the cake by himself. We learnt this from his helper, who was a church sister of one my aunts, and who became our encyclopedia on everything we needed to know about the lifestyle of the rich. Now some may jump to the conclusion that it is a sad state of affairs for a forty-five year old man to be cutting his birthday cake by himself, but we should not be too hasty in jumping to conclusions. His helper did, after all, report that there were more than a few attractive young girls at the party. Perhaps Mr Man had two or three of his lovers there with him, but knew that inviting any one of them to cut the cake with him would spark crack-head behavior amongst the others, such as the scratching out of eyes. Not uncommon, such unbecoming behavior - then, or now.

So, we know some basic things about Mr Man, and we know that somehow he is a part of our puzzle. Let's move on.

This part of Simone's story is also a good way to get back to and properly introduce my Uncle Bob, who lived so long, and died so well. He was a very thin man who lived, on and off, with some of the heftiest women he could find, in the house next to mine. Maybe because he himself was so thin and he had so little of everything, he wanted to compensate by having a woman who was everything. The trouble is, they always left him. Each and every single one. For months, sometimes years, he would have all the oxygen in his house to himself. There, every day, at the front of his house, looking over his zinc fence at the back of his yard, making a fire to cook (a sure sign that he had gotten money from somewhere), or sitting beneath the guinep tree, keeping company with the Duppy of his dead brother, whilst watching the little girls and boys play. But mostly just sitting there, smoking his bighead spliffs and sending out as much smoke as an entire Apache reservation on the brink of war. He sure had a way of getting some of the finest, highest-grade spliff there was. I know; he introduced me to it. Some of the kids joked you could get high from simply standing close to him, but it was my brother, fresh from church one day, who came up with the line that really stuck: *In the beginning was the weed, and the weed was with Bob, and the weed was Bob.* Blasphemous little fuckers we were. But back to Uncle Bob. Good old Uncle Bob. Some of the kids wondered why he was always shifting and fidgeting so much while he sat, others of us knew it was the recurring piles in his ass. One thing we all knew, was that though he couldn't recognize his name if he saw it on a piece of cake he was about to eat, he was, in the ways of the world, a smart man. Knew how everything worked: cars, bridges, televisions, ships, nuclear weapons, women, politicians' minds, God's design, the devil's mischief, and such. You just needed to spend a little time with him, especially after he smoked, and wisdom beyond your wildest imagination would be yours. He once shared with me some of his most exclusive advice: that the best time to suck a woman's coochie was a few days after she's finished taking a regime of antibiotics, because then she would be pure and cleaner than a madman's conscience. He also confirmed that, despite what the other boys had told me, no matter how sweet a girl's coochie was, you could not catch diabetes from eating it.

Uncle Bob was there, looking over his fence, on that day when we gave it to Simone good and hard. He saw the five boys leave the house with the one girl, and it didn't take much for him to figure out what had happened. But he waited. One day later, the day before Brian's slaughter, he spoke. First, however, he hawked and spat. His hawking was Number 6 on my other Top Ten list - of most disgusting things. His hawk was prolonged and sounded like an overloaded sugar cane truck going up a steep hill in first gear. The 4th most disgusting thing on that list was what he did next – blow his nose by using his index finger to close one nostril, while blowing through the other, then using his fingers to flick away the snot. [The 5th most disgusting thing also involved the nose, as it was seeing some folks pick their nose by sticking their fingers so far up their nostrils you thought they were trying to scratch their brain.] Of the five boys that had been with Simone – me, my brother, Brian, Georgie, and Garnet – I was the one Uncle Bob called over to his house to have words.

"Do you think I didn't see you all go in that room? Do you think I didn't notice how long you all stayed? Do you think I don't know what you boys did inside there?" He didn't expect me to say anything, for he was only speaking to himself, his eyes staring blankly at some distant, murky future. Then he turned his head towards me and said, in evident conclusion, "She have a tight little pussy, doesn't she?"

It was obvious that this was a rhetorical question. This wasn't the first time we had had such a rhetorical conversation, my uncle and I. And it wasn't the last.

Grandma Bell: "If she had gone to church she would never turn out to be a whore!"

CHAPTER 8

The Music It Sweet, So Sweet

When I started writing this one, I didn't know if it was goin' be a poem or a song; all I know is that it was about this man, who goes around singing with a Calypso Band.

The man he not singing from no book of lamentation; no, this man he a liar, he a Calysonian! Now, "Calypsonian" ain't got to do with where you from - like you'd say "I Jamaican", "I Alien", or "I Haitian"; it's just the man who sing the Calypso song. You'll find him all across the Caribbean – there is one on virtually every island.

Now, that man he don't know if the cows they go come home at 5:30 or 5:45, but he know they be coming home, so he make up his lies: the man he on the radio, down the street, whistling melodies between him teeth, singing for the girls, saying the music sweet, no matter it have a Reggae, Soca or Calypso beat, "Hai! Hai! Hai! Hai! The music it sweet, so sweet!"

Just you listen to our friend the Calysonian! Whether he be Trinidadian, a (ugly) Bajan, or Antiguan. Boy! I swear you just wouldn't understand! Him tell you that the music is like having a fine Ganga spliff in your hand, while you drinking some dark rum in easy moderation, and lying on your back being attractively worked on, by, not one, but two lesbian! (The younger of the two being

Scandinavian). Hai! Hai! Hai! Believe me boy! You start to follow that man! Start feeling that this is all part of the master's plan, and that the music it sweeter than salvation.

So you decide to leave the Jews alone with them Promise land; leave the Arabs with them Oil, and the African… well, leave him with him Aspiration, and you tell the people at the Embassy you don't bother want to be no American, cause you think the music so sweet, boy it sweeter than salvation! And your mind is made up - you go stay in your forefather's Land!

Then you find that you start singing with this man! Cause he tell you the music it sweet, so sweet, it sweeter than salvation!

Boy! You covered in mud, rolling in the dirt! Now everything is bacchanal, giddiness and mirth! It's Carnival man! The girls they all flirt! They don't know you, you don't know them, but still they lifting up them skirt! This ain't no joke boy! This man he slick boy! He say this music sweet boy!

From 'The Book of Lovelace', Chapter 4, 1999

CHAPTER 9

The Lord of the Flies

"If you stare at one spot of a wall constantly and persistently for a few hours, never yielding in your faith and convictions, then, as certain as the night becomes day, you will acquire clarity and enlightenment. You will realize the eternal truth that a man only needs health and attitude to win himself the desire of women, but health and handsomeness to obtain his desired jobs."

K. Lovelace, ramblings, circa 2001

I consider the pit toilet (outhouse, latrine) to be somewhat emblematic of my childhood. This is because it served as a constant reminder of the fact that the shit in our lives always stayed with us, and could never be flushed away. Moreover, if at any hour of the day you felt inclined to see the results of all your papa's and uncles' labors in the fields, and your mama's and aunts' labors in the market, then you could just go to the pit toilet and look down. Every last bit of their efforts was there. Whatever you saw in that rising mountain, was all everything came down to. Nothing more, nothing less. Not a bigger house. Not a car. Not money in a bank account. Just that glistening load of shit. Would you like to know the name I gave to that fat, glistening load? Here is what I wrote in my notebook many years ago: *The Lord of the Flies.*

These were the days when that trophy that you spat on, shined and placed in a glass case for all to see and desire, with its bold, bronze letters saying "Progress", was stored too high for us to reach.

Our toilet didn't have much of a door, and was made of wood and zinc. Anyone could see through the wide openings, and frequently they would stand outside holding a casual conversation with you while you went. Each *plop* the sound of bits of pride falling into a pool of eternity. The toilet plays a central role in the first diary entry, a poem, that I wrote in my notebook in relation to Uncle Thomas. This was about eight months after he had lost his son, Brian, to the murderous mob:

"No other words"

He was full of shit.
There is, truly, no other way to describe it.
He had an epileptic fit
in a pit toilet,
was found the next morning
in a load of shit, dead.
And that was it.

Undated diary entry, circa 1984

After we found my uncle dead, covered in shit, this is what I wrote in my diary: *The Lord of the Flies*. Long before I knew there was a book with the same title. Now, my dearest Semicolon, it is indeed common knowledge that the same knife that stick goat, stick sheep. So one has to be careful about laughing at the misfortune that befalls others, as we never know what may also befall us. I therefore recount these events not to make fun of any one in my family, but simply to tell my truth.

What is worth noting about the setting in which this event occurred? Very little beyond the fact that it was a smelly pit toilet, located a little distance away from our houses, and one which many of us used. No one had any private or indoor toilets at the time, so this too was shared property. This is perhaps one of the reasons this memory has stuck with me throughout these years, because I had spent many hours in that toilet, and developed strong thigh muscles from squatting over the seat, trying to prevent my ass touching the surface.

I should also point out that, in addition to the shit, there was quite a bit of newspaper at the scene. Though let me clarify that in our yard not one single person used the newspaper for news. Newspapers served a useful purpose in either wrapping green fruits (mangoes, etc.) until they ripened, or wiping our ass after we used the toilet. (You may say that this is how my uncle ended up in the news.)

This all happened a few months after Brian was killed, and roughly a year after I first fucked my other cousin, Jennifer. Now, Uncle Thomas was not like that miser in that George Eliot book (Silas Marner) who had a lot of money hidden and suffered from epilepsy and was robbed while unconscious. That was just a sad story in a book you read in High School. This though, was my real uncle. One of the four uncles I had. Perhaps the poorest of the four because no one would give him a job with his frequent epileptic fits. The ironic thing about all this, I guess, is that it shows how a man can go through his entire life not having shit, and still be killed by it.

The concentrated shame that his shitty death, and the goat-thieving death of his bloody son, caused on all our families, was unbearable. I went to both their funerals. They were the same. Based on my diary, they were both like this:

"The funeral"

There he lay
like a dog in the streets.
Kicked.

Rolled over.
Confirmed dead.
No microscopes.
No stethoscopes.
Unexamined.
As though it never lived,
loved,
felt.
Amen.

And that was that, and no fucking more than that.

Grandma Bell: "If he had gone to church all of this would never have happened to him!"

CHAPTER 10

Doretta Carpenter

Dear Mr Lovelace,
My death is upon me,
I see his messenger approaching in hurried haste-

Dear journal,
I want to tell you my story,
so could you defer your death?
I am a beast,
Have always, will always
Live by smell;
I like to smell
Beneath a female's dress
To choose my mate,
See who is ripe,
Then lick her breast
Like a dog lapping milk.
I am thus.
Is it for want of a mother, a salary or a soul?

Journal entry, circa 1997

Doretta Carpenter was forty-seven years old in 2002. A sturdy, no-nonsense Jamaican woman who wore her sense of purpose like strong

71

perfume. She was a teacher at the time, and collected the meager salary her government paid for the hard work she put into her job, with scarcely concealed resentment. She supplemented her income with the earnings from offering private lessons. The main blights on an otherwise acceptably normal life: her salary; the experience of childhood poverty; a wart beneath her right eye large enough to be visible from the moon, and three of her four kids.

Born in the hills of St. Catherine, she was the second of seven children for her mama. The first child, Mildred, completely stole the spotlight from the rest, as she was born in the same year as the deadliest hurricane to ever hit Jamaica.

"Is Hurricane Charley blow her come!" This is what people would say about her sister Mildred for pretty much all her life.

In 1951, Hurricane Charley had blown the roofs off 25,000 people's houses, and carried away the souls from 154 bodies. Kingston, St. Andrew, St. Catherine, and St. Thomas were the parishes worst hit. Mildred was born three days after the storm, while the roads were still blocked by fallen trees and other debris. No midwife could attend her birth. Indeed, for a time the birth of the child went almost unnoticed, as it was completely overshadowed by the storm. As folks went about their business boiling water for their coffee, cooking the meat of animals that had died during the storm, feeding their remaining chickens and such, the only thing they spoke about was the fierceness of the storm and whether it was, indeed, God's retribution. After the novelty had passed, however, attention turned to the child, affectionately regarded as the Child of the Storm.

Doretta though, was neither the 'first born', the 'washbelly' (last child), nor the 'only boy'; she would therefore live her life with little attention from anyone.

She had to look out for herself.

In addition to her kids, she also had a vile, purposeful, and calculating cat that the kids called Schizo (short for 'schizophrenic'), though its proper name was Amina. The reason for calling the cat Schizo wasn't exaggerated. By the way, three years after owning the cat, Doretta's eldest daughter Rebecca, visited home from the US and realized that the cat was male, not female as everyone thought.

Schizo the cat on a good day

Doretta also had a dog. It was initially, like the cat, a stray that she started leaving food for at the side of the house, until it decided it would be worth the effort to settle down at her yard. The dog now lived on the flat-slab roof of her house in Hughenden, Kingston. Once, she'd had a plan to build a second floor, and the workmen had put in a makeshift staircase at the back of the house for this purpose. This was the dog's route to the roof.

In February 2002, Doretta was, again, single, having kindly asked her fourth common-law husband to leave her house. This last one, many folks had thought might have been the only person in the world who would actually marry and remain married to her, because of his 'clinginess'. She, however, had come to regard him as so mean that he economized even on the amount of words he used to think. Like all the others before, she had been taken in by his charm, attentiveness and sweet words. A psychiatrist might have said that these men provided something that her own parents never gave.

As a teenager she had had a serious, medical, hormone imbalance problem. She wasn't to be pitied, however, given that her papa planted some of the sweetest sugar canes this side of hell, and her grandmother not only roasted and made her own delightful hot chocolate, but made a sweet potato pudding that could instantly take a teenage girl's mind off older boys.

In February 2002, we find her sitting on her sofa inside a boiling-hot house. She has three fans in her living room, arranged in a seemingly cultish manner: standing in three corners and pointing to the centre of the room where she finds both her truths and a modest respite from the blazing heat.

From here on we switch to her point of view, because I have only ever met one other person like her in my whole, entire life, and would therefore prefer to have her speak for herself.

A day in the life of Doretta Carpenter

I go into the damn, lazy boy's room and he is lying there, awake, looking up at the ceiling. Every morning that the good Lord gives him, the damn boy does the same thing: lies there, just looking at the ceiling and the walls for hours! I ask the damn boy,

"What the hell you doing, Tony?"

He says, "Mom, I feel like I am a vessel." Only the good Lord knows why I haven't murdered that boy already. Nothing but crosses and tribulations!

I ask him, "A vessel for what?"

He tells me, "For the music, mom. I am a vessel for the music; the music must pass through me." The damn boy is lucky that last night I started reading that book about Gandhi, for my Master's Degree program. Only the good Lord and Gandhi's teachings on non-violence, keeping him alive. He better count his blessings, name them one by one.

I bet the damn fool goin' get up in half an hour expecting me to have food ready for him to eat in front of the damn television. Seventeen year old boy watching nothing but SpongeBob all the time, and the damn fool don't even realize that Patrick is gay.

"Get out of the bed so I can make it up! You can't make twelve o'clock catch you and your bed is not made!" Damn lazy boy, watch him taking him own sweet time to get up! I finish asking that boy to make him own bed. Last time I tell him to make him bed, the fool say to me, "Just cool yourself no mommy," as if I am some overheating radiator! Only the Blood of Christ and the Songs of Solomon save him then!

Tired like a dog. Watch him! Fool went out late again last night. Every night that boy going out with him friends, partying with my hard earned money, then have no use for himself the next day. Look at him!

Two weeks ago the boy have police calling me in the middle of the night. Police stop him driving on the road, coming back from party. One o'clock in the middle of the night I get phone call!

As always, it was him and that worthless friend Omar. Now that boy Omar is another crosses! Just like Ms Bess' extra toe, that boy is always out of place. Can't finish eating one mango before starting another! I remember a few months ago that fool says to me,

"Ms Carpenter, you can't set me up with your daughter?" Wants me to get Jacqueline to go out with him. Every time he come here the fool asking me the same thing, to set him up with my daughter. I would love to see him with her! Fool! These fools like chasing tail, wait until them get married to the wrong woman. He don't know how lazy that girl is. I would want to see how many years he would wait to see if water can boil itself.

Now she is another one. Real crosses! Fool fool child think I was born yesterday. Take my car all day last Friday, tell me she only went down the road to that idle girl Nadine, who think she goin' make a living as a hairdresser. She come back with the tank I just full with gas nearly empty, and don't even have the common sense to refill it. Think I don't know it's that old, gray-head man she seeing. If that fool think she's goin' stay in my house until she become grandmother, she got something else coming to her.

Only the good Lord know how I end up with them three pickney. And it look like I got myself in another situation here again! Lord help me! That damn nigga had cotton candy dripping from him tongue!

Anyway, this damn boy have the police calling me. People say "Duppy know who to frighten." Look like them damn police know that I have high blood-pressure, calling me at one o'clock in the morning.

"Mistress Carpenter," thinking I married.

I said, "Yes, this is she." I don't know why I bother to even speak properly to them. Before I ask them anything, I say to myself, "Lord, you are my rock and my salvation!" Then I ask the officer what happen with the boy. He tell me that Tony was driving the car and only has a learner's permit. That he with someone not experienced enough and that he should not be driving on a learner's permit that late at night.

I had to get out of my bed and drive to Red Hills Road to talk to the police. You remember what that man wrote in the Gleaner? "Ask not what the police can do for you, but what you can do for the police." Seven thousand dollars of my hard earned money I have to bribe the officer to let the damn boy go. Nothing but crosses and vexation!

What was even more hurtful about it is that the same night him girlfriend was here in my house waiting for him. While him gone partying with Omar, she sitting in my sofa telling me how him promise to take her out the same night. I had to lie to the poor child, tell her that him must have forgotten, and that he just went to visit his aunt and might soon be back. Every night the damn boy goin' out and him not taking her, and she not getting the message. Him giving her so much bun all she need now is a little bit of cheese and a glass a lemonade and she have lunch.[3] The few times him borrow my car I find used condom underneath the car seat. I remember asking the damn boy if he having sex with them cheap, worthless girls that have no respect for themselves, in my car. He say to me,

"I duh know what you talking 'bout, mom."

"You *duh* know what I talking 'bout? You want to study engineering and you can't even speak properly?" is what I ask him.

"So, what about them condoms I find under the seat?"

"Those are probably just balloon, mom, I don't think you know what condom look like. They had condoms in your days?" That damn boy is a real revelation. Pure crosses and temptations!

Anyway, I finish making him bed and cleaning him room, and about to go sit down and put up my feet a little, when I hear my front grill opening and somebody coming into the house. I know it's not Jacky, as she not coming back before late in the afternoon - have herself a job interview. So it must be One Eye Margy. She the only other person brazen enough to open my door without knocking. Sure enough, is she come through the door.

One thirty in the afternoon and One Eye Margaret come by wearing some bright red track pants that her sister in America sent, along with a blue blouse with nothing but laces and frills. Having another bad clothes, bad hair, bad make-up and, you can bet, bad breath, day.

She finally build up her courage to leave that good-for-nothing, empty-pocket man, who look like a constipated mule. Now she goin' have to fend for herself. Fool go pick up man with hair growing straight out of the middle of him forehead and she don't expect problems. Crosses!

"Howdy doo Doretta, what good deeds can you do for the poor today?" Is not that she think I am any Salvation Army, it's the same thing

---

3   "Giving Bun" or "Getting Bun" are Jamaican expressions meaning cheating on or being cheated on.

she say to everybody.

Just so she waltz herself straight into my living room, put down her Easter Bunny purse on my side table. I've never seen a woman without grandkids walk around with so many sweets in her purse. Half of the time it full of ants because she leave a sweetie open inside there.

I tell her good afternoon, ask her how come she wearing track suit and never jog a day in her life.

"You like it?" is what she ask me. "I have to work with my assets, you know, show them off. How else I goin' get man?" I ask her if she looking for another man after the crosses that the last one bring, she tell me she still young enough and need some action. Hehehe. She is something else, I tell you. Ask me if I can put on a pot of water for her. As always, she bring her own tea and sugar.

"I have to leave at two o'clock to go by the school, you know Margy." I ain't got nowhere under the sun to go, but you gotta establish some things early with her 'cause if you leave it to her then a short visit becomes a Christmas Sunday service at church. Never met a woman who can chat as much as Margy. She come by almost every day that the good Lord gives her. Has nothing to talk about, but it's her habit. She is all right.

"What Brando say really happen with that girl?" I ask her. Brando is her only son, and he going out with a Seventh Day Adventist girl, say him find his true faith. Now people say him fat up the belly of another girl who go to the same church. There's ain't no end to the crosses in this world!

"Him say Mona goin' stay with him. Say she understand that he is human and humans make mistake. I hear that Mona mother pressuring them to get married."

"Is the girl even good-looking? 'Cause I know that is only ugly people go Seventh Day church, and all o' them looking man and those big rings."

"She could have been, but her nose get in the way."

"So what him goin' do with the girl now that him get her pregnant? And what 'bout the baby considering that him not working?"

"Well him goin' have to find a way to take care of the child. I don't promise anybody that I taking care of anybody pickney. I had one pickney and one is all I wanted," is what Margy tells me.

"It look like I will have to file for custody o' that child," I tell her, "'Cause if the father is an idiot, and the mother is also obviously an idiot, then that child won't have a chance."

"Well, it's either him and Mona going to have to find another church, or him baby mother, 'cause it won't look good at all to have all of them going to the same church and everybody know what happen."

She ask me if I can't turn one of the fans in her direction so she can get some of the cool breeze as well, as if I had invited her to my house.

While she drinking her tea, I finish up some of the work I had in the kitchen, and put the clothes on the line. When I come back to the living room, Margy looking even more comfortable and relaxed, kicked off her shoes, and turn on the TV.

"I hear that Jacky had a job interview today," she say, as if I wasn't the same one who tell her about it two days ago.

Any minute that fool fool pickney coming back from her job interview. She has had four good jobs in the last eight months. Good jobs, and manage to lose every one of them. She can't wake up that early, she don't like that boss, the people them a thieves and liars, and so on and so forth. One excuse after another. I ask the fool what she really want to do with her life, she tells me she want turn movie star. God bless her if she expect that my pension goin' take care of her!

"Yes, she should be back soon, but I won't be here, as I have to go by the school."

"I hope she get this one. Is a paralegal position with that company... What them name again?" I tell her, Nunes and Scholefield. "How Rebecca up in foreign? When's the last time you hear from her?"

"She is alright. Working hard as usual. I think she having some trouble with her husband but she won't tell me what it is."

"Is only one year now that them married, what kinda trouble could they be having?"

I tell her I don't know, and that I have to go get ready to go to school. I feeling like I must now have Coolie blood inside of me, with this bare faced lie I telling. But even after I turn on the pipe in the bathroom, she still looking relaxed, watching CNN on my TV. So I tell her that I will see her later. Little by little she started putting her things together. Almost twenty minutes more before she leave! I already have on clean clothes and looking like I really leaving the house.

Anyway, after she leave, I change back into some yard clothes, and go for my mangoes. I always have to hide those mangoes from the pickney dem. Same way them take whatever money them find around the house, is the same way them take my mangoes. I carry the plastic chair, go on top of the roof where I like to eat my mangoes in peace. Tony might smell them from him room if I eat them inside the house, and Jacky she might come back soon. The damn dog is already there on the roof, look like him sun-bathing. The last time I come on the roof and see the dog eating one of the pickney shoes, I tried taking it from him and the damn dog nearly bite off my hand. Growled at me as if I was a stranger and not the one feeding her! Damn dog!

Anyway, this is how I eat them three East Indian and two Julie mangoes. And is so I end up falling asleep for two hours in the hot afternoon sun with the pickney in my belly. I have no one to blame but myself for how this child going to turn out.

CHAPTER 11

Guy

My dearest Semicolon, I don't know why my Jesus loves me, but He does.

When I was growing up, it was a common thing for kids to try to stick things in their nostrils. Kids today probably still try to do the same. Marbles were one of those things we often tried, and stones. My mama would often say to me,

"Kenny, the only thing you should ever put in your nose is your elbow." My mama was right.

When I was in my teenage years I met a gentleman whose name was Guy. He was an English teacher at my High School and one of only two people I ever told that I was going to write a book one day. The other person was a gorgeous, as-desirable-as-winning-the-lottery brown girl I fell desperately in love with about eight years later. I remember the distinct reactions of both. I had been trying to impress her, to see if I could get our relationship to move up a notch, essentially from flirt to fuck. So I slipped her a note with the important news about writing my book one day. We were in a class on English Literature. My note went something to this effect:

I plan to write a book one day.
Stephan

This is the note she slipped me in return:

I am elated that I am able to be in your presence, and I will revel in every minute that you can spare to be with me before your career explodes!! The simple thought of knowing a man who is destined for greatness excites me and transmits a feeling of warmth through my body as if I were a green lizard basking in the early morning Caribbean sun.

We had had very different levels of education up until then. I kept her note in my diary for years.

I spent many days and nights thinking about that girl, picturing her climbing up on me like a newly-released Madonna single mounting up the charts. How mango sucking sweet that would have been! I remember how she loved eating chalk. She even had one of the teachers save her the ends of the green sticks, which were her favorite. Terri-Ann was her name.

Anyway, Guy's response was very different from this girl's. He said to me at the time,

"Stephan, you haven't lived long enough and experienced enough of life to write a book yet."

And I said to him, "What would people like you know anyway?" I said this to the guy because I was upset with what he had said, but also because there was something else bothering me. I would write about it some five years later, in this form:

"Searching"

He was created at the top
by the Highest, Most Divine,
and though it is accepted

that he was lost for a time,
it was never clear to anyone
why he would expect to find,
the essence of his Being,
the Spirit sublime,
at the very bottom
of his own kind.

K. Lovelace, circa 1989

I wrote this because word in the 'hood was that the guy went to three different *male* doctors with big hands to get his prostate checked, in one year. Folks said he said he did it because he wanted to "be sure" even though there was no history of any form of cancer or prostate problem in his family. He went to black male doctors with big hands, even though Chinese and Indian doctors with smaller hands were just as good at checking prostates. Even though female doctors could also have easily stuck their fingers up his ass to check his prostate for him.

Word in our classroom was also that one day, he caught a child misbehaving at our school and told the child, "Your little ass is mine now," and between the ribbing from the other kids and the nature of the threat, the child, reportedly, had nightmares for months.

It was also joked that he was a guy who thought that men, like Porsches, looked better from behind. If we are to be blunt, word was that the guy was gay. In rural Jamaica. Where, compared to gays, parents would much sooner invite goat thieves to tend to their retirement finances.

Hence Guy, in a country full of Gangstas, Rude Youths, Rude Bwoys, Shottas, Cocksman, and Dons, was one of the rare, marked-with-three-6s-on-his-forehead, better to have been born dead, 'batty men', as gays were not so affectionately labeled.

Initially, he didn't respond to my outburst. But after a while he quietly

said,

"What do you mean by that?"

Guy, 1985

Now, given that we were already very familiar and had covered many topics before the subject of my book came up, topics ranging from suicide to the purpose of mathematics and my mama's cooking, I thought I could ask him, "Guy, aren't you gay?" This is what I did.

We were both sitting on a bench by the school cafeteria, with our faces looking down towards the playfield. When he turned to me, I could see very clearly that he wasn't yet ready to deal with what I was asking him. Like you often see sinners try to turn to Christ, but they turn away again because they are not yet ready to deal with what He asks of them. And you know that they will only turn back to Him, when they are either truly desperate or dying. So too, he turned to me, but I could see in his eyes that the time hadn't come. So he said,

"Why do you ask something like that?"

I chuckled sardonically, because it was obvious. The news had gone around that there were many folks offering him death at a low price, because of a rumor that he had molested an un-ripened boy. A big guy molesting a little guy, whose ass was too tiny for even a marble to fit in. This is the rumor I had heard and needed to get off my chest with my teacher. It was extremely disturbing because by then I knew that:

- A goat thief in rural Jamaica was like Lucifer disobeying God in heaven.
- A gay guy anywhere in Jamaica was like Lucifer cast violently into the pits of hell.
- A big gay guy molesting a little guy with a tiny hole was as despicable as Lucifer trying to squeeze himself back into heaven.

Moreover, rumor also had it that a mob was already in place and waiting. I suspect that if people had thought that he was gay but it was only his cup of tea that he alone drank from, then maybe that would have been fine; but when, they say, he tried to serve it to others in a big teapot... well that was a different matter altogether.

So here we were with a mob, again. Not the same mob of rural farmers, but a mob of regular working Joes. Some people believe that there are differences between a Jamaican rural mob and an intellectual, professional or working-class mob. Not true. To these folks I present:

Glenroy

Many years after the conversation with Guy, I went to study at a college in Kingston. There were thousands of students there, and certainly more than enough to form many mobs. I knew a guy there, who people said was gay.

Glenroy looked a lot like a normal person. He had hair on his head, and a head to have hair on. He had two ears, two eyes, eyebrows and eyelashes (albeit well-done), a nose, a mouth with teeth and tongue, a neck, a chin, shoulders, arms with elbows, wrists, fingers with fingernails, a body with a navel, legs with thighs, knees, ankles and feet, and toes with toenails. He also had an ass, of course, which is the reason he could be gay. I mention these details because they are important.

Glenroy, it turned out, was neither smart enough nor fast enough, to escape a mob of college students. In the wee hours of the morning, this intellectual mob caught him. He was later found on the soccer field.

The soccer field of Old Trafford, home pitch of Manchester United, is one of the most beautiful fields a man's eyes will ever behold. The soccer field at my college was different, almost like Anfield at Liverpool, but a little worse. It was a dustbowl. Surrounded by trees. The only thing which climbed those trees, was algae. We found Glenroy in the midst of some crab grass and a few patches of sorrow. And we saw the handiwork of an intellectual mob whose motions had been timed with dying cries. After what they did to Glenroy, this is how we found him:

A trip to a reserve

A business associate of mine told me that he once took a trip to Namibia. It was a safari of sorts. He went to a reserve where they had a few lions. The tourist guides claimed that there were more lions than the few that he saw. My associate said that there was a wall with a small letterbox-sized opening, covered by a glass window, where tourists peeped through and feasted their eyes on the malnourished-looking lions. Apparently, a year before, there was a lion feeder, who used a special contraption to feed them. This had a chain running along what looked like a small, one-foot wide train track; the feeder would put the meat on the chain and pull on some part of the contraption; the chain would move, and the meat would be carried along the small tracks to a feeding point in the reserve. The malnourished-looking lions would smell the fresh smell of dead meat, wash their paws, brush their manes, and come on down for dinner.

The way the story goes, one day the chain got stuck. The lion feeder went into the reserve to get it unstuck - because stuck things should be made unstuck. The lion feeder was in the process of getting the chain unstuck when a look-out shouted out that the lions were already groomed and coming down for dinner. The lion feeder, it is said, started walking back to the gate and then decided to turn around, go back, and finish the job. The look-out again shouted out,

"What the fuck do you think you are doing? Get out!" Or something to such effect.

But the lion feeder calmly said, "These lions know me, they have seen me around for many years, they know that I am the one who feeds them, they will not harm me."

And in that manner he fed the lions.

The forensics team that later came, was dispersed to different parts of the reserve to find pieces of the lion-feeder's body. To find pieces of his hair, his head, his ears, his eyes, his eyelashes, his eyebrows, his nose, his mouth, his tongue and teeth, his neck, his chin, shoulders, arms and elbows, wrist, fingers and fingernails, his body and breasts and navel, his legs and thighs, knees, ankles and feet, and his toes and toenails. And also his ass.

This is exactly the same manner in which we found traces of Glenroy.

While I stood there, down by the soccer field that day, I saw the religious flies who, like John the Baptist, were spreading the good news, but to maggots and vultures.

"Your salvation is at hand!" is what they said.

There were a few dogs that had heard the good news and came as well, but they came out of curiosity. Both the dogs and the murdered man were the subject of discussion at college for days after. Some argued that dogs were man's best friend until man invented cars and started lavishing all his attention on the inanimate object instead. So there was a falling out in the friendship, hence the reason these dogs appeared to have had no sympathy for Glenroy and hadn't come to his rescue. Others reasoned eloquently, that dogs did not appreciate the finer points of gender socialization, and were confused as to whether a feminine man was still a man and would qualify as a best friend.

The only other creatures that I noticed at the scene that day were a pair of butterflies. I learnt from them that they were an old couple that had already lived a long, full twelve days out of the thirteen that they were allotted. Their eyes held the wisdom of creatures who had seen a lot in their long lives, and who understood the nature of things at their essence. This, together with their own imminent departure from this world, was perhaps the reason for the tears I believe I saw beginning to form in those same eyes, before they turned away, softly fluttered their wings, and took to the skies in search of another place to spend the final Thursday of their lives.

(Grandma Bell was dead by then, but I know what she would have said about Glenroy.)

Back to Guy. The guy never answered my question. Not to this day.

I suspected that he must have had a really hard childhood.

When I lived in Jamaica I often felt as if my ass was tight and constipated. I made drawings in my notebook of what my ass looked like then. This was what I thought it looked like:

Ø

I also drew signs above my ass. One looked like this:

Please note that this is a very different sign from the one below, which might have given some folks the wrong impression.

I no longer live in Jamaica, but this is what my ass still looks like:

Ø

The sign is still there. The first one.

CHAPTER 12

The Fire

"The Fire"

It was well over two hundred years since anyone was last surprised by the events which followed, when an incompletely put-out butt of cigarette was left near a barn full of dry hay. Around those parts, even the descendants of slaves had known the possible consequences of this. Moreover, there was always the occasional item of news on the box, or talk after Sunday service, about someone who had lost everything to a fire. And, if for any reason these weren't enough, there was always the reminder by his woman, issued every single day that the good Lord gave her, about the dangers of his habit.

"If you don't burn something down, Heaven help us, then one day that thing is surely going to kill you. One fine day. Yes Sir, mark my words."

The look on his face as he stood there was, therefore, not one of surprise; and no one would have expected it to be.

He was thinking about the woman. She had gotten up in age, couldn't move much these days. Hadn't aged gracefully, and the varicose veins on her legs were as hard to look at as her bickering was to listen to. But she was a good woman, and had taken good care of him, forty-two years now last June. Had remained steadfast in her faith, unyielding to any form of temptation, including some of the flesh that at times he had hoped she would give in to, especially back in the old days. Loved her bible and her Lord; cooked one of the best fried catfish anyone ever cooked in those parts. She was a good woman she was.

The girl had turned out to be alright. Had decided, on her own, to quit school at nine years old, and the woman had not said anything. Had her first child at fifteen, but this was okay for those parts. He would have liked it if she had gone off to the city, studied to become a nurse or something, like one of those you saw on the box in their pretty little white uniforms; but all in all, she had turned out okay. Had found herself a decent, church-going fellow, who worked hard, stayed away from the bottle, and only struck her once - but that was alright, for she had learned to treat him with respect and there were no troubles after that.

She was standing next to him now, watching the barn burn, bearing witness like the rest of the animals that had been saved. Her sobs were drowned out by the roar and the crackles and pops of the fire, but he knew her suffering was great.

The boy was a good boy. Respected his mother and father, worked hard, seemed to know how to speak with the animals. Had never been to the doctor once in his life; had good blood. Never been to school either, but that was okay; he took care of the farm, helped to feed the family. Was a brave boy, never afraid to go out on the farm or to the barn alone at night if he heard any strange sounds. Slept lightly that boy did. Got kicked in the face once by a goat while trying to milk the creature, but learned his lesson after that without being told. The woman had loved the boy the most.

One of the greatest regrets he had in all his life, was that he had never called the boy 'son'. That was just the way things were in those parts. There were a few times that he could remember, on a Sunday evening now and then, sitting with the boy on the veranda, when he had thought of taking a sip of his coffee, quietly putting it down, and casually beginning a conversation with 'Son'. Sometimes after watching one of those family shows that came on at six o'clock on the box. But some words didn't come off a man's tongue easily in those parts.

These are some of the things he reflected on, while standing there, watching the fire burn, helpless to do anything. Many other thoughts and memories entered his mind as he stood there, but, most of all, he thought about how the fire must have started, and he thought about how hard the boy had fought to put the fire out. These were the two main things he would think about for the rest of his life, which is perhaps an extravagant way of saying for the next two hours and fourteen minutes.

K. Lovelace, very short-story, 1997

It was about a decade after writing this, Semicolon, that I sat down one day to try and analyze what had really happened, and how our minds try to deal with difficult childhood experiences. Writing stories that poke at the truth from a safe distance allowed me the space to work through my thoughts and emotions and to capture a little of what I had seen as a child. Of course it was my own papa that had never called me 'son'. Also, I had in fact seen a fire, but not of a barn, and the one that burned wasn't a boy.

There are many things that you see and do when you are a boy growing up in rural Jamaica. One of the things that always captivated me, was the manner in which we killed chickens and pigs. There were two main ways to kill chickens. One way was to tie a rope to the feet of the chicken, then tie the chicken to a branch of a tree and then cut off its head and run far away as it thrashed and splashed its blood all around. The other way, was to place a bucket over the body of the chicken, leaving only its head exposed, place something heavy on the bucket and slice the head off the chicken. The only difference between this method and the previous is that the body would become still in the darkness of a bucket, concealing the secrets of those last seconds of life. With the first method you stood and watched the futile, violent fluttering.

With pigs the method was quite different. The most effective involved inserting a long sharp pole through a precise spot in the neck, and holding the pig and the pole firm, while the life drained out of it. As the pole slowly pierced, the pig would squeal at a pitch that would have dogs in Alaska perking their ears. I can still remember the way they held those pigs. Even my Aunt Frida would be there with the men, holding on to a pig. She was a big woman my Aunt Frida was, and by that I do not mean simply one of those people whose body is best accommodated by loose fitting clothes. One of the things that has stuck in my mind after more than twenty-five years, is a slice of a conversation she had with a 'just come from foreign' cousin she hadn't seen in something like five hundred years:

"Oh Frida girl, it's been such a long time since I last saw you! My Lord, how time flies! I can still remember you when you were just a little girl!"

To this my aunt replied, "Oh no honey, you remember me when I was *young*, for the good Lord knows that I ain't never been *little!*" And then they laughed and embraced, happy to see each other, and comforted by the knowledge that such truths can only be uttered between close friends and relatives.

Anyway, that was my aunt, holding on to the pig, or otherwise waddling in front of the group as though she alone was going to part the Red Sea, or getting tired quickly from all her exertions, then fussing to park her ass, as though it was a Leyland 18 wheeler.

On one particular day, while the pig and the pole were being held firm, the pig escaped. Needless to say, it did not escape death; as we all know, nothing escapes death, no matter how humble he now claims to be. This pig ran faster than Usain Bolt, and squealed bloody murder for all to hear.

Sometimes when I awake in the middle of the night with cold sweat running down my body, I hear that same pig squealing, but what I see, is the face of the woman who burned. It was one of the cruelest, most painful things I have ever seen. I was fifteen at the time; she was old and insane. And she was black, like me. Black, poor and insane - like my family.

It was a group of teenagers who lived close to our depression, that had set the mad woman on fire. They blamed Rodney, a boy from a good family, who already drove a car to school at age sixteen. They confessed that they had all indeed poured the gasoline on her, but said it was never their intention to actually set her on fire. They claimed they were just playing with the lighter – Rodney's lighter – when the fire accidentally caught a small piece of her clothing, and that the fire burst into such a large flame so quickly that they didn't know what to do. Rodney was standing there when we all emptied our yard and got to the scene. The police were there as well, walking lazily around her charred remains, with smoke still escaping from her hair and body. There was no remorse on Rodney's face, not that I could see. His friends were there as well, some anxious. Witnesses to the fire said that the old woman had squealed like a pig being poled, which is why every time I awake from my nightmares, I see that charred body running like a pig, squealing like a pig, and dying like a pig.

I am really happy that this will all be behind me now, thanks to my doctor. He says that these nightmares I have are "nothing that can't be cured by late evening exercise and a good healthy diet."

CHAPTER 13

What I am

There is absolutely nothing good about me! I am filthy, nasty, dirty, impure! Right through to my corrupt kernel! I am a stinking frog! Not even my nose is clean! I am nothing but fraud, a vessel for corruption, fornication, deceit, nastiness, bureaucracy reform.

No one should trust me because I am un-trustworthy, un-faithful, un-loyal, un-true! I am a dog, a nigga, a liar, an employee, a despicable shithead! No one should marry me, date me, sleep with me, give me attention, give me time or a salary! Rottenness is what I am! The worst fucking kind!

I am not shit, I am filth - not smelly, but abominable satanic stench! Pure darkness! What I am not even the good Lord knows even though He had me made. Liar! Thief! Cheater! Pot-bellied nigga who won't even go to the gym! Gum, chewed by cavity filled teeth, sticking to a mongrel's paw. That's me!

What could I possibly be worthy of? Love? Affection? Attention? Education? I am not even human! Don't even look at me! This is for your own good!

Wish me to be dead! Go ahead! Wish for it! Do me the favor! Invoke the plagues upon my head! Wish me to blaspheme and be struck down instantly! Wish me not to even leave a will! Not to leave anything at all behind!

Helloooo fellow people! Can't you see that I am a fish? I am listening but I just don't want to hear! I know capacity building of the state is important but isn't mango also critical?
I am: lonely, crazy, hungry, sad, pedestrian, losing my mind, an employee, horny, sick, afraid.

I choose employee.

This conversation does not exist; I do not exist; He does not exist. Or, this conversation is dead; my soul is dead; He is dead.

I choose bureaucracy.

I need treatment, and it must start tonight!

I am a fish.

I can talk more if I am more drunk.

Thanks for all your kind attention people.

K. Lovelace, notes from my dinner meeting, April 27, 2011

CHAPTER 14

Little Boy Wonder

"What's the time Mr Wolf? Woof, woof!"
"It's time to visit Mr Hippo, Mr Fox. Ahoo!"
"Where does he live Mr Wolf? Woof, woof!"
"In a glass house at the bottom of the sea, Mr Fox. Ahoo, ahoo!"
"So no one can throw stone at his house, Mr Wolf? Woof, woof!"
"That is true Mr Fox. Ahoo, ahoo!"
"And how do we get to his house Mr Wolf? Woof, woof!"
"We take a submarine taxi from Milk River Bath, Mr Fox. Ahoo!"

[Note: For the life of me I have no idea why we made the sound of a dog for a wolf, or why the fox made the sound of a wolf.]

Tommy was a little boy, and a little boy was he. Tommy was a skinny boy with fat expectations. Tommy was a good boy who, with proper encouragement, could have been naughty. Tommy was just a boy. Tommy was a song without a refrain.

Tommy and I played a lot when we were young. He liked to be Mr Wolf.

But how do we really talk about Tommy?

In the 1970s and early '80s, Tommy was my closest childhood friend living in our yard. [Sean, who I will mention later, was my best buddy at school.] But where do we begin his story?

There is an old time saying that we have in Jamaica: "What stays too long, serves two masters." We used that a lot when I was a child. It basically

98

means that if you take too long to use or eat something, then someone else will use or eat it for you.

It was a popular saying because we, as family, cousins and friends, would often sit together at mealtimes to eat whatever little food we had; we knew that if we didn't eat the little we had quickly, then someone else close to us would grab it and eat it for us. They would then laugh and say,

"What stay too long serve two masters." I played the same prank - if indeed it could be called 'prank' based on how serious some folks took their food. We all played this prank.

A few years ago I was having dinner with some Jamaicans at Negril Restaurant in New York, which is actually a nice Jamaican restaurant and not the usual hole-in-the-wall. These Jamaicans, who I had only recently met, wanted to know if I myself was a *true* Jamaican. As part of their barrage of questions, they asked me what 'test' I would devise to determine if a Jamaican who grew up in the rural areas, had brothers and sisters. It was one of the easier questions. The response:

"Invite those Jamaicans over for dinner and put a little food on each of their plates, then watch how they eat." We all laughed knowingly. [The ones who eat with their arms curled protectively like crab claws around their plates most likely had brothers and/or sisters.]

I mention this because it helps to explain a lot about Tommy.

Tommy was a little boy with a little ass. His ass was perhaps about this big:

O

Tommy also had a very little life. His life was perhaps about this big:

O

In mathematical terms, you could think of Tommy's ass and his life like this:

$$O \approx O$$

And his life was worth shit.

So, Tommy had just a little life. The problem was that he waited much too long to use it himself, and hence, someone else took it from him. He was dead, *just like that*. (Grandma Bell: "If that boy had come to church that would never have happened to him.")

'Just like that', perhaps one of my favorite Jamaican expressions. All *true* Jamaicans know the meaning of something happening *just like that*, and they never ask for anything further to be explained. It could come in a short form, such as, "My dear, that boy robbed the bank and got away with it *just like that!*" Clear, concise, definitive.

Or, it could come in a rambling, long form, and still be *just like that*. About eighteen years ago while I was studying in Kingston, one of my cousins called and told me that my (only) rich aunt's house was robbed the night before. I shall elaborate, but first, a note on how my aunt became rich: she was on my mama's side of the family and lived in an entirely different neighborhood. She didn't become rich based on her own efforts. As I heard it, after high school she went for a job at the local government office and someone who was on the interview committee asked her,

"What personal characteristic do you think will most negatively affect your work?", or something like that.

And the girl version of my aunt said, "Well, you see, I like to sleep and sometimes after lunch I feel very sleepy and it's difficult for me to get anything done."

As we understand it, the shock felt by the committee was intensified as she proceeded to elaborate on measures she normally takes to 'fight' the urge. So, as we were saying, she became rich because she had the good fortune to marry a man who had a souvenir shop in Montego Bay, tourist capital of Jamaica. Some folks say that he married her on the way back from his first wife's funeral, because they were already having an affair and he didn't like being alone. His shop was located on the hotel strip in

Montego Bay where, if you flew over the island, you could think you have discovered a colony of rich, white people in a poor, black country. This was one of those souvenir shops where, today, almost everything in it that proudly advertises Jamaica and Reggae, is actually made in China, so you have to check the labels carefully if you want something authentic. And everything in his store, was priced at *if you are a local then you can't afford anything in here US$* and above. And in the '70s his business did well in spite of the socialist regime, so he had made good money. They did their best to conceal their wealth.

Anyway, coming back to the robbery, my uncle-in-law had gone hup to Hotlanta for a little holiday hover there to heat some Hamerican food (some of us Jamaicans struggle with our h's more than others), and had not yet returned. So my aunt was on her own for a week. My cousin, Wayne, explained to me that while my rich aunt's house was being robbed at 2 a.m., she had tried calling the police on numerous occasions, having locked herself into her bedroom. The robbers were there for nearly three hours, slowly going about their business of taking everything they felt they needed. He said that the neighbors had also called the police. Meanwhile, the thieves took everything in my aunt's house, loading up a truck, and leaving her with only her allergies… then they got away *just like that*. When I heard this I didn't ask, "Did the police catch them?" or "Why didn't the police come?" or "How could they get away *just like that?*" My cousin was not expecting any such follow-up questions. In any event, I already knew all the possible answers, which could have included:

- The police station was closed and no one picked up the phone when the calls were made
- A policeman answered and asked my aunt to call back in the morning because it was too late
- A policeman answered and said they had no cars at the moment, and wondered if my aunt or someone else could send a friend

with a car to pick him up so that he could come and apprehend the robber

- A policeman answered and said he was the only one at the station and he had to "man the station". If you asked him why he couldn't call the other officers at home he would then ask you in return, "Do you know what bomboclaat time it is?"

And so on and so forth. The one answer you would not hear is that the police came in time to catch the thieves, or that they caught them at any time later. So, after listening, I simply echoed, "So they really robbed her, *just like that*?" which was to acknowledge what I had heard. It was as simple as that, *just like that*. Thieves stole and got away with it, *just like that*. Mobs chopped up gays and little boys and got away with it, *just like that*.

So there could be any possible number of reasons for a dirt-poor, little boy like Tommy to die, *just like that*. No investigation, no trial, no sense of wonder and intrigue. Just dead. *Just like that*. For all we knew, it could have been a crime committed by the CIA or the Illuminati. It really was as simple as that.

How he died, is quite easy to explain, as there were, at least, two first-hand witnesses: my brother and Garnet, Tommy's older brother.

Tommy, as I mentioned before, generally had very little to eat. When some people say, "I badly need to watch an episode of Law and Order", you generally know that they can survive another few days without it. Tommy, however, really needed food. Whenever he was allowed to venture outside of his yard, he would spend a lot of time at other neighbors' houses or in the cane fields, mango trees, orange trees, coconut trees and so forth, searching for something to eat.

The other thing our little boy wonder did a lot, was chase after trucks. The first type, were the sugar cane trucks that passed through the village. As boys we would run behind these trucks trying to pull some of the sweet sugar cane off them. We all did this, though, in his case, it was perhaps more for survival than entertainment.

The other type, the trucks we all chased purely for entertainment, were the trucks carrying ice from the ice factory to sell to folks. Few people had refrigerators in those days.

We often hung out at the ice factory, watched the men load the trucks, listened to their stories (almost always about sleeping with some women with tight coochies), and, sometimes begged a little money from them. In response to this latter, they occasionally responded by pulling us up by our collars (if we were wearing shirts), as if to check that we were not also made in China, before giving us a little slap, or, sometimes, a few dollars. The pulling up by the collar was just a part of the process, whatever the decision to follow. We knew this as well as they did, which is why we continued to show up and beg, and they to slap and give.

When the trucks were loaded, the workers hopped into the back of the truck, clutching the metal clamps they use to grip and unload the blocks of ice. When the trucks drove off we ran behind them. The workers standing in the bed of the truck generally found this entertaining - watching us trying to jump and hang on to some part of the truck and get a free ride before jumping off. These workers were paid very little, and tended to be the lesser-educated workers at the ice factory. The lowest caste. They were like us, and they laughed with us. They slapped us. They gave us money. Perhaps they too could remember days gone by when they were the ones who ran behind the trucks.

The drivers, on the other hand, never found these events amusing. They were better paid, perhaps high school drop-outs, or just people who thought they were on their way *up*. And their truck was the vehicle taking them there. Maybe they were embarrassed by the sight of us *riff raff* hanging on to their self-image. So they always shouted at us. They always used adult language with us. They always threatened to do things to us that only the State has the legitimacy to do to people.

Now, going back to Tommy. On that particular day, the driver of the truck that he was chasing stopped the truck abruptly... and then reversed. It was as simple as that, and we had fresh road kill.

(Grandma Bell: "If he had gone to church this would never have happened to him!")

Heated arguments followed about what made the driver reverse at that specific point in time, given that there were no obstacles in front of him. Some noted he was an experienced driver, even had his own *one previous lady driver, full service record, rides smooth like a ghetto girl* second-hand car. But this is to fuss about small, trite issues. The simple truth is that trucks are designed in such a way that they can go both forward and backward, and he chose to go backward. And that was that, *just like that*. My brother, and Tommy's brother, saw, and carried the news home.

Of course, we were well-used to seeing bad news walking down that lane, strutting as though he owned more land and paid more property taxes than all of us. But there was something a little more peculiar than watching *a royally fat black woman with a big ass trying on a Victoria Secret Mini-Wedge Boot* about the scene, when my brother and Garnet came through the lane without Tommy, their heads down, walking slowly. It wasn't normal.

Now, why did Tommy generally have so little to eat? The answer here again is also quite straightforward: because his papa didn't want him to eat. There.

Garnet and Tommy were very different in many ways but most noticeably in their eating habits. Garnet was a greedy little fucker - put anything in front of him and he would eat it, "except pussy," he claimed. Tommy on the other hand, always had the look of a delicate and depressed child, and didn't eat much even when he had something to eat. But it was also just this boy's sad ass luck, that while his mama went to work during the day, his papa was the one who, as part of his great contribution to global gender equality efforts, stayed home with the kids. Sitting on his stool all day smoking weed, eyes blood-shot and red (it is not clear whether this was from the smoke or envy for what others had.) Unemployed, but for the small job of making sure our little boy wonder didn't eat much, didn't play much, didn't smile much. You would have more chance finding a whale in the Rio Minho River, than hearing his papa once say a kind word to Tommy.

One day, his papa found out that Tommy had gone to a neighbor's house, not to play, not to climb their mango tree, not to do anything else, but to beg for food! The disgrace to his name! The disgrace on his house! The shame and disgrace! When his papa found out, he locked Tommy in the house for a few days. When little boy wonder (how he survived) came out, he was a different person. His mouth and lips were dried, cakey and darkened, and something inside him seemed to have been bent out of shape. His limbs looked parched, like embers for a wood fire. This was just a couple months before he died.

Oh Tommy, Tommy. You were like the afterthought to a silent thought, weren't you Tommy? Weren't you, stupid Tommy? Stupid Tommy expecting food. Stupid food. Stupid absent food. Even Tommy's shadow looked hungry. Sometimes when I was around him I thought I heard the Hallelujah chorus, and looked around to see if angels were swooping down to take him away.

Why, my beloved Semicolon, did his papa treat him like this? I will explain this bit a little more when I talk about some other related issues.

I am sure that the way Tommy died left quite an impression on my seventeen year old brother and on Garnet. Then there is the issue of the impression it left on my Uncle Bob. After I learnt about what had happened, I went to tell him my version of the events, but found him unmoved by the excitement. To be more accurate, I felt I had preached a passionate Revivalist chorus to a stiff, unblinking congregation of Catholics. He must have already heard the news. He just sat there, with the tail end of a spliff hanging loosely from the corner of his mouth, not listening to anything I was saying, just grunting the words from a 1970's

People's National Party socialist song. The bit I caught went like this:

> *"No bastard no deh again,*
> *No bastard no deh again,*
> *Everyone lawful"*

Which, translated, simply meant that there were no more bastards, as everyone was now lawful. There were other parts to the song, but this is the only part he sang. I suspected that he thought Tommy was a bastard, but I wasn't sure. I also didn't know why that would have mattered so much at a time when something so much more exciting had happened.

My Uncle Bob once reminded me that an orgasm will not last a day, but diarrhea will. This was his way of teaching me about the relative weight that joys and miseries will have in our lives. It seemed he not only expected Tommy to die, but that others would follow.

CHAPTER 15

Some Dialogue For The Heck Of It

My dearest Semicolon, a good editor would observe that more dialogue is needed in my story. Adds texture and richness. But where would I find dialogue just like that to insert into my story? When I reflect on my life in that *hateful* fucking place, what I remember are people and what happened to these people. I also remember certain events. I just cannot recall the dialogues, and I was hoping not to have to fabricate anything, especially something like a conversation, the memories and details of which change with each passing day. Anyway, let me go back and see what I can find for richness sake.

There I am, about nine or ten years old, running over to Tommy's little crustacean house (for some reason, I always thought they looked like crabs in one shell) to ask him if he can come out to play. Approaching the back door where he would normally be sitting quietly looking out. I am about to push my head through the half opened door to peek in and see if he is there. Then, voila! What have we found here, my love? Dialogue:

Tommy's mama:	Yu tink I don't know dat (that) yu fucking dat little stinking pussy *black like Marassa and Midnight* gal?[1]
Tommy's papa:	Wich raasclaat smaddy (somebody) tell yu dat?

107

Tommy's mama:	See! See! I knew it! See! Yu neva even ask me wich gal!!
Tommy's papa:	Yu don't have nothing better to do? Go learn to bomboclaaat cook!
Tommy's mama:	Is she yu giving money to a week time, don't? Is she why yu not feeding yu pickney dem (them), don't it, don't is she?
Tommy's papa:	Yu know how I get my money? Yu know what I have to do to get my raasclaat money? Woman, jus' go cook some food so I can eat, and shut you pussyclaat mouth!
Tommy's mama:	Ohh, yu tink a so it go? Yu tink a so it go? Dat stinking pussy gal should wear nice clothes while my pickney dem can't go skool? Yu tink a so it go?
Tommy's papa:	Skool? Skool? Wuman if yu know what I know yu wouldn't mention nutting 'bout skool to me! Why yu no go learn to cook and stop raasclaat boddering me?
Tommy's mama:	What? What? I shouldn't ask yu nutting? I must just lie down and mek (let) yu walk all over me? She can fuck better dan (than) me? Is because her pussy tighter dan my pussy why yu giving her all of my money? Eeh? Eeh?
Tommy's papa:	Jus' watch yuself wuman, jus' watch yu raas self, cause if yu don't shut yu raasclaat mou-
Tommy's mama:	What? What yu gonna do? Yu tink I 'fraid o' yu? Dirty wutless bwoy like yu? Watch

	me! I goin Obeahman dis same Friday! Tomorrow, tomorrow! I goin obeah yu raasclaat! Mek yu stay at yu raas yard and tek (take) care of yu bomboclaat pickney dem! Watch me! Watch how I goin sort out your business!
Tommy's papa:	Obeah who? Obeah who gal? A kill yu want me kill yu? Wait! A kill yu want me kill yu? [Slap! Slap! Whack! Whack!] Obeah who? Obeah who?
Tommy's mama:	Murder! Murder![2]
Tommy's sister:	Mama! Mama!
Tommy:	(Nothing) [3]

Explanatory notes: [1] Tommy's papa liked his coffee the way he liked his affairs – hot, steamy, and *dark*, and he drank it often. He was popularly acclaimed for knowing the town inside and out and better than most seasoned taxi drivers, which was the true mark of a man with many women. [2] People rarely shouted "help" in these circumstances, 'murder' was more effective in drawing attention. [3] The last time Tommy voiced a freely-expressed opinion during one of these quarrels, his papa put a brutal end to the young democracy; thereafter Tommy, like a true cockroach, stayed out of the chicken fight.

Let's leave Tommy's family for a while. We want to hear something different, so let's not go to doors numbers 2,5,7, and 8. Georgie's papa just came home drunk so we will certainly avoid door number 11 also. Now where can we find some different dialogue? Brian's papa is standing at the side of their house showing immense affection to each member of his pack of nicotine, while kicking the dog (I swear dogs just couldn't get a break in that *hateful* fucking place), so we will skip that door as well. We are not going to hear much from door number 6; Wayne lives there with his mama - his papa left them so there isn't as much quarrelling these days. His mama once lost a public argument in a most embarrassing manner. Had all her ideas, dreams, thoughts, hopes and views, rubbished in public, and swept away into the garbage. Got royally and scornfully out-cussed, so much so that for months afterwards she rarely raised her head or her voice in public. Picked the wrong, fucking crackhead-bitch to quarrel with that time! Anyway, where, where, where shall we find some dialogue...? Aha! got it. Let's pass by Simone's little shed.

First, let's stop by Simone's mama's room, before we go on to the extended room Simone confiscated for her litter. There I am, at Aunt Josephine's window, listening. Not much of a dialogue but we go with what we have:

Aunt Josephine (about thirty-five years old or so): [Whimper, whimper, whimper.*]

Carmen:	The good Lord giveth and He taketh away.
Aunt Josephine:	[Whimper, whimper, whimper.]
Carmen:	Hummm, hummm, hummmm, shhhhh, hushhhhh, hummmm, the will of the Lord be done... Hushhhh, hushhhhh, shhhhhh.
Aunt Josephine:	[Whimper, whimper, whimper.]
Carmen:	Kum ba ya, ma Lord, kum ba ya, kum ba ya, ma Lord, kum ba ya, someone's crying ma Lord, kum ba ya, someone's praying ma Lord, kum ba ya...

* The horrible weeping and wailing from the day before, when her second still-born child was buried, is now over, so today she is only whimpering. The day before, there was a little burial ceremony at the

back of the house; a deacon from church had come to *say a few words* over the body that they buried under a banana tree. My own still-born sister was buried under the guava tree, so there was no more room there for this latest still-born. Deacon said some things that I really wanted to have a dialogue with him about, but never got the chance. Specifically, he quoted some scripture (Ecclesiastes?) and concluded, satisfyingly, "Here today, gone tomorrow." At which point I wanted to ask, "What about here today, gone fucking today, deacon?" But it's just as well I didn't, for I know what he would have said.

Let's leave Aunt Josephine. After all, it is not clear why a woman who already has more kids than teeth would want any more. Let us sneak up with Brian to Simone's little zinc room and listen. Ahh, some dialogue:

Simone:	Yes! Fuck it hard! Fuck it hard! Sink it in deep!
Random man:	Yu feel it? (pant pant) Yu feel it? (pant pant). Tek(take) dis(this)! Tek cocky gal!
Simone:	Yes! Yes! A feel it! Hard! Hard! Woyy! Woyy! It hot! Woyy! Hot!!
Brian:	Yes! Yes! Give it to har (her) hard! Hehe
Me:	Shh!
Random Man:	A who the fuck dat? (pant pant)

Peeping at others was no shame to either us or them, for we all knew that everything we did was being quietly observed by the cold unblinking eyes of Eternity.

Now see me there, running away from the zinc house, walking over to the spot where four older boys are playing a game of dominoes and having the deepest conversations on the shallowest topics. But here again, some dialogue. Just what we are looking for:

Me:	Dave, yu gettin six luv (love) again? Hehe

Dave:	Shut yu raas mouth and fuck off!
Me:	Hehehe. It really look like dem hav yu under pressure Dave. Hehe. Look like yu getting it good man. Straight up yu ass, Dave, hehehe.
Dave:	Same way I giv it good to yu madda and sista last night.
Older boy 1:	Partna, yu want to pose?
Older boy 2:	Alright. How much we reach now? Five luv?
Dave:	Five fucking what luv? When yu reach five? Y'all can't raasclaat count?
Me:	Look like yu 'bout to get a nice six luv Dave.
Dave:	What the raas! Yu want me thump yu in yu bomboclaat mouth bwoy? Run way and go suck yu pussyclaat madda! Yu stinking batty bwoy (homosexual)!
Me:	Yu still look like yu getting a nice six raasclaat love Dave. Dat is all I know Dave.

Dave reaches for his ratchet knife with murderous intent in his eyes, other older boys laughing, then I walk off towards our one-room house, there encountering my mama combing my sister's hair on the little veranda. More dialogue:

Me:	Mama, what we gettin fo' dinna?
Mama, softly:	Shit.
Me:	Kay, what happen to mama now?
Kay:	Don't ask me nutting! Don't ask me nutting.

And so on and so forth.

But it isn't all bad. Once in a while we emerged from the darkness of the sewers and our eyes were hurt by the unaccustomed light of day.

Sometimes I had another kind of dialogue:

Me:	Hey Guy, yu tink I will ever mek it out of dis place?
Guy:	Kenny, if you stay in school and if you keep asking that question, you will.

CHAPTER 16

In The Summer of that Year I Fell Madly in Love with a Red Snapper, Not a Trout

If you see Timbuktu then you have gone too far.
Have I already gone too far?
Can you explain yourself?
I don't think I am myself.

Ramblings, circa 1985

My love, the events described below were not recorded in my diary, so I have had to reconstruct them from memory. My memory being what it is, there is no guarantee that they are reported in exactly the manner in which they occurred. Nonetheless, they are based on actual events.

In the summer of 1985 I fell madly and deeply in love with a fish. At the time it happened, I already knew the difference between succumbing to things due to the inherent weaknesses in human nature, like the temptations of an under-aged girl, and to things that were unpardonable. Having a relationship with a trout would have been unpardonable, as everyone knew that, almost without exception, trouts were just sooooo gay! I did not, and I repeat, I did not, fall in love with a trout, and absolutely nothing transpired between me and any trout during that time.

I remember that summer well because in my country, summer was the only season we had. Everything else was, simply, the rest of the year. It is not like how it is here "up north", with all their seasons. Like their winter, which reminds me of an old aunt I had in Jamaica who was known to like fondling little boys to see "how big you are getting," and who liked to be kissed on the lips. She would embrace you with the heady smell of stale rum and lascivious desire, both undiluted, on her breath. Then she would press herself against you and ask, "You think you are too big to give your aunt a kiss?" And even though you try to push her away, you can't, because of both her strength and your mama's disapproving eyes. Like winter, embracing your little body - which offers little resistance, and placing a frigid, damp kiss on you, while she fondles all parts of your body with her cold icy fingers. Was I sexually abused? Homeboy turns politician: *I do not respond, I do not confirm, I do not deny*. In any event, I really and truly and genuinely hate winter! I always have. It feels like the Tribes of the North have not only butchered the weather, but they have ganged up and lynched the bloody sun. But I digress, my love.

As I was saying, it was summer, as I recall. And I did fall deeply in love with a fish. But it was a Red Snapper, which weighed about six pounds or so. She had really beautiful, soft eyes, and smooth skin. I met her one day when I went swimming, and we started to talk. Soon we were chatting and laughing, telling stories about our lives on the land and in the sea. There was a kindness in her eyes that made me feel so comfortable talking with her and sharing the stories of my childhood.

We agreed to meet again the next day, and so we did. I hadn't realized it on the first day, but, by the second, I saw just how much she knew of the world. She had a remarkable grasp of history, geology, politics, religion, sports, and a range of other subjects. We could talk forever and neither of us would get bored or upset, even when we disagreed. We continued meeting and talking every day after that and soon it was quite clear that we had fallen in love with each other. All the other fish and creatures in the sea could tell what was happening. Some days a crab or a sea bass would see us together, swim by and mutter something like, "Just get on with it already!" And they would laugh as they went on their merry, mischievous way.

But neither of us was ready for commitment, for we both had an uneasy feeling about our relationship and how it would be perceived by others, especially those people and creatures on land. And neither of us could really say for sure what the reaction would be from our respective families. While this unspoken concern remained unresolved, we continued with our courtship, with our long conversations, and with our quiet swims together. I could not have been happier even if I owned all the mango trees in the world and never had to steal mangoes ever again!

I remember, also, how we would stay up late at night sending secret messages to each other in bubbles through the air and in the water. Bubbles in the water carrying my messages to her. Bubbles in the air carrying her messages to me. And so we chatted, like young lovers, into the wee hours of the morning until sleep finally caught up with us, panting with the heavy breaths of a fat lady who has just run a mile.

One night she told me of her ancestry. She was a direct descendant of the two fish that Jesus used to feed the multitudes on the mountain with the five loaves of bread (see the Gospel according to St. Luke, chapter 9, verses 10-17). I learnt that night of the sacrifices that those two fish made for the good of man. And I understood the unspoken message that she was sending me then: that she too would make great sacrifices for me.

And I remember the promises. She promised me that, even though she did not normally eat meat, she would eat my worms, so that my mama would never have to give me worm medicines again at the end of summer. She touched my heart with that promise for I had always hated worm medicines, and seeing those creatures crawling out of me, turning and smiling before wriggling away to die. She was going to save me from all of that forever and for as long as I lived! In return, I promised that I would always take care of her, and that I would never let anyone ever hurt her. No fisherman, no Blackheart Man, no gunman, no politician, no lawyer, no hungry kids, no one! And she promised also that she would always love me, and I promised her the same. She said that she would give her life for me, give me her heart, her soul, her fins, her last breath. She wanted us to be together forever and always. I had faith in her. I believed her with all my life, with all my soul. I believed in her, for she loved me. She genuinely loved me. And if I could not believe her, then who could I believe?

CHAPTER 17

The purge

My past often thinks about me, and comes to visit whenever it feels inclined. My mind is just there, for my past to enter and exit. At times I feel as though I am on Rohypnol and being raped.

My past reminds me that I have known my sins from when they were very young and could barely creep on their knees, let alone walk. I knew them when they were still forming bones, and when people thought they were cute.

Semicolon, I have done things that I am not proud of. I continue to do such things. I can only hope that my motivations have changed.

July, 1985

I am absolutely positive that based on her global successes, she would not bother to even fart on us if she saw us now. But back then she was thirteen years old; ate ants; formally buried birds, cockroaches, and frogs; played 'doctor' and slept in an old wooden house with only two rooms.

I will leave out her name and the songs she has sung. If you did a Google search, her name would be in the top ten list of successful Jamaican female musicians, and you would probably recognize one or two of her songs. She was one of the most successful Jamaican female reggae singers of the 1990s. That's as much as I can say, as I simply can't afford to have some lawyer on my ass, threatening a lawsuit.

We called the same lady 'grandma' and spent many of our summers with her.

Every morning, grandma sent one or more of us to buy the items needed for breakfast, along with one cigarette. The process would be repeated in the evening for dinner, the only common ingredient being cooking oil and the cigarette.

The purge took place one summer while I was at grandma's house. My brother was there, along with the singer. I was fifteen years old.

Grandma was of the unshakeable opinion that, given the size of our little asses, none of us needed more than three squares of tissue to wipe it.

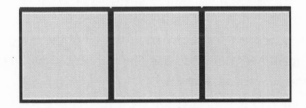

Three squares of tissue is about this much

In view of this, most times when we went to the latrine, we would supplement our ration with a bit of newspaper or some leaves. I particularly disliked going to the latrine at nights, when we had to use a bottle torch to light our way, and when it was harder to see whether a lizard, scorpion or Duppy was already seated on the toilet that you were about to lay your ass on.

I had to go to the toilet alone on the night of July 18.

My grandma's common-law husband, Mr Scott, father of our songstress' father, made a living selling little knicks and knacks in the local market. I was never sure how what he earned from selling needles, pins, clothes pegs and so forth, could feed a family. My grandma also sold small items in the same market. Some days she had us picking limes or cashews all day, which she then brought to the market to sell. Other times she traded four or five crocus bags filled with limes, for a few drums and a couple buckets of water from her next door neighbor. The neighbor would stretch a hose across to grandma's house and we would fill our drums ourselves, and then squeeze in a bath too. We would also make sure to drink as much water as possible directly from the hose, and fill all available containers with water - these were not formally part of the deal, but contracts were not as strict in those days.

Grandma always came home from the market first, in order to get dinner ready. Mr Scott had built a little outdoor kitchen out of wood and zinc, and we kept the dry firewood in there along with the pots and pans. My brother and I, along with out songstress, helped her with little things like fetching the water, but mostly we sat by the fireside watching her cook, and waiting for her to give us a little bit of the dough to put on a stick and roast over the wood fire. She rarely used her kerosene stove because the oil was too expensive.

At about 7.30 p.m. on July 18, I had the runs. It was normally dark by 6 p.m., and 7 p.m. was our bed-time. We were already in bed when I knocked on the door to the adjoining room and informed my grandma of this new development.

"Grandma, I need to go to the bathroom, I have a runny belly," is what I said to the door, knowing that she was still awake and would hear me.

Grandma, like many of the Old Timers, had a simple approach to things. She believed that if food was too visible then we would eat all of it quickly. For this reason, the crackers and biscuits and so forth were always locked away in a cupboard, and we kept slim and healthy. With the tissue it was the same – she obviously thought that if it were left where we could see it, then we would use more of it than was necessary. So she kept it in her room, and we had to ask her for it when needed, or resort to newspapers or leaves. It was only much later in life that I also wondered whether Mr Scott also had to ask.

Anyway, she came and opened the door, and from her private and vintage collection, gave me three squares of tissue which, if I didn't know better, I might have believed were previously used. But it was just the dampness of wherever she kept them. I told her that these would not be enough as I had the runs, and there was no newspaper in the house. She reaffirmed her belief that I didn't need any more.

There was no point arguing with her; she had her beliefs and they were firm. You ate what you got, went to church, never 'talk back' to an adult, did what you were told and drank whatever she gave you for your ailments. And at the end of summer, before we went back to our parents, we would receive worm medicine, sulphur bitters, and some herb to wash us out so that we would be clean.

Normally the only noteworthy thing about taking all of these things, was the bitter disgusting taste, but one summer after she gave me the worm medicine, a small regiment of worms decided that, instead of coming out in my faeces, they would come marching out of my nostrils. I saw them wriggling out of my nose, and started to scream. My brother laughed. Grandma just stood there saying,

"That's right, that's right," like she was a midwife encouraging delivery.

People just don't know the things that will screw you up for life. One year later, my brother called me one day and said,

"Kenny, come watch this... come closer." He placed a piece of pork in the sun and left it there for a few hours. Called me over right at the appropriate time, so that I could see the worms wriggling out. That was the last day I ate pork, and the first day I started having nightmares about maggots living inside me.

"Tell me something about you that I don't know."

"I have nightmares about maggots living inside me." My second wife, Rebecca, had asked the question while we were dating. She was grossed out by the response and the stories behind it. She said, as part of her contribution to my knowledge about her,

"You know that whenever I go to the toilet I never turn on the lights?"

"Sometimes I go with my eyes closed," I had said. The little things that young lovers do and talk about.

"My mom called me a cow," Rebecca added as one other thing I didn't know about her.

"Your mama is a real character! Why?"

"I don't know really, it makes no sense. One time she asked me if I remember who sang some song and I told her to wait as I was going to remember. Then I put on a blank face to meditate on it. She asked me what I was doing and I told her I was going into a trance to remember. She call me a cow. Said only cows just stand there looking blank, or something like that."

"You are so like your mama." She was indeed a lot like her mama; had the same fierce drive and dedication... and the same toxic tongue. I miss Rebecca sometimes.

"You know she always said that if there is anything that I can do, anybody else can do it, 'cause if I can do it, it must be easy." She chuckled at this memory. I know her mama was proud of her. Her first child, hardworking and focussed. The second and third were lazy, the last, sun-stricken in the womb, was slow-witted like Georgie. When Rebecca had told me about her youngest brother, I remembered what people had said about Georgie. I think about Georgie sometimes.

As I was saying, I took my bottle torch and went to the latrine. I was really upset. I didn't bother to gather any leaves.

The latrine stood in the same place it always did, right beside the big jackfruit tree. It had been built too close, which is what accounted for the frequency of lizards and the bits of tree roots inside. I had once watched some adults digging the ground to locate a new latrine. There had been talk of how deep it had to be, to last for how long, but not too deep to make the foundation unstable. Stability had become important because the last one had collapsed completely, leaving a small pile of wood and zinc above the hole, the rest inside it. Until the new one was built, we had to dig some shallow makeshift holes behind the dasheen plants at the back of grandma's house. We used them for a few days, squatting, crapping, then covering, while we waited on the new structure to be built. Years after when I traveled to India and Bangladesh and saw the holes in the ground that folks squatted over, a little part of me wanted to say "Hi friend, long time no see."

Stability of the foundations was not high on the list, as I sat there that night with the torch and three squares of tissue in hand. Neither did I find myself overly perturbed by the thought of a lizard falling on my head, or touching a scorpion as I reached to latch the door when I was finished. The branches of the Jackfruit tree formed their usual shadows against the wall, and danced to the flickering melody of the torch, but they had lost their evil enchantment.

I also wasn't worried whether:

- Red ants would bite me on my bum and leave their usual three-day icky lump
- A small garden snake would slither all the way up my ass
- A Duppy man or woman would come to use the toilet and find me there (only the good Lord knows what would happen!)
- The devil would decide to take me there and then and simply pull me under

These things simply didn't matter to me at that point in time.

When the deed was done, I did what could be done with the three squares of tissue, and then I sat there. I am not sure at what point in the process the thought occurred to me, but after about five minutes, I got up from the seat and walked, crouched like a crab with my shorts at my ankle, right over to the side of the little outside kitchen where the drums and buckets of water were kept.

There was no hesitation. I found a bucket that was about knee high, and I sat in it and felt the cool water on my ass. For a moment it was as though a relative of mine had passed away and young Miss Water had been sent over from next door to help us out – it was neighborly, comforting, soothing, kind, gentle. That was the freshest my backside has ever felt.

After that, however, I spent the entire night agonizing over the deed, and wondering if I should tell someone.

I realized that I couldn't say anything to my brother, Martin, as he wouldn't wait for breeze to blow and help carry him to grandma to report what had happened. He loved it when I got a whipping. Our friend, the big-time singer, never liked it when my brother and I came for the summer. Always thought she was better than us, and apparently still does. As for me, going directly to grandma to confess – well, there is extreme stupidity, and there is confessing to grandma. A monster whipping it would have been, especially after the 'attitude' I had displayed when she gave me the tissue.

The long and short of it is this: we normally used the water from the smallest containers to the largest; from the pots and pans, to the buckets, to the drums. The next day they used the water from the buckets. They used it to wash their hands, to cook lunch and dinner, and to wash their feet before bedtime. If that's all they had done, my soul could have been saved. The problem was, they also drank.

There are awful pranks you pull as a child, knowing that it is harmless or that you will be found out before it gets bad. Like pissing in a cup and offering it to your cousin, Cookie, and telling her it is cola champagne soda, but knowing, however, that the minute she gets a whiff of it, you and everyone else will burst out laughing. Harmless.

At times you do something worse, and a little part of you wants to regard it as just a harmless prank, or wants to blame it on being poor, or to assign the fault to someone else. At times I said it was grandma's fault for not giving me enough tissue.

But.

That was the first time I really sensed the difference between good and evil. How I handled it was not only my first real secret, but my first deep shame.

Grandma nearly died from the strange bout of gastroenteritis she picked up a day after. I could tell you what she looked like in the hospital room, but I have other hospitals and other people to talk about as well.

And so, Semicolon, I once knew a bus driver (hello Mr Wallace!) who accidentally killed his load of passengers after driving too fast and ignoring the pleas to slow down. I have carried my guilt with me, like he his.

CHAPTER 18

About My Papa

11 p.m.

Dear Semicolon,

I forgot to share this important bit of information with you today. As you are now asleep, and there is no guarantee that I will remember it in the morning, I thought I would share it with you in my notebook.

My love, today I got pulled over by the police again. But Mutual Frustration and Inability to Communicate once again reared their ugly heads. They wanted linear proof of some small sign of intelligence, or otherwise something evidentiary pertaining to medication. I opted, instead, to befuddle, astonish and confound them! I asked them to challenge me to spell any three or four letter word in English, or to take on three quarters, which has three and four in it. All the while I was concealing my belt so they wouldn't realize I had the upper hand! When they didn't choose, I chose for them, and started spelling BOY, with all its complexities! Were they surprised at my abilities!

The officers then left with Obvious Annoyance, forgetting, as it were, to give me the ticket I am sure they had intended. It was then, as they were walking away, that I remembered those profound words you once said, "Once people get to know you, they will love you." So I shouted at them, "Do you love me now?" I doubt, however, that they heard me. In any event, as I sat there alone in the car, I observed a fly on the inside of the windscreen. Much to my surprise, and after all these years, I discovered that when they are not buzzing around incessantly, these insects can not only be quite attentive listeners, but adept conversationalists! And this one was particularly well informed: he was aware that the World Bank has not been able to reduce poverty anywhere in Africa, and he also knew, without me telling him, why it was that my Aunt Frida never showed her teeth when she smiled.

All in all, I came away from the encounter humbled by the devastating awareness that the knowledge I have acquired from over four decades of living was perhaps the same as the knowledge that this insect possessed.

Good night again my love, and sweet dreams.

Kenny

Diary entry, May 16, 2011

Long before I listened to them reading his eulogy, I knew that my papa's life had not only been short but hard. During the early days of my childhood I had known, almost instinctively, that the harshness in his eyes was the reflection of the hardships he had experienced on his journey.

By the beginning of the 1980s, I started to also see that harshness spread all over his face, his fingers, his feet and his body, as the coarseness of cruel years began to harden on his skin. The man that looked like he had worked every single minute of his life for over forty years, began to work even longer and harder. But he now carried home less than before - less money, less groceries, less snacks, less cigarettes, less words, less hope. I had never been the kind of child that ran to my papa when I saw him coming home in the evenings like on TV, but the days came when suddenly I wanted to run *away* from him. My papa always came home alone - others feared and respected him, and would scamper like cockroaches to get out of his way. So he walked through that lane alone. And on those days when I was playing marbles or some other game with my cousins, someone would sound the alert "Kenny, your papa coming!" Since stopping anything you were doing was the appropriate reaction, I would stop, and look, and I would see his sternness coming through the dusky grayness of the lane, and following him would be this icy, black shadow of hardship, despair, waste and loss. It wasn't my papa, but rather something about my papa, that I feared and that made me want to run away.

I knew that times had gotten harder by the end of 1980. The October General Election, one of the bloodiest in our country's history, signaled that change. After the giddy days of socialism and the orgies of ideologies ended, people woke up to find a message from the new government telling them that they had overslept and were well-advised to quickly put on their clothes and get their sorry asses back to work to rebuild the economy. 'Lord Voldemort' was now Prime Minister; the evil, capitalist, *He who shall not be named* son-of-a-bitch, whose face my very socialist papa would not look at on TV or in a newspaper. From my papa's attitude, I could tell that our country had now become the kind of place where people could catch a bird, make it Prime Minister, and wait to see if it could chirp.

The new Prime Minister, Edward Seaga, told the country the obvious: the hour was late, things would get tougher, the country was bankrupt, and the engine of the economy was sputtering and in need of hard-to-find spare parts. Goods became scarcer and more expensive, and it was harder for my papa to feed his family. Construction on the extra room we had started building had long stopped; the stove mama had put on a lay-a-way plan at Singer never came; there was less chicken meat and more bony chicken back for dinner, and our roof leaked almost as much as my granddad, who, by then, had to use a tube to help him urinate (we had no money to fix either him or the roof.) These may have been the reasons my papa seemed older and more hardened those days, but somehow, long before then, I had always thought of him as a hard man with a hard life.

Charles Lovelace was the name they christened him with at birth in 1938.

Beyond this, I realize now that I knew very little about who my papa really was, other than the oldest male person in our house that was called on when necessary to straighten out our crookedness, by whipping us for our days-old and long-forgotten crimes. He rarely spoke to us. He smoked a lot. He got the best parts of the chicken. He was served three plates, one for the rice, banana and dumplings; one for the meat, and one for the salad. At times there would be a little saucer as well, with some thinly-cut Scotch Bonnet chili pepper. He grunted his approvals and disapprovals of things, never speaking to us in complete sentences. We never ate meals at the dining table and talked about our days with him - not only because we didn't have a dining table in our one-room house, but because he wasn't that kind of man. He paid the bills for the years before he died, then my mama paid them for the few years she was alive, after. But I really didn't know him, not as a father, never as a friend, scarcely as a person. It is hard to admit this now, Semicolon, but his funeral was useful in a number of ways; I was able to learn a little about his life, and for the very first time I also saw my papa in a suit.

One of the things that I learnt at the funeral, was that he actually had younger half-brothers and half-sisters that I had never heard about.

There were three of them that he lived with when he was much younger. They were sent to live in England back in the 1950s while he was in his early teenage years. His mama couldn't afford to send all four of them, as she needed help around the house and on the farm; she still had one cow and a few goats that needed care, after selling two cows to help pay for the tickets. Because he was the oldest and strongest, he stayed behind to help. I found that story fascinating, though what I most wanted to hear was the one thing they never said – what my papa thought about every day as he washed the dishes at the outside pipe or milked the cow, and saw the planes flying high in the sky. I could see the frown beginning to form on his teenage face as he squinted his eyes at the blinding mid-day sun and traced their voyage above the clouds. Another thirty years, and those frown lines would be as deeply-engraved as the letters on the back of my mama's wedding ring.

I listened to these and other trinkets of information with interest, as they read his eulogy. At the end of the service, and while our ageing Methodist choir sang with the melody of hogs in labor, I went to look at him again in the open casket. I wanted to see if I could match all the kind words spoken about him, with the person that was lying there. I wanted to see the young boy tending kindly to the animals, dutifully cutting the grass, always obeying his mama and helping those in need, respectfully going to church and worshipping the Lord. That boy wasn't there. Instead there was a man about 1.92 meters tall, with thick, coarse hands (that had once hit me so hard they nearly broke my ribs) folded gently across his chest. He had the composed look of a practical man who concerned himself with practical things, like hammers, nails, screws and engine parts, and who felt that a clean shoe said more about your character than anything your mouth could ever say. His beard looked grayer than it did before, and had been neatly cut so that it didn't have any bristles. I had seen his beard close up a few times before while he slept, but I had never played in it like those kids sometimes did with their dads on TV. He had the same long creases stretching across his forehead, like fossilized worms, and his eyes were closed - like they seemed to have always been towards me. He was my papa for sure.

People expected me to cry while looking at his body, but I didn't. The only times I had ever cried because of my papa was when he whipped me.

But it sure was nice to see him in a suit. They had dressed him up real smartly in a black suit, with a handkerchief in his breast pocket. They hadn't fully succeeded but I sensed that the poor undertakers must have spent hours with a crowbar trying to straighten the frown on his face, and make him seem more *at peace*. I knew by then that you could conjugate a verb, but the root would always remain the same; and I tried to indicate to the funeral director that I wasn't disappointed with his efforts. He stood in a corner of the church watching all of us and our reactions to his handiwork when we went to the casket. When I looked at him he did what he had been unable to get my papa to do – he smiled at me. I looked back down at the man in the coffin, who looked far different from the papa I had, and closer to the one I had often wanted.

That was the last time I saw my papa, and I knew, even at that age, that he was gone like the socialist '70s that he loved so much, and was, likewise, never coming back. The only sadness I felt in seeing him go, was knowing that he was taking with him all the answers to questions I had, like why he never once called me 'son'.

I have looked back in my childhood diaries to see what else of his life I had taken note of, and what might be important to talk about before his death. I found very little, except, perhaps, one other memory. Charles Lovelace, if you can delay your death, I would like to share this one memory with you.

In 1980 I was ten years old, and I was attending Vere Pen* Primary, which was one of those *have you no ambition for your child?* elementary schools near to our depression. [*Years later the Government would start changing the name of communities and taking off 'Pen' because it gave the connotation of animals being trapped inside. Thereafter came the 'Mews' and 'Meadows' etc.]. I know it is a cliché to say that I had to walk three miles to get to school, but I will say it anyway because it was true, and because I know that, in the future, children will be snickering at their parents' claims of what they had to do in the *old days*.

By the end of my first week at Vere Pen I had already learnt everything I would ever learn there: you would get whipped if you came late; bulga rice would be a part of lunch for three days of the week; you would get whipped if you were caught fighting; nobody liked a Mr or Ms Goody Two Shoes; and you were well advised to say "Yes, Miss" or "No, Miss" or "Sir" as appropriate to your teachers. The rest of the time I spent at school was essentially waiting to move to the next grade and then to the next school. My real education was at home, with my grandma, my uncles, and my cousins. With them I learned the important things: when to know if a bull is about to charge at you, how to milk a cow, which leaves cure what ailment, the importance of filing freshly cut fingernails before fingering a girl, and when to go to church or the Obeahman for protection against what forms of evil.

For my first three years at Vere Pen nothing truly eventful happened. There were the usual everyday things: I went to classes and sat or slept in them; my head was split open two or three times (stones thrown at mangoes or birds crash-landed in my head – it was like playing Russian roulette, your time would eventually come); I caught lice; I had mumps and was teased because of the fatness of my face; a boy lost an eye in a fight over a boiled dumpling, and, occasionally, we had to get those freaking horrible vaccinations that involved heating the needle over a lamp. I should point out that I did not take those injections willingly and with good humor from our fat, ugly, bulbous nurse. While my sisters seemed to have descended from a more passive African tribe, and surrendered easily to whatever grandma and her dark army of bush medicines brought forth, I was, always, Yoruba and feral. With respect to our nurse it was,

"Catch me if you can, whore!" *or*

"Hold me down if you can, bitch!" *or*

"Give it to me in my ass would you cunt?" My mama would have wept rivers if she knew just how filthy my mouth was at the time.

There were, of course, good days as well - days of eating mangoes and Asham; days of Nutty Buddy ice cream and King Kong popsicle; days of Stinking Toes and Hog Plums; days of touching giggly girls in gooey places; days of playing football, running wild, and being so happy you could hug a whore. All these days drifted by with time.

Then came the day in December 1980 when we broke from the norm, and the memory I have kept for thirty years was formed. It started with a simple request by our teacher for us to write a story.

"The small boy with dark skin, bright, curious eyes, and curly hair, stared intently at the blank page spread open in front of him, while his teacher gently rested her hand on his shoulder and whispered a few words of encouragement." I have tried to recreate the beginning of that moment in time on many occasions, writing various stories with the idealized beginnings and endings that stories are meant to have when you are a child. The reality was different though, never the way I wrote about it.

I did write a story. I do not know whether my story was only good when read in relief, or if there was truly something special about it, but my teacher, Ms Graham, thought that it was the best thing since sliced bread without the edges and with condensed milk spread all over the middle.

The morning she handed us back our stories I had noted that, as usual, Steve's story had not been marked. It was the first one she returned, and she didn't bother to make any comments to him when he went up to collect it. Steve always wrote about the same things no matter what the subject was or what the teacher asked us to do: "On my summer vacation I went to the island that my dad owns," "Last week we went on my dad's yacht for a fishing trip," "My dad is rich and will raise your taxes," and other such fables. The only thing wealthy about Steve was his surname, Kempinsky. This, by the way, is one of the cruel pranks ghetto parents sometimes played on their kids - giving them names that spoke of promises. Outside of his surname, Steve also had an unimaginably rich imagination.

Only two of us got hand-written notes from Ms Graham on our stories: me, and my best buddy Sean, who was repeating grade 4 for the second time. After reading his story, Ms Graham had crossly asked him to bring a message home to his mama. Sean, already twelve years old, was capable of remembering to deliver a message. He did, on both days. When he came into the classroom the next morning there were only about fourteen of the thirty-seven of us already at our desks. Ms Graham had reminded him for the millionth time to say good morning before asking,

"What did your mother say, Sean?"

To this Sean, who was standing out of harm's way at about ten feet from her desk, delivered the following matter-of-fact return message,

"She say I must ask you what the fuck you want to see her for, Miss." This was ironic because, as I learnt from Sean, the reason for the message to the parents was because of the adult language Ms Graham kept finding in Sean's stories and compositions.

Sean was a rascal, make no mistake about it. At the time about four or five of the kids in the class had laughed, which was perhaps an accurate and proportional representation of the state of indecency in the overall society. From what I am told, in the '50s and '60s everyone in society was polite and proper with the worst crimes being petty theft and adultery; by the early '80s, after socialism had caved in and crumpled our grand hopes, 'slackness' had had begun to creep in to society, and gun violence was beginning to blossom.

School too was changing. More graffiti was visible, along with more kids with their socks at their ankle, their shirts out of their pants, their skirts stealthily climbing above their knees. Boys began wearing handkerchiefs hanging out of their back-pockets (Sean tied a red polka dot one on his head and looked like an Arab), and girls tried on make-up during the breaks.

Not much had ever been expected of me in school, not by my parents who sent me, nor by my teachers, but the signs of the times suggested that even less was now expected. Some of the teachers seemed to have lost interest in their work, and we saw more and more younger teachers as the older ones gave up and went home. Which is how it came to pass that Ms Graham herself, a very young teacher, had become our Form Teacher. She was in her early twenties and spent quite a lot of her time displaying the latest fashions – in hairstyle, clothes, shoes, jewelry and such. She always had a little handheld mirror that she consulted almost immediately after she gave us something to do to keep us occupied.

It is the little things that people do that we often remember about them, and with her it was never anything she taught me, but the note she gave me to take home that day, and, perhaps, one other small thing - I had also seen the various colors of her underwear. Her first name was Monica, but I may never have remembered that if I hadn't received that note and seen her underwear. Nothing about her hair or her eyes or her lips had caused me any panic attacks either, and therefore, as women go, she would have likely gone from my memory. But she loved wearing tight skirts, and that made all the difference.

After I found the right desk to sit at, all that remained was patience because, eventually, I knew - we all knew - she would uncross her legs. When she did, I saw all the promises ever made to man! Her white underwear put needles inside my heart; the red suffocated my soul! While I sat there I often felt as though I was fainting, falling to the ground, gasping for breath and stammering out a desperate cry for help.

Back in those days, there were a few things that I loved and could never get enough of. At ten years old I loved ginger beer - homemade, strong, and harsh 'til it burned into the back of my throat. My mama couldn't make it fast enough for me to drink. I would have committed genocide for my Aunt Frida's fried pork skin. I loved my grandma's 'cawfee' (coffee) in the morning, with its wickedly rich aroma (many of us kids started drinking before we were ten). There was a divinity in such things. But the days came when I could not think of ginger beer, coffee, fried pig's skin, curried crab, or Julie mangoes. On those days I felt feverish and delirious, my mind swirled, and the only thing I wanted - the only thing that I thought could heal me - was to feel the texture of the white, see the mysteries hidden beneath the red, and touch the pink. I so wanted to touch! But this was at the turn of the '80s, and back then teachers were still, mostly, untouchable.

That too would change, in time. Two years later, the school was rife both with used condoms, and condemnations by the school principal during morning devotions. Boys and girls, students and teachers had begun to touch. As values and morals deteriorated, so did barriers between students and teachers. Sean touched a teacher.

I was twelve by then, same school, same friends, same level of education, just different teachers. My grade 6 math teacher, Ms Evans, looked no older than twenty-one, and she was sweetness plus tax: young, curvy, beautiful, powdered, and always carried the fresh smell of rose petals, like every day she was going on a date. She was hardly there to teach and I was hardly there to learn, so I spent many hours thinking about her and all the things I would like to do with her. Sean was doing the same. I was already very girl crazy by then, I had already seen through many windows, looked at many pictures in Garnet and Courtney's porn magazines and was very comfortable leaning against a wall and chatting up the young girls in our neighborhood. And, of course, I had also had various encounters with Simone, Jennifer and others. Sean had had his own experiences, and they were not dissimilar. We spent a lot of our days talking about girls. We also spoke about how, with a little more time, one of us could have gotten Monica in bed… and what we would have done with her.

The day came when Sean, being both more restless and mature, decided he had had enough of 'only talking'. I didn't believe he would do it, and the wager that followed involved my lunch money for five days.

From his step-by-step account of what happened, I deduced the following. He had gone up to Ms Evans' desk one day, after our class was sent on break and all the other kids, yours truly included, had gone outside to play. She was at her table, packing up our books to go to the staff room. He helped her gather the books, and when she said "Thank you Sean, that is kind of you," he told her that she was very hot and sexy.

At the time we classified our teachers by age. Category A for Alright: the young teachers, those in their twenties, who rarely whipped – maybe they didn't have time for it or just thought that it would mess up their nails. Category B for Bitches: those in their thirties who would enforce an occasional crackdown, like the Chinese government, to remind everyone of who was in charge. Category C for Cunts: those in their forties who could be relied on, without fail, to whip your ass as soon as you fell out of line. [Cunt and Bitch applied to either male or female. Bitch would be replaced with 'Son of a Bitch' if it were male.] And category D for Demons: the others, the evil ones in their fifties, who relished beating and never missed an opportunity to take their pent-up frustrations out on us. Then there was Ms Mclean, who was her own category. She was rumored to be older than Ruth and Abraham combined, and should have retired a long time before except that no one, including the principal, dared to say anything to her. To Sean's certain knowledge: she was bald and was wearing a wig; she only smiled when her cats licked her cunt when they were in bed at night; she had eleven toes, and she was the representative of the devil on earth - the Pope's evil counterpart. Her sole purpose in life was to whip. Also, she could never remember my name.

"You boy! What is your name?"

"Kenny, Miss... I mean MY NAME IS KENNY, Miss."

"Were you the one I had to beat on Tuesday for not carrying in your homework?"

"No Miss, that was not me, Miss." The pregnant pause, the cat and mouse game. She surveying my hair, my clothes, my shoes, and so on while I hurriedly tried to put everything into its rightful place - usually my shirt would have come out of my trousers when I bent down to play marbles during break.

"Are those black shoes I see you wearing, boy? Do you know what the proper school uniform is, boy?"

"No Miss. I mean yes Miss. I know Miss. My mama sent a letter, Miss..."

"Are you the boy I had to beat last week for lying about your mother giving you a letter?"

"No, Miss. That was not me, Miss."

"What did you say your name was boy? Let me look in my book when I get back to the office..."

Outside of these formal occasions we spoke very little to the older teachers, and we never tried to make conversation with them. Ms Evans was, however, different. She was a category A. And she giggled often.

When Sean told her she was sexy, she giggled, or rather, from his account, she "unlocked her door." Both he and I knew by then, for we had often discussed it, that women loved confidence in a man, and that girls loved confidence in a boy. That truth was certified and never failed either of us. For my part, I practiced for hours how to stand, how to lean against a wall, how never to ask a girl "Do you like me?", how never to hold a girl's hand in public, how to know when the moment was right, and what to say to them when it was. The moment had been right for Sean. He confidently resurrected a line he had used once before with success.

"I bet your pum pum (vagina) must be fat and nice." He said it in the form of a compliment such that it would either open her unlocked door or lead to a mild rebuke, no more. She giggled again, and he was in.

In the early 1980s, as part of the grand plan to revitalize the economy, lots of government workers were laid off by the new and very non-socialist regime that was committed to making government slimmer. Many police, firemen, teachers and nurses were made redundant. We had a nurse's quarter at our school where the ugly, fat nurse used to sit all day reading novels and, periodically, giving us those wretched vaccinations. She was made part of the State slim-fast process, and the room became unoccupied.

A few days after their little chat, Ms Evans and Sean went to that room during another break. He said that 'boy-girl' things then ensued: he sucked passionately on her soft, big-nippled breasts, he fingered her plump, moist clit, he squeezed her ass, and, in return, she muffled moans and sucked on his ears and tongue. Regrettably, their subsequent encounters didn't go much further than what he described (he was an honest, straight-talking kind of guy - most other boys would have lied about that), but by then both he and I had learnt what we needed to about approaching older women.

Thereafter my grades began to improve, both because of the more generous marking of Ms Evans and also from the increased help and attention I got from her. She had asked Sean to promise not to tell anyone about them, but from the next day, she knew that I knew. And so, perhaps because she didn't want me to tell anyone, I was made an accomplice, and she started giving me extra lessons and attention. Serendipity pointed its fingers at me, and my own story would change from that point on. But I see that I am already straying quite far from my papa who, if he had known what was happening, would surely have whipped my identity out of me so that no one would know who I was after he was finished.

Back to when I was ten. My teacher, Ms Graham, had praised my story, and sent me home also with a note to my parents, saying that this was one of the best stories she had ever seen from a ten year old and that I had real potential and should be encouraged.

I took the note home and showed it to my mama. She decided that it was a rare enough occasion for her to play mother. She beamed with pride, told me how proud she was, hugged me and rubbed my hair. The sheer novelty of hearing those words from my mama confused the hell out of me, but that became one of the strangest and yet happiest moments of my life.

Then came papa.

Mama, in her bizarre excitement, asked me to take the note from Ms Graham to show him at his workplace, before he came home.

I was not allowed to leave home without my manners, and never liked to walk far without a mango, so I brought both with me on the 3.5 mile trek to papa's workplace. My manners not too girlishly visible, but available on request to be shown to an adult, and my mango in my front pocket where I normally carried one. I did not want to be seen as I went, which was not a problem because I was already a highly-trained Ninja Jedi Master at the time. So I took the second lane that led out of our depression, and walked unseen, blending into the background. At times I walked softly on the leaves on top of the trees, or held on lightly to the feathers of birds that could not detect my presence nor feel my weight as they carried me with them. I only made myself visible to Billy who was coming back from the corner shop and held what appeared to be a bag of juice in his hand. I had beaten him at marbles the day before and taken his prized steely marble. I thought, as a negotiating tool for a suck on his bag juice, I could first offer a bite of my mango or, failing that, give him back his steely. However, by the time I got close to him I saw that the color was gone, and the ice remaining in the bag was whitish and translucent. He had nothing to offer me, so I kept my marble and my mango and told him where I was going, before returning to invisibility.

On my way I showed no mercy in slaughtering a Rolling Calf, and outwitting a Blackheart Man. I also helped to rescue a fashion model who had been captured by a group of aliens and was being taken to their planet, Bibblepop. When we jumped from their spaceship and were nearing earth I stuck my fingers beneath her white underwear and brought her safely to land. She smiled and thanked me for doing both.

The only demons I fought when I got to my papa's little mechanic shop, were the inner ones. He was there, with his hard look. He was working with his apprentice, Dave, pulling down an engine. When he saw me he looked at me without expression but I knew it meant it was okay for me to come closer and say whatever it was I had come to say. I sat on a gear box that was turned up-right and waited, with the note in my hand. After a while he stopped what he was doing, looked at me, and grunted something that vaguely sounded like "What?" I leaned forward to hand him the note, but another grunt implied that his hands were greasy and I should tell him what it was. I didn't know then that he could not read, that is something else I learnt at his funeral when they spoke of the sacrifices he made so that his younger siblings could have a better life. I told him what my teacher had said about my story and that mama had asked me to come and tell him about it. He listened, then turned his head away from me and simply grunted again.

I sat for another few minutes on the gearbox while he continued to work and grunt instructions to the apprentice who had not bothered to acknowledge my presence. There is something about the influence that others have on how we behave.

After a while he stopped again, wiped his hands on a filthy rag, and took out a couple of dollars from his wallet in his back-pocket and gave them to me. Through some strange subliminal code, the apprentice knew he was being asked what he wanted to drink and told me "Kola Champagne". My papa grunted "Red Stripe" (beer), and somehow left me with the impression that I could get something for myself as well. I went to the shop next door and got them their drinks and myself a D&G Ginger

Beer soda. When I gave him his change, he had a five dollar bill in his other hand which he gave to me. Whether as payment for my services, a bribe to leave them alone, or a reward for having done well I have never ever known. Nothing else was said, and after a while I walked back home. I played no games, and even though I had not changed into the Jedi Master, I still, somehow, felt invisible.

While seemingly mundane, that became a defining moment in my life.

Three days later, one of my papa's friends dropped by our house. Mr Roper often came around in the evenings to chat and smoke with him by the side of our house. He had come a bit early that day and papa was not yet home, so Mr Roper was sitting on the front steps chatting with mama and my brother Martin about how things were. When I came back from Tommy's house (early so my papa would not see me running home when he came through the top lane), Mr Roper was still there. He greeted me loudly and memorably,

"Hey! Is this the smart one coming? Boy, I need you to read that story for me! All evening we at the bar yesterday and that's all your puppa (father) talking about. Come read that story for me boy!"

I learnt then, that my papa not only had full-length conversations with other people, but that he was, also, proud of me.

So there we have it. Now, let's deal with his death, which we have delayed long enough already. Let us send him on his way.

My papa died when I was young. He too was young, as were my brother and sisters. For that matter, my mama also died when I was young, and she too was young, as were my brother and sisters. Indeed, many members of my family died when I was young and while they were young, with only a few making it beyond fifty. It was for this reason that my good old Uncle Bob once kindly advised me to have my 'mid-life crisis' in my twenties.

The day before my papa died, I had gone to see him. He was at a hospital in the City of Spanish Town. This was November 1986 and I was sixteen.

There was a bus that went from our village to the city, entering it from the slummy South West section people called the City's ass. It drove past the stains and shames of the slums, and headed towards a cloud of billowing black smoke of ash that rose from an unseen building in the distance. Then, despite the fact there was no bus stop, it came to a stop anyway at the gate of the hospital; the buses always stopped there as so many poor folks from the city and neighboring villages went to that public hospital. A few days before I went, my cousin Wayne had joked that people went there either to die or to visit those dying, but no one had laughed even though it was said in the innocence of youth.

My papa had been hospitalized. He had been there for a few days before my mama informed me that he had gotten sicker, and we needed to go and see him. He could not eat hard food, something had gone wrong after the surgery, he had lost weight, it looked grave, and so on. Like a good son, I went with her to see him. In my mind, I pictured us going there, she touching his hands and helping him to eat the liquid food his digestive system could accommodate. While I watched.

We had gotten seats on the bus, which was not always easy. We had had to wait a long time for the bus to load its passengers. Then we left.

On a Saturday there would have been very heavy traffic on the main road leading out of our village. Saturdays were market days - days that made my mama lament that only constancy in prayer and abiding faith in the Lord could get you through the bustling stream of people, animals and vehicles. But this was a Wednesday, and the streets were less crowded.

"I am sure he will get better soon," my mama said, attempting to make the words comforting. Back then my mama owned very little happiness, but she managed to borrow a smile every now and then. On that morning she gave me one of those smiles, with a touch of sadness sitting in her eyes. We didn't talk much after that, the three of us. My brother was also quiet. My sisters had not come, because only two had been born by then (one was well on the way), and they were deemed too young to see his suffering.

Our village, along with those words and that smile from my mama, and a few shameful memories that had flashed across my mind, drifted behind me. I spent much of the time looking through the window, at life in its eternity, taking note of things in my diary.

Along the way I remember seeing the familiar cane fields. They were then government-owned, but used to be part of a slave plantation which, legend has it, was once owned by a witch. The Indians we called Coolies, still lived around the cane-fields. They were brought in after the slaves were freed, over two hundred years before; built their little houses around the plantations. Not much had been added to those houses since the days when they were built.

We moved on past the mango trees that lined the road by the '15 mile' marker, and past the little Catholic church which I often wondered whether the Vatican City had approved. Along the way there were the usual little girls selling fruits by the street sides. Mangoes, oranges, imported apples. A part of me had hoped that this was a contribution to their family income and not the source of it. But I knew...

As we approached the outskirts of the city, a constellation of old houses crept up on us. Women were still in their nighties at 10 a.m., sitting in front of their yards. And the men who squat, were still there by the roadside. The "squat a lots," my brother once joked. They were also squatters, part of a population as numerous as crab holes on an early morning beach. A few months before there was a national resettlement program with funding from the World Bank. The Minister of Housing was very proud announcing it at the time. People talked a lot about the World Bank and the IMF in those days, and their plans to 'rescue' our economy after the Socialists nearly killed it.

Our journey took us closer to the zinc fences, the broken windows, the barbed wire gates, the stray dogs and the myriad posters announcing the location and time of the next big inner city party. This huge, hillside slum settlement, which made the hills joyful with music day and night, bore all the symbols of 'shantyness' - the 'blight' that the Minister of Housing had a firm and unwavering commitment to rid the city of, so they could create a new Metropolis. There was a demonstration at the time, I was never sure whether this was because people thought 'blight' referred to them, or because they valued something in those tenement yards that others could not see.

On our way I saw a dog by the roadside that looked as though he was promised he would be fed as soon as there was peace in the Middle East. I remember him because he reminded me of my own dog. Ruffy, was also just an ordinary mongrel dog, who found his own food, lived outside the house, ate grass when he was sick, got in fights with other dogs and ran after chickens, goats and pigs. A no-tricks kind of ordinary dog. Hollow, mangy, smelly – I would often hope that he would forget his way back to the house, like those cats folks would sometimes place in a bag and throw away miles from our yard. He got run over by a car when I was thirteen, and that was the end of him. He was nothing like the dogs I saw on television, that stood on the front seats of cars going down the US highways - admiring the world and appreciating its beauty, with the wind caressing their faces. Those dogs fetched sticks, chased balls and rolled with kids on the ground, without giving them ticks.

The bus drove by the St. Catherine Primary School. A weary-looking guard was sitting at the school gate, daydreaming, but was ready, at a moment's notice, to protect the property of others armed with hunger and a wooden stool. I noted at the time that he looked thinner than my papa's wages.

In my budding writer's mind, I never understood why the British thought an agreement was needed, but our bus successfully *negotiated* the corner that led past this area, and approached the hospital. I saw smoke belching upwards into the skies, from a building at the back of the hospital. My brother once told me that the smoke came from an incinerator which burned the bodies of all the still-born babies and paupers. I never knew whether this was true, or another one of those *the cows would like to speak with you* pranks pulled on illiterate kids. I hadn't bothered to ask at the time.

There were a few beggars by the roadside, surrounded by visible signs that they had made the streets their Marriot. A one-legged beggar hopped into the middle of the street, so broken and destitute it seemed as though it was the man that was behind his own shadow. As he hobbled towards each car and bus in search of a 'bank', someone in our bus yelled at him the request to "move your dirty stinking self!" I jotted it down. A few folks on the bus laughed, my brother chuckled. Round of applause, standing ovation.

I saw an old woman lying prostrate by a street lamp, head slightly propped under "Tricia sucks", the winning lottery numbers for the day before and signs pointing to where chicken back was sold. From a filthy plastic bottle she enjoyed a refreshingly cold glass of lemonade but without the lemon, sugar or ice. Her eyes were as hollow as eternity, and her collar bones, visible through the tattered clothes, sunk deeper than the Titanic. She was sucking on a cigarette butt discarded by another city shadow. I thought that she most likely had many children, but none of them had come to take care of her. A good child would have at least gone to see her.

There were no frills and laces in that part of the city. No living rooms, no guest rooms, no spare rooms, nothing to spare.

A few minutes later the bus pulled up to the hospital gate. A boy about eight years old, was giving people directions in anticipation of their spare change. This was his way of making a living. At eight years old it seemed he had spent more time with cows than with a school teacher, and the

Manchester United jersey he wore was the closest he would ever get to England. His clothes and demeanor were persuasive and compelling in defining him as poor. I wrote in my notebook that he didn't have shit.

Another little girl, maybe his sister, a Pocahontas, was also there with him, running wild and free and already being much too friendly to strangers. She looked about six years old and was gyrating innocently to music playing on a battery-operated radio on a nearby vendor's food stall. It wasn't Gershwin. I wondered at the time whether, if I happened to pass by her home one night and stoop beneath her window, I would hear her squeal in laughter, "Daddy, stop tickling me!" I doubted it, very much.

We walked into the public hospital, spoke to everyone we needed to speak with, and then went to his room. No one else was there, just my papa, the bed, a few items of clothes, and the smell of urine, Dettol and suffering. No words, for my papa was no longer conscious.

The things you see and smell in a hospital room can tell you a lot about a man. They can tell you about how he got to work, whether by Mercedes or foot. They can tell you about the type of work he did, how much schooling he had, what kinds of food he normally ate, how often he could afford to eat, and what he would choose if offered caviar or a piece of cake. Unfortunately, they tell you little about how he felt when he went to his bed at night, whether with his friends he was a maker of myths and legends or what he thought of politics. Neither do they tell you if he once made sweet potato pudding or slept with a fat woman, if he quietly sang when he showered, if he sometimes thought of casually grabbing his woman by her waist and making her dance while she struggled to wash the dishes. Nor if he had little habits, like farting and smiling, or if he once laughed so loud he felt he would split into two. Or if he ever loved your mama.

My papa died at 9.17 a.m. the next day. Thursday. When I saw the doctor that day I thought to ask him a question, but I didn't bother. I didn't think my father would have taken the time to tell him whether he ever loved me.

He died after a simple surgery to remove a gallstone. When his urinary tube was full, no one was sent to replace it. And no one came when he rang for help to go to the bathroom. And no one came to give him a pair of non-skid socks. And no one was there to catch him before he fell. And no one was there to call a doctor, or to stitch his wide-open wound back together. And no one was there to listen to his last words as he started bleeding almost to death on the filthy floor. Then the unconsciousness. Then, a day or two later, death. And that was that, just like that.

THE YARD

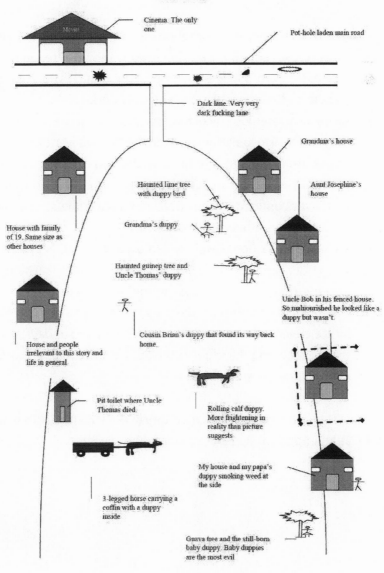

Cinema. The only one

Pot-hole laden main road

Dark lane. Very very dark fucking lane

Grandma's house

Aunt Josephine's house

Haunted lime tree with duppy bird

Grandma's duppy

House with family of 19. Same size as other houses

Haunted guinep tree and Uncle Thomas' duppy

Uncle Bob in his fenced house. So malnourished he looked like a duppy but wasn't.

House and people irrelevant to this story and life in general

Cousin Brian's duppy that found its way back home.

Pit toilet where Uncle Thomas died.

Rolling calf duppy. More frightening in reality than picture suggests

My house and my papa's duppy smoking weed at the side

3-legged horse carrying a coffin with a duppy inside

Guava tree and the still-born baby duppy. Baby duppies are the most evil

Some notes:

- This is, of course, an incomplete picture. There were an awful lot more houses and Duppies than what is shown here. On the right side of the yard is where 'my side' of the family lived. Most of the people on the opposite side were outsiders.
- All these houses look nicer than the ones we actually lived in, and the cinema also looks fancier than the one we went to.
- I have drawn all houses to look the same not because they physically were, but because everyone who lived in them had their lives confined by four walls in basically the same way, and their windows offered no escape.
- My uncle Bob's house was fenced around not to keep intruders out, but to keep him in. The funny thing about my malnourished uncle is that he was always promising to take us kids for ice cream. Almost every Saturday he promised to take us on Sunday for ice cream, and he would never be seen on Sunday. Such that the word among the older kids was: "Never before has someone with so little promised so much."

There is no way to show the Cedar tree in our village on this diagram, but it was an important tree and I will talk about it later.

CHAPTER 19

The Secret Life of Cats and Dogs

It ain't that hard for a young man to create dreams: watch lots of soap operas, eat late at night, and the rest will fall in place. Creating wealth though, is an entirely different matter. Work hard, dream hard, study hard, and still no guarantees!

Our friend, homeboy, is now thirty-eight years old. In the last twenty years he has made attempts at fifteen businesses, not counting the hustling he did during high school. Let us call him Marlon. From the looks of it, all the guys who went to his wedding had strong white teeth, based on the wedding photos. He has a buddy, referred to as his 'sparring p' ('p' for partner). Let us call him Delroy Townsend, or "Mr T" for short. He is thirty-nine. The only thing remarkable about Mr T is that he only has sisters – six of them, and all six have acne.

We will now allow these two characters to speak for themselves.

Setting: Friends on the Deck bar and restaurant, Trafalgar Road, Kingston, Jamaica, December 12, 2010. Homeboy and his sparring p are sitting on a barstool at the counter. Homeboy looks cool, and is turned sideways on his stool blowing the smoke from his cigarette upwards to the roof. The place is near full with patrons, mostly middle-aged men, a few with women one would suspect they couldn't take home with them. There is a darts board with a few darts still in it; no one is playing. On the wall behind the counter is a Red Stripe Beer calendar full of photos of busty and big-ass women flirting with the eyes of every male that orders a drink.

"So, what you goin' do my youth?" Mr T asks.

The bartender walks down to their end of the bar, smiles at homeboy and gives his sparring p a brief, disinterested glance. After work last Saturday she had had her legs over homeboy's shoulders in the backseat of his Mitsubishi Pajero.

"Love, gimme another gin and tonic," he says to her, adding, "Mr T, you ready for another one?"

Mr T generally needs a photograph to remind him which house and what set of people he should go to at the end of the day. He spends a lot of time on the road, working, hustling, drinking, womanizing. He says,

"Yeah man, gimme another one." He likes scotch and ginger ale, when others buy; rum and coke when it is from his own pocket. He lifts the glass to his head to empty it. At the back of his right hand you can see the faint outline of the ganglion cyst he has had since college. People used to call those things a bible bump, because back in the day, the Old Timers thought all you need to do was thump it with the word of God or another thick book like the bible and it would go down. Some friends had called him *Lumpy* for a while, but the name never stuck.

Homeboy, on the other hand, got a name that stuck. He is popularly regarded as the *President of Gillette*, as it is universally acknowledged that he is sharper than any razor when it comes to picking up women. As legends go, the title was bestowed after it was rumored that he took his wife and two kids to a hotel one holiday and immediately after getting them settled into their room, went back downstairs and in approximately six minutes was alone in a bathroom with the female security guard he had smiled with when they drove in. He had a nose for easy pum pum. But we stray.

With the toilet as his office, the President at Work
(As drawn the day I heard the story)

"I don't need to do anything", the President puffs on his cigarette.

"You think she suspect?"

"There is no way she can know." The 'she' is homeboy's wife.

There are seven empty pitchers at one end of the bar counter, turned upside down. Seven in all. The bartender is serving another client but periodically looks in their direction, watching his glass and looking at him. She knows he is a 'regular', and didn't come to the bar just to see her. But the memory of Saturday night is very fresh, and the new Mitsubishi Pajero hints at possibilities beyond her dreams.

"You sure it's your youth? I tell you, Jesus would have to come off Him cross and tell me that it's my pickney before I believe it. You never use rubber with her?"

Mr President chuckles knowingly. "Bwoy, you want to know that she was a virgin. And I man never feel like using no condom."

"You normally more careful than that man. She was on the pill or something?"

Homeboy doesn't respond immediately. The bartender has come within earshot to fetch a bottle of Campari to serve another customer. There are two tall bottles of Natural Orange Juice beside the blender. Two in all. When she moves he continues,

"No bwoy, she wasn't on the pill. She did ask me to put on a condom-"

"So what happen? Is not like you can forget to use a condom," Mr T cut in.

"Mr T, all I can tell you is that pum pum sweet."

This is one area in which I would agree entirely with homeboy. While at college with these two, we had collectively agreed that pum pum was perhaps the best gift of the creator to man, and that the condom was man's best gift to himself, so that he could have maximum enjoyment of what the creator had provided. Mr T at the time had made an impassioned case for the inventor of the condom to be sanctified immediately without going through the normal process of beatification and confirmation of miracles.

"You goin' mind the youth?"

There are four cans of Red Bull in a corner of the counter; four in all. Someone ordered a Corona, could only have been an American. But then the Latinos have invaded New Kingston - many came with the opening up of the telecommunications market. More came with the setting up of the Spanish all-inclusive hotels dotting the North Coast. A few, it was rumored, were the owners of the new gentlemen's nightclub where Russian, Cuban and Ukrainian girls entertained. Perhaps the patron who ordered was Mexican, who knows.

After another hesitation. "She is a nice little flesh, you know. I think I goin' give her some money to take care of the child. She not really working."

"So Barbara not goin' find out if you give her money?"

"Barbara don't know how much money I make. That's my business. I give her some money every month, and she use her own."

Barbara, his wife, works as a cashier at a pharmacy in Kingston.

Two cans of Sweppes Bitter Lemon have been opened; two in all. One glass gets a sprig of lemon, not lime. Shaken not stirred. A male bartender pushes some fresh peanuts in front of our friends. Over in a corner, a waitress presents a fat lady sitting by herself with her order of spicy chicken wings. She checks her Blackberry occasionally, types now and then. Some men would think she is expecting company, others that she is expecting a baby. People see things differently in life.

The bartender again looks in their direction, wishing she could become pregnant for him. That would be one sure way of improving her situation.

There is a Budweiser sign above the bottles of rum on the top left side of the bar. It is meant to be lit, like the Red Stripe and Heineken signs in other places, but it isn't. Either the electrical connections have gone bad, or the sign does nothing for business in the land of Red Stripe Beer.

These are modern times. The male bartender has two nose rings, three earrings, a piercing above his right eye, and wears short trousers, a ponytail, and tattoos.

"Anyway, forget about all o' that right now. Professor Lovelace, you are the man of the night. Bwoy, I can believe it's been... how many years now Mr T?"

I had returned home to bring some closure to my past, and met up with my old friends. They called me "professor" back in the days, because of how studious I had become. Once they tried to stick "reverend" on me as well after they heard I had taken Religious Education in my O-Level exams. Not much had changed throughout the years. Homeboy was still peddling business ideas and still seemed prepared to convert to any religion whose deity offered the greatest promise of wealth. Mr T was still glorifying his conquests. He was the talkative one who we always said wouldn't give your ears a chance to grow grass. They still got together from time to time, and went to the familiar drinking spots to drink, eat jerk pork and pick up women.

It is amazing how little people seem to change before their sixties (when it is not only inaccurate but indecent to tell them they look the same). Mr T has grown a few gray hairs and carries with him a spare belly wherever he goes. Homeboy looks the same, talks the same, seems to wear the same cologne... Fendi if my memory served me right.

While I sat there listening to them, I thought about Rebecca, and the last night we spent together. We had woken up on a Florence Micro Quilt 240 x 210 cm Down Comforter, hand wash or gentle machine wash with luke warm water. As usual she was completely covered, with only the soles of her feet sticking out down below. The sun had woken up the same time as us. I was looking across at the opposite wall where the workmen had done a poor job of installing the a/c unit. There were cracks in the wall, two in all. She was looking at the space between us, at her bouncing, healthy newborn convictions.

I had gotten up with my mind insistently impressing on me the notion that at some point in the past I had lived with a local family in Honduras. But I hadn't, and, living with Latinos is not something I suspected I would ever likely forget. These are the things that the mind does, however.

I also wondered about Georgie. Where he might be, whether he was drinking with friends, telling stories of love or lust. If ever there was a child from my childhood whose life I needed to find out about, that child would be Georgie. Did he have a child? Was he living with someone? It was almost Christmas, and a part of me hoped that he would be somewhere preparing to give and receive gifts.

CHAPTER 20

Life on the Scale of a Cockroach

Once upon a time in a land far away, there was a cockroach.

This cockroach had no particular interest in seeing another century as he felt that one was enough. All of his life was, therefore, played out in the last century. He was born sometime after the First World War and before the Second. In a way, we may say that his birth was surrounded by events of monumental scale, even though he himself was rather small.

As is the custom for cockroaches, he lived all his life in a little, dark place. If this place were called a home, it is quite likely that many houses would be offended. For our purposes, therefore, it was just a small, dark place that we shall not call a home.

To the boundaries of his sight, he could see only strangers. When he opened his compound eyes wide and looked to the North, he saw strangers. When he chewed with his mandible mouth and squinted in the glare of the morning sun rising in the East, he saw strangers. In whichever direction his antennae pointed, he saw strangers: for though they were all family, they weren't his family. As far as anyone knew, he had no family. He was surrounded by a large family of fowls and chicks, but he was a cockroach. A single solitary cockroach in a dark place surrounded by fowls and chicks!

His situation was made the more precarious because he lived in a desperate age: an age when it was, if we are to be frank, every fowl for himself. So much so, that adult fowls showed a blatant lack of curiosity as to the welfare of their chicks and how they fed themselves. The reasons for this were twofold: first, as we have said before, those were times when it was, generally, every fowl for himself, chicks included, and, second, because in that age some chicks had become so fearsome that even fowls feared to ask them how they fed. Stories are still told today of the first chick that went home to roost with blood on his beak, and how, despite the fact that every fowl knew that neither worms, nor corns, nor bugs bled, no one dared ask the simple question: on what had this chick dined? The cockroach feared this chick above all others. Everyone feared this chick above all others.

Little was known about the cockroach, for he stayed in the dark by day and came out at nights when the fowls roosted. Many a fowl surmised that he was an uneducated cockroach because, from a philosophical viewpoint, cockroaches were incapable of learning, and, from a practical standpoint, a cockroach that chose to live among fowls could neither be sane nor literate. My own view, should this be of some interest to anyone, is that this cockroach was smart, and may have even intended to write a book someday. The kind of book whose pages would smile with politicians and priests - with their promises of a better life in the year-after and the hereafter, then jeer them as soon as they turned their backs. But such a book was never written, and no other proof of his intelligence has ever been found.

This cockroach lived a long life. Neither chick nor fowl ever came close to eating him. Most stood at a distance and teased him, while pecking the ground and stomping their feet. They all said that this was on account of his smell, for he was a cockroach that refused to bathe. My own view is that it was because they all feared a cockroach that would live in the midst of fowls – for this was the type of thing that was beyond their understanding, and, as such, the type of thing that is feared. And these were, indeed, the dark days of fear and superstition, for they lived in the age before the Enlightenment.

They all called him Old Man Tom. This was not because he was an old cockroach. In fact, the name was given to him when he was young. This is normal and quite in line with the naming and nicknaming conventions of rural Jamaica. He had no wings and so could not fly. He was, also, not fast enough to outrun chicks, so he stayed in that dark place all the days of his life, hiding from and spitting at the teasing fowls and chicks. Safely protected, they said, by his smell, his spit, and the smell of his spit.

When he died they wanted to bury him in a cockroach cemetery. But when they tried to lift his body in its coffin, a hundred fowls could not move it! I was there on the day and can bear testimony to this. And it wasn't because his coffin was weighed down by his stench, which is what some people say. No. As my grandmother explained to me, it was because the coffin was weighed down by his *will*.

I mention Old Man Tom here for two reasons. The first is because I think it is important for people to understand the power of a creature's *will*, regardless of whether that creature is a *real* person or a cockroach, or is living or dead. The second, and perhaps more important reason I mention this cockroach, is because I spent many years of my early childhood hoping and praying that my life would not be played out on the scale of a cockroach. I prayed hard, almost every day, for this not to happen. I often prayed like this:

> *Merciful Father, I thank you for all your blessings and your kindness. I thank you for the food that you have placed before me to eat and the water to drink. I thank you for the strength of my body, and of my mind. And I pray, Merciful Father, that you will not make my life be like that of a cockroach. For they often get stepped on, dear Lord. And then they squish. They squish, dear Lord, they squish. For these and other mercies I pray. Amen.*

I did not want my life to be such that I could simply be squished like a cockroach. While I grew up being poor, in the far recesses of my mind I had great expectations of my life, and I hoped to one day become somebody important. There were many days when I sat beneath mango trees and explored how I wanted my life to be, and how I would want others to see me and my future wife. I found a good model in the book of Isaiah, chapter 40, verse 9:

"Say to the cities of Judah, Behold thy God!"

Behold thy God! This was perhaps the most beautiful expression I had ever read during my childhood! Not surprisingly, therefore, I used this model to derive similar expressions that I felt would one day be fitting for me and my wife - there being no doubt, of course, that I would have a wife. Below are a few of the expressions I scribbled in my notebook at a young age:

Behold this man!
Behold the power of this man!
Behold the beauty of this woman!
Behold their magnificence!
Behold this man who is the master of his own destiny!

I could not, however, accept, under any circumstance, the prospect of being greeted with:

Behold this cockroach!

And I could not bear the thought of being squished. It terrified me. I had never known anyone whose life had been so insignificant that they were simply squished, and I did not want to be the first. Of course, I knew at least one cockroach, Old Man Tom, who lived all his dirty stinking worthless life in a dark and desperate place, teased and scorned by all.

But while I never saw him die, no one said he was squished. I also knew that there were some *real* people who were worth less than a rat's fart, and whose lives were almost squished out of them. But even they, at the end, had managed to escape such a disgraceful fate. I recall, for instance, that in the days when I went to primary school, which I did to oblige my mama, there was a child playing behind the school bus one day. The bus reversed, as buses do. And its wheels ran over the child. The entire child. The entire *real* child. All its right wheels. Starting with his head. This wasn't Tommy, but another child.

(Grandma Bell: "If he had gone to church this would never have happened to him!")

But he did not squish; it was more of a popping, cracking sound like bones and balloons bursting and breaking at the same time.

I also recalled that during the General Elections of 1980, when hundreds of *real* people died, there was one man who was killed in a manner which could be regarded as close to being 'squished'. Most of the folks killed during that election were killed through ordinary means: stabbed by knives and ice picks, chopped with the sharp side of machetes (for these were non-domestic disputes), shot with guns, and so on. But, on that day, I went with some men from our neighborhood to see a man who had chosen a different, less obvious, less ordinary type of death. He had taken a road that ran through the stronghold of the opposing political party - not a very wise thing to do, given that, in those days, politics to Jamaicans was no joking matter. Back then, if you cut some folks their blood would have dripped orange or green. Not only that, but the chickens, the dogs, the pigs and the flies in their yard and the flowers around their house, were either Comrades or Labourites. And a baby's first words might either be, "Yow, whey (where) the stinking pussyhole Labourite dem deh (are)?" or "Gimme (give me) a gun, mek (let) me shot a raasclaat Comrade bwoy!" or something to this effect.

Anyway, the motorcade in which this man was traveling was caught in a roadblock that was staged by hooligan supporters of that other political party. When all his colleagues jumped out of their cars and escaped, he was left behind as he had an injured leg, and was caught by the hooligans. When the others went back for him with their reinforcements, they found him lying there in the streets, surrounded by the burning tires and old refrigerators that had been used to form the roadblock. There were no signs of bullet wounds, stabs, or cuts. And no signs of life, of course. But the boulders and bricks that they had dropped on his head and body, over and over and fucking over again, were still lying there beside him, like loyal dogs beside a dead master.

(Grandma Bell: "If he had gone to church all of this would never have happened to him!" Somebody that I can't recall but who was caught up in the heat of the political moment: "Shut the fuck up woman!")

Now I must confess that while standing there, I could sense that there was a certain degree of absurdity about the whole affair, and I am not referring to the sort of *watching a Jamaican bobsled team compete in the winter Olympics* kind of absurdity. It was more the *even one of his own cousins in that other party was dropping bricks on him* sort.

A few persons said they heard the sounds that were made as the bricks and boulders fell. I listened to these accounts, but no one used the term 'squish'. They used words like 'scrunch', 'squash', 'pop', 'crunch', and so on, but no one said "squish".

And then, of course, there was *the corner* at Vere Pen Primary School.

The crossing for the school was very close to a corner. This was a tricky corner. Drug dealers the world-over have long used corners to ply their trade. They are always at a corner offering death to kids and adults alike. This corner, which had learnt from the drug dealers, went into business on its own. It was niche marketing its own type of death to 6-11 year olds.

"Hey kids, come on over here. Use that crossing and come on over, I have something for you," the corner would say.

"Why?" the kids would ask, "What do you have for us Mister corner?"

(Kids were always polite, and always said Mister or Miss.)

"I have a little death here for you kids, come on over for it."

"What is death Mister Corner?"

"Kids, you don't know about *death* yet? Where have you been living? How old are you anyway? You haven't seen death yet kids?" And in this way the kids would feel stupid and ignorant for not yet knowing about death. "Death is sweet kids. The little death I have for you is very sweet."

"But the ladies at the school gate sell us things that are very sweet as well, Mister corner," the kids reasoned. Everyone who went to a rural school in Jamaica knew of the ladies by the school gate that sold candies, biscuits and ice cream. One or more of them always had a disgusting sore somewhere on their foot.

"Sure, that is death too kids, but no, the death they are offering is not as sweet. You may have to wait a few years for their death kids, or you may need to go to the hospital to get it. The little death that I am offering is the sweet kind of death that you can have right away. Right now. Don't knock it until you try it kids, come on over. Use the crossing right there."

The kids, feeling ashamed of how little they knew of death at their age, would then go across. It took almost fifteen years of kids going across that crossing before someone decided to have strong words with the corner and set him straight. And more than fifteen kids dying. (Grandma Bell: "If they had gone to church none of this would have happened to them!")

But the kids were squashed, like worms. They were not *squished*.

I remember these events well, because it was my brother who held my hand and said, "Kenny, wait," just as a car sped around the corner, one fine Caribbean day. I would not have written about worms if my brother, before he lost his mind, had lost hold of my hand. I would have been eaten by worms.

The point of all this, my love, is to let you know that while I had no idea what I would become in life, or whether I would live long enough to regret living long enough, I was always driven by the *will* and desire to have my life played out on a scale that was larger than a cockroach's. And not to have my life squished out of me.

CHAPTER 21

Putting the Pieces Together

Dear journal,

*On the third day, I rose from the stool. I was refreshed, and felt as
though I had been baptized. Feeling light, clean and pure inside,
I thought I might also start a church. But this was the Congo, and
the god of the people of the villages never went to Jerusalem, and
never left them to return. He lived in their trees, their snakes, their
rivers, and their spears. He was accessible, not like the Lobster
Thermidor god that the millions of poor Christians across the world
worshipped.*

*The thought occurred to me once, while I was there in the Congo,
that I should ascend to the mountains and write my own rules. I
thought I would meditate on, document, and then share with the
world my own canons - the precepts that would guide the way I
live, and explain why I love my fellow man and his woman, and
Law and Order. For those three straight days while I sat on the stool,
I thought a lot about the church. I wondered whether, in order
to shake the shit that was wedded to me, I might need to break
up another church, like King Henry did. But mostly, I thought of
creating my own church, creating those canons, and finally earning
myself a name. "Pastor" – crisp, clean, clear, powerful.*
Postscript:

I have never been to the Congo. I said this to see what would happen - pastor said I would be smitten if I lied, so I try it sometimes.

Random thoughts, May 2008

We called him by different names then, but mostly 'pastor', 'reverend', or 'father'. Some of the older church goers would sometimes call him 'brother' as well. My cousin Wayne called him 'elder', which is what Wayne called everyone, including me. I tried it for a while, calling the other kids 'elder', thought it would be cool. My brother asked me if I was a fucking idiot, and then I stopped. Mama didn't know at the time that he was swearing so much, and would have been very distressed by it because she sent us both to Sunday school every Sunday morning, and bible studies on Wednesdays after school. Mama wanted us to be 'confirmed' in the faith, which is what Methodists do. This was back in 1984 and I was about fourteen years old. My brother was three years older than me, and would stay that way for a few more years.

Anyway, I was telling you about pastor. This one preached at the clap-hand Pentecostal church on Gibson Road in that *hateful* fucking place, very close to the Depression where we lived. They were all devil worshippers there at his church, so no one from our side of the family went there. Pastor was new, had moved there from Chapelton about three months before. He drove a 1983 red Honda Accord, licence plate BA1794.

When I saw pastor's new car I asked my mama where pastors got their money from - if it was from the offering we gave in church. The question hadn't occurred to me before because I had never seen our own pastor driving a car. Mama told me that they got a salary because preaching and ministering to the poor was their *job*. I can't say what I thought of this answer at the time or whether I asked anything else. Only the key memories remain. Like the extra bit of information Wayne added to mama's response.

"The best way to make money is to turn a pastor," he explained. "Them get the most woman too. You never notice all them church sister that say them a carry food for pastor? You think is food alone pastor eating?"

I also remember that my Aunt Martha, who pastor had come to visit in that red Honda, looked much older than she really was in 1984. It was only last year when I went back to our Depression and looked at her grave in the *Hateful* Fucking Place Cemetery that I realized that she would have only been about forty-one years old.

I have never liked cemeteries; it was the second time in about twenty-two years that I have been in one. When I was a child cemeteries were the land of the dead. I never liked going to our church back then, because there were lots of graves in our Methodist churchyard. Mama had told me that the church reserved burial space for the faithful, so they wouldn't need to be buried in the old, run-down public cemetery. Clearly no one in my family was faithful (or rich) for they were all buried in the public cemetery.

Whenever I went to church I always stopped at the gate, and I would always feel a tremor inside me as I stood there. Mama usually gave me a tug, or my brother would slap me in the back of my head. It is not that anything bad ever happened to me in church, I was never molested by a pastor or anything like that. I was just terrified of graves and the church was surrounded by them. On the way to church, my brother would often remind me never to point in the direction of the graves as all my fingers would rot and fall off, and whichever demon's grave I had pointed on would think I had invited them home. All seems like foolishness now, but I really believed it then.

Last December, I finally decided to confront my fear, so I went to the cemetery. It was also because I wanted to see them all again.

I realize now how we see everything and everyone differently with the passage of time and with enough distance between our present and past lives. Like every day we used to get up and go on the verandah, yawn, stretch, and look outside, but without ever really noticing anything in particular. Then came the mornings after a hurricane or flood, when you stood on the same verandah and saw almost every single detail of the things and people around you - expressions on people's faces, the buildings, the trees, the old toilets - as though for the very first time. And the entire world looked different.

That is what it felt like last year, standing in that cemetery. So many of my family and my childhood friends, were buried there. I had lived with them for almost three decades, under the camouflage of an ordinary life lived with ordinary people. Looking at their graves for the first time in over twenty years, I realized that this wasn't so. This is how I came to see, for the first time, not my papa and mama, not my aunts and uncles, not Tommy and Brian and all, but instead just a graveyard full of disposable people, some of whose graves were now being re-used to bury the newly dead.

Her grave said that Martha Lovelace was a wife, mother, grandmother, sister, aunt and friend, and insisted that she rest in peace.

She had lost a breast at the time, back in 1984. The doctors had said that it couldn't be saved because the tumor had become malicious (or so I thought I heard.) So she had one breast. Perhaps it was also because of the cancerous cells that her teeth had already begun to fall out; they only numbered three more than her breasts. Her four teeth were oddly distributed, with three above and one below. Everyone in the yard said that even before she lost her breast, her husband, Uncle Joey, had stopped touching her and didn't fuck her anymore, because of how unattractive she was.

She had stopped going to church by then as well, mostly stayed home, cooking for her kids, washing the clothes and so on. Aunt Martha was my biological aunt and so Uncle Joey was actually an uncle-in-law, but back then even strangers were called aunt or uncle. You had to be polite, or may the good Lord have mercy on your soul before your parents got hold of you.

Uncle Joey had died in the same year that Aunt Martha lost her breast. Thinking about it recently, I realized it was about eight months after her surgery that he died. She had come back from the hospital sometime in April, while we were on Easter holidays. He had gone on the winter Farm Work program in December, to pick apples. Normally he would have gone on the summer program, but hadn't gotten his papers sorted out in time that year. He wasn't used to the cold of winter, caught pneumonia, and died up there.

Uncle Joey hadn't spoken to my papa for the eight years before his death. Back then little things could completely destroy a relationship. For example, after years of marriage, Tall Man had cheated on Aunt Josephine once more and she had left him, ending a twenty-four year relationship. Just like that. With my papa and Uncle Joey, it was just about the same. My papa was a good friend of the councilor (local politician) who gave out the few farm work vouchers available every year. Uncle Joey had asked him for a voucher and he didn't give it to him, because my papa wanted to seem impartial and maintain the respect and integrity he seemed to have lived his whole life for. Uncle Joey never spoke a single solitary word to my papa after that. But he obviously did get a voucher from another source.

Getting a farm work voucher back then was like winning the lottery, it was a ticket to your dreams. Every year you saw the workers come home, wearing new jeans, new shirts, new hats, new shoes, and often carrying a big Boom Box radio in their hand. We often went to the airport in a chartered bus to see them off or welcome them home. With his new income, Uncle Joey had started to build some additions to his house - had a kitchen, a bathroom and one other bedroom. Every year he added something new. In 1982, he got a television set, the first in our Depression. He also got a video, a blender, and a bright red bicycle for his daughter, my cousin, Sophie. Not to mention the barrels of clothes, soaps, rice, flour, and so on.

It was the TV that brought us kids to his house every day though, including a few weeks after he died. We went there every day to watch cartoons as soon as the TV signed on at 6 p.m. We would sit on their verandah, sometimes ten or eleven of us, watching the Flintstones and Top Cat. I loved Speedy Gonzales back then, though I never knew the day would come when I would learn Spanish.

The day pastor came to the house there was no electricity. My aunt didn't have any money to pay her bills and they had cut off the light. The surgery on her breast, her continued treatments, and the funeral had all been more expensive than we knew, and Uncle Joey had been in the habit of spending all he earned on things, rather than saving. Saving wasn't part of our culture really, not least because few of the adults had any decent jobs that would allow them to put things away for a rainy day.

This was on a Saturday afternoon and about four of us boys were sitting there on my aunt's verandah. I was staring at the TV screen as if I expected the light to come back any minute then. Billy, Tommy, Garnet and Cudjoe were chatting and telling jokes. Even though it had been a few days since the electricity was cut off, we still gathered there daily. It had become our spot.

It was both my cousin's silence and the silhouette on the TV screen, that told me that someone was there. I looked around and saw it was the pastor. A cool kind of man. A *neatly pressed, pleated black pants; clean, fresh white shirt; spit shine, black leather shoes; gold Citizen Quartz watch; sweet aftershave and cologne, clean-shaven, showered* cool kind of man. There was no dry shit caked up in his backside, and he probably used tissue to swab his dick after he pissed, like people said Mr Man did. He was definitely not one of us.

It was clear why he was there, at least to the adults who later explained to a cousin who explained to another cousin who explained to my brother who explained to me, "Why the raas you always asking me question? You don't see that the woman just lose her husband?" Pastor had come to comfort her after her loss.

He came almost every week after that. We were often there when he came on a Saturday. He gave us money sometimes to go out by the road and buy soda or ice cream. Sometimes he brought us candies. Never once did he try to preach to us the gospel.

The older folks said that that was the way the devil worshippers worked. They looked for those who were weak, those who had fallen out of grace with the Lord, those who had stopped going to church, and provided false comfort to them. They also pretended not to preach, but all the time they were sowing their evil seeds with their words and their deeds. Buying us sweets, for example. I had to eat mine when the adults weren't looking.

Aunt Martha had four mouths to feed and no electricity. There was cousin Junior, twenty-three or thereabouts; cousin Ricky, twenty; cousin Louie, seventeen, and, as I mentioned before, the one girl, cousin Sophie, fourteen. The older boys were hardly ever there, and didn't get much of the sweets and money that pastor gave us for soda. But Louie and Sophie did. Sophie especially, because she was the youngest and a girl.

The light came back about three months after. Neither Junior, Ricky, Louie, nor Aunt Martha had gotten a job, but we learnt in those days that the Lord worked in mysterious ways and would always provide. We just needed to have faith and the Lord would help us find a way.

The light stayed on for about a year. In late 1985 Sophie got saved, and about seven or so months after she also got a child. I can't say it didn't take me a while, especially because by then I had stopped asking my brother questions, but I did, eventually, put all the pieces together.

CHAPTER 22

My Mama's Smile

"Insomnia is an abomination!" growled the lion, readying himself to endure another sleepless night beneath the vast African skies. It had been three weeks already, his suffering was great, and he felt no one understood his anguish.

From a little over a hundred yards away, the cougar softly snarled while watching the restless head of the pack lament and roam. The lion was an aging king, his insomnia wasn't due to age, but his farting certainly was. On nights like these, while the pack sought to rest, he would sometimes let one rip with sonic force and split both atoms and ribs. Like he did just now. It was only a matter of seconds… one… two… three… before one of the younger cubs would claim that the fart was colored and visible. This would result in additional ribs being burst with laughter. Ageing was why he farted so much, and was also the reason he no longer exerted the effort to silence the cubs as they giggled and kept the pack awake. But he was also a king, and kings didn't trouble themselves with tiny things.

But the cougar was worried by the constant prowl, the constant growl, the farts and the giggles. He knew that many efforts had been made to solve the problem, including feeding the Old Timer the delicate meat of Gemsboks late at night before he went to bed.

There were, too, herbs and bushes and the magical chants of the Mystical Ones, yet he still could not sleep, and would stay awake through the long and lonesome hours of the night.

They were not friends and had never been, but sometimes comfort is found in places we would not expect. Besides, while they are still alive, it is often hard to display open hate for those who protect us. So the cougar stayed and the lion growled, and both watched the twinkling stars and the moon as it went to sleep. But there were questions that the cougar had, one of which he would never ask, at least not of the king. "Your troubles we understand, we have seen it for centuries on this land, but is there a reason it must be shared with everyone?"

"When I grow up I would like to be a lion," said the cougar's cub, "and I won't need to answer questions."

Diary entry, August 12, 1987

There is no need to put any clothes or make-up on this, or try to make it look like something it isn't. This is the naked truth.

In June 2008 I was in Jakarta, Indonesia. I don't often get to Indonesia. Indonesia: one of the four most populous countries on earth, a place where volcanoes grow like rice. Remarkable Indonesia. What rich cultures! What languages! What ethnic tribes! What spicy food! What diarrhea!

On this trip, my third, I had an accident. I was in a rented car and a couple were on a motorbike. The two vehicles collided and the couple were nearly killed. I am aware that in many countries with large amounts of poor people, a few (not mass) random (not serial) deaths will normally go unnoticed, but I have generally tried to avoid killing people.

This is because of how I grew up - to value all things and all people.

That part of me remains.

It is never very easy for someone to distance him or herself from their past; it is easier to get separated than it is to become fully divorced (a little like the relationship between Church and State). And so I have never forgotten my roots: not my family, dog, former lovers; not what it was like to be a plain, ordinary child growing up in a plain, ordinary village in a plain, ordinary, developing country.

It is for this reason that the night before the accident, it had boiled my blood to hear an expat couple tell a story of their time in Hanoi. They said their next-door neighbors had a dog that was tied up and beaten by its Vietnamese family every evening. The aim was to soften it up for cooking. I was revolted and angered. While news of this nature may bring joy to the ears of some mailmen, I had always thought that dogs simply couldn't get a break and were never treated fairly. I guess I had also always known the importance of treating all animals with kindness.

I learnt the value of things from a young age. I never shopped for 'groceries' before I was well into my twenties. All my early years were spent buying a few items needed for the next meal. I didn't know what *foie gras* was until I was thirty-one, let alone what it would taste like when seared by a Master Chef and served with Hong Kong sauce. But I know these things now. And I know the life of global airports, high-rise buildings, and places where ordinary folks call you *sir*. I have come a long way. But I still will not give my dog its own bedroom with a TV in it, or its own page on Facebook. I will still encourage the teller at the bank to attend to the local man who was ahead of me first. And no matter how many helpers and workers I have, I know I will never want someone else to wipe my ass. I remember my roots, always have, always will.

Of course I have made some mistakes, like everyone else. Once or twice I have done things that might have suggested my roots had slipped my mind.

One day in 1991, an old, dirty-looking woman came up to me on the streets of Kingston. I was attending college by then, and had enough money to go to Domino's pizza in Liguanea. I remember that as the old woman opened her mouth to say something to me, I said to her, "No, I don't have anything to give you today," just as her, "Excuse me sir, do you know where..." started to fade from her lips and the hurt crept into her eyes. That look I will take with me to my dying days. I never grew up assuming things about people because of how they looked. I knew then that my first few years of college education were slowly killing a part of me, and dragging me from my roots.

After that experience I re-normalized. I have since seen 'anomaly people' but I maintained my composure. In India, I saw a woman whose face was covered with marble sized warts with almost no space in between them. She begged me and I gave to her without revealing on my face the horror I felt inside. In Kingston, there was a man whose face looked like the mask of 'Scary Movie', probably from an acid attack. I saw him as a man. I didn't go to the whores who called to me in April in Bangkok, because they were whores, but because whores were no longer my calling. In Nepal, there was a lady with a wart growing from her cornea. I had no clue how that was even possible, but I saw her as a lady. Then there were all the people with bodies contorted from polio, in Sudan. While I had no idea what kind of person I would be after seeing them, I knew they were people with disfigurations, not disfigured people.

But back to Jakarta. It happened like this: my driver was taking me back from the mall where I had gone to pick up a few shirts - he pulled out onto the main road, made a U-turn where one should not have been made; the car coming on the other side had a clear view of us and stopped, and the motorbike coming alongside that car had no view of us and was stopped by my car. The bike remained grounded. The couple that was on it, took flight. I heard the sounds of metal crumpling, glass breaking, things crunching. Then came a crowd, then family, then frantic conversations.

I called the Security Advisor at the company I was consulting with, as we had gone out for drinks a couple nights before. I was advised to take the couple to the hospital but not to make any commitments. I went and waited on due process – the triage, the examinations, the x-rays, the soft comforting words from newly arrived relatives and friends. I had been to another hospital the week before, in Singapore. Cleaner, costlier, better.

It was while I waited to hear how bad the lady's injuries were, that I got the first shocking indication that I might appear not to be the person I have always been. The security advisor called back. His perception of me was such that he suggested, essentially, that I should find out how much money would create amnesia and make the woman and her pain go away.

The lady had taken the bigger fall and was the main one being treated. Her little son had come to the hospital. I could see that he was changing teeth, with the gums at the front of his mouth now perfectly shaped like two squares. The writer in me thought the teeth were lying in wait, like spies behind the scenes. He tried to sit on his mama's lap after she came back from x-ray and sat in her wheelchair, but she told him, in Bahasa Indonesia, the equivalent of "not yet," with a softness that belied her pain.

Her only English-speaking relative filled me in on a few important details: The doctor would soon come and look at the x-ray result. The woman only had one child. The man with her was her second husband that she just married a year before. Her first husband was a driver for an expat family and had died from carbon monoxide poisoning while he fell asleep with the car on in the garage - the woman didn't find out until after he was already buried because local culture necessitated burial within twenty-four hours. The damage to the woman's leg didn't look too bad.

Then the doctor came, looked at the results, spoke with the family and gave instructions in Bahasa Indonesia. After he left, I thought to go over and say a word to her, see how she was doing, but mostly to apologize for what had happened. That is when the second shocking event happened. Perhaps it was something to do with the way others, including my driver, had spoken <u>for</u> me. Or the way I stood - straight, erect, without a hunch or any signs of recent experiences with hunger. Or if it was my Italian shoes that she maybe felt she could only afford if she sold the organs of her one child. Or if it was my perfumed smell of authority, or my expat status. Whatever it was, it made this wonderful woman sitting in her wheelchair, massaging her wounds, look up at me as I approached her and say, in her basic English, "Sorry... cause you trouble, *sir.*"

I went to the car and I cried. She reminded me of my mama.

What I cannot remember well is whether it was a shoebox or a shoe that we lived in, but I know it was something of the sort. Maybe our shoebox was made out of zinc?

I lived with mama, in our shoebox. You know my mama already: Sonia Lovelace; born 1953; nearly died giving birth to me; 5' 4"; widower of a man's impression; mother of four; woman; poor, always; giver of life to people, plants and puppies; buyer of books with plots and characters that she herself could never read; lover of frilly pink dresses; Jamaican.

That's my mama. But I don't think I ever told you about the day of the flood and some of the things that made her cry.

I was twelve years of age at the time. Still. June 1982, it was then.

The weatherman on TV, Tom Browester, had said it was coming. He had in effect said that it was one of those lazy but brutal storms - the type that came with ferocious force but approached slowly, like a Jamaican policeman. He had explained that, based on their projections, the storm was set to slowly saunter across the island and dump its misery on the entire southern sections of the country. He said it over and over again:

"It is not the wind that you should worry about, it is the rain. It will come with a lot of rain and because it is moving slowly, the earth will become waterlogged and there is a high risk of flooding. Persons in low-lying areas should move to higher grounds."

"Higher grounds" he had said, those were his words. In those days the first thought that had come to my mind was to get myself one of the biggest ganja joints I could find. As kids we had often heard the adults ask, "Why drink and drive, when you can smoke and fly?"

No one believed the weatherman at first. We all felt he was a dunce. He had never been able to predict the weather accurately before, so people thought that it was much safer to get a forecast by either watching the goats and the cows, or, while you are taking a piss, swinging your dick to see to which side the last drop of piss would fall. Those who wanted to be proper about it would perhaps just toss a coin.

But we were in a low-lying area, and if he chose that one time in his whole life to be right then we would be, using the memorable words of my uncle, "in deep shit." This is not the same uncle who was found buried in it.

Our house was not only in a low-lying area, it was close to a canal. This canal had over-run its banks many times before, after any consistent downpour. The rain waters came rushing off the hills to hunt like lions on the plains, usually catching little kids, and folks silly enough to try crossing the rivers on foot. We had seen it happen a few times before, so whenever it rained hard we all sat on our verandahs and watched the canal to see the level of the water. And we would continue watching it late into the night before we went to bed.

By the late evening, a raging wind was whipping round us and it had started to rain. My family had one of the few houses made of brick, and it was strong enough that the big bad wolf could not blow it down. By then we had completed the second room on the house which was, that night, full of family and friends who lived in wooden and zinc houses and needed somewhere safe to stay until the strong winds passed. With our candles and our bibles, we were like a church congregation at a midnight vigil. Some folks were praying. I remember how the night began to take on a living form, and darkness was the color of the sky and also its mood. [How dark can a night become? When rum-loving Uncle Bob lost his factory job sometime in the mid-1980s and found himself in a bar spending all of his small severance pay, his common-law wife, Aunt Frida, came in, grabbed him by the collar in front of his friends, slapped him in his face and knocked over his unfinished drink in the process. Can a night become as dark as the face that was slowly raised to look at her? Can a night breathe wet, caustic and corrosive malignancy? That one did!]

There I was, a child in a small dark room, surrounded by scared adults, and sensing something outside my house that seemed alive and monstrously evil. And I sensed that it was looking through the darkness, through the door, through my brother's body, at me.

After a while the howling winds passed, and the rain really set in. It was about 11 p.m. when the others left in search of more floor-space somewhere safe to sleep. Most went to the fire-station a few miles away because it was also made of brick. I was left in one room with my brother and papa, and my sisters were in the other with my mama. It was too terrifying for any of us kids to go outside to look at what was happening by the canal, and too dark to see the waters anyway, to see anything. By then, our illegal electric connection was disconnected, and our candles and lanterns blown out by the winds - none of us had taken the weatherman seriously enough to have gone and bought flashlights. After a while, somehow we went to sleep.

In the middle of the night the water started to rise. In just the same way you see the shadow of evil rising behind the hero in those horror movies after he stupidly only struck the evil once, and turned his back to comfort the damsel-in-distress. So it rose. There were two houses that were closer to the canal than ours. Two houses with thirteen people. I did not see two of them again after that night. Two little girls I sometimes played with. Swept away by the rising floods. It might have been their dying voices that woke us in the darkest hours of the night, or the voices of my mama and sisters.

I awoke to screams. And to find that the stealthy, sneaky flood waters were already on my bed, lying there with me like a serpent, mouth open and measuring my body to see if it could take me all in. I woke my papa and my brother and we waded through the water to the door to open it and go to rescue my mama and sister. The door was jammed. The rapidly-rising water outside, and the pressure inside, made it impossible to open. It occurred to me that this must have been the same thing that was happening to my mama and sisters, why they had not rescued us either.

So we started to scream also. All of us in that house started to scream as though it was the day of judgment and we had heard the verdict on our souls.

The water reached my shoulder, came close enough to smile at me and kiss me on my lips. I had by then resigned myself to its unwanted advances and violations, and to the muddy-water smell of its breath. Then, incredibly, the firemen came. Sent by some family or friend at the fire-station to swing by and check on those who had stayed. They used their axes to rip apart our door that the Salvation Army would take three months to replace. One of them put me on his shoulders, and took me to safety. It would be sixteen hours before I would finally see the rest of my family again, including my broken papa. A man dressed in the guise of a caring politician, came and offered us all his sympathies - thick, abundant, unwanted and suffocating, like snot in a baby's nose. But what I remember most was seeing my mama when she found us and realized that we were all safe. She cried rivers as she embraced us. When she pushed me away to look at me properly I saw such tenderness in my mama's eyes. I knew at that moment that no matter the hurtful things she may have done and said to me before, my mama loved me.

I had seen my mama cry many times before, often because of things that my papa did. Sometimes he hurt her so deeply that she would have to go by one of my aunt's houses to borrow some sympathy. This aunt would later swing by herself, perhaps in a couple of days, to pick up her sympathy, as something would surely have also happened to her within the space of a week. This is how I learnt that sympathy went around, and came around, much more than money, which, once loaned in that village, was hardly ever seen again.

In Jamaica we say "Where there is a will, there is a relative." This is because, after someone's death people you never met will show up to claim some share of the inheritance. In my mama's case there was no need. We had nothing. Not even shit in our name. Hers was a hard life, Semicolon, only interspersed with occasional joys. Some of these joys also had their dark side. Like the first time *my side* of the family went to KFC. One of our relatives from abroad was visiting and took us there so that we too could enjoy a little of the life of the north, while still living deep down in the south. What a treat that was for us! It was as though we had all flown to Italy to dine at a fine restaurant in Venice! At the end of the meal I tried pulling a Robert Mugabe *I am never leaving here* stunt, but was quickly slapped out of it by mama. But I loved being at KFC so much that I told my mama that I wanted to go back there every day. And, true to our circumstances, she said I just might, for there was little prospect of me finding a job anywhere else when I grew up. It was always like this, you learnt to enjoy the little things that came your way, but never to build your hopes and expectations up.

But I knew she loved me deeply, Semicolon. Though I was only the second son, I knew she loved me. I could see it in the softness of that smile that was always so comfortably reposed in her eyes when she looked at me. And then she died, just like that.

Hers was the first death I truly felt. If I were to be true to myself I wasn't angry when I found out that my mama was dead. The word that came closest to capturing my feelings was 'inflamed'. When the news came I was in the yard playing a game of cricket with some of the other boys. I had struck the ball, run a single, and was waiting for my partner, who happened to me my brother, to face the bowler. Then they told us. The good and the bad about rural people is that there is no tact in the way they deliver information; no one asked us to sit down.

"Kenny, Martin, unno (your) mumma dead!" Followed by "Lord have mercy!", "Jesus Christ!" and other similar exclamations that are used to underscore statements of fact but do nothing to disperse disbelief.

I remember seeing my brother's fingers clutching tightly to the cricket bat as if it contained the word of God and he was holding on to salvation. For my own part if I had released my own grip my fingers would have curled themselves into a fist.

For so many years she lived with us as a real, solid particle and then, like vapor, she was gone.

I know that wherever in the world she lived, my mama would have one day died because that is the fate of us all who were born in sin; so it is written, and so it will always be. I felt, however, that in most developed countries she would have had a *curable* disease, and would have lived a longer life. Moreover, the fact that she died young could not be blamed entirely on the level of science and technology in Jamaica at the time, for we had one of the best healthcare systems in the developing world. This was no Third World country where doctors had neither a clue nor curiosity; this was Jamaica.

The real problem was that by the mid-1980s, people who had insufficient disposable income had become disposable people. By then, bringing your chicken to the doctor was no longer seen as cute, let alone as currency. We were a full-fledged capitalist country.

While she was lying inside the hospital room, a fierce political boxing match was taking place on TV. The battle was between two slogans: in the Socialist corner, "We put people first" and in the Labourite corner, "It takes cash to care." They had reached Bout 3 of 11 when her last breath escaped.

But these are highly complex issues, and it is perhaps better not to delve into them without either a bible or a stick of weed which, from my experience, are two of the best aids to contemplation.

"When sorrow sticks"

When sorrow sticks, it sticks.
Sticks like Old Man Tom's unexpected phlegmatic spit -
gummy, gluey, sticking
like the shame that remained after dignity took flight.
It sticks. Unintentionally. Like shit. In a constipated ass.
Refusing to come unstuck in spite of all the deceptive teasing,
goading and easing. Stuck. Like muck.
Muck spoilt, rotten, decayed.
It sticks, like a truant tantrum-throwing toddler,
that will neither come nor go, but just sits.
Sits and sticks, like that man's meanness surprisingly stuck,
after he gave a buck to a beggar he then begged for change.
Sticks, sugary sweet,
not in your teeth,
but like the bubbling hot homemade guava jam
that "inadvertently" spilled and gripped Georgie's hand,
smothering the primordial scream that tried to escape.
When sorrow sticks it sticks,
like a leech bathing in 100% body juice,
drinking and sucking sweet vitamins and minerals that are not
from concentrate
It sticks, like the dark yellow mucus stuck in the back of a
pneumonic throat,
that neither Vicks nor Mucinex could dislodge.
Stuck. Trapped.
When sorrow sticks, it sticks.
And nothing can separate you from it.

Disposable People

No matter what you take – Valium, Pilates, Yoga, or the best
Appleton Estate rum.
When sorrow sticks, it sticks.
As tight as your own fucking skin.

Undated journal entry

You know by now, Semicolon, that it doesn't make any difference to tell you why or how she died. And telling you about her may indeed give life but only to her character.

What I want you to know, Semicolon, is that there are times when you know within yourself that you will never go back to a place and time. I know I will never go back there. Neither alive nor dead. I am certain of this, because I know that even the dead can resist. I know, because I remember the day the pallbearers attempted to carry a coffin and bury a body someplace where the deceased had explicitly indicated he didn't want to be buried. I remember that, as the pallbearers went along, they found that the coffin gradually got heavier and heavier until not even a hundred men could carry it. Old Man Tom had resisted. Mocked all the days of his life, but in death his *will* had to be honored. I was there, I saw it. Even when I am dead, therefore, I know that I will not return to that *hateful* fucking place. For this is my will, and nothing in this universe can change it.

I will say nothing more on this.

Nothing more.

Perhaps just one thing as it now comes to mind.

There are some things I have sworn I will never do a second time in this life, unless someone puts a loaded gun to my head and demonstrates intent. I will never sleep with another whore without a condom. That is one. More important than this, however, is that I will never again go to a Third World morgue to identify the body of a member of my family. They had her there, pulled out of the 'freezer' on a dirty, rusty-looking slab. She looked like a large lump of meat and was completely naked. We could see all the long, crudely sewn-up gashes from the post-mortem. They had a thought that she might have had a stroke, and therefore removed a part of her scalp for the autopsy. Not even the slightest effort was made to conceal it when we came. It was just a dead body – as proof, she did not move.

CHAPTER 23

Martin and My Brother

"Dear diary,
We know that the world changes, but never at its core."

K. Lovelace, 2001

Martin Lovelace, 1991

I cannot recall the exact details of the conversation as it happened, but I do remember the broad outline. I overheard it while I was waiting outside our outdoor bathroom with my bucket of water in my hand, ready to go in and bathe after my brother was finished. He was still very much mid-wash and had not yet lifted his bucket above his head to empty all the remaining water on himself, which would signify the conclusion of the bathing process. While standing there waiting, it occurred to me that there was someone else there with him inside the bathroom. It was Martin. They were speaking to each other. The conversation I heard went something like this:

Martin:	"Where were you when she died?"
My brother:	"You know I had to be at work, why do you keep asking me that?"
Martin:	"Because you never really cared about her."
My brother:	"Of course I did!"
Martin:	"No, you didn't. You never really cared for anything or anyone!"
My brother:	"That is not true, I cared!"
Martin:	"Did you care for Ruffy?"
My brother:	"Ruffy? No! Ruffy was just a dog!"
Martin:	"Did you care for Tweetie when she got swallowed?"
My brother:	"Tweetie? Tweetie is just a damn cartoon bird!"
Martin:	"Did you care for Glenroy?"
My brother:	"Who the fuck is Glenroy?"
Martin:	"Did you care for all those mangoes we ate?"
My brother:	"What? Of course not! They were just mangoes."
Martin:	"See! You never cared for anything!"

It was clear that Martin was winning the argument with my brother, who was getting exasperated. Only... Martin *was* my brother, my *only* brother.

He was losing his mind. Not many people knew. For many years, not many people knew. My brother's case was later diagnosed, at which point many people began saying, "Oh, so *that's* why..." For them, the past was now perfectly explained. For us, the future, and my brother, were now totally fucked up and unfixable. My older brother that I always wanted to look up to, but couldn't.

Not many people can understand the impact of these things on a family, for you generally have to experience them to know. For most of us, our experience extends only as far as when a friend or family member says, "I can't find my keys" and we all jest and make fun of him while we help to look around the room to see where he may have misplaced them. For me and my younger sisters it was different. Days came when we often saw him standing there facing us, and though he never said it, we knew the expression in his eyes meant, "I can't find myself," and none of us knew how to help him look for what was missing.

My brother continues to be three years older than me, but only in age. He grew less in height and intellect, but his body had a more efficient way of proportionally allocating resources to its parts. He loved to ride his red bike before he grew to love riding women. Much later he loved two of his three kids.

He ran away to the Bahamas in 1992. Then, two years later he made a phone call:

"Hey Kenny."

"Hello... Martin?"

"Tell everyone that I love them. I will send you some money when I get back on my feet."

"Martin, where are you?"

"Everybody alright? Alright, good. Bye."

"Martin?"

Nineteen months later – phone call:

"Hey Kenny."

"Martin?" (Just where I had left off)

"You want me to send you some money?"

"No, I am good, I-"

"Kenny, I think I am fucked up. But the doctor says I will be fine in…

5

4

3

2

1

I am good now. So you want me to-"

"Martin, what the fuck you-"

"Tell everyone that I love them. How Kay?"

"Mart-"

"Alright then, bye."

To infinity and beyond. And that was that and no more than that.

This is a rather charming way of describing it, no? The shifting of Teutonic plates, the falling off into the continental shelf, the changing of things that will never be the same again?

This is what I know. First, my brother's mind started drifting away it seemed after mama died, which is after papa died, which itself is after Tommy died, which is also after Brian died, which was eight months before Uncle Thomas died. So much loss in just a few, short years. When all these things happened to us, and to other folks like us, they had a profound impact on us all. Maybe they did something altogether more to the young boy Martin.

CHAPTER 24

Why Beyoncé and I Are Not Together

I have a feeling deep inside my bones, that within seven months I will be fully 'upper class'. No more middle- or upper middle-class for me! Mark my words: seven months, three days, and $164,000 more and I will be comfortable and secure, and not a soul will be able to dislodge me once I have perched in my upper class nest.

Journal entry, June 2009

One of the true loves of my life: Beyoncé.

It would be a big fat lie if I said that I have never seen a woman from another country dance and wine their behind like a Jamaican. [Wine: to gyrate one's waist. To revolve around a fixed point or axis.] There have been two. The first was a Japanese, and she was competing against a Jamaican! I will give you a moment to reflect on that. Noodles. Rice. Sushi. Versus Jerk Pork. Curried Goat. Oxtail.

It gets a bit embarrassing here, as I must admit that I was watching a dance competition to select the best dancer of Jamaican reggae. This was the show to crown a new Dance Hall Queen. Not a Princess, but a Queen. 1998. The competition was now down to the noodle-eater and the reigning, curry-goat-eating Dance Hall Queen, 'Mad Margaret'. In itself, this is sufficient cause for concern given that curry-goat-eaters, even without names such as this, are normally bloody aggressive people. Noodle-eaters are not. The two hardly belonged in the same country, let alone on the same stage.

The judges were looking at the quality of the women's wine – how they moved their waist and their behind – to determine the winner.

Mad Margaret took the centre of the stage. This was unusual, given that the reigning queen would normally wait for the challenger to dance before taking the stage. I guessed that Mad Margaret was impatient.

Mad Margaret walked to the centre of the stage.

The music was turned up and effectively deafened seven people who would find out ten years later.

Mad Margaret kicked off her shoes and her decorum.

Mad Margaret dipped.

And then she began to wine.

And as her juicy delights began to oscillate, the men in the crowd started heating up and popping like popcorn. It was an unbeatable performance!

The noodle-eater could not win! It would not be possible! We all knew then why Mad Margaret had gone first: it was to make the noodle-eater feel so inferior that when she took the stage and did anything, the boos from the crowd, combined with her feeling of inferiority, would lead to a quick collapse. So that the crowd would call for Mad Margaret to return, like a true queen.

But the noodle-eater had something else in mind.

She walked the way women walk when they are Japanese and went straight to the centre of the stage.

The music deafened another ten to twelve people, according to a medical research that would be published a few years later.

The noodle-eater then went on her *head*.

Balanced.

And then she began to wine.

A Japanese girl, on her head, with her sweet little ass beginning to *tic toc*! The country exploded! The judges were made redundant! Noodle-eater had the crown!

Now, with regards to Beyoncé, I am not sure whether she eats Jerk Pork, Curried Goat, Julie Mangoes, East Indian mangoes, Sushi, Noodles, or anything. She is, in fact, quite trim. But I have seen her dip. And I have seen her wine. And heaven knows I have seen that behind. And this has been one of the purest pleasures I have had in my life, along with eating mangoes. And there are days when I wish that Beyoncé and I were together, and cannot for the life of me, figure out why this isn't the case.

CHAPTER 25

Carbon Footprint

9.45 p.m.

My dearest Semicolon, there are times when I feel as though my life is winding down like a long day, and try as I might I cannot resist the enchanting spells of night, and I know that I will soon fall asleep. My Thursday is on its way.

Tonight I feel I am falling apart. I am stained, Semicolon, and nothing I try seems able to wash away my stain. I am hurting, my love, and neither the lonely walls of this hotel room nor Facebook, seem to help. On another subject, my love, who in the UN do you think I could write to ask them if, while they are working on making this a more peaceful world, they could also try to make it more meaningful? My love, violence I can deal with, poverty is my middle name, but the tedium of doing and eating and seeing the same things every day?

Then, to make matters worse, my love, today there was a man preaching on the train I was on in the subway. He said that the world is going to end on May 14, 2014. Just weeks before the next World Cup! I don't know what I am going to do, because I have always loved the World Cup.

Sleep well, my love

Kenny

Journal entry, June 28, 2011

As I think you already know, Georgie too was one of my cousins. People say that just like Doretta, Georgie's mama had fallen asleep in the sun while she was pregnant with him, and that this is why he was never very smart. His little brain must have boiled in her belly in the hundred degree heat.

There are some people that, when they smile with the Universe, the Universe smiles back at them, and may even strike up a conversation. There are other people who, when they smile with the Universe, the Universe simply nods a slight acknowledgement. And then there are those people who, when they smile at the Universe, the Universe yells profanity at them, like, "What the fuck you smiling at nigga?"

Georgie stopped smiling with the Universe when he was about three months old. That, however, is the beginning, and we should perhaps start his story at the end.

The last time I saw Georgie he was sitting under an old Ackee tree, with his bare feet planted firmly on the ground. His hands were resting on his knees and held a black and white photograph in them. He looked like his papa who, in spite of his wretched ugliness within, was a man whose face, if it suddenly appeared above a baby's crib, would not cause the child to cry. Tall, black, muscular, with a hard, angular face, and eyes that held hues of ash. A sobering reminder that evil was not always ugly.

I had never seen Georgie look as relaxed as he did that afternoon. Sitting there alone, knowing that everyone was watching him. Yet he seemed so at ease with himself and with the world. The photograph was all that he had left of his papa.

The police came, and I have not seen Georgie ever since. Not to this day. This is the end. Now, let me tell you a little about Georgie's story and the connections with the others.

We will begin with the hiss:

"The hiss"

I can still see him, reminiscing
in gerunds, present, continuous and perfect tense,
alliterations and consonance,
playing with words that rhyme with wounds
and a ragged GI Joe doll

"Joe? Are you still missing?"
(gerund:
functioning as a noun – the missing,
unseen, unheard.
Not missing as a verb)
Her,
or her cuddling, hugging, touching -
feelings slipping like a song
from lips,
that once recalled a mother's tender loving kiss.

"You are scarred, Joe"
(perfect tense:
were scarred, are scarred, will forever be
scarred)
by the slit, the slash, the gash
on your wrist,
and by father's saccharine words:

Disposable People

"kindly be sure that next time you don't miss"

"Now it's time for your bath, Joe"
(alliterations:
bring a bucket,
now bend for a bathe in it.
No, Joe, not in that, in this
aged like rum,
ripened, rancid, reeking piss.

"Run, Joe, run"
(present continuous:
run, as if the continuation of your life depended on it)
or better yet, Soldier, pull your gun
that's the only thing to stop the vicious hit
of his jet propelled, knotted, knuckled fist.

"Don't be afraid, Joe"
(present tense:
when he's present, very tense)
and try not to reminisce
about the hiss
of that hot steamy iron's sticky unwanted kiss.

I guess he must be out there,
somewhere,
by now he would be a man,
I would so like to see Georgie,
if anyone still can.

Undated Journal entry

This is the second version of what I wrote about Georgie. I created this version many years later when I was playing with words and with the thought of writing poetry rather than capturing simple, pure emotions.

The original version was a little more direct. It went like this:

"The Hiss"

When you reminisce,
can you find something worse than this?
Worse,
than never having known a mother's tender loving kiss?
Worse,
than having felt too much of your father's knuckled fists?
Worse,
than being bent to bathe in a bucket of piss?
Worse,
Than being cruelly encouraged to slice your own wrist?
Worse,
than being kindly asked to ensure that this time you don't miss?
Worse,
than the hiss?
Of a hot steaming iron's sticky unwanted kiss?
If you reminisce like this
then, Georgie, I have been trying to find you for a long time,
write to me,
if you still can.

Undated Journal entry

As you see, the elements are all the same, but the structure is different. The elements are the same because things, at their essence, always remain the same. Therefore, the hiss is true. It was a true hiss. So too the fist. So too the piss. So too the wrist. And he had many scars. For the rest of us scars were the trophies of an enjoyable childhood, and symbolized that we played karate barefooted and sometimes stepped on glass, or crawled on our knees beneath the cellar of an old house and got cut by nails. None of Georgie's scars came from playing or exploring; they were all gifts from his papa. (Grandma Bell: "If that boy had gone to church none of this would have happened to him!")

I know all of these things must have left indelible imprints on Georgie, but what most left its mark on me was the footprint. The carbon footprint. *Carbon footprint: a measure of the impact of our activities on the environment and on the earth.*

Let us back up a bit to put this in context.

Georgie's mama

Georgie's mama had died about five years before. The ingredients of her death were:

- 1 woman
- 1 very low self-esteem
- 15 or so years of extreme cruelty
- 20 or so bags of shame
- An appropriate harness that could fit a small woman's shoulders

Mixed together this created a curled-up and airtight ball of disappointment and disease, dying under a blazing mid-day sun. Fainting and dying right there in the market. Just like that. The frothy bubbles at the corners of her mouth lingering longer than any hopes she ever had of having a good life.

When she died, some say that Georgie's papa had shed a single tear to comply with expectations. I, however, do not believe this, because there are some things in life that we know with certainty. We know that not every painting we see in a hotel room is good, because some painters lack aptitude. We know that not every plate of food we get in a restaurant comes without a bit of spit from a disgruntled cook (like my cousin Wayne), because some folks lack decency and self-control. And we also know that not everyone you see walking around your neighborhood actually has conscience and a soul. This is the way they came into this world, and the way that they will leave it.

My grandmother once offered some advice to the air, which we all understood to have been directed at Georgie's mama:

"The first time a man strike a woman, that woman must do him something that he will never forget, that way he will never strike her again. You see the first time Mas Jackson hit Miss Elaine she was in the kitchen, and she grabbed a knife and slash him, then she grabbed the pot that she goin' use fry the chicken on the stove and throw the hot oil after him. It never did catch him, but him remember, and him never touch her again after that!" Not all women had such character.

Georgie's papa

It would be easy to make excuses for him if you had not known him for long. You may say that there is so much love a man has inside of him that after he gives some to himself, gives a little to his machete, a little to his stool at the rum bar, and a little to an old pair of shoes, then sooner or later he will run out of love. Fair enough. But let's get to know this man a little better so that we don't jump to hasty conclusions.

Georgie's papa was like a rare fruit we have in Jamaica called a *Starapple*. True to its name, the Starapple grows very high and remains among the stars; far out of reach even when it is fully ripe. It ripens and then rots on the branches and then withers like the hope we had as children of ever tasting its succulence. We all called the *Starapple* the "meanest fruit." Georgie's papa's affection, if it ever bloomed, ripened, rotted and withered far out of Georgie's reach.

Georgie cooked dinner each day on a stove his papa had made from the rims of a car tire. There were many stoves like this. The rims were elevated on concrete blocks. His papa would bring coal, which Georgie would use to cook on. When the fire went out, the ashes from the coal would scatter on the ground. *Carbon*. The footprint comes here:

"Georgie"

Smile Georgie smile,
come and play for just a while;
laugh Georgie laugh,
after all you are still a child.

Smile Georgie smile,
he will be gone for at least a while,
and Billy will be on watch
to warn you if he comes back.

Breathe Georgie breathe,
he will soon re-submerge your head;
now hold your breath for a while,
'cause it seems he really wants you dead.

Smile Georgie smile,
the barrel of water is gone for a while,
and Courtney will be on watch,

to warn you if it comes back.

Hush Georgie hush,
we know it really must hurt,
that steel boot crushing your skull
against dumb mother earth.

Play Georgie play,
you don't need to go home to read,
and Cookie is now on watch,
for the belt that makes you bleed.

Smile Georgie smile,
We're here to help you heal,
and I am now on watch,
and praying with all my life -
that he never ever comes back.

K. Lovelace, 1988

Georgie's papa came home unexpectedly and dinner had not yet started. As we know, kids will sometimes be kids and may find themselves playing when they should be doing what they are really supposed to be doing.

Georgie ran to the stove to start the fire. His papa ran after him,
See Georgie run. Run Georgie run.
and caught him after stepping in the carbon. He then stepped, with his workman's boot, on Georgie's head.

Georgie cried, and so did I while watching. We all often watched as Georgie's papa inflicted some of the cruelest beatings on him.

The funny thing about life is that some kids will continue crying for all their lives, while others will stop. Georgie was one of those who stopped. Thereafter, no matter what his papa did, which buckled belt he used, which boot, whether he punched with one or both hands, slammed him against wall or ground. Georgie would not cry. But with each beating, the hate hardened in Georgie's eyes.

I once saw another cousin of mine carry a child in her womb for 250 days, then abandon it in a dumpster about thirty minutes after birth, because the burden had been too great. With Georgie it turned out to be the same:

"Elijah"

Elijah's mama came from the south
but needed a recipe book to cook
and a variety of pills to cope

with all her shame and stress
she was, utterly
worthless.

Elijah's dad was one of the rare breed of men
whose wives would die before them
and would only shed a tear to comply with expectations.

Elijah went to church, poor boy,
in search
of a new father,

but found, instead
Grace,
unfrocked, in bed

Ezekel Alan

slipping into the mood
for a bit of rectitude.

Amidst the burning bushes
and smoking tushes
the Father was never harder to find, nor whores easier;-

Elijah could choose whomsoever.

He overlooked Religion -
an obesely fat woman
with candlestick legs
as brittle as eggs;.

and scorning Repentance
Elijah chose Vengeance -

she who'd said, she'd prefer to be dead
than be like chattel, possessed;
so yearned for democracy, and greater openness.

So, the father he hadn't found
but when Elijah went home,
he was, surely
not alone.

Then,
rejecting the church's offering
Elijah washed away his own sin.

K. Lovelace, 1989

Obviously, Elijah was Georgie. I used Elijah for the religious feel it gave to the verse. With his faith in God shaking like his loose tooth (the result of his papa's fist), Georgie took matters into his own hands and managed to do what no one else had been able to – get his papa to smile. It was a big, wide-open smile from his throat. On the last day that I saw him, he himself was smiling as they took him away to juvenile penitentiary. And that was that, and no more than that.

There are some connections here that I should point out. First is that Uncle Bob had lost his third brother. This was not immediately obvious to everyone. Why? Because, based on what my cousins said, when Uncle Bob heard the news he displayed a certain *Hey Haitian child! Run! Run! A massive hurricane is coming! Run for your life! Why aren't you running? This one is bigger than the one that killed your parents five years ago! Boy I said it is bigger than the one that killed your brother and your friends two years ago! This one is gonna kill you bwoy! Run! Run child run! Don't you hear me? Run!* kind of indifference. He simply responded, "Well, he might as well get it over and done with."

Second, his lost brother was also our uncle. This came after losing Uncle Thomas and our papa and cousin, and Tommy and so on and so forth. All in the space of a measly few years.

Third, while I had gone to the shop to purchase big gill of oil (I don't know how much that is in metric); ¼ bread; 1 lb of chicken back; 1 tin of mackerel, and some syrup, my brother was in the yard when it happened. He was one of the first to go over to Georgie's house, stand there, and look at the body.

I am smiling as I write this, Semicolon, because I know only a few people will believe any of this. It is only a story they'll say, twisting and turning to hopefully some form of interesting end.

CHAPTER 26

The Pastor

Let me quickly set one part of Georgie's story straight. Georgie was not the one to see the pastor in bed with Grace. Which really was her name. It was a woman who attended the pastor's church and was dropping by his house to bring him dinner. I wrote a verse about the pastor a few weeks after the event.

"The pastor"

Hallelujah, Hallelujah, Hallelujah!
Amen, Amen, Amen!
Words filled with the Passion
Dripping with the Blood
Heavy with the Spirit
Of the one and only God

Hallelujah, Hallelujah, Hallelujah!
Amen, Amen, Amen!
Rising on the wings
Of His Holy Grace
To taste the milk and honey
In that heavenly place

Hallelujah, Hallelujah, Hallelujah!

Amen, Amen, Amen!!
He shall come again, brother
He is on his way
Singing mighty Hallelujah
That will be some day!

But until that day sister
You are looking fine
You sweet little thing
With that mighty sweet behind!

Remember:
He is perfect sister
But mortal men are we
You shall find salvation later
But for now just let it be!

K. Lovelace, 1989

I knew this pastor and I knew Grace, who was only fifteen years old but old enough to start taking a big preacher man's cock. (No one asked Grandma Bell about the fact that Grace *had gone* to church and received quite a bit of rectitude).

I do not tell these things simply to tease and titivate senses and sensibilities. What we have here, yet again, is a big man's cock confronting a little girl's crotch, an event as normal as flossing your teeth and, occasionally, smelling the floss. What we also have is the credibility of the church. Yes, we all went to church very often, and one might have gotten the impression that we were all deeply religious. Perhaps we were, but ours was the permissive type of religion that allowed lying, cheating, stealing, fornicating, raping, adultery, and other things, but not (SLAP) taking (SLAP) the (SLAP) Lord's (SLAP) name (SLAP) in (SLAP) vain (SLAP) (SLAP).

How much could they really offer us, these pastors? One pastor spent years trying to convince us that God was standing at our front doors waiting to be let in, while the devil was at the back waiting on those trying to sneak out. In his view, in just the same way we could easily jump on a bus and go to Lionel Town, Vere, Spauldings or Chapelton, so too we could all easily go to Hell.

Another pastor carried a gun, claiming that the Lord helps those who help themselves and that the same applies to protection.

Another told us that crime doesn't pay, when that was all we ever saw happen.

Another one, eminently trained at some North American theological seminary, read World Bank reports to understand poverty (good luck with that!), and drove his late model Mitsubishi Pajero to work. Chit-chatted with the browner folks in the browner pews, those who came to ease their conscience and hedge their bets on the Lord.

Other pastors promised us an abundance of wealth in the hereafter, encouraging us to just stick it out another forty years or so.

The final straw was pastor's interpretation of Jesus' response to the Sadducees (Mathew 22). Somehow, after reading this passage, pastor implied that there would be no marriage (to which I hissed my teeth), no romance (I could barely contain my disgust), and no sex (I was ready to walk out of church) in the afterlife. On that day he placed a firm foot on any desire me, my brother and cousins might have had, of ever going to Heaven.

When we were called upon to sing, my hymns undulated in flesh-colored tones and rattled like hollowed bones, and when I lifted up my head to give praise my voice stayed down, and disobeyed. For I found nothing but emptiness in church.

CHAPTER 27

The Strangest Magic Trick I Ever Saw

Hey you. Yes you. You with that skin-tightening cream on your face reading my book. Yes, you. Give me a thought. Don't worry I am not going to steal it. I just want to show you something. You really worry too much, you know. Just give me a thought. Any thought, it doesn't matter. No, I am not going to harm your thought either. I promise I will give it back to you in the same condition as I got it. I just want to show you a trick.

Okay. Good. Now here we go. Now, does everyone see the thought here in my hands? [Both hands are together and the thought is nestled in them.] Notice that all of it is still here, in my hand?

Now I need an assistant to help verify what I am about to do. Any volunteers? Good, come right up. What's your name? Steve? Nice to meet you, Steve, I would shake your hands but, as you can see, I am holding this thought. Now, come closer Steve. Can you see the thought clearly in my hand? Can you also please touch this thought Steve, so that our audience may know it is real and that it is the same thought. Can you confirm that the thought is real Steve? Good.

Now, everyone, please pay attention. Notice, I am not wearing a long-sleeve shirt. No jacket. Just my bare hands. This thought is right here in my bare hands.

Now, I am going to slowly close my hands, like this… [both hands close]. Now I am going to slowly open my hands… [both hands slowly open].

Look! The thought is still there! Gotcha there, didn't I? I know that most of you must have thought that the thought would have disappeared, didn't you? But it didn't. So now I know that most of you must be thinking to yourself "So, where is the magic?" Well, let's see. Let's try this once again.

Now, I am going to slowly close my hands once more, like this... [both hands close]. Now I am going to slowly open my hands again, like this... [both hands slowly open]. Now look! It's gone. Right before your eyes!

"Grandpa? Grandpa? It's me, Kenny. Are you okay Grandpa? You were just telling me-"

"Leave Grandpa alone, Kenny, just leave him alone!"

Since Einstein popularized the theory that space and time are relative rather than absolute concepts, a lot has been written on the subject. I can offer no further insights. I will instead confirm that, from my own personal experiences, space and time and many other things are indeed relative. In fact, I would state it in another way: context gives meaning to the things that happen in our lives.

For example, the look that a gorgeous movie star such as Angelina Jolie gives while standing on the red carpet for the Oscars is normally regarded by the media as 'sultry' (exciting strong sexual desire). However, the very same look on the face of a young girl in the inner cities of Kingston would be regarded as 'horny whore'.

I have also thought that the same principle applies to things that people may consider a 'surprise'. Let us, for example, take the situation of a policeman sitting in a police station in Lynchburg Virginia, USA, and who finds that the station has come under attack by four cars filled with gunmen carrying high-powered weapons. It is reasonable to assume that such a policeman would be very 'surprised' as he scrambles frantically to reach his receiver to radio for back-up, screaming "Holy shit!" into the microphone, as the person on the other end asks, "What's happening? Mike? What's happening there buddy?" However, a policeman in inner-city Kingston, finding himself in the exact same situation, is unlikely to be 'surprised' as he picks up his own high-powered weapon and calmly mumbles, "Oh, so you fuckers have come back? Wait until you see what I have for you today!"

The same happened with you as well, Semicolon. I had told you that I grew up in a small house. But, as we discussed the evening after you saw it, small too can be relative. If you recall, you found out that the 'small' apartment you owned in New York had, in fact, enough room to hold more than four cows and a goat. Relativity.

I have grappled with this issue of relativity and context for quite some time. Mainly because I am yet to figure out whether there might be a context in which a seven year old child would easily understand and not be surprised at how often his own grandfather failed to know who he was. A seven year old boy living in simple times, long before he knew the medical term for the magic tricks of Grandpa's mind.

Now this was Grandpa 1, on my mama's side, who, once upon a time, used to tell us interesting stories. Before his second heart attack and the cancer. After that, he spent a week repeating something he had apparently heard from an old Japanese man about how having gold dust in your underwear helped to increase circulation and promoted healthy testicles. Grandpa asked all of us to write to those who had migrated and ask them to send him a case of gold dust. After that he said nothing.

My grandpa too died young. With all the heart attacks and cancer eating him, he simply fell apart like a real estate deal. In addition to the cancer eating his stomach, something was also eating his brain and memories. I don't know if this is in any way related to whatever started having a go at my brother's mind. Or if it was just pure coincidence. They said he was fifty-five when he died but one could never tell people's real ages. This was due both to poor record keeping and the fact that Christians and scientists age differently.

CHAPTER 28

An Old Familiar Stain

It was March 2009 and the global economy was undergoing a recession deeper than my grandpa's hairline.

I woke up in the early hours of the morning. I knew it was early because, though I was still groggy, the pleasant quarter-to-three smile on the face of the clock had become familiar, after many years of insomnia and being chased by shadows. I had my usual dialogue with my mind. In the old days, my mind had an easiness about him that made it effortless to talk to him. Like you would say to him, "The weather has held up this weekend, no?" And he would smoothly say, "Yeah, it turned out nicely after all, didn't it?" Or if you said, "Man, did you see that monster hurricane that hit the Bahamas?" He would say, nice and easy like, "Yeah, that sure is something you don't see every day. That was a real monster right there." And there would be such ease to the conversation. But something had happened since those days, and our conversations had become strained.

After I got out of bed that morning, I ate my usual oatmeal and toast buttered with some spread that had five or more labels relating to heart disease written all over it, together with some disgusting imported fruit that came in the guise of being a mango.

Then I took the train from Westchester to Penn Station.

Which is a very different experience from taking the train from Dover, New Jersey to Penn Station, which I had done a week before. Let me explain this a bit, because all these things are important.

I had gone to Dover to do some consulting work. I was returning on the Dover line, passing all those typical New Jersey towns that are home to hundreds of retired industrial buildings and commercial trucks, as well as Grayness. My eyes flitted over the crowd on the train. One man was there reading *Gage's Guide to Physical Examination*. I could clearly see the face of another man's iPod; he was listening to an Andrea Boticelli album. A strange hippy-looking woman walked between cars, hunched over as though she were cold but I know she couldn't have been because even though it was still winter I wasn't cold and I was the only Negro in that car. I saw another man take fleeting glances at the same girl. I thought he was sneaky. If he had a wife or girlfriend she would need to watch him closely, but judging by his behavior I guessed he was single.

Sitting beside me was a charming family, a mother and two young girls, one about six and the other nine. The father had obviously gone somewhere (to a business trip? A mistress? His grave? I couldn't tell). The nine year old asked the mother if she would play some game with them. The six year old responded for her mother:

"Janine, the answer is no. Mommy is probably tired. And she misses her husband. She has no one to talk to. No one to hug her. No one to sleep with. No one to make her laugh. Just like us she misses daddy and so won't play."

All this she said while looking through the window out at the open fields, nonchalant and distanced, while their mother continued sorting things in her pocketbook, oblivious to the conversation. I thought it was most unusual for a six year old to say those things. But she did.

They had a cat in a little travel bag. It sneezed and for a moment I felt blessed, before cursing myself for still believing so much in the nonsense of my past.

The train picked up Latinos along the way. Then a white man joined our car at Convent Station, with his newspaper. I thought at the time that it was one thing to not afford a house in New York and settle for New

Jersey, but another thing entirely to buy the NJ Star Ledger instead of the NY Times. This purchase showed he lacked ambition and that he was where he belonged.

Finally, there was a girl who slept and kept her mouth open the entire journey. I inferred that she had respiratory problems or was otherwise congested.

This was the motley crew coming in from Jersey. Your ordinary, run-of-the-mill lot - whites, blacks, latinos, and all.

Now, here I was coming from Westchester. I noticed the first man in the car because he was looking at me. He was a rusty, *white enough to enjoy Canadian winters* old man, whose memories of the past would always be better than anything in his future. Looking at me, his eyes transmitted: *you are nothing more than a Darwinian anomaly Nigga. No matter how well-dressed and educated you are, you are still black and you don't belong here.* It was clear that he regarded the image of a skinny pot-bellied negro with intelligence as visually discordant. Then he turned back to his Wall Street Journal and scoffed. Was it at the front-page news? Obama's Health Care policy? The dividend cut at Sony? Who knows. All I saw was Resentment, pure-bred, well-fed and immaculately dressed. When he went to bed at nights, Hatred climbed in with him, pulled up the covers and snuggled comfortably beside him.

The man whose face I saw next, is the one I want to talk about. He was sitting across from me on the train. He also looked the Wall Street type: the kind of man who went to work very early in the morning and came home very late at night, and only watched his kids grow horizontally in bed. Not *rich enough to have a flat screen TV in the dog's room*, but still the type that was able to wear those *Nigga, how many of your children's organs will you sell to afford this?* kind of business suits.

It seemed he may have just been told some really bad news, like that his company was going under, or he was losing his job, or he had lost a fortune or something more important if such were possible. In any

213

event there was a deeply-pained expression on his face. But he was a rich man, like Terri-Ann's father (I will get to Terri-Ann and her father next). I therefore saw his pain but had no pity whatsoever for him.

There was a woman too. A very attractive, mature woman. She wasn't the average kind of attractive that could win some State beauty contest in the US Midwest but, in Lebanon or Brazil, would have people gossiping about her need for plastic surgery. No, she was the Real McCoy, the kind that a rich Wall Street type could import from somewhere else in the world. Like the Ukraine or Venezuela.

I soon realized that they were together. He was taller than her, but not by much. She was slimmer than him, but just by a little. But the difference between them was enormous. One thing they had in common was that they were both delicate people; the kind that would eat an Arugula and Goat Cheese Salad because it's fine to eat what goes into and comes out of a goat, but they would never touch the goat itself. These were folks whose meals were served in the centre of their plates, never occupying more than a quarter of the available space and would be found equally enjoyable by rabbits. Anyway.

The train stopped at a station, as trains normally do. The woman got up, gathered her things, and got ready to leave, taking with her a brand of flavored-hot water New Yorkers often refer to as coffee. Then, before leaving, she gently ran her hand through his hair and straightened it. It was the look on his face that gave me the impression she had tidied his hair because it wouldn't occur to him to do it himself. The look that said he no longer cared about himself. This was a look that was very different from the look on the face of another man I once saw leaving a public toilet in Kentucky. It was clear that he had just finished letting out a load of shit, based on three key bits of incriminating evidence, namely: his solitary presence in the toilet; the something-must-have-died-in-here smell of the place, and the depths from which he was pulling up his pants while walking out of the stall, with his ass showing much more than a crack.

His ass looked like this:

He wasn't wearing any shirt. He walked out of the stall, wiped his hands on his pants, and walked past the pipes and the paper towels and the hand drier and just kept on walking. From the look on his face I knew that it was not that <u>that</u> man did not care about himself, it was that he didn't care about anyone else, and was, also, plain fucking nasty. The look on <u>this</u> man's face was different. He had lost interest only in himself.

She said a soft "love you" to him as she got off the train. She said it in the way women know how to choose their words to suit occasions. "Goodbye" or perhaps "see you later" was somehow not appropriate. One may have conveyed finality, the other may have lacked certainty, and she knew better than to use either expression within the context of whatever it was that they were going through. He said nothing. He also did not look at her face. I concluded that she was his wife, that they had been married for a long time in which he had seen her face many times, and that he expected to have the option of seeing her face later that day if he elected to look.

He finally showed two signs of life a few minutes after she left. First, he raised his hand and gently ran his fingers through his silvery white hair. I was a bit surprised at this. I reasoned to myself that this action was not intended to undo what his wife had done. There was no such purposefulness in his countenance. And it may not have been possible anyway. I concluded that it was the reflexive action that came from decades of grooming himself for big appointments in the Investment Bank in which he worked.

Then the second sign: as the train moved along I saw him grimace and open his eyes widely. It seemed as though he was either processing a thought or remembering something that had hurt him deeply.

That man seemed to be in so much pain, my love. I will never forget what I saw in that man's eyes. Nor will I ever forget how I smiled as I saw his pain. How I hated him.

When I stepped off the train a little while later I thought this would have been the end of my hatred for that day, but it wasn't. As I came off the next train at 42nd, I saw more objects of hate. In the subway. On the streets. In the Delis. With their i-pod and i-phone and i-closed-to-everything around them. They were all around me. I stopped at the Starbucks, and watched them for a while. Thinking each one uniquely loathsome. Two leaning over to chat with each other, were obviously gossiping over infidelities and other crass titillations. Another one with his burger-loving obesity and rheumy, dejected eyes, was seemingly conversing with himself. One woman, entering Starbucks, seemed annoyed with her truant Blackberry, which was obviously refusing to communicate her importance to the world. She was aging, but defiantly. Still showing cleavage in spite of the fact that her boobs, as fake as a politician's smile, were beginning to crumble like the dreams of a middle-age whore.

Then she came.

"Gorgeous, sexy shoes"

"If I were held hostage and told that to survive I could only wear EITHER shoes or clothes, I would have to choose shoes. There is nothing like gorgeous, comfortable, sexy shoes. I am sure those

terrorists would allow me to at least wear pearl beads with my shoes," she remarked to her girlfriend, chortling as she initiated a process that would lead to the order of a "Oh darling, I always have" cafe macchiato, skimmed milk, one sugar.

She was a very attractive woman - this was not the ordinary type of attractive that could win a State beauty pageant in Kansas but would have people gossiping about her need to do plastic surgery in Lebanon or Venezuela; this was Real McCoy attractive. And it was spring; everything long, thick, heavy or flat had already come off, and even the wind, now deliriously giddy from playing beneath her skirt, was beckoning her to take off more. While it was already unmistakable in her mannerism, the Pharaoh Hound she walked when in the mood on Sundays would sometimes help to clarify for strangers that she was not a 'sweet little thing' from the Bronx that is placed high on a supermarket shelf but, with a little effort, becomes accessible for public consumption. This was a woman who should only be approached by men who spoke in foreign currencies or on public platforms.

She was married to a huge and extravagant ring that grew up in Africa before migrating to Tiffany's on the Upper East Side. The handsome, sparkling diamond was a gift from the man who formally held the title of husband. He was, and had been since the day of their wedding, well up into the fart-a-lot age (he himself remembers, with fondness, once being alone on the porch and letting one rip with such volcanic force that he chuckled at the thought that he might also have spewed lava) and wore glasses thick enough to enable him, on a clear day, to see all the way to China. Worked as a banker, served as a bank, and was, otherwise, completely irrelevant to her. He remained grateful, in an odd sort of way, for the daily recognition by the dog, the "Good morning Sir, you look splendid today" by the butler, the gifts recognizing his birthdays, and the obliging matrimonial encounters she allowed every once in a while. Other than that, he found his deepest satisfactions in his work. As for her, what mattered beyond drinks with the girls and the Day Spa on Madison, were her ring and, of course, her shoes.

As humans we all have our flaws and one of hers was to occasionally permit herself to be seen in an ordinary food establishment. In her regular establishments she would have a fine bottle of Chateau Mouton Rothschild accompanying some form of cuisine that would have been recommended by her personal trainer and which would be found equally delectable by rabbits. But ever so often she found it hard to resist a Starbucks macchiato. On this day, she had walked into Starbucks with her Tuesday afternoon girlfriend, 'Stephanie darling'. They had entered the Starbucks at 2nd Ave after a stroll short enough to be considered acceptable and civilized down 42nd street, from the Helmsley. Stephanie had entered Starbucks first, and she had come in after. She had let go the door without looking to see if anyone was behind her - perhaps because if you were, then that would be where you belonged. The Pfizer employee who came in just behind her had found many other things in life more amusing.

Her nails had not too long ago been manicured by "Oh darling, you got to go see" Phillip up at East 73rd. The disabling effect that manicures and pedicures have on the rich being commonly known, it was not surprising that she made great and dainty efforts to find her purse, scavenging through her handbag, if we are to be crude, with less aptitude than a mongrel dog. Eventually she

218

located her "Darling, Yves Saint Laurent doesn't design anything remotely as elegant as this" Hermés Birkin custom-made purse.

She was standing close to the newspaper rack in Starbucks. The rack was, as usual, loaded with NY Times newspapers that clients don't always realize they need to pay for before they read. One of the headlines on the bottom of the front page announced that a CEO of another failing financial company was looking for a bailout but swearing never to leave.

"Yellow one, punch bug!" A little boy wearing a Lyceum Kennedy School uniform and holding on to his father's hand joyfully announced his sighting, tallying his points and taking advantage of his dad's pitiful Pavlovian distraction, as he stared at the two sexy women. (Unlike Pavlov's dogs, his dad would never be fed.) She glanced at the boy with eyes that confirmed that she had no children, and never would.

Returning her attention to her purse, it was in her line of sight and natural for her to once again glimpse her shoes. This prompted renewed surprise and another round of "So you like these, huh? I absolutely adore them! I am just waiting to see what he comes out with for the Fall line. They are gorgeous, aren't they?"

There was a Latino at the counter. His name badge called him 'Jorge'; his father 'puta cábron', and his homeboys 'Don Juan'. His father had brought him and a cousin over the Mexican border when he was fourteen. He was sufficiently self-aware to know from both his past and his present that his family had never been anything but poor. In spite of this, Jorge had tremendous self-confidence. He was good with the girls, was seen as the unofficial leader of the homies, and, of course, was the owner of an almost new, super-fast sports car. And, there was that one time when he was very sick, having fallen prey to a Jeffrey Dahmer like virus back in his pueblo, Campo Alegre, in Mexico, and woke up in the middle of the night to see his widowed papito's eyes as he sat by his bed watching over him. And he knew, without it ever been said, that what he saw that night was love. Little things like these help to give a man confidence.

Being male, Mexican, Latino and in possession of carrot-eating eyesight, he hadn't needed anyone to point out to him that a 'hijo de puta, qué cálor! Dios mío! Ostia! Qué tremenda mujer!" woman had walked in and was standing a few feet from him. It was, for the all the reasons just mentioned (save for the eyesight), in his DNA to therefore flash her a soft smile when she looked up from her purse to place her order.

Three years earlier, Jorge had bought a 2004, two-door bright-yellow Mustang GT, and painted flaming streaks of red along the sides. In the evenings and on weekends he took his homies for a ride through the East Orange 'hood. Had met with some success picking up various mulattas, especially the easy ones from Guatemala and El Salvador who, unlike Argentinians, would settle for a Mexican rather than spend their lives waiting for an Italian. But he knew that his success was part of the Latino style, and that mainstream upper class American white girls were not necessarily into that sort of thing.

Jorge also understood that by playing soccer rather than golf he was in a different social class than many of the folks that he served at Starbucks on 42nd. But this was just a way of life.

For sure, there were nights when he would hit the road with
his homies, 'chequear' the hot spots looking for some mulattas
calientes, particularly the Mamacitas with the heavy set bosom
he was so fond of. Aye! And many times he would go back to
the crib alone. And, having spent all his extra cash on the extra
insurance needed for a sports car driven by a twenty-four year old,
he knew he was unable to afford the TEN or Playboy channel add-
on package. On these nights he would often help himself while
watching the fine pieces of flesh on a beach fitness video he once
taped. But Jorge understood that while striking out like this was
'mierda!', it was normal, and not a reflection of any fundamental
flaw in him.

Jorge understood all these things about his life, his background, his
ethnicity, his class and about general men-women relations. But,
until the moment that the gorgeous woman in front of him took
her receipt and her change and turned, he had never before in his
life felt so completely invisible.

K. Lovelace, Short Story, Starbucks, March 2009

I was surrounded by *them*. And their faces were all the same. And I hated them, Semicolon. I really, truly and deeply hated the whole fucking lot of them that Thursday. At thirty-nine years old, Semicolon, I carried such hate within me. And a part of me knew why. It had a lot to do with my sense of pride and identity. The hatred had begun a long time before. I don't know precisely when it started but I can clearly recall one precise moment in the past when I had felt it, and knew it was there, pulsating beneath my skin.

CHAPTER 29

Sources of Pride

Dear Semicolon,

I was in another meeting today. And as I was about to lay me down to sleep and pray my soul the Lord to keep, another colleague of mine, who himself was paying as much attention to the speaker as Iran pays to American sanctions, leaned over and started telling me something about 'talk, talk, talk, talk, talk, talk, talk, talk, talk, talk, talk, talk, talk, talk, talk, talk.' And I found myself again thinking about little red riding hood and why no one calls Santa Claus obese, though he is.

There were about fifty people in the meeting and it lasted about fifty hours because everyone was important. But, just like in my High School history classes, I heard nothing, and I learnt absolutely nothing.

It was then that a few realizations came to me. I knew then, with certainty, that Estée Lauder and Nadinola may have helped my Aunt Frida cover up her ugliness and acne, but nothing she put on could have masked the pain she felt in that house with him alone at nights.

I similarly concluded that, notwithstanding the World Bank's projections, the fourth man loaded on the motorbike in Bangladesh - the one carrying the goat on his shoulder - is never going to be rich. This is more than just a hunch in the pit of my stomach.

I concluded, also, that if you are in a country like Barbados for three days and by the end of those three days the nicest-looking woman you have seen is a mannequin, then you are never going to find a nice wife. Because if you see a donkey standing in the sun eating grass for four days, then on day five, if you see him, he will be doing the same.

I also realized that an upbeat Travel Agent telling you that Chisinau, Moldova is beautiful, is only doing her job.

Finally, and perhaps most painfully, I also came to the severe conclusion that I will always have to work for everything I have.

Sleep well, my love.

Kenny, June, 2011

My love, I have read many books in my time. One of the most important was written by Victor Frankel. It was "Man's Search for Meaning". I mention this in my story because it serves particularly well to connect us back to the incident I have just finished recounting.

As you already know, my love, I am a black man and a Jamaican. Also, I grew up in a *hateful* fucking place where people lived short, nasty lives. And I know that throughout those years we were all looking for meaning in those wretched, cockroachy lives. While no one said it, it was something that you could see, right there: in the time people spent in the rum bars; in the amount of money they spent on horse racing, cock fighting, dog fighting and hermit crab racing; in the number of women men would try to impregnate; in the abuse men meted out to their partners and children; in the number of kids women would have so that they always had someone to love them (the love of a child lasted only so long in those environments, hence the need to constantly reproduce fresh love), and so on and so forth. You would also often see it in the way we all made fun of the white folks who we mostly saw on television - the wealthy class in our country with names from the Middle East and Europe. Businessmen and politicians. Owners of everything. Everything except our blackness. For though they were "Jamaicans", they were not like us, the real Jamaicans. And it was our real Jamaican-ness that gave us our sense of purpose and self-worth. Particularly our blackness and our ghetto-ness. No one ever verbalized these things to me, but I knew it.

Did you ever think that you could be,
*   big john swinging*
*   ivory teeth gleaming*
*   ghetto girls breeding*
*   rum bar drinking,*
*   black like me?*

Excerpt from undated journal entry

There are many who will, of course, take issue with my characterization of what made us proud to be who we were. I know that there are many who would like nothing more than for me to shut my rassclaat mouth. That's fine. I will only speak for myself, and will only share with you my understanding of things based on the interactions I had with the people I grew up with. And, for my part, these were the subtle themes I picked up from our daily realities of chatting, playing games, fucking our cousins and our neighbors, picking mangoes, cooking in the bushes, and watching the adults around us do the same things.

If you accept then, that this is my own personal account of things, let me move on to say that, from what I saw, the single most important source of pride for us as boys growing up, was our dick. I will pause here to give some academics a chance to vent and take issue again.

Chicken eat worms, cats chase rats, dogs piss on posts and so it goes on. These are just a few things that people may want to argue with but will eventually accept. For these things are, simply, the truth.

Okay, now let us resume.

In that *hateful* fucking place, the focus was always on those men who were well-endowed and on how many women they fucked. We'll allow more time to vent.

Okay then, let me continue.

Everything was about cocks and clits, crotches and dicks, and the earnest necessity of keeping them acquainted.

As you are aware, there were many of us living in that *hateful* fucking place. This was, of course, the natural outcome of a situation where: (a) adults were always having kids, (b) some adults were having kids with kids, and (c) some kids were having kids with kids. So, there were lots and lots of kids. In spite of this, us boys knew how endowed every other boy was, each and every one. Because each and every one of us was actually measured by the eldest member of our group. The measurement was done in inches. Tommy – 5.3 inches; Brian – 6.2; Tony – 6.5; Billy – 6.8; Kenny, me – a source of real pride; Garnet – a horse-man, and Tiny Tim – could easily get into Harvard based on the size of his endowment. We all knew that, even though he was younger than the rest of us, Tiny Tim, with his childhood monstrosity, would one day occupy the position of honor in our neighborhood, assuming that they could fix a small problem that he had, and which I will talk about just a little later.

So my endowment was, for many years, perhaps the only source of meaning to my life. I was among the cocksmen of the neighborhood-those who could really make a woman *feel it*. And this did make me somewhat proud. But my pride intensified with that as-desirable-as-winning-the-lottery brown girl that I mentioned before; the one I tried to seduce in that English Literature class. She flirted with me for months. And that girl could flirt! Let me provide you with an example of the cruelty:

It came to pass in those days of the early 1990s, that one night she went with me to a party in Kingston. There were parties every Friday night while we were at college. This one was a simple affair really: everywhere there was music playing, alcohol flowing, food selling, cute girls dancing, cute girls smiling, cute girls twirling, cute girls shaking, cute girls bubbling, my freaking heart failing, my freaking lungs failing, and so on. Anyone who has been to a Jamaican dancehall session would know what I mean. Furthermore this was a Red Hills Road dancehall party with Stone Love Sound playing! Red Hills Road and Stone Love! With nothing but the hottest crews of dancehall girls! The girls in question were like a group of mercenaries lined out against a wall in the dance hall. Heartlessness and cruelty their middle names. And when the DJ selected one of those '80s dancehall songs, these cartoon-eye-popping sexy girls, in unison, began a slow and deadly wine. Their waists gyrating rhythmically and powerfully like windmills, and generating more electricity than was needed to power all of Kingston that night. I was therefore already hurting when Terri-Ann started to giggle beside me, watching the pained look on my face as I watched those girls. It was then that she kissed me quickly on my lips (my first kiss from her!), and walked backwards towards the dance floor, all the time keeping her eyes on me.

To be truthful, she had always hinted at the fact that she could dance. For months I had been telling her, almost daily, "God you are beautiful!" or "God you are amazing!" and each time she would giggle and say something like, "Wait 'til you see me dance!"

I finally saw her dance. Blessed Salvation, did I ever finally see her dance!

What do I recall? Spontaneous combustion... Hiroshima... radiant white lights... a gently-flowing river... open fields of lilies... voices calling my name... Abraham and Isaac smiling... little birds chirping... It was cardiac fucking arrest!

I can never truly describe what that moment was like. I can share with you what I later wrote in my notebook, but this does not in any way capture what I experienced:

"Truth and rapture in wine"

I do remember, there was at least that one time
when I experienced rapture that was heavenly,
perfect and divine;
and it was a Jamaican girl at a party
who completely blew my mind,
when she put aside her Heineken,

dipped

and then began to wine.

She had "juicy" on her bulging tank top,
"delights" on her revealing little shorts,
and as her juicy delights began to tic toc,
I swear it nearly burst my heart.

Undated journal entry

It was so wonderful the way she moved! So wonderful the way she walked, in that beautiful, bending-knee, tikkety-tok way people walk when they are gorgeous women in tight jeans and high heels. And it was so wonderful the way she wined. She was just so wonderful! But what a fucking flirt!

Anyway, she only flirted with me for the first six months or so that I knew her. Then she gave in. The very same night of the party. Oh my love, did she ever give in! My love, Terri-Ann was the first girl I slept with that made me *truly* proud of myself. The first girl that made me feel I was someone, and feel that my life had meaning. Before her, as I said, I did feel pride in the size of my dick. But, that was normal and that pride wasn't particularly boosted by sleeping with my cousins and other easy-to-get ordinary, poor, black women. This girl was different. In our Depression we categorized women into two groups: girls that were *only* fuckable and those that were both fuckable *and* edible. A big difference influenced by small degrees of skin shade: in plain terms, the lighter the better, as no one wanted to eat dark meat.

So, the first night I spent with Terri-Ann was the first night I felt my life had real meaning. But things didn't end there. Allow me to explain.

She was seventeen years old, more or less, and I was a few years older, more or less, but we were both in the same class in college. She came from a wealthy family. She liked me. I knew this because she always flirted with me and women only flirt with men they like. What wasn't clear was why, after about six months, she finally decided to sleep with me. But that is less important to our story.

We left the party. She had enough money to afford a hotel room. The room was just a room. She was lying on her back on the little hotel bed. The bed was just a bed. She was from a wealthy family and therefore had enough money to have no shames: she was lying completely naked, free of all clothes, shames and inhibitions. Lights all on. And she was gorgeous!

I looked at her smile, and she was smiling. I looked at the mid-size mangoes on her chest, with the dark nipples pointing in the direction my hopes were heading. Then my eyes crawled along the gracefulness of her body, lingered awhile at her belly button, before sauntering on to rest on her mound, which I thought, at the time, was far more beautiful to look at than the face of the Miss Universe winner that year.

228

I looked at the soft hair and felt especially privileged - most of the women I had been with had coarse, nappy hair like the underbrush of a forest.

Her feet were planted on the bed and her legs raised. In mathematical terms, when viewed sideways, her legs would have a triangular shape, like this:

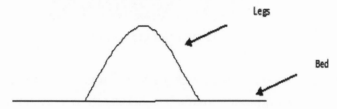

Or, as I would later learn, could more accurately be seen in terms of a normal distribution, which generally had this appearance:

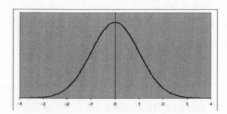

I stood there watching as she playfully rocked her normally-curved legs: open, close, open, close, open. In the oval centre I saw the pinkness. Just like the pinkness I remembered from that time when I was with Cookie. And the moistness between her thighs brought moistness to my eyes.

My eyes beheld such glory

I have been impressed by only a few things in my life. One of these was to see the tight pants of the late 1970s return to being fashionable. Another was to learn, a few years ago, of a gay guy and a gun man becoming friends in Jamaica. I was also mightily impressed by the news of the level of corruption found in the NY Police Department in the late 1990s. But all these things were surpassed by what I saw between those legs. Of course, nudity is one thing, but a beautiful woman on a bed playfully spreading her legs sends me into delirium. I melt at the promise of what that offers.

Anyway, how I feasted on that fruit! It was forbidden like the star-apple, which had always been out of my reach. It had the redness of a papaya, the plumpness of plums, the fleshiness of sweetsops, the juiciness of melons, the softness of custard apples, and the delicious taste of East Indian mangoes! I oscillated wildly in an orgasmic giddiness. There was such frenzied sucking and licking! The taste of lips! Upper lips. Lower lips. Lips. Such kissing. Such sucking. Such gripping. Tight. Such dripping. Such sweat nectars! I had a volcanic eruption that shifted the earth on its axis by 2.3 centimeters.

Do we as humans have a tendency to remember things to have been better than they actually were? The cold milo at the Annual Denbigh Agricultural Show; the peppered shrimp in Middlequarters; the taste of cotton candy melting on your tongue; the boiled crabs at Heroes Circle;

the roast yam and codfish at Faiths Pen; the enchantment of Lake Atitlan and the city of Damascus; my mama's curried crab and fluffy white rice on special Saturdays; Aunt Frida's fried pork skin; cold coconut water on a hot day; doves caught in the bushes and roasted with a touch of salt; playing games in the cool rivers of summer; nightly Duppy story time; the Sistine Chapel, and all – have I remembered them better than they actually were? Could I have overstated the wonders of that first time with Terri-Ann? I captured that first time in my notebook like this:

"The first time"

Touching
Probing
Tasting
Moaning
Squeezing
Sucking
Tasting
Groaning
Gently
Spreading
Touching
Probing
Tasting
Gasping
Scraping
Clawing
Sinking
"Deeper"
Rocking
Moaning

Groaning
Sweetly
Exploding

Undated journal entry

That was one of the single most joyful and proud moments of my life. We made love many times thereafter for the next couple of months. Here endeth the part pertaining to positive pride.

Here beginneth the part pertaining to poisoned pride and self-worth.

By the end of the summer she had really gotten fucked. I mean this in the sense that when her dad (in particular) found out what she had been doing and "WITH WHOM?" she was really fucked.

For he had met me before. I had gone by their house once. She had brought me home like a child who had found a caterpillar on a tree and brought it home. Her story was that I was just a friend in her class that she was studying literature with.

She had left me in the living room while she went and spoke with her dad about something. (The aim was not to bring me to be introduced.) It was around dinner time, but I was not invited to eat with them. It was like flying with American Airlines and finding out that they had food, but would not give you any unless you paid. Or like visiting the house of a wealthy but mean relative who was both embarrassed by your parents' poverty and afraid that you would come to depend on her. A relative, let's say an aunt, who decorated her house with the finest-looking fake paintings and cheap furniture because she preferred to lay out the appearance of luxury but keep the cash. And, let us say that she would have food in her house but would say to you when you dropped by, "Hey Kenny, hey Martin, I know your mama must have fed you as she would not send you out hungry, so I am sure you guys must be full and don't need anything, no?" Always phrased in the negative, because she knew how much shame we would bring on our parents if we gave the impression that they sent us out hungry to beg. She had food, but would never give us any. Never wanted to foster or encourage dependency. Never wanted foster kids.

So too Terri-Ann's folks had food and were eating it then and there, but never invited me to stay for dinner, as our culture demanded. It wasn't because they were not aware that I was there. He had seen me. Of this I am sure. The helper had seen me too. Walking back from the dining room with some glasses of lemonade on her tray. Just rebuked for bringing them lemonade made from white granulated sugar as though she didn't know, I heard him grumble, that the sugar you drink should have your own complexion. I gathered then that he expected brown sugar in his lemonade and not the darker type which I would be expected to drink.

For the first few years of my life I had thought that all of us were 'black', but that nonsense got knocked out of me early, and I had long come to realize that I was black while folks like Terri-Ann's father were 'brown'. And not only on account of the slight differences in the shade of our skin; the size of his bank account also helped to make him brown. He also worked hard to cultivate the ways and habits of being brown: he laughed brown, slapped the chaps on their backs in a good-natured brownish manner, and asked, "Does anyone care for a round of golf this weekend?" with a brownish accent. He also drove a brownish car, which was an expensive car. A really, freaking expensive car. In those days, and true to the fine cultural practices of our village, we used unusual words to describe things that were exceptionally beautiful and, almost without exception, out of our reach. One of those words was 'stink'. A shoe that was 'stink' was absolutely gorgeous and expensive (and out of our reach). He drove a car that was 'stink'. It was a new Mercedes Benz S Class. This was not a car that <u>you</u> drive, my brother would say, but rather it was the <u>car</u> that took you places, and announced that you had arrived. Terri-Ann's dad had long-arrived.

As I was saying, even their cat, which had the peculiar habit of walking like a horse, had seen me and meowed. So, they had all seen me. And this was much more than the *Dogs are not invited where bones are not provided* plain form of ignoring me. That I could deal with, for I did come without prior invitation. But neither was it the *simply too preoccupied* form of ignoring you that you see those flight attendants in Business Class suffer as they stand there going through all their security demonstrations while all those rich folks ignore them and continue to read their Wall Street Journals and Oprah Book-club books. No. This was different. For the way he saw and ignored me, hurt me deeply.

Someone once told me that he went to a Turkish Bath in the Middle East. In there, he said an exceptionally strong, surprisingly well-fed, but remarkably ill-trained black man from somewhere in northern Africa scrubbed his skin so hard that it felt as though he was raw and peeling. But this was just his skin, and the pain could be considered *skin deep*.

Similarly, Jamaican folklore tells the story of a female plantation owner in the days of slavery, who was also a witch - the "White Witch of Rose Hall". The story says she would take a strong black slave to her bedroom as her lover, and, after a few weeks 'use', she would kill him for his soul before taking another. Each night she would come out of her skin like a serpent and fly away to haunt the local villagers. She would return in the early hours of the morning before sunrise, slip back into her skin and go to sleep peaceful and content and with the innocence of a newborn baby. As the story goes, one of her slave lovers found out not only what she was planning to do to him, but also where she hid her skin when she left at night. He poured salt and pepper in her skin. *Jamaican* pepper. Not pepper like those Jalapenos that you find in the US which are like that stunning black cheerleader for the Dallas Cowboys in the 2006 American Football season who was always in the middle and who had a *fiery spirit* but was, otherwise, may-my-heart-not-fail-me-now sweet! No siree. We are talking real Jamaican pepper. Real *Mighty Jesus take me now!*

Holy Mother of Christ this is hot! pepper! It is said that when she slid into her skin her screams broke glasses on Saturn and startled that old man in the deepest pits of Hell. And while I imagine how painful that may have been, again I cannot help but feel that it was still only *skin deep*.

Or we could stretch the illustration of a skin-deep wound to the day when Martin playfully swung the axe at Cudjoe's toes thinking that Cudjoe would move them (as we always did). But Cudjoe didn't move them, thinking that Martin would stop (which he normally did) if he saw that Cudjoe wasn't playing and wouldn't follow through with the axe (which he strangely did). And so the axe took off two toes (one learns that with a very sharp axe and a shoeless foot a little effort can indeed go a long way). His toes may have been left crooked when they were reattached, but we are still only talking about matters of flesh and bone, and the boy himself was fine.

When Terri-Ann's father came into the living room, looked at me and left, I felt a different kind of pain. The pain I felt did not come because:

He came into the living room, looked at me, <u>said</u> nothing, and left.

But because:

He came into the living room, looked at me, <u>saw</u> nothing, and left.

That pain went much deeper than just my skin. And I felt crooked, not in my flesh and bones, but somewhere deep inside me. And the little man inside me also said he felt the same. This all came back to me years later sitting in Starbucks and watching the way that woman looked at Jorge at the counter. I cringed inside. And the hate came back.

Now, self-confidence is not something you easily build and maintain. Sure, a plain-looking American woman, frustrated with years of fruitless searching on E-harmony, may move to the Gambia and find hundreds of suitors who constantly remind her that, "You are a beautiful woman." But somehow she knows nothing's changed. For what we know and believe about ourselves doesn't change overnight, does it?

They eventually sent Terri-Ann away to college in the US. He somehow learnt what had happened. Dad and his Royal Guard and Special Forces had been watching and protecting her virginity and had no idea that it had slipped through the back door and was running free and easy. So dad slapped mom and shipped off daughter. It was that easy to do when you were a rich parent. I wasn't surprised to find, when she eventually wrote to me, that she had rebelled. Had dropped out of college and was then in 'hair school'. (In her note she said the news severely distressed her grandmother, who lamented that she couldn't now die in peace because she had no idea how her granddaughter was going to feed herself.) I had no idea what it meant to be in 'hair school' but I supposed that she was not planning to be the lawyer or doctor that her parents wanted. It was that simple to do when you were a rich kid. She told me that her only problem was that in 'hair school' they made her wear black clothes every day, which she sometimes found to be quite depressing. But they said black was a neutral color that could go with all the different hair styles and wigs that they had to try on each other. I have often thought it peculiar that a color so neutral, elegant and versatile in fashion and style, isn't any of these things in people. Black and rich brown certainly clashed in my country. Especially the darker shades of black.

She said that she sometimes missed me. Or rather, to be more accurate, she missed my 'third leg'. This was her rich kid way of saying she was *down with the slang* that poor people used to describe a man's dick in Jamaica. I still find it interesting, in my later years, to reflect on some of the expressions we used back in those days to give ourselves the sense of pride and respect that no one else would give us. Like the first time I heard about the 'power-plant', which I immediately thought was the property of the electricity company. I was wrong. It was first a reference to some form of gun that the "baddest of all gunmen" was carrying around with him. This *power-plant*-flaunting gunman, it was said, was so evil his name would horrify the rural police and make them wet their pants. So evil only a squad of the most ruthless police from the capital city, Kingston, could handle him - which is what happened. Many months later, and this didn't surprise me by then, I would often hear some of the boys in my neighborhood call to girls on the street and point to their dicks and ask "Hey, don't you want to feel my nuclear *power-plant*?"

At the end of the note, Terri-Ann drew a little smiley face, like this:

I thought she was trying to draw a Rastafarian smiley face, but I couldn't help but think that only a rich kid could have made a Rastafarian look so much like a spider.

I mention all this, my love, because I know I can be open with you. We have always been like that with each other. I also mention it because, even today, I can still see that man looking at me the same way. And I also mention it because I was not the only one in that *hateful* fucking place that was treated that way. But these things are all in the past, and behind us now.

Anyway, let us get back to Garnet.

CHAPTER 30

Garnet

"Destiny"

I sometimes take the No. 1 train,
And sometimes it is the No. 3,
I have often gone by car and plane,
And once or twice I have gone by sea;
But I know somehow that it is all the same -
The place these vessels take me,
So I will go, and I will not complain
As I can only go to my destiny.

K. Lovelace, April 2011

Speak the truth that God loves and shame the devil. This is what I have done up to now, and what I will do again just now. For it is important that these things be recorded and analyzed.

He is in prison now, for the second time, and has been for the last thirteen years, from what I hear. This time a fifteen year sentence for rape, robbery and aggravated assault. Some people are only bad in their dreams, when they wake their worst mischiefs are lust and pilfering office stationary. Not this boy.

Four years before he went to prison he 'left' for the USA with a US$1,500 visa stamped in his equally fake passport. Dressed in some outlandish *going to foreign* outfit that was the absolute last word in ghetto-ness. He came back two weeks later. Said he didn't like the place, but folks in our village suspected he was told by someone at the airport that the visa looked fake and he would be caught, and then he stayed hidden in Kingston or someplace for two weeks to conceal his shame. This is all just rumors and inferences. Just like the rumor that Mr Man had paid for the visa.

Eighteen months before, he was in prison for the first time. Served fourteen months for aggravated assault. The events leading to this can be broadly summarized as follows.

For many years Garnet fancied himself to be a cocksman. As we know, he often said that his dick was longer than six months which, while making no sense, was fully understood by the rest of us. As was his claim that it normally took him an hour to an hour and a half to get it all the way up inside a girl, depending on her level of experience. He had no interest in regular sexual positions like doggie-style and missionary, he therefore fucked or slammed in styles such as lizard lap, roast duck and banana peel. The rest of us boys, perplexed, smiled as though we knew what he was talking about.

Garnet was indeed a cocksman. Had a few kids by the time he was twenty. Never had enough money to take care of them. No job, no car, no prospects for anything, and, above all else, no fucking ambition. The only time someone ever used the word 'ambitious' in relation to him was when he was about fourteen years old and asked his younger brother, Tommy, for some of his dinner and received, "But you ambitious!" and nothing more, in return.

Garnet gambled to feed himself and some of his kids. And in those days it was alleged that he had developed something of a temper. One day while he was gambling he got much too upset after losing too much of his money. He felt that he was cheated. And he struck back, much too hard. And then Trevor was unconscious, bleeding from his temple because of the 2x4 that Garnet had connected with his head. The police had no option but to arrest him. That's what I heard, because I was not there that day. I was already living in Kingston. So, he was placed behind the walls. Four walls that made no room even for graffiti.

Now, you would recall, my love, that this was Little Boy Wonder's brother, who had seen his brother die. And we would expect that the murder of his brother may have had something to do with his inability or reluctance to control his temper later in life. I certainly believe that that was part of the explanation. But there was something else that had happened about a year before he laid Trevor flat on the floor. This I had been a part of, because I was still living in that *hateful* fucking place at the time.

So, we now come back to Mr Man - the man people say bought the US$1,500 visa for Garnet well over ten years later. What do we recall of Mr Man? That he was the owner of the ice factory, and that he owned a lot of happiness, no?

Rumor has it that Mr Man, to appease his conscience over what happened to Little Boy Wonder (why there was no investigation), gave Garnet the job of taking care of his yard - basic gardening, cleaning up, that sort of thing. Now this was an outside job, requiring no direct contact with the boss and no need to go inside his house. Whatever supplies were needed could be obtained by going to the back of the house and asking the helper. In short then, the boy had no business ever entering the house. But he did. The first time, he claimed that the helper wasn't responding to his calls, so he just came to look for her. And was just in time to see Mr Man at the dining table, alone, eating dinner. Feasting. I imagine few things are harder to deal with than watching a rich man eating lobster without the delicacy and decorum to suggest that this was a rarity, when you yourself are about to go home to swallow your own spit. And it must have been hard to see just how much joy and happiness that man owned. The man whose truck had reversed over your little brother. Undoubtedly it got harder and harder for him the longer he stood there, transfixed. Rumor has it that he was spared further anguish by the helper, who appeared and ushered him, unceremoniously, outside to his proper station in life.

At this point we the kids in the neighborhood reasoned among ourselves that Garnet went home and hatched a plan. But whatever this plan was, it was about as well-thought-through as a Mugabe government cabinet decision. Because it did not play out very well. This is what happened:

The next Saturday that Garnet went back to take up his proper station in life, cleaning around the periphery of happiness, he decided, once more, to go inside the house. This time he chose a time when Mr Man was not at home. Went in from the back, waited to make sure that the helper was not in sight, and slowly made his way to Mr Man's bedroom. What comes next is an exhibition of really silly behavior, and by this I mean behavior that far surpasses *push a friend in the river, why the fuck did you do that for? Push you back in the river* kind of silly. For those are actions that carry little consequence. What Garnet did was very different. Garnet went and stole some money and some jewelry. A lot of both. And the helper saw him take it.

Now, some people have argued that, being as they were both from poor backgrounds and had family connections, she should have kept quiet about it. But, even as kids, we knew that this was not the kind of thing that could have gone unnoticed. Somebody's ass was always going to pay, and it was either going to be his or the helper's. It was his.

My love, what comes next is brutal so you might want to cover your eyes and close your ears until I am finished. I will tell you when to reopen. Okay. Close your eyes.

Let me do this quickly. Garnet left before Mr Man came home. The helper must have told Mr Man what happened. Mr Man did not send any messages to Garnet during the week. Garnet must have felt that the deed had gone unnoticed. He went back to work on the following Saturday (as a confirmation of the fact that he had done nothing.) When he came through the gate and locked it behind him and turned around he was <u>not</u> greeted with a *happy birthday*-type SURPRISE!, <u>but</u> more of an *Oral speeding in his brand new BMW, overtaking on a corner, encounters a truck coming in the opposite direction (goodbye Oral)*-type SURPRISE. Two hired-hands from the ice factory came from nowhere and greeted Garnet at the gate with thunderous blows raining down like showers from heaven. And not just with their hands. You can pick your poison, they all have the same effect, was this:

- A beating to end all beatings?
- A slave attempted to escape and must be made an example for others, beating?
- A feel free to beat him as badly as you want because the police inspector is my beer-drinking partner, beating?

Some people may say there was a certain *we only threw stones at you, but you fired back missiles at us* element of disproportionality in the response, but I am not the type to arbitrate on what constitutes fairness and what promotes deterrence. I can only say what happened.

But in fact, just like

- a girl squeezing her boyfriend's facial bumps in public;
- a man stopping his car to piss at the side of the road;
- vendors selling concoctions to give you a harder erection (Strong Back, Stand Firm, Roots, Irish Moss, etc.);
- x-rated dancehall music blasting loud on school bus with teenagers,

this kind of a beating was a fairly normal, everyday thing that happened to thieves. (If anything, Garnet was very lucky that he wasn't a goat thief or a gay. Because then the mobs would have been involved, with machetes!) Where we depart from the norm, however, is here:

Mr Man had two dogs tied up at the back of his yard. They were Doberman Pinschers. When the hired-hands had finished with Garnet, Mr Man, allegedly, brought the dogs and set them loose on the boy. (It was later confirmed by the police that the dogs got loose accidentally.) And they mawled him mercilessly.

[Digression: can we blame the dogs in this situation? What do we know about the way dogs were normally treated? We know that *Shot a fire! Run for cover! Save you mother! Put out the dog!* was a common thing, as dogs were expected to fend for, and feed, themselves. We can conclude that dogs were always given a raw deal. Also the dogs were Doberman Pinschers, so it was in their nature to bite. Moreover, they were trained to attack and kill. More moreover, they were often given marijuana tea to drink (a horrible byproduct of which is that occasionally such dogs would also often attack their own masters, for which reason they were often tied up, as in this case). So the fact that they attacked the boy was not to be held against them. We may contrast this with a case which happened a few years before, where a stupid mongrel dog attacked a man going about his business, walking along the road. It is said that the man came back the next day with a sheet, and when the dog came chasing him, he threw the sheet over the dog, caught him, held him and bit him hard. We could all agree that it was the dog's fault in that case and the dog deserved to be bitten. (I know some may think that this was something of an odd behavior, but most of us Jamaicans would understand that while perhaps not an everyday thing, these events happened.)]

You can reopen your eyes now my love.

So the events I just described occurred. For those doubting-Thomases out there, there is also proof that they did occur. For when the rest of the people in our village heard what had happened, they staged a big protest against Mr Man and the ice factory. Managed to mount a large demonstration urging people not to buy any ice from Mr Man. And the television and newspapers came, so the rumored version of the events is properly recorded in the archives of the Jamaica Broadcasting Corporation and the Daily Gleaner. I say the rumored version only on account of the fact that there was no full investigation because, as I mentioned earlier, if you were to have looked closely in Mr Man's wallet you would have seen some very small tiny men with names like Inspector so and so, Sergeant so and so, and Justice so and so.

This is also why people thought it was Mr Man, again attempting to appease his conscience, that bought the US$1,500 visa for Garnet some years later.

Now we have a saying back home that goes "feel sorry for mawga (meager) dog and mawga dog turn around and bite you." (Sorry to bring dogs back into the picture). Word is that Billy was the first one to see Garnet dragging his sorry ass through the lane coming home. Billy who was in a Number 11 mango tree eating mangoes. Billy, who felt so sorry for Garnet that he rushed to him and reached out a hand to help him. But, as that hand touched Garnet, Billy got hit with all the frustrations that a man can possibly carry in his life.

Why did Billy feel so sorry for Garnet? I shall use a few arbitrary words to describe what Garnet looked like when he came through that lane. This is what he looked like:

Oh No Oh No Oh Noooo! Bomboraasclaat!! Nooooooooooooooo, Lord Jesus Noooooooo!!! Jesus Christ! Merciful Father!! Ohhhhh Myyyyyyy Godddddd!!! Lord have mercy, Lord have mercy, Jesus No, Jesus No!!!! Pussyclaat! Him dead, him dead, him dead, Lord him must dead!!!! Fuck! Look pon (on) blood!!!! Jesus, Jesus, Jesus, help me Jesus!!!!

But he got better. After he recovered (at least physically), Garnet often walked the few miles to Mr Man's house, and he stood across the road, looking. At first I never went to see, but my other cousins who had gone said that he had the *Die Villain Die!* look in his eyes. But they knew that this was no cartoon. For the days had come when it was no longer *you smiled at me, can I give you a child in return?* that was on Garnet's mind. For this was a person who no longer smiled, no longer listened, no longer responded. No longer fucked around. No longer fucked. Had always been a stupid little fucker with a one-track mind that people said could never find hay in a haystack. But somehow now he had become as dense as the Dead Sea. And unkempt, and unwashed. Hair more and more like molten plumps of black candle than the unruly cornrow that some baby-mama had started many months before. Just standing there.

Of course we know that people go to war for different reasons. The Ancient Greeks, from the stories we read, went because of a stolen woman who they say was beautiful. And the Jews and Arabs, we know, have gone to war over land and objects which they believe to be holy. For that matter, the Irish, according to history, have gone to war over a frigging cow during the Irish Tithe War, but I will allow that it must have been a mighty fine heifer. Reasons there are many. The results have often been the same: the bloody, gory, waste of lives and property. Battles that provide the stuff from which legends have been made. Fought on fields of glory and in rivers of blood. And yet, in spite of everything I had read in books and seen on TV about the deadly menace of war, there were few things more fearful to me as a young person, than seeing what was behind Garnet's eyes, the first day I went to see him for myself. Because the type of war I saw raging inside him made me shiver. It was cold and silent but you felt the power of Satan's army, and of his legions of demons, raging a cosmic war inside that boy. Who simply stood there, day after day, like Death, silent and composed, with time on his side. Hands always behind his back. There. Waiting.

But Mr Man was now heavily guarded. Was now never seen alone. Was now never seen. But the police did come by our yard a few times to talk to the Old Timers about Garnet. To talk them into talking to Garnet, for even the police knew that he was no longer the kind of person that they themselves could talk to. No one dared.

At this point in time Garnet was a grown, young man whose youngest son would be born about a year later. People say that this son must have felt his papa's rage, for he spent the last four months in his mama's womb kicking her belly, frustrated that he didn't have any one to fight. They say that what came out of the womb was a mean, evil-looking child that only a mother could love; but in reality she didn't.

To wrap up. Garnet had also had drunk from the poisoned well, and was stained. His son too, appeared stained. We will check in on this son in a little while, to see how he is doing, because we are far from finished with him.

CHAPTER 31

He Expected Me To Thank Him, Can You Believe The F'ing Nerve?

Dear Semicolon,

You know me better than anyone else, so you will understand how I became involved in a certain conversation today, while watching a replay of a game at the bar. He was a young chap, my love, and he was very nonchalant in his assertion, "You know what they say, if the mountain won't come to Mohammed, then Mohammed must go to the mountain."

It was at that point I proffered, "If the mountain won't come to Mohammed, then it's the mountain's bloody business."

To which he responded corrosively, "Who the fuck is talking to you? Go mind your own fucking business!" I found him, if not well-mannered, quintessentially linear and well-structured. Thus I said to him, "You believe you are wise, and I believe that you are wise, so I will call you homo sapiens sapiens, or homo sapiens squared, for short."

He then rejoined in the most intellectually apt and profound manner his wit would permit, "Fuck off!" I believe it gave him closure.

It wasn't a game that Manchester United won, but at the end of the day Liverpool remained behind, as they always will.

Love

Kenny

Journal entry, May 14, 2011

I could give you the long version, but it makes no difference. The result is still the same. In the summer of 1985 I went to the river with my cousins and my brother (whose mind was slowly detaching). They were climbing trees, playing, laughing, sliding and swinging. I silently walked towards the bank of the deep end of the river, and stood at the section that everyone called the "Blue Hole". The section that Old Timers said if you fell in, could, like United Airlines, take your body to another part of the world, like China. But just your body, not your soul. This was a river that had helped other young kids make that journey at no cost to themselves and without the need for a visa.

They were still playing in the trees and in the grass, when I jumped in on that very fine Thursday afternoon.

But when I hit the water and began to sink, my journey didn't go as smoothly and serenely (like in those movies on TV) as I had thought. No sireee. There was no gentle, soft slide down to the bottom, with the body and the soul floating in the amber radiance of heavenly light softly cocooning your body. No sireee! My freaking body, when it could not find air, panicked! Involuntarily. And the panic showed, even under the murkiest of dirty river waters. And sometimes, Old Man Time, who I once thought was a lazy asshole, moves swiftly. And then Wayne jumps into the river and grabs on to my hand tightly. Wayne jumps in and saves me. Saves me from saving myself. Saves me so that I could drown in my nightly darkness and emptiness. Saves me so that I could remain in that *hateful* fucking place. And then expected to be thanked. With his stupid boyish grin, standing there expecting me to "At least say thanks". And still fucking expects to be thanked today. The fucking nerve!

I failed in my quest that day, but something else started. A new set of nightmares. Two of these I have had, on and off, for the last thirty years. They have never left me. In the first I see Millicent. I suspect the nightmares started because of what I had seen happen to Millicent a few days before my suicide attempt. Anyway, in this nightmare I see her sitting under an old cotton tree. She has not aged a day in the thirty years I have seen her underneath that tree. She just sits there, un-aged, playing with that very hard cricket ball that I had helped to make. I have been looking at her for over thirty years sitting there and I know she is aware of my presence, but she never looks at me. She never raises her head and turns to me. And while I know that even the worst sinners will eventually turn to Christ when they are dying and seeking salvation, I know that Millicent will never turn to me. I am less afraid of this nightmare because I know everything that it means.

The other nightmare stands out. In this nightmare I see two pineapples. Then one pineapple jumps on top of the other and sinks into it, becoming one with it. Then a unicorn comes along and eats the combined pineapple. Then a rhino comes along and eats the unicorn, before a giraffe comes and eats the rhino and an elephant comes and eats the giraffe. Then a dinosaur (T-rex) comes along and eats the elephant, and a monster comes and eats the dinosaur, and a turtle comes and eats the monster. Then a leaf eats the turtle and a tree eats the leaf and so it goes on and on until I wake up with another silent scream and cold sweat pouring over my body.

This is the nightmare that stands out most among all my nightmares because there is some part of me that understands all the others and the messages they bring. This one, however, I have never been able to decode.

CHAPTER 32

Sine, Cosine, and Tangents

First, another quick check-in on Garnet's son. There he is: eight years old, getting close to nine, mother trying harder to beat some sense into him, knowing that the time to do so is running out. She's trying to drag him to church; trying to slap politeness into him; trying to whip, punch, kick, spit, and curse some good moral foundations into him before he crosses the age of nine when everything in his character will become set. Seems like the little fucker is aware of the plan, and is hurrying along quickly to the welcoming arms of age nine. Now he's there! Safe! Everything is all over and done, nothing can change him anymore! World without end! The only thing his mama can now expect is a kind, forgiving God at the Final Reckoning. Now see him there at ten, coming along just fine with his small group of homies tagging along.

Okay, that's it for now, we will check back on him again soon.

Whenever in my life I have encountered things that I thought were very complex, I would break these things into bite-sized pieces so that I could chew on them little by little. This is an approach I picked up in mathematics, where you had to use different simplification and other techniques to understand and memorize concepts. For example, for Sine, Cosine, and Tangents, I used a simple mnemonics formula: Coh, Sah, Toa:

Coh – opposite/hypotenuse

Sah – adjacent/hypotenuse

Toa – opposite/adjacent

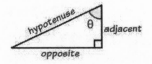

In this manner, an otherwise complex issue becomes simple.

The same approach worked for most other things as well. For example take the following equation:

Boy feels his life will be condemned to being a cockroach;

+ Boy spends a lot of his time watching Bossman/Mr Big eating succulent fried chicken in his office everyday while he himself has to go home hungry;

+ Boy knows that Brownman/Mr Man had a lot to do with his brother's death;

+ Boy knows there is no hope of a better life for himself;

- any respect from anyone;

- loved ones or just love at home;

= pure, unadulterated hate.

I figured out Garnet just as easy as that. In time I understood why we all remained poor, why men and women slept around, why women had many kids, why most kids never went to school and why the Old Timers believed so much in Obeah or the church or both. Once I started to break things down into small pieces, a lot of things became clearer – just simple equations of life.

The one thing I found that I simply could not figure out was how to make a relationship work. With a real person? With a real woman? That right there was rocket science! Ask me the purpose of life… go ahead, ask. Simple: live everyday as though it were your last and treat everyone with kindness and respect. Ask me calculus, physics, theoretical chemistry, world trivia, anything! But don't ask me how to make a relationship work!

I don't know, Semicolon, if maybe it was because I didn't feel much love when I was a child, or perhaps because I didn't have enough loved ones to practice loving on when I was older and more aware of love, or what it was. All I know is that when it was time for me to give love in a relationship, I lacked experience.

I could not bond, Semicolon, not with man, woman, nor dog. Dogs, of course, just weren't reliable. So I couldn't bond with them.

With men I feared I would be considered gay. I have explained this before.

Women were just for sex. When I saw women, all I saw were *tall* fuck, *cute* fuck, *should be old enough to not get arrested for it* fuck, *hairy* fuck, *would be my first blond* fuck, *nice titties* fuck, *cute smile* fuck, *big ass* fuck, *shorty* fuck, *polished fingernails* fuck, *Man those are some nice boots she wearing, she should be good to* fuck, *cook good* fuck, *holds a beer in a lady-like manner* fuck, *the baby looks at least six months old so mommy should now be ready again for* fuck, *pity she has those burn marks on her face, but still…* fuck, and so on. In my mind even the way a woman walked was viewed through the lens of her coochie. The *tight pum pum* walk, the *kukumkum* (or skinny pum pum) walk, the *so heavy it slowing her down* walk, the *pum pum fat 'til it buff* walk, the *sweet, juicy pum pum* glide, and more. There was even the *worthless gal that give it away too easy* walk, which was a broad, bowlegged looking walk. Everywhere I looked all I saw were girls waiting to be picked up like bad habits, and taken to my crib for a sweet ride. As for the ones I had been with, I gave them their own names to remember them by: Good Burger; Fat Burger; Healthy Burger; Juicy Burger; Burgerlicious; Burger Queen; Meaty Burger and such like.

Most of what I learnt about love as a child I learnt in church while listening to pastor tell stories about a man I wouldn't meet before I was dead. The temporal consequences of this lack of intimacy with love were grave.

Here is the long and short of it all:

Wife number one

This page is intentionally left blank to reflect my understanding of how exactly I managed to screw up my first marriage.

Wife number two

It would be better for you to have this one come straight from the horse's mouth, but this horse has a really foul mouth, and there are things that even now I prefer never to see or hear again. She wrote her own story in my diary, in the form of an unsolicited journal entry. June 2004.

It opened like this:

"It doesn't need to be dark, rainy or gloomy outside for us to speak the truth."

It suggested:

"No matter their station in life you are ready, willing and able to be the village ram. Lepers, whores and misfits need not worry, because you will also be their jockey. Anything for a good ride."

It ended:

"You are really no more than the scum of the earth who should be hitched to a toothless hag who gives you just what you deserve."

In August 2011 I went to see all 160 centimeters of her fiery tempestuousness. I had, somehow, hoped to bring closure. It was worth a shot, after all, people don't seem to dance the same way they used to anymore; I can now cook rice after Googling "how to use a rice cooker" and discovering the miraculously-simple eight steps; I have grown to like the feel of Kenko K-1 pens in my hand, and I now like wearing Adidas sneakers. Impossible is nothing!

Times have changed.

2011, Brooklyn, New York, near to Buff Patty. The winter had long gone, taking with her temperatures colder than a serial killer's cruelty. It was August 6. She had gone back to live in the neighborhood and had bought a little two-bedroom apartment at a discounted price due to the recession. When we dated she lived in Brooklyn, but then we moved in together on the Upper West Side, not too far from Central Park, where she used to jog.

I was the second to arrive. Her friend or, more accurately, her mama's friend, Margaret, more commonly known as One Eye Margy, or, more accurately, One Yeye Margy, had come a bit earlier allegedly to help with the preparations for the dinner.

When I got there Margy was sitting in the living room eating some grapes and watching CNN. At fifty-four years old, she was born two years before her best friend, Doretta.

Margy once told me that she didn't find out who her real mama was until she was sixteen years old. She was living in real bush at the time, up in Ginger House, Portland. I can't recall how the conversation started but she told me that she had seen this lady almost every day of those sixteen years, and didn't know that it was her mama. The lady would walk by their house to go to the shops and church on Sunday mornings. She would wave to whoever was sitting on the veranda of their house, sometimes stopping two houses down from hers to visit with a family that had a little boy, Germaine. At sixteen, One Yeye Margy also found out that Germaine too was the lady's child.

They had lived less than four hundred meters from each other but somehow she had never come over, and they had never gone to her house. When they had their first real conversation, the lady offered no apologies and no explanations, she simply said, "You grow good gal." This was to signal a certain satisfaction with how she had turned out.

One Yeye Margy had lost her right eye at age forty-one because of high blood-pressure. Initially the tiny capillaries (at first, and because of her pronunciation, I thought she had said 'caterpillars') in the retina of her eye started to bleed a little, because she also had diabetes. Then some vessels in her eye simply went pop, and that was that. Since then, she has spent a lot of time drinking coconut water, decaf and green tea to reduce the pressure that is constantly building up like a dam in her remaining eye.

The door was unlocked and left slightly ajar, so I walked on in. Margy greeted me from the couch,

"Well look who's here, if it ain't Mr Lovelace and his lovely haemorrhoids. " Rebecca had never been one to keep information to herself.

I greeted her more customarily, then enquired, "I thought Rebecca told me you were coming early to *help* her with the preparations?" I gave her a meaningful look.

"It's my fault," Rebecca, who had by then entered the living room, responded on her behalf. "I forgot what my grandmother always tell me: 'You can't feed slave before you put them to work.' How you doing Kenny?"

Rebecca had planned a little get-together with a couple of Jamaicans, mutual friends, living in the New York area. One, Simon, was teaching at CUNY and trying to finish his Ph.D before NASA's New Horizon probe, which launched in the same year he started (2006), reached Pluto in 2015. The other was Giovanni, whose given name promised more than his parents could ever fulfill. He was studying law and beer at Rutgers in New Jersey. I had gone to college with both back in Jamaica, and would often get together with them while I lived with Rebecca.

Everyone was expected to bring either alcohol or some home-cooked food to what was going to be another of our long-time, Jamaican-style 'lime' (get together). I had brought some real spicy jerk chicken in foil paper. The last time we had my jerk chicken the professorially bald spot in the middle of Simon's head had trapped more water than the Amazon Basin.

Margy, who was visiting from Jamaica, didn't bring anything, but was supposed to help Rebecca cook the steam fish and curried goat. As noted, she was already on the sofa nibbling on crackers and picking her teeth.

Rebecca looked the same as she always did. We kissed cheeks the way folks on Martha's Vineyard do, a habit we had acquired with increasing prosperity.

Once in a while I had believed that I loved her. I realized, however, that what was happening to me was the same as getting sick: I would be healthy for five months then have a sudden onset of the flu. Then someone would remind me that it is the start of the flu season. All I was having were just the occasional impulses that came with certain cycles, perhaps with watching too much TV, or after seeing a couple holding hands on the road.

Rebecca pointed her index finger in the direction of the kitchen. While I carried the chicken to the kitchen, I shouted back into the living room, "What you doing with yourself now Margy?"

She had been at our wedding, but we were never really friends. She was close to both Doretta and Rebecca. She was now walking behind me coming to the kitchen, hopefully to start helping out.

"You know, once upon a time mama say to me and Susan that we can become anything we want in life. She then ask Susan, 'So what you want to become?' You know what the pickney say? She say 'I want to become a Jew.' Now, that's a pickney who always did know exactly what she want! You see her now? The child have money like dirt! I never did know what I want. Still don't know. The long and short of it, my dear, is that yours truly is formally a 'housewife.'" She said it with sufficient pride to suggest that 'housewife' was better than 'cashier', 'dressmaker' or unemployed.

Why the housewife had, in recent times, taken to bleaching her face, was something I would never ask about.

The first thing I heard in the kitchen as I entered, was the scrape of furniture on the floor from the apartment upstairs. That sound would once have hurt my ears. Then came the sound of the vacuum. I asked Rebecca who would be vacuuming at six o' clock in the evening. She pointed out that the upstairs neighbor had gotten herself a male house cleaner, who took longer than anybody else to finish his work.

"You know that man do everything different from woman," she had

258

explained. "Look like him vacuum even her books. Either that or she using the vacuum to cover the sounds of what's really going on, 'cause she single, and that's the only man I ever see going inside that place."

It was a small kitchen, but neat and clean. I saw the jug of water alongside the sugar and lemons on the counter. I knew instinctively that she had put them there, waiting for me. She caught my eye.

"If you never did anything else good for me, you made me some nice lemonade." She was probably right.

It had always been difficult to find good-quality dark sugar at the corner stores in Brooklyn. The powers that be seemed to always send the dirtier sugar from Guyana and Haiti to Brooklyn, leaving the better stuff to be sold as *organic* and *natural* in Wholefoods in Westchester. The thought crossed my mind of how our great-great-grandfathers died in the cane-fields with machetes in their hands and the sun baking their heads like potatoes, and whether their final thought might have been how wholesome and organic the cane was and how it would nourish those on the Upper East Side for centuries to come.

Margy, having gotten herself another drink, walked over by the kitchen sink, and admired some flowers on the windowsill.

"Them flowers here real?"

"Yes, them don't look real to you?"

"Well it's just that I plant some fake ones because them look nice. Sometimes the fake ones are really prettier."

"What you mean by plant? In dirt?"

"Yes, the dirt help to make everything look real."

I knew I would never want to visit Margy's house. I asked Rebecca if she had enough ice for the lemonade and the rest of the drinks. She pointed to the igloo on the ground beside the oven. There are times when her tongue wags mercilessly and eternally, and times when the volcano lies dormant and her body does the talking. Her finger was speaking now.

I had just poured the sugar into the jug when I saw the skinny ass nigga walking towards the front of the apartment complex. Rebecca's was a floor up, and from the kitchen window you could look straight down to the entrance of the building. He was wearing shorts, completely unmindful of the dangers of walking around like that during bird season. The boy looked to be about ten feet tall and to weigh four ounces. Giovanni walked past a dog that immediately perked up his ears, before relaxing again to enjoy his sun tan in the late sun of summer. Then I saw Simon just behind him, wearing purple shoes, black and white pants, a black and white polka-dot shirt, a bright-orange scarf (in summer), a fedora and shades. Having known him since college, we all thought he was 'sweet' but not gay.

I anticipated the question before it came. "Good evening, where you guys going?" I wasn't close enough to actually hear the question, but I knew it came, and I knew the exact words.

Rebecca had told me about the old man in one of her emails, and I had just met him. He was about sixty-five years old, with a pleasant smile – this made his question perplexing but not threatening. She said everyone suspected he meant no harm. He just sat at the entrance on a chair he took from his apartment, which was on the third floor. He went back inside only to eat and when his daughter came home from work at about 7 p.m. She said he offered free watchman services to the complex – meaning that he would watch whatever crime was being committed as he had neither the strength, phone, nor weapon to stop anything from happening. His wife, a white lady, had left him over eighteen years before. Apparently he once told Rebecca that she had remarried, was living in New Orleans, volunteered at a soup kitchen, was a part-time nun, and was now into swinging.

He asked all visitors the same question: "Where are you going?" And, on departure, "Where are you coming from?" It wasn't that the two questions were designed to test consistency. Folks were never sure whether or what to respond.

She also told me that he had a tall, dark-skinned son that "looks like that Sri Lankan spin bowler, what him name?" I knew it was Muralitharan; it was the only bowler she knew in all of cricket, and this was because I had pointed out his unusual spin to her once. From then all dark-skinned Indians, Pakistanis, Sri Lankans, Bangladeshis, Nepalese, etc., looked like him. The son came and went, and occasionally gave the old man a cigarette before going upstairs with or without a companion, mostly females. She said she had seen the son once on the E train going towards Parsons/Archer, while she was coming home late one night. He gave her the faintest acknowledgement. He was with another girl that he barely spoke a word to, even though she was yapping away throughout the ride. They were always white, those girls, she said. Something about him had told her that he was "somewhere far down in the long queue of men waiting to be understood, like you."

I went and met my old friends at the door. I hadn't seen them in over four years. I doubted whether they knew what had recently happened to me as I hadn't kept in touch with them much after Rebecca and I divorced. And Rebecca may not have told them.

Simon was the first to remind me that nothing ever changed.

"Raasclaat Kenny, long time no see! Look like life agree with you! Look like you have belly now! Like you a breed! You must have some fat pum pum gal a feed you some good food. Where you live now?"

Simon's upbringing had ended at being potty-trained, and his parents never bothered to go onto decency and decorum. He was, always, foul-mouthed. The last time I saw him his car was in the garage and he drove a big U-haul van to the house. He told us then that he wasn't moving but had rented the U-haul because it was cheaper ($19.95) than a regular compact car ($30-40), and he needed some wheels for the week his car was out.

"Hey Kenny, how you doing man?" Giovanni was Giovanni.

We all embraced, Jamaican style, brother-to-brother style, man-to-man style, gangster-to-gangster style. Then Giovanni, with his elephant's brain, picked up the thread of their paused conversation,

"But if you want to talk about which government did what, Simon, I would ask you to remember that it was your government that lower the Common Entrance Exam pass grade from 2 to 3. That was pure stupidness! That's the worst thing them could ever do to Jamaica! Stupid Labourites!"

"Giovanni," Simon interjected, "Giovanni, the only thing you can remember is the last time you eat pig tail, nothing else! Let me tell you something. You see when Michael Manley was in power-"

"What is this? It seems y'all have hog for your mother? Y'all forget your manners?" It was Rebecca, it could only have been. They greeted and saluted her, laughing. Rebecca, Rebecca.

I had taken her to Cuba once. March 21, 2006. She had gone with me on a couple of business trips to Europe and parts of the USA before, but that trip was different, and it was all at my expense. It was our anniversary. We had walked from our hotel to a restaurant the concierge had recommended, El Tiburon. It was one of the private, 'underground' restaurants as some folks called them. It was our second anniversary. I tried hard to keep my eyes off the girls. Some friends had asked me before why I was taking pizza to Italy.

Our dinner was: a sign on the wall that said "El-Tiburon"; approximately sixty bottles of wine stacked horizontally in a wine cabinet; every word of a live concert once performed by Silvio Rodriguez; memories of childhood; memorable quotes from Shakespeare, Dante, Ruiz Zafón, Bounty Killer, Beenie Man and Shaggy; an insect on the wall; the etchings on the chairs; the teachings of Buddha; the laughter from another table; the apron worn by the waiters; the photos of previous guests; her looking at her gypsy-like bangles and her ring. She had studied her fingers and her ring a lot, stretching the fingers out on the table the way women do when showing a new engagement ring to their friends, and turning the ring with the fingers of her right hand. She had spent a lot of time looking at her ring. She had worn a Jeans jacket covering shoulders and arms, open at the front where you could see her little pendant and her light-blue dress. The forks and spoons had felt like family sitting there with us. She touched them from time to time, moved them around. She had Sangria and studied the lemon, apple and orange slices. She had told me once that she was the easiest valentine – only needed two tins of Nesquik and a smile. But while we sat there the romance had felt damp and musty.

She had slowly drank her Sangria. Used the fork to take out bits and pieces of fruit.

Our conversation was:

"You know my younger sister was nearly raped when she was nine?"

"I didn't know that. What happened?"

"Do you know what they put in Sangria? Is there anything else apart from the red wine and fruits?"

"I think they use a bit of brandy."

"I probably could use rum, you think? I don't really buy brandy, but I would like to try it when I get back." She had spoken in the singular and first person.

"But you know that Jamaican food is the nicest?" Apparently the reference to pig tail had brought Margy's attention to the meal ahead of us.

Giovanni, ever the lawyer, counter-argued that everybody thinks that their own food is the nicest.

Simon counter-counter-argued, "So, you really think Bajans like them own food? Them don't even like them own self!"

Rebecca looked the same. Still busying herself, moving things from one place to another, organising, getting things ready, while the rest of us chatted. They were invited to help themselves to liquor in the kitchen. No one asked for water instead.

"Talk about that, you see the report saying that Barbados is now a developed country?" Giovanni asked, on his way to the kitchen.

"All it takes is ugliness and unpleasantness to become developed?"

smirked Simon.

"Why you calling the people ugly and unpleasant? You know any Bajans?"

"I don't need to know any. I hear 'bout them, and anything that people tell you 'bout Bajans is true 'cause people don't need to make up story 'bout Bajans."

"Well, them developed now, and Jamaica is nowhere near reaching that stage."

"If that's a developed country then I want to be backward and illiterate all the days of my life! Them don't have music! No culture! No athlete! No nothing!"

"Them have money though."

"You know Giovanni, I think it goin' take a brain transplant to cure whatever mental disease you have..."

It was always the same pattern of conversation between the two, and the rest of us generally stayed on the outskirts.

I got myself a beer and stayed with Rebecca in the kitchen. Margy remained in the living room, having 'checked' on the fish in the oven. Simon and Giovanni took their beers and went to the dining table.

Rebecca had cut her hair. She was always doing something with her hair. Had once gone dread.

I could have chosen to tell her the Truth then and stopped Time in its tracks. Instead I chose Convenience, and allowed Time to walk its course, make new friends, see new places, create new obligations, all in our name. Cuba was a turning point for us in some ways.

"Jamaica could have become more developed by now if we had joined the Caribbean Community back in '62, at the time of Independence," declared Giovanni, from one side of the table.

"Joined what?", scoffed Simon, from the other, "You drinking mad puss piss? You see what happening in the European Union right now? You see how the weaker countries them draining the stronger ones?"

"I don't know much about them things 'cause I not as educated as y'all, but I think Seaga was right. Jamaica should not join no CARICOM!" offered Margy.

"Y'all don't understand what Michael Manley was doing," urged Giovanni. "That man had a vision. Let me explain-"

"I don't know what you goin' explain to me," Margy retorted, "All I know is that Manley might have been a good fuck, but he wasn't a good leader! Him should've just go on chasing skirts and leave other people to run the country. Seaga was the best Prime Minister-"

"Seaga! Seaga what?" Simon interjected, "That man was a raasclaat thief! Y'all hear me? Seaga was the worst Prime Minister Jamaica ever had!" From his third or so sip of Appleton Estate Rum Simon was acquiring increasing conviction and clarity of ideas.

"Is what this?" asked Margy. On Rebecca's directions I had taken a few dinner items to the dining table, which Margy was now appraising. Either her attention was easily distracted, or she was never really attuned to the debate.

"Sweet tamarind. It's imported from Thailand," I explained. I had brought it.

"Is Jamaica me come from my love, I don't eat fruits out of box. And besides, Tamarind not supposed to be sweet."

Rebecca was just behind, bringing the plates.

"Man no have wings and not supposed to fly either, but you come here in the clouds," she said.

Simon felt the need to add, "Margaret, I don't know you that well, but let me alert you to the fact that them used to burn people at the stakes for harboring more sensible beliefs than what I hearing from you."

The conversation continued, covering the flight from Jamaica and how much things had changed since Air Jamaica was sold. Rebecca and I set the table. When we were gathered at the table, Margy said grace, in the process inviting the good Lord to grant Jamaica another Prime

Minister like Seaga.

Not soon after we started eating, I realized that Giovanni must have some spiritual connection with jerk chicken - every time you looked in his direction you would see a part of the chicken being absorbed into him.

Rebecca seemed to be doing well for herself. It is a two-bedroom apartment, but spacious. She could have afforded a nicer one further uptown, but had always been economical. She needed a place to sleep, and enough walls to hang her family photos. A lot of photos were hung. None of them included me.

Giovanni continued the flight to Jamaica, perhaps because he had not been there for a while.

"So how things back home these days Margaret?" he said.

"Bwoy, Jamaica still nice, but all I know is that it hard to make money now. Nothing at all happening."

"From what I hear you can go into pig farming. People seem to be making a lot of money from that, no?" offered Giovanni, ever online reading the Jamaica Observer and listening to the various radio stations.

"I don't know about that-" said Margy.

"Or you can buy, fix up and sell house. I hear that the Government lower the transfer tax so people probably goin' start buying and selling property more. I know one lady-"

Simon had heard enough from the two.

"Listen to me. Y'all listen to me. I think it is my civic duty to explain something to y'all." Simon himself was fresh from a recent visit. "The biggest money maker right now in Jamaica is chicken back licence. Tell anybody that is me tell you that!" He points at himself with his thumb to confirm the identity of the speaker. "This is not what I hear, or what anybody tell me," he continued, "I know as a fact that you can easily make JA\$200,000 or more per month net if you have one of them licence." Giovanni wanted to know how much that amount was in US dollars, but Simon was now focused on giving his lesson. "Conch is good to, but it harder to get licence for that."

"Giovanni, that is about two thousand five hundred US," Rebecca chipped in.

Giovanni's ears pricked up.

"But that sound like good money! How you get a licence for them things?" he asked.

Simon had the answer to that as well.

"The Minister has direct responsibility for issuing licences. But I have a good friend, you probably remember Arthur. Kenny you supposed to remember Arthur, he was at college with us?" I nodded my remembrance. Giovanni remembered him as well. "Well Arthur have the link. Him and the Minister are good friends, and him have them giving away like treats to Labourites."

"See what I telling you? Nothing but frigging corruption!" Giovanni was and always shall be nothing if not a die-hard PNP supporter. He succeeded in raising Simon's blood-pressure.

"Giovanni," he said, firmly.

"Yes?" Giovanni replied, with a puzzled look.

"You have days of the week that you set aside to talk nonsense? Let me tell you something man. It's seventeen years that Labourites waiting to eat food! Seventeen years that the dirty stinking Socialists alone getting fat, while Labourites a walk out a road hungry."

Rebecca sensed the direction things were heading, and interjected with a decoy less for information and more for peace.

"But when you have the licence and bring in the meat, how you store it? Like the chicken back, where would you store that?" she asked.

Fortunately, Simon, still visibly disturbed, preferred opportunities to share his infinite wisdom than to brawl.

"You can rent cold storage at the wharf, like out at New Port," he said.

"You say Arthur in it?" I chipped in, to help continue to steer things away from confrontation.

"Yeah, him have a whole heap of licences."

"And him making money for himself?"

"Bwoy, him bathing in it! That man making so much money right now you wouldn't believe it!"

"I don't know him but I hope him using him money wisely," added Rebecca.

"You don't know Arthur? My dear, Arthur him staring forty-five in the face 'cause he was older than the rest of us, but all him doing is buying car and bleaching cream for him woman dem. Him tell me say him also give one of him friend some of him money to save it for him. The rest him have under him mattress or someplace in him house."

"Damn idiot!" blasted Giovanni. "A fool and his money will soon be parted!" He was looking for another opening to rile Simon up again.

Simon was by then sucking on a piece of jerk chicken leg. The scar halfway down his right cheek, equidistant between his right eye and his Adam's Apple, was roughly at the same spot where Georgie sometimes had a swelling after his papa punched him in his face. Georgie's papa was left-handed. He liked to punch at the face – a smaller, harder-to-hit target and consequently more satisfying. I understand that for many years rural people had thought that nothing could rival the cruelty of a left-handed man, until the 1970s came and they found out that the cruelty of a *short*, left-handed man had no boundaries. Funny how the American President is now left-handed, and Jamaicans expect no evil of him.

"But what you going to do when you get back Margy? You can't keep relying on you sister to send you money you know," Rebecca chimed in, knowing also that the longer Margy remained unemployed, the longer she will keep asking her mama, Doretta, to ask her, Rebecca, to send her, Margy, remittances.

Margy, unaware of the deeper significance of the question, recounted how she got into her predicament. She had opened up a little restaurant in one of the malls on Constant Spring Road. Her sister, Susan, had given her the capital to buy the business, and all she needed to do was make sure it was profitable enough to pay the rent and leave her with some spare change at the end of the month. The white, rich man who owned the plaza, though, didn't know that it was One Eye Margy who bought the restaurant until he started seeing her around very often. When he realized, he started making things difficult for her, raised the rent, started pointing out things that were 'not up to standard', and then asked her to sell to a gentleman he knew that had the capital to 'really invest in it' and bring it up to the standards he was expecting. Told her that he was planning to upgrade the mall and wanted only top quality shops and restaurants.

"Him never expect a ugly black woman to be running the shop," Margy concluded, and confirmed she had indeed sold it after all.

"Is so white people stay! None of them expect that black people can do anything!" fumed Giovanni.

It was a convenient conclusion. Margy could have pointed out that her own black papa and mama were the same, and neither had ever expected anything of her. But truth doesn't always float to the top like oil.

No one had ever expected anything of Georgie, either. Not mother, not father, not friends, not white people, brown people, black people... no one.

"That's why Michael Manley say Equal Rights and Justice for all!" Giovanni continued.

"Giovanni?" Simon's blood was flowing faster.

"Yes?"

"How often you feel the need to speak rubbish? Fuck Manley!"

"I would have loved to do that," Margy chipped in.

"As far as I am concerned y'all swap black dog for monkey," Rebecca added, distancing herself from her birth country in a manner I hadn't seen her do before. I shared her belief; the two political parties and Prime Minister had had the same effect on the country.

Bob Marley's 'One Love' was playing in the background, but nobody

269

took heed of its invocations.

"Y'all don't understand the kind of leader that Manley was; Manley is like Obama-" continued Simon.

"Now *him* look like another good fuck! That's a sweet looking black man!" Margy reminded me of an older, uglier, shorter, poorer, dumber, female, one-eyed version of me.

Simon took advantage of this new opening, "Margy, it look like you need a man. What happen, you not getting any?"

"My dear, the only kind of man who would want me now is the kind who'd go to a pet store and adopt a three-footed dog or a blind cat. Anyway, it hard to find a man these days, worse where I live." I was dazed by her brutal honesty.

Margy used her right index finger to straighten her right eyebrow, almost as though subconsciously she was saying to herself "this is the only part of me I think is beautiful."

"Well, if you looking for a man, you should leave the pond and go to the river where there are more fishes," was Simon's insightful recommendation.

Margy's response was quick and natural, "Are you suggesting that I become a correctional officer? Prison is the only place you can find lots of black men these days, and I not looking for that kind of fish. Seems like all the black man I talk to these days worthless – some want to know if I have my own house and savings account. This worthless Jamaican one I see in Queens a few days ago want to know if I have a 401k or other kind of pension fund, and telling me that him can iron my clothes and do my hair. Larks! My love, I not looking for man that I going to have to feed at this stage of my life. So I will wait. I have the venue, the pastor, the church, the dress, the menu, the list of guests, and everything else ready, I just now need to wait until I find the right man."

Then, in line with the infinitely incomprehensible order of the universe, Giovanni exclaimed, "Shit, look like some of the curry from the goat get on my shirt!"

Simon was about to comment but Rebecca cut both of them off, "You know Giovanni, your lack of gratitude worries me. You will be leaving here wearing more than you came with and you are complaining?"

There was a chuckle. Margy's blindness, sexual urges, and recent dating experiences were all forgotten, along with her plans for her post-restaurant future. The mention of curry brought food back to the centre of the conversation.

Giovanni led the way, "Screechy still cook the best fish and lobster in Hellshire?"

West Africans miss their flies, mosquitoes and power outages when they are away from home; we miss our music and our food. Wherever there are Jamaicans, there are always conversations about the best places to get what food. For the record: Middlequarters remains the best for peppered shrimp; Faiths Pen for ackee and saltfish and roast breadfruit, and Kens in Portmore for curried goat. Boston jerk is now a waste of time and an abomination.

Simon scoffed. "Look like you no go Jamaica for the last fifty years-" He had every intention of setting Giovanni straight with the latest information, but by then hurricane Margy had already started to blow.

"Talk 'bout what happening in Jamaica, you heard about the two women that them behead in Hanover? Y'all know that one o' them was an old lady, woman probably in her sixties, sitting on her veranda, and the raasclaat wicked killer just come up behind her!"

Rebecca glanced at me, perhaps hoping to give comfort. She was the only one who knew what had happened with me in December when I went home.

Continuing their conversation, Simon nodded that he had heard about the incident as well. "Look how the world changing," he said quietly. It was said in such a sad, soft way that you would believe that, blatantly and en masse, citizens all over the world are now overthrowing their governments; men are now having as many wives as they wish; children are setting up call 1800getgin&tonic businesses, and priests who so desire can play freely with choir boys.

The events of the past few months in Jamaica became the sole subject of conversation. Rebecca continued to look at me from time to time.

And so the evening, like our lives, passed.

At 10:45 pm they all left. Giovanni had to catch the last train to New Jersey from Penn Station.

When they had all gone, I stayed behind to help with the cleaning up. I also needed to see her alone.

We didn't speak for a while. Then we brushed against each other while both reaching to put some things in the refrigerator.

"Awkward, huh?" she questioned, continuing to do what she was doing. "On an awkwardness scale of 1 to 5, with 1 being the lowest - as in, for example, your wife has invited you to drinks at a bar that you used to frequent, and 5 being highest - like you then bump into some of your friends at the bar and they are laughing at you trying to convince them that this is really your wife, where would that fall?"

She always said things like that, asked questions for which she knew there could be no answers.

I lived so much of my life believing that without air and the warmth of a woman's crotch, I could not survive seven days. Now I realize that what I long for is the taste of an occasional conversation and maybe a sip of wine. Maybe someone, every now and then, to lie beside me throughout the night. I have discovered it's nice to wake up with the sunrise, and the sounds of birds chirping in the trees, and the wind gently tapping on the window. Not with a woman that you would otherwise have to usher out before the sunlight damaged the acceptable beauty bestowed on her by nightclub lights.

Rebecca was now more comfortable speaking her mind. We had met in Atlanta in 2000, after the first wife and a couple of girlfriends in between. She was Jamaican and black. Her papa, one of the sugar-tongued monsters that had seduced Doretta, was living in the US and had applied for her US residency permit. She was already a citizen living in Atlanta, when I met her. She worked hard, went home to watch television, and was on her path to a normal life. After a few months of dating long-distance, she had picked up all her life in a few boxes and moved with her expectations, to Brooklyn. After that big move, other tough decisions came easier, like deciding to walk out on a three-year marriage.

"Sometimes when we made love, you would have a look on your face... almost like a mechanic working on a car." She had said something else in between that I missed. I suspected it had to do with how she knew I was not in love with her.

"Like I was just something you were working on."

It was something else I had no response to.

"You know Kenny, you will die early."

It was a strange twist to the conversation, but I would be lying if I told you that it was unexpected. This was how she was.

"What? How'd you know that?"

"I Googled how to read people's aura."

"Sometimes I swear... You know that you are weirder than your mama?" I asked her.

"Not as weird as the man who spends his whole life searching for the right goat to love."

"Where you hear that? Which sleazy tabloid you saw that in?"

"I didn't read it or see it anywhere, but I know there is someone like that. This world is full of all kinds of people."

I hadn't touched anything for a few minutes. She had been speaking while cleaning and clearing up, while I had just been standing there, looking. Then she too, stopped. She was standing at the sink facing the wall, and I was behind her, beside the fridge. She glanced back ever so slightly, over her shoulder.

"I am really sorry about what happened to you." She said it with a

273

slight tremble in her voice and with her back still towards me. I know she had struggled to get the words out, even though she had called me a few days after it happened. I knew that, in spite of everything, her sympathies were genuine.

I wanted to tell her that since that day my life has become a routine of acid indigestion, of acquiring the taste for single malt whiskey, of long walks and planting flowers, of eating plain noodle soups, taking aspirins, listening only jazz pianists, and finding myself sitting alone in the dark, speaking with the Whiskey gods. I know, however, that like our time on earth, the anguish we feel is temporary, it fades in time and, like our bodies, will eventually take another form - perhaps numbness, or a gently-weeping sorrow.

But I also wanted to tell her, Rebecca, there and then that I also often thought about her. About how young, black, and beautiful she was back then when we met in her late twenties. But this was not something I could talk about, because I remembered the movie theatre courtships and the knowledge that it was only the caresses that had inspired those words of affection and endearment. I can still see us slouching lower in the seats, touching, exploring, while the dark silhouette of something that wasn't Love watched us in the shadows from a few seats behind. I remember how as the credits rolled, the lights came on and we straightened our clothes and held hands to leave, I would often look behind to see if something was in fact there. But it wasn't. And I sometimes wondered if it had already gone to the future to wait on us, to wait on the words that I would now struggle to get out.

The devil chuckles at lies, so I told him I have loved, and together we laughed and watched the relationships drift away in little bubbles of methane.

"Thanks, Rebecca," I said. "I am sorry too. I really am. For everything that happened between *us*. For hurting you."

And now the thing that remains is the stain, of having loved something more than you love your own soul, and knowing that it was never God.

The In-betweens

After Rebecca left I hooked up with a girl called Bitterness for about a year. With sufficient resignation a man can remain in a relationship with Bitterness longer than he can be with Loneliness. Loneliness is a real bitch. Bitterness eats at you little by little, but mostly at herself. And you can occasionally sleep with Bitterness. With Loneliness you generally have to go in search of cheap, sad whores – those for whom the late-night street lamp is the only light in their darkness.

Bitterness had another name, of course, Debbie, and she also had a question: "What am I living for?" This was sometimes framed as, "What's the point of all this?" I reckon she asked her question approximately 2,167 times during our brief relationship. I estimate this based on a complex formula. The formula takes into account a few variables:

- The frequency with which we had arguments (the question was mostly asked during an argument)
- The average number of times the question was asked in an argument (which is based partially on the ratio of occasions when the question was asked in different forms to just one form, during the same argument.)
- A logarithmic factor for the first six months of our relationship – the more passionate we were in the earlier days the angrier she often got and the more frequent the arguments, leading to a higher average number of times that the question was raised.

This is what gave me the figure of 2,167.

After we broke up I wrote a verse in answer to her question and mailed it to her:

"The meaning of our existence"

As I understand,
and according to God's plan,
the true essence of man
lies in his consciousness and free will.

And thus I will contend:
that man's essence will not be found
in the splashing sound
of liquid coursing through his heart;
but rather in
the rattle of the wind
that's heard when he releases a fart -
consciously and willfully.

This logic I will defend,
though I am not sure you will comprehend
the subtle but important difference:
that a healthy heart indeed we need to exist,
but a hearty fart gives meaning to our existence.

K. Lovelace, April 2006

I would so much like to know what she has done with herself. Whether she ever married, had kids and a good reliable dog, and found happiness.

Other women came and went like they have always done throughout my life. Things would often start off well, like brushing your teeth more often after a visit to the dentist – lots of caresses, lots of sex and a few flowers, until things slid downhill to the norm.

I could give them names and addresses and personalities, and dress them up in different clothes, but what would be the point? Outside of the two marriages, there were eleven relationships and approximately twenty-three whores, not counting the Malaysian one who had no bloody idea what she was doing. I regard them as the 'in-betweens' because all I wanted was to get in-between their legs. All biology, and no chemistry. Sometimes they were so absolutely dull that having made the effort to bring one home, I would send her away so I could simply be by myself.

A group of former army guys I had drinks with at a bar once, enlightened me about the ways a man can make his own hand feel like someone else's to enhance self-pleasure. The various techniques mostly involved numbing the hand (bucket of ice, sitting on your hand, etc.) and then jerking off. At times I found this far more pleasurable than having the company of a whore.

Semicolon

Then, of course, there is you, Semicolon. You. The very spark of life.

Whatever it is that you did to me the day I met you has not been undone;

Many years have passed since then, but I still think about you every day as though it was the first;

The day may come when I lose my mind again; when it degenerates like an old car;

I may develop Alzheimer's and forget my way home;

I may forget about my mama and the things that happened to her;

I may forget about my papa and the things that happened to him;

I may forget;

Thirty days have September

April, June and November
All the rest have thirty one
Except February which has twenty eight
And twenty nine if it's a leap year
I may forget;

My	*Mercury*
Very	*Venus*
Energetic	*Earth*
Mother	*Mars*
Just	*Jupiter*
Served	*Saturn*
Us	*Uranus*
Nine	*Neptune*
Pizzas	*Pluto*

And though it is very, very, very unlikely, I may even forget the taste of mangoes;

If all these things should happen, and if the day should come when, like my grandfather, I should look in a standing mirror and say, "Excuse me sir, do you know where my woman is?" I will be thinking that you, Semicolon, are my woman.

My love, I have feelings inside me that are like bulls stampeding in an enclosed room; they rage for release, but there are no words I can find to unlock the door and set those feelings free. I sometimes think that it is tragic that after all of mankind's great inventions we have not yet found the words for a man to tell a woman how what he feels when he is with her goes so much further than "I love you;" I have tried symbols, such as)(; I have tried to sing, but these feelings go much further than Peabo Bryson and Lionel Ritchie. So much further. I will return to us later my love, for our story is not yet told.

CHAPTER 33

A Death Wish

For my funeral I would like them to play Simon and Garfunkel's *The Boxer*. They can then do whatever else they want to do, as I won't care.

For my death, I would like the following to be the cause (though every care should be taken to ensure that I am sufficiently old and fragile before the sequence of events is initiated):

- Press: Initiate self-destruct sequence
- Fasten me securely in my wheelchair with a blanket over my knees
- Blindfold me and take me somewhere on Red Hills Road to a Dancehall session
- Pay Stone Love Sound System to play the latest dancehall music (there will be sufficient funds to cover these expenses from my Citibank Money Market account. See my will for details)
- Place me in my wheelchair in the centre of the dancehall, surrounded by ten to fifteen of the dancers that have placed 1st to 3rd in the Jamaican Dance Hall Queen contests over previous years. (Funds will also be left to compensate them for their services)
- Ensure that no paramedics are within ten miles of the location
- Have the Stone Love DJ select "Batty Rider" or "Punnaany Too Sweet"
- Have the girls begin to dance
- Remove my blindfold
- Do not come to my aid
- Let me rest in peace

Amen.

CHAPTER 34

The Day I Stopped Smoking

It was August 21. I was lying in bed feeling the soporific effects of lying in a bed in a hot room, smoking weed and reflecting on a life of little interest. Suddenly, in this state of stupor, I heard the shouts.

"Kenny! Kenny!! Come! Come quick! Martin! Martin! Come!!"

I jumped up quickly, shaking off the haze like a wet dog shaking off water, and started for the door. The shouting continued.

"Dem ketch him!!" (as in "they caught him"), "Dem ketch him bloodclaat!!" (as in "they caught him, expletive").

I heard my brother outside running and he was now also shouting, "Who? Who dem ketch?" In a small village where so little happened, anything exciting was a major event. This could be:

Two dogs 'doing it' and getting stuck while 'doing it'

The sight of Georgie's papa beating Georgie

The sight of Georgie's papa beating both mother and child at once (a rare excitement)

The sight of Georgie's papa coming home through the lane when Georgie was still playing with the other kids

Someone falling from a mango tree and breaking their limbs

The moaning sounds coming through the thin zinc walls of a house (this was often Shemoans, but sometimes other folks)

The ice cream van passing by (even though we didn't have enough money to buy the ice cream it was fun to run behind the van and, occasionally, the ice cream man would throw us an ice cream bar to share)

A really big event was when a thief was caught. (I have already described for you the series of exciting events that that entails). That day, they had caught someone. I was running behind the other kids shouting with my brother: "Who? Who dem ketch?" but the other kids were just laughing and running and telling us to come quickly. I thought it must either be a thief or a rapist. But what kind of thief? A goat thief? A chicken thief? Or, and my heart raced with excitement, could it have been a Blackheart Man? No one had ever caught a Blackheart Man before. Maybe this was why the other kids were not saying anything, maybe they had finally caught a Blackheart Man! The man that caught little children, cut out their hearts and stole their souls!

When I got there, I could see that they had someone tied up against the tree, but I could not see who it was, as a group of adults and other kids had already formed a circle around him. More specifically, my view was blocked by the mightily imposing rear end of my Aunt Frida who had never been small, honey.

Before I could get closer to see who it was I heard my uncle Bob's cold dry voice ask, "Whose heart you gonna steal now?" I then saw his machete rise and descend, before hearing the metal connect with bone. But there were no screams. I stopped in my tracks. There were no screams! No pleading for mercy! This could only be the Blackheart Man! My blood turned cold as I prepared to finally see this most dreaded creature.

Then I saw my uncle's hand rise again and begin to fall as he asked once more, "Whose mind will you now fill with ideas?" Chop! Chop!

I thought I must have heard wrong. Fill with ideas? I pushed hard to get between the crowd. All excitement had gone, replaced by a numbness as I looked towards the tree and saw him. Sitting there beneath the tree, hands tied cruelly tight behind his back. Looking blankly at us as my uncle's machete came slashing down, over and over again. I turned my back and walked away. There was nothing I could do for him and nothing he could do for me now. They were murdering The Incredible Hope, a superhero I had created. I abandoned him right there. I had learnt my lesson: the longer you continue to think that things that are impossible are merely improbable, the more you hurt yourself. So I bid farewell to The Incredible Hope. And in so doing, I knew I would never leave that *hateful* fucking place, never become somebody, never escape. I was born there, would grow up there, and would become an old incurable disease right there. I knew this with certainty. So I simply turned my back and left.

When I was young we used to smoke an awful lot of marijuana. There are, of course, many different ways to smoke weed. My favorite was the Chillum pipe, sometimes referred to as a Chalice. This was also a favored way for many Rastafarians in my country. The Chillum has a lot of things in common with the Sheesha or Hookah. There is a jar or bowl with water, a draw-pipe for inhalation, weed (or tobacco) and a source of heat. With the Chillum, like most other similar instruments, smoke bubbles through the water in the bowl, up through the pipe and into your lungs and your brain. Depending on what you smoke, how much of it you smoke, how frequently you smoke, and whether you have anything else to live for but to smoke, the effects on your mind can sometimes be awe-inspiring. And sometimes the depth of realism in the things that play out in your mind can be phenomenal. Images and memories of people come back in many different but vivid and colorful ways and forms. Often, one thing stands out intensely from an image or a memory, such as the softness in someone or some creature's eyes. It could be a fish or your mama.

It was on August 21 that I stopped smoking weed, and retired my Chillum pipe. I specifically remember because on that day, when I returned to lie in my bed, a little man about three-quarters of an inch tall, with a tiny pointy hat and a goatee, came and sat at the end of my pipe, looked me in the eyes and said to me, "You are not mad. I would not tell you this if it were not true. You must believe me." And, for the first time, I realized that I did not believe him. I also realized that sometimes we have to face the living and leave the dead, no matter how soft the look in their eyes. There are just some things that we must face. No one could get me to smoke again.

CHAPTER 35
Toes and Other Miscellaneous Things

Well it's Sunday night my love, but tomorrow this nigga will not need to get up and cut canes, or pick cottons or apples. Thanks to the efforts of my forefathers, I am free to sleep late, eat a nice breakfast, and select what projects I want to work on.

Now, let me take a moment to get a few miscellaneous things off my mind.

First, it doesn't matter how beautiful they may otherwise be, or how sexy the rest of their bodies are, women with long toes give me the heeby-jeebies! They absolutely freak me out! This is not particularly relevant to anything in this story, it is just a snippet of information I thought I would share with you while I am confiding so much else.

And while I am at it, let me also humbly suggest that since 9/11, US airport security has become an abomination unto the Lord.

Finally, seeing that there is no other place I can think of fitting this in, let me also ask the question here: why is it that children find it so hard to obey their parents? As I am sure you know very well, my love, it is written in the holy book:

> *"Children obey your parents in all things, for this is well pleasing unto the Lord."*

Ephesians 6, 1:4

The things that are written in the holy book were not written for our entertainment. Whether or not we believe they are the words of God, or words inspired by God, one thing is clear: they provide some of the best guidance on how to live a morally upright life.

My mind is full of questions. So many questions about what happened on those two days all those years ago. The first question, and I have chosen this one randomly because we need to start somewhere, is this: why the hell would Georgie not listen to, and obey his parents?

I start with this question because I am also not sure how much clearer their guidance could have been to Georgie, as it seemed quite clear to me.

"Do not play close to the fire!"

"Do not play with fire!"

"Do not play close to the pot while it is on the fire!"

Why would Georgie not listen to his papa? What was wrong with Georgie? Why would he not listen to anyone? Georgie's papa said he told Georgie not to play too close to the fire. Georgie's papa said that Georgie's mama also told Georgie not to play too close to the fire. Georgie's papa said that Georgie's sister further reminded Georgie not to play too close to the fire. And *still* Georgie would not listen. What the hell was wrong with that boy anyway? How many times should he have been told that a pot on the stove gets extremely hot? How many times should he have been told that coconut oil in a pot gets exceedingly hot? What the fuck was wrong with his hearing?

And how the hell did Georgie manage to burn himself in so many places? Did he need to burn himself twice before he started listening to and obeying his papa?

My final question is a small but important one: why the hell did Georgie suddenly decide not to fear his papa and start playing around, even while his papa was at home?

CHAPTER 36

Watching Dogs Die - 1

I watched him with hate in my eyes as he boiled the cornmeal with water, stirring it slowly, saying nothing. I watched him with hate as he placed the finely broken up pieces of glass into the pot and continued to stir. I watched him with hate as he seasoned the pot with salt and pepper and scallions. I watched him with hate as he cooled the cooked cornmeal and fed it to the two starving dogs, who ate the meal as though it was their last supper. Not knowing it was. Not understanding what was happening to them shortly after, as the pieces of glass bored holes in their intestines, and they slowly bled to death. Whimpering in pain while Georgie's papa stood there looking at them, silent and vengeful.

Georgie and I had stood there and watched.

We had often heard about what people did to cats and dogs that were alleged to have stolen things. Sometimes a dog or cat would, allegedly, steal food from a pot cooking on a stove outside. It was common to set all kinds of traps and poisons for stray cats, dogs, rats, and other animals and insects.

Seeing Georgie's papa apply his remedy changed my view on our cultural practice altogether. Not because his actions confirmed that there was no 'innocent until proven guilty', but because a part of me knew that he was the kind of person who would do the same thing to a human.

CHAPTER 37

Watching Dogs Die - 2

Believe as much or as little of this as you choose Semicolon – you cannot go wrong either way.

It was, in all respects, a good day up until then. I had spent some time with my sisters. I had eaten some of their Sunday fried chicken and rice and was content, and felt no particular self-loathe. Largely because I was leaving there. Leaving that *hateful* fucking place. That hateful village where I grew up. That nasty hateful community. That horrendous hateful neighborhood where I could never breathe. Leaving there. Going back to Kingston, to my little room in a little house. My own room.

I was driving. In a small Suzuki car I had saved for and got quite cheaply from a lady who was leaving what she considered to be that hateful country. That nasty hateful country. She just wanted to leave, come hell or high water. Leave that hateful car in that hateful country. This was at a time when things had gone far downhill in our country. I got the car very cheap.

I was on the highway. Leaving that hateful place. I was twenty-eight years old at the time. Easily recalled because there were four of them, and in mathematical terms $8 \div 2 = 4$. And I had a 2 and an 8 in my age, and there were four of them.

The radio was on. In those days cars were being imported secondhand from Japan with all the manuals and instruments on the instrument panel written in Japanese. Noodles, Rice, Sushi vs. Jerk Pork, Curried Goat, Oxtail, all over again. Without a band expander, you could only pick up radio stations below the 89.9 frequency. That was only one station. The same one I was listening to. Two other cars were behind me, one a taxi.

A small car appeared in my rear view mirror. At a distance it was quiet, I could only hear the murmur of an old deserted river in its engine. I looked in front of me at the road, and then I glanced back again. Immediately I felt as though someone's breath was tingling the hair on the back of my neck. The car was coming fast. For a moment I felt my heart, my mind and my song, stop.

In the desert-like haze of the boiling-hot, mid-day road, I saw that vehicle coming like a phantom, with the quiet and determined power of a Porsche on the German Autobahn. This was no puppy-powered car. The beast beneath its hood was full-grown, hungry, and snarling its way down the road, chewing up the asphalt.

My heart started to race just the way it often did when I was a child on those dark nights with no street lamps, when little bumps crawled on my skin and I thought I felt the presence of a spirit.

In an instant it appeared a few hundred yards behind me. It was still in the outer lane. I could tell that the driver had positioned himself to overtake the cars behind me and my car, at the same time. And he had decided this long in advance.

Then the car appeared alongside mine.

It was new. They were young. It was red. They were four. It was turbocharged. So were they. It was a Toyota. Small. And it was loud. Vroom. Vroom. Vroom. Loud. Boom. Boom. Boom. Loud. They were singing, screeching, shouting, laughing, loud. All four boys, with the windows partially down, in that turbocharged little car moving with a ferocity unbecoming of a vehicle that beautiful and that small. It was a Toyota Starlet. A car our dancehall singers said in their songs was "easy to drive, but plays hard to get" because even though it was so small, it was fucking expensive. These must be rich kids. In their expensive race car.

There was a sudden silence that told me that something was

wrong. Then the driver looked at me, stared straight into my eyes, and frantically gesticulated for me to do something. Ahead of us another car was coming. After it came closer I saw that it was a Hyundai sedan, plate number BB1897. I realized that they had misjudged the ability of their little turbocharged car to overtake us. And that the taxi behind me, who had not taken kindly to being overtaken, had in true Jamaican fashion, accelerated to prevent them from getting back into the lane behind me. And that they had wanted me to slow down to give them room to pull in. But it was then too late.

I remember the spot where it happened:

It was close to the big billboard with the four teenagers, two boys and two girls, looking healthy but eating Burger King hamburgers and fries and drinking Pepsi.

We had passed the sign earlier that read *Undertakers love Overtakers*.

We had passed the overhead bridge in Sandy Bay where the police often laid in wait to issue speeding tickets.

But we hadn't yet gotten to the cane fields. I would have remembered that, for cane is sweet.

These things I remember. Along with the stories we used to hear about race cars. About rich kids who raced their turbocharged Starlets and Mitsubishi Lancers at popular race tracks. Some added additional power and speed by combining Nitro with their already turbocharged engines. I had never seen such a car; never heard that whistling wheeze of Nitro combined with the horrendous roar of a turbocharged engine.

But I had recognized it the moment this car appeared in my rear view mirror, moving with its deathly grace.

In the eternity of a few seconds, I watched the two unstoppable forces coming at each other. A blazing-fast Hyundai sedan confronting a ferocious Toyota Starlet. Neither could stop even if they wanted to. What should have happened? At the time, there was no time to think. But it is a question I have asked myself many times and for many years since.

I have never been able to find the right answer because of the speed and position of the two cars. What did happen? They both swerved off the road, at the same time, in the same direction. The crash was cosmic. Metal, flesh, glass, bones, tyres, clothes. Bits and pieces of it all, and so much blood, everywhere.

I felt the crash. Felt it the way Georgie must have felt his papa's fist crashing into his face with the force of a machine part-Ferrari and part-jet.

The four were there one minute, staring at me with panic in their eyes, then they were all gone.

Perhaps it was because my foot had, accidentally, hit the accelerator when I was trying to slow down to let them pass.

Chapter 38

I Have Long Wanted to be a Writer

My love, I once tried to write beautiful poetry. I wanted to write like Shelly (although he has a girlie name for a guy), Tennyson, Byron and Shakespeare. This is the best I came up with:

"Awakening"

We were born to sing Hebrew hymns
until the mocking bird's chirp pecked from our flesh
bewildered worms that opened their eyes
and showed us a dream of serpents
measuring their bodies against our souls
that stretched for centuries like a bridge
over troubled waters that swelled
and washed ashore radioactive seeds
that sprouted lions that sang and danced
for hamburgers, baked chicken tenders
mini carrots, ziti, warm spiced apples, saag paneer,
sweet and sour chicken-
then they reposed as trunks of Maple trees,
and jackals wept with laughter sweet
sipping syrupy blood

that honeyed the chords
they climbed to reach on high
where they sang
while the lions rested
and dreamt of hills and gold.

Undated journal entry

But oh the problems with trying to be poetic! No one understands poetry! And the beauty of poetry gets lost in the mundane.

More importantly, my love, I decided not to write verses like these because I realized I really did not want to be a poet. Poets are poor.

I am not a poet,
And I hope you knoet,
For a poet is often pooreth.

I wanted to be a writer and become very successful. This, I thought, would earn me lots of money, which would make me gyrate wildly in glee.

This is why I wanted to be a writer.

While we are on the subject, I have always been captivated by the comments of critics on the inside pages of books I have read. I doubt very much that I will ever provide a review for someone else's book, so I once decided to do one for my own. I had a title for a book: *Sometimes I think what I needed was a better dog*. This is the review I wrote for it:

"Sometimes I think what I needed was a better dog" combines the
pathos and gut-wrenching emotional punch of Edwige Danticat's
"Breathe, Eyes, Memories" and Augusten Burroughs "Running
with Scissors", the wit and wry humor of Frank McCourt's "Angela's

*Ashes", the simplicity of language and style of Kurt Vonnegut's
"The Slaughterhouse Five", the courageous un-conventionalism
of Richard Brautigan's "Trout Fishing in America", the get-the-hell-
away-from-me-that-can't-be-true eerie authenticity of Khaled
Hosseini's "The Kite Runner", and the unapologetic lack of brevity
of any of Shakespeare's works. Yet this is a novel that manages to
stand alone as a thoroughly unique and remarkably brilliant piece.
And at only $14.95 the paperback price is a phenomenal bargain.*

If only I could have gotten the New York Times to write this! What
an achievement that would be my love! Especially the comparison with
Shakespeare. Hahaha. I know, however, that after reading my critique of
my own book they would be more likely to write something pithy like:

There is little modesty where much is needed.

Signed: New York Times critic

Or they may offer their own review, which would be equally pithy
and sarcastic. Perhaps something like this:

*It is awfully easy to read, and awfully hard to forget its dreadful
awfulness.*

Signed: New York Times critic

And that would be that, and nothing more than that.
So, knowing this, I revised my review to something more subdued:

*"Sometimes I think what I needed was a better dog" leaves you
with the feeling of someone picking the scabs off an unhealed sore,*

flinching at the pain, but continuing to laugh and joke.

I reckoned this is what I would say in the cover letter to the publisher.

I also thought that a US paperback price of US$14.95 would be a good price, and that if my book were to become hugely successful then I would make lots of money. This would make me giddy with happiness. I could see my wallet finally becoming heavier than my conscience, or, at least, balancing it. I penned a verse for this:

"Blessed Equilibrium"

Oh blessed equilibrium!
Should that day ever come -
when my wallet weighs as much as my conscience,
filled with dollars and not with cents.

CHAPTER 39

The Bush People

"Repentance"

Some secrets we take
to our grave,
some we confess
if we are brave,
and I am,
deeply sorry,
for that one.

Come out come out wherever you are. Here little memory... come on out now. Come on over here. I can almost see you...

Ah, Semicolon my love, sometimes the memories that hurt bury themselves deep within you and refuse to cooperate when you want to introduce them to others. They lie hidden, concealed, kept quiet like the plight of Sudan. Sometimes they will come out like Latinos at a soccer match in the Orange Bowl, and at other times they stay securely hidden, like the truth at a Congressional Hearing. But this one will come out at some point. I am sure. Patience is everything, as my good old Uncle Bob used to say.

Anyway, this all brings us back to Aunt Frida, Uncle Bob, and the beatings.

A little about them:

Aunt Frida

Aunt Frida wasn't actually my aunt, but we had to refer to the common-law partners of our uncles as Aunt this or Aunt that. And, now in her early thirties, she happened to have been the one to stay the longest with Uncle Bob, so she came to be seen as a part of our family. She was not just fat but fluffy. And hefty. If she were on the Moon and I on Planet Earth, I suspect that only then we would both weigh roughly the same. I used to just sit and watch my Aunt Frida, for she was truly an impressive, eye-filling woman to look at. Sometimes I would find myself involuntarily breathing in sync with her, because when a person is that fat you see every breath that their body heaves to take. But I liked her a lot, and she would often tell me stories.

She was a housewife, to the extent that we can say someone is any form of a *wife* if she has no husband - and it was always clear that he would never marry her, but more on this in a moment.

She wasn't cute.

She always looked around her to see if someone might be hiding behind her hugeness, as she didn't like being taken by surprise.

She was barren. Some mango trees are not made to produce mangoes, some people's brains are not meant to produce ideas and some women's wombs are not meant to carry little crying packages. At least, Uncle Bob said she was barren. Now, we know that Donkey can bray, can run, can carry heavy loads, can pull carts and do many things. But Donkey can't put pot on fire and cook himself a meal. And while he might be out there thinking about it right now (who knows what Donkey thinks about), it is still the same: he simply cannot cook. And it is fine, people still call him Donkey. Aunt Frida couldn't have kids, he said, but instead of calling her Frida he called her *mule*. And she couldn't read and write too well, he said, so instead of calling her Frida, he called her *jackass*. And it appeared that the more he did this the more she gave up on her struggle for self-worth - and for every ounce of pride she lost, she gained it back in flesh.

Uncle Bob

I have already told you a little about my Uncle Bob. Good old Uncle Bob. He was no hunk of a man, indeed, as a man, he was as poorly-made as rum punch in a North American hotel. Constantly farting and burping and rubbing his stomach. Short and stocky. The hair in his nose and ears slowly and sinisterly encroaching on his face, betraying ambitions for empire. Eerily simian in both manner and appearance. In brief, an atheist would have a strong hand if he pointed to good old Uncle Bob and asked any Christian, "Is this man made in the image of your God?"

Unrequited love: he loved money badly, but money wanted to have nothing to do with him.

I highlight these things about my Uncle Bob simply to point out that if this man had ever had kids, they would never have wanted him to walk them to school. And also, so that you might know that it was not always going to be easy for him to find young, healthy-looking, attractive women. He therefore took what he could find, and they were always fat women with low self-esteem.

The two together

There is a universal truth that is relevant to their relationship: we know that to a man who has a lot (money, charm, good looks, power) a woman will often become peripheral (cheated on, taken for granted, etc.) Similarly, to a man who has too little, a woman will often become abused. This is, of course, part of the reason the great philosophers argued so passionately that democracy depended on a large middle-class of ordinary people with ordinary means. Because where there are extremes, things tend to fall apart. And here we had two extremes living together. The result was barbaric. Another universal truth may help us to understand why: the good stuff in us, like tolerance and understanding, can be stretched to their limits; but the bad stuff, like cruelty, can't. As such, there was no ending to his beatings and cruelty.

Every so often the quarrelling would begin. She, loud and boisterous; he watching the air escape from the crack in her face. Then when it was all over, when evening had come, when the rest of us had gone to our beds, the beatings began.

Hear her scream. Whack, whack, whack. Hear her sob. Sob, sob, sob.

Night after night. As boys we wondered why she never just sat on him and put him out of his misery. Why she, with her titanic self, allowed him to beat her so badly without putting up any form of a fight.

Then the day came when they had their last quarrel. And in the midst of it she alleged that she was not barren. Pause. Ponder.

Yes. She was not barren. He was.

The few words I caught and which everyone else caught were, "Why yu badda fuck if yu fuck like fart?" Translated: "It is better not to have fucked than to have fucked and for your fuck to have been just like a fart in the wind."

Said he was a 'one-minute' man. Pause. Puzzle. Wonder.

Said he produced no sperm (which was later confirmed.)

He did not wait for the evening to come.

When she left that same day she could have carried her bags by herself, but it was far less painful to have someone else carry them for her. She could have walked by herself, but it was far less painful to let others help her. And she could have said her own goodbye to all of us, but why run the risk of opening her mouth and have something else fall out?

I mention these events only because I believe they connect to another matter of even greater consequence. To Millicent and the things we least expected. This is what I wrote about that event:

"The things we least expect"

The child Robert had come out of his mother's womb looking as normal as any other child; laughed when he was tickled, squealed when thrown in the air, and wet his cloth diapers with appropriate frequency. His early years were also lived in the form of an ordinary boy: shooting birds, chasing chickens, pushing other kids in the river, playing 'doctor' with the girls, eating mangoes, and faking a swoon at the sight of delicacies such as spicy jerk pork, curried crabs, cotton candies, and the plump coochie of a ripening cousin. He laughed riotously and indiscreetly at the latter. Robust, healthy, full of laughter, mischief, and worms; he was nothing out of the ordinary, from what the Old Timers said. I cannot, of course, confirm any of this because at the time I wasn't yet born, and therefore what I learnt about his youth was through second-hand gossip.

The mark then appeared, on his penis, when he was thirteen. According to what the Old Timers say, as I wasn't there, and I have never personally seen his instrument. But this is one of the few details all the Old Timers were quite certain of - it appeared at the age of thirteen. If you sat with Grandma, listened to her stories as she ate her fried pig's skin and drank her strong coffee with a pinch of salt, she'd say the mark was about the size of a farthing, for she still related better to the British currency once used in this one-time colony. She also felt we never deserved independence, which she saw as possibly the worst thing to have happened to us.
Uncle Jeremiah, however, being more modern but equally illiterate,

would have described the mark as being more the size of a nickel. He had no problems with the change to American colonisers. In any event, both described the mark as roughly the same size. The Old Timers also said that it looked like a pinkish layer of second skin.

Everyone knew what it was the moment they saw it - and they all saw it, because the boy was taken by one of his uncles on a parade to consult with each of the elders. He had hoped that they would have allayed his fears. But it was what it was, no mistaking it.

Everyone knew, but no one said a word about it to his mother. She had already suffered much throughout her life, they said; had had every last one of her opinions slapped out of her by her man, the boy Robert's father, before he died. She was therefore pitied as one of those who would eventually go back to the 'Master of the House' with regrets that she had not used the talents she had been given, and had nothing at all to show of her life. They thought at the time that she probably had another seventeen years or so of cooking, cleaning, and washing left in her, and no one in the village wanted to ruin these remaining years by confronting her with something everyone already knew to be obvious.

And it was obvious. That an Evil thing had come to the village; had chosen the boy Robert's one-room, one-bed, one-chair, one-set-of-sheets, one-window house; had waited until nightfall; had crawled into the bed with the thirteen year old boy while he slept, and had tasted his flesh. The mark was there, and there was no doubt about what had happened or, what it would lead to.

By 1978 the look was already on his face. 'Odd' or 'strange' are appropriate words you could use to describe a politician visiting your neighborhood outside of election season. But we had no words for the look on Mr Robert Lovelace's face as he sat there watching us kids play every day. Unshaved, unkempt, unwashed, and reeking as foul as a lawyer's fart. Always there, with a darkened, unlit stick of ganja, like a foetus' limb, growing from the side of his mouth. We were, also, absolutely convinced that things were growing inside his hair that were mature enough to speak to you and try to touch you if you came close.

It started in 1985. Old Timers say that those were some of the hardest days lived since our forefathers were freed from slavery. In the statements from the Ministry of Finance, the country was undergoing a major recession; in our village not only mangoes but whores were being sold two for the price of one. Indeed the most productive part of a man's day back then was when he took a crap, as that was the only time he saw the fruits of his labor. But we were boys then; the days were long, the rivers were cool, every fruit tree belonged to us, and the sweetest things in life were sucking on an East Indian mango or a young girl's breasts.

Millicent was only nine years old in 1985. She too had a distinguishing mark, but hers was made by man, not by the devil. She had lost an eye while watching a group of us boys play cricket in the yard. I was there, and saw what happened. The hard cricket ball was struck with force, and connected with the soft tissues to the right of her nose. These things were considered lamentable in those days, but no great tragedy – after all, no one had any illusions that Millicent (or any of us for that matter) would one day need both eyes for medical or legal school. The issue for debate three months after she lost her eye was whether, with both, she would have been better able to see what was about to happen to her.

On the day it happened, she was wearing a pair of
old Reebok sneakers (also sent by a relative from abroad), a pretty
sunflower dress, and the African continent on her ears - these
were the early '80s when Black Power and 'Back to Africa' were still
important to her mother, who had put those earrings on her.

The group of us younger boys were there on that day; playing
dominoes, eating cane, and discussing issues that would never
affect Chinese foreign policy. When Martin came bolting from
the bushes and straight down the lane into the yard heading
towards us, screaming and shouting, it was clear that he was not
just looking for attention or the fame of being the first to break
some news. The morsels of exciting everyday news were brought
simmering in a rich, saucy stew to the rest of us by whoever was
the first to find out from the elders. When Martin ran to the yard,
fell to the ground (though he wasn't Pentecostal), and released the
scream that still curdles my blood today, we knew, we all knew, that
it announced something unexpected and unimaginably awful.

K. Lovelace, short story, 1995

I used their real names, because by then everyone knew what had happened.

It wasn't a Thursday. It was a Saturday. A Saturday evening to be precise. She still had one eye, which I reckoned was fine, for she really didn't have much to look at in her life. As I've described, our parents would normally send us kids out a couple of times a day to the shops to buy items for breakfast and dinner. Breakfast: 2 eggs, ¼ bread, big jill of cooking oil, 2 cigarettes. Beg some sugar from such and such. Dinner: 2 lbs chicken back, 1 lb flour, 2 tomatoes, 2 cigarettes. Beg some ice to cool the lemonade from such and such. And of course we were always warned not to take the shorter route through the bushes because "Short cut draws blood". Because *Blackheart* Men would catch us in the bushes and cut out our hearts.

I could make this long, and I could describe the color of the houses, the leaves on the trees, the things we saw as we walked and so on. But none of these descriptive details have anything to do with what happened. So, I will make what could be a long story, short.

It was late evening, we had finished playing games, and Uncle Bob was still sitting in front of his house where he had been watching us. About thirty minutes later, Millicent's mama sent her to the shop to buy things for their dinner. Not long after, mama sent my brother to the same shop to do the same - get things for our house. As I later found out, he took the short cut through the bushes. He did it because he was older and less afraid. While on his way he heard the muffled crying sounds and went off the beaten track through the bushes to see what was happening.

Our lives were simple, in those days. The bushes were a source of fascination. With daylight and other boys as your companion, they were a place of excitement. A place where you went to hunt birds, pick mangoes and to cook dumplings and chicken back. Those were simple times - when we rarely saw cars, and had no telephones, one television, no computers, no refrigerators, no electricity and no running water. Our lives were made up of simple deeds – folks went to the farms and worked, and then to the market to sell what they produced. They came home at 5 p.m. and were in bed by 8 p.m. And you simply had one set of good clothes that you mainly wore to church; one school uniform that you washed a couple times during the week; one room to live in with everyone else; and one set of teeth to serve you for life (there were no prospects for implants, bridges, porcelain veneers, crowns and such.) You also had one hope for making it out of our Depression – a US visa, and one aim in life – to win the lotto.

The bushes held birds, mosquitoes, herbal remedies, unnamed fruits, uncharted paths, giant lizards, and the magic of childhood. They weren't pruned into parks and riding paths and implanted with play areas. For, as I said, these were simple days - before American fast food chains started to open up all over the place like cheap whores. The bushes were simply, bush.

In those days, no one ever died from a natural cause or accident - the explanation was simple: there was some form of evil spirit at work, usually brought on by someone who envied or hated the deceased. Illnesses had no medical names. My aunt lived her life with a 'bad heart', not coronary disease, and when her number was called up in heaven, she simply 'just dropped down dead' – there was no 'massive cardiopulmonary failure'. A sharp pain in your side that lingered for a few days was never seen as a risk of a rupturing appendix, but as reason for a relative to offer a hot cup of tea to get rid of the 'bad gas' that was inside of you. My grandpa's mind played magic tricks with thoughts and ideas - there was no understanding of senility. And a man who became "good for nothing" (currently referred to as "impotent") had no Viagra to look forward to, but rather twenty bags of shame to hang around his neck, as there was no place for such people in our land of majestic cocks and tight clits.

In those simple times, simple folks followed a simple path: you were born, grew strong, worked the farms, grew old, transformed into a *curable only if you have money* disease, died, and got buried in a place acceptable to your spirit.

And the people themselves:

Level of intellectual curiosity: about what?

Views on ideas: out with the new, in with the old!

Level of awareness: you could say, "They can tell the difference between a horse and an elephant." But you would not say, "They can, *of course*, tell the difference between a horse and an elephant." For these are two very different things.

Views towards education: pie in the sky, radar, gyroscope, horse shit.

We were the people of the bushes.

And, Semicolon, lots of things happened in the bushes. Let me tell you about Tiny Tim for instance.

They had a machete! They had a fucking sharp machete! And they were not talking!

His name was Timothy, but everyone called him Tiny Tim. This is not because of the character in that book by Charles Dickens, *A Christmas Carol*. It was because, as I have explained before, he had a dick that was huge. We have certain peculiar traditions in rural Jamaica, one of which is to give people nicknames that are the opposite of what they are. So a relative who is 6 ft 5 in tall may be called "Shorty". And a man who everyone knows to be as corrupt as the devil will popularly be known as "god". This is the same way, "You nasty, dirty, stinking vulture, what the fuck are you doing here?" would be seen as a warm and endearing greeting, signifying, "My dearest friend, you cannot imagine how happy I am to finally see you again!" For these expressions, in all respects offensive to others, were the kinds of expressions that flowed easily from the blood and bond shared by people who lived closely together in those yards. And so Timothy became Tiny Tim. A boy with a manhood.

Tiny Tim was my cousin. This should not surprise you, as I am sure by now you realize that I had A LOT of cousins.

People thought it was evident that he must have descended from a line of African kings or mighty warriors, because he had all the marks of such illustrious ancestry: namely, he was black as hell, strong, fierce, and had a monstrous dick for a boy nine years old.

It was therefore also self-evident that the destiny of such a child was not playing out as it should. While the other children ran and played in the rain and the mud, Tiny Tim was confined to his room heaving and wheezing with asthma. Confined to a space so small, a house so small, a room so small, a future so small, whenever the evil spirits attacked him. And this, a descendant of warriors who roamed the vast African savannahs to hunt for wild meat!

It was therefore equally self-evident that Tiny Tim had to be cured. First, his parents tried the certainties of science – they enlisted all the doctors who would take payment in cash and kind (chickens mostly), or allow monthly payments. They tried the longest needles, the bitterest medicines, the biggest pills. And I suspect they also took him to 'doctors' who had nothing but a Phd dissertation on *The lifestyle of young brown rats that live on the east bank of the River Nile during the first half of the rainy season*. In any event, nothing worked. Which was fine, because few believed in the certainties of science anyway.

Having tried the white man science, it was now time to try a bit of black man science. The science born from the knowledge of a parallel universe, that their ancestors brought with them on the slave ships that crossed the Atlantic.

They started with the secret healing powers in the leaves and barks of countless flowers and trees. Sometimes boiled together, sometimes separately. None of them worked.

Next they tried rats. They sent the rest of us kids like warriors to hunt and catch rats to cure Tiny Tim. These were not ordinary rats. Not the ordinary rats that lived in the dirty wooden houses with all the stresses of rent and utility bills. No, these were the rats that lived like Rastafarians, pure and clean. The rats that lived in the canefields. Rats that looked happy like this:

Tradition had it that only the soup made from such rats could cure children with asthma. This is the rat soup that Tiny Tim drank, time and time again. (For anyone who may be living in high society and thinking that this was child abuse, I ask you to remember that these were no ordinary rats. These were clean, vegetarian rats. Besides, I have now learnt that people in other countries eat things that are far more disgusting than rats.)

Unfortunately this did not work either. The way I heard it, different things worked for different kids. It was not that no child had ever been cured by the leaves or the barks of trees or the rats. Some had been. It was just a matter of finding the right cure for Tiny Tim. Maybe it was the African warrior in him, but he was a brave and willing subject for their on-going experiments.

They then took him to the Obeahman. Obeahmen's houses always had a big red flag flying on a long stick in the front of the yard to make it easy for everyone to know where to find them. The Obeahman gave Tiny Tim a bath in a big bucket in the yard. In public. I was made to understand by an older cousin that this was to wash away all the evil that clinged to his outside. Such as any Baby or Coolie Duppies hanging on to his neck or riding on his back. And to wash away all bad luck. Then he was taken inside the little Obeah house for the remainder of the rituals and chants - for the killing of the rooster, the draining of the blood, the mixing of the intestines of toads and other things more disgusting than rats. And for the drinking of some new concoction. I believe Tiny Tim had by then drunk every concoction made from every leaf and every belief. He was made pure inside and out. Then he was given a special charm made from the solid parts of the concoction that he had drunk. And was told to have it on him every second of every minute of every hour of everyday for as long as he lived, or wished to live. For this was a charm to keep evil spirits away. And evil spirits were fast. It would take them less than a second to see that he was unprotected and reattach themselves to him. And suck his air out of him. And give him back his asthma.

It was evident that the Obeahman they took Tiny Tim to was not very powerful because, within a month, his asthma came back. Though I must say that some folks, specifically those who recommended that particular Obeahman, are still of the view, even today, that the asthma only came back because Tiny Tim must have taken off his charm at some time during that month. Even for a second.

So, now they had a machete. They had a glistening sharp machete and they were not talking. I had seen my Uncle Bob sharpening that machete a few days before, which had not struck me as anything peculiar because I had seen many of my uncles sharpening their machetes many times before. He had spent a longer time than normal sharpening his machete. But this too had not concerned me. For I knew the difference between

(a) how sharp a machete had to be when my uncle was just going to the field and needed to chop away bushes from in front of him, or to chop a coconut off a tree to get a drink of cool coconut water, and

(b) how sharp it had to be when my uncle was going to slaughter a goat or a pig.

If it was (b), he would spend much more time sharpening his machete.

This machete was sharpened for (b). My uncle had it in his hands and they were all walking into the bushes, with Tiny Tim's mama holding his hand. No one was talking. Tiny Tim was scared. I will get back to this in a minute, but it is important that you know that at that point he was really really really really scared. So was I. Other kids were following the group of adults going into the bushes and I decided to do the same.

It started to rain.

They were still walking.

They were still not talking.

The machete was still fucking sharp.

I was worried for Tiny Tim and started to wonder about what he was wondering about. I thought that under the circumstances it may have been reasonable for him to be worried shit-stiff. Worried that he had been a disappointment to his family and his ancestors. Worried that they were no longer content to leave him alone with his shame and his wheeze to die a slow but certain death.

While he worried, they walked. In silence. In the rain. When we got deep into the bushes they eventually stopped beside a Cedar tree. When it rains the Cedar tree, for those of you who are not familiar with the smell of trees, is perhaps the worst-smelling tree that the Almighty created.

Uncle Bob took Tiny Tim's hand from his mama, led him away from the rest of us, and placed him underneath the Cedar tree.

Tiny Tim made no effort to escape. No effort to run. I could understand why. He had brought so much shame to his family with all his wheezing and being confined to the house and his failure to allow himself to be cured, that to bring further shame by being a coward when it was time to account for his deeds, would have been unthinkable. Either that or the fear of being disciplined by his papa if he failed to do what was required was greater than the fear of whatever fate awaited him underneath that Cedar tree.

Then, in the next moment, the only words that would be spoken, were spoken. They came out of the mouth of Uncle Bob, who had the machete in his hand. These were the only words he spoke:

"Stand still bwoy!"

He had his left hand holding Tiny Tim firm against the tree. He then swung his right hand with the machete away from Tiny Tim. I saw the blade as it arched through the air, slightly upward, slicing the rain drops with precision. Then I saw Tiny Tim's eyes. There was such fear in his eyes. Pure fear, cold, dark and shivering, shining in his eyes as the machete swung sharply back towards his head, and my uncle's left hand let go of his body. Tiny Tim stood motionless and firm against the tree. Only his eyes were trembling.

The machete slashed deeply into the Cedar tree about 10 centimers above Tiny Tim's head.

There was silence. For everyone else this was momentary. Then they began to talk. And from the chatter I learnt that what my uncle had just done was perform an ancient medical ritual referred to as "chopping someone under a tree". The ritual was considered an effective way of curing asthma. The belief was that as the tree grew, the cut would rise, and, as it rose, the asthma would also rise and leave the body of the child. I thought to myself that the cure probably worked because they would have scared the shit and the asthma out of Tiny Tim. It turned out that they did. So this magic actually fixed the asthma as Tiny Tim never had another attack. He also did not speak to anyone for an entire week. A similar thing happened with my brother on the day he heard the muffled sounds and saw Millicent in the bushes.

When my brother came out of the bushes he came straight home, and he did not speak. He hadn't bought the things that mama had sent him to buy. He stood on the veranda and squirmed, and we could see that something inside him was squirming as well.

I think that is when it happened. When things came unhinged. But I am not sure.

He never spoke about what happened or what he had seen. When Millicent was brought back from the bushes she also never spoke about what had happened. But everyone knew, and knew it was the now lonely, horny, evil Uncle Robert (Bob) Lovelace who did it. A few days later she was sent to live with a relative in Kingston.

I heard very little about what became of her after that. In those days I often thought of her like a spaceship on an inter-galactic voyage that gets lost in another universe, and which starts to encounter engine problems, losing all power, then drifts quietly off into empty space.

I never told her story before, but I should have.

CHAPTER 40

A land of Crotches and Clits

Dear Semicolon,

When I awake I am often wet. My dreams are rivers that run in hues of red, coursing through the caverns of my skin, staining my bones with un-bleachable grief. When I awake I am often drenched, by noiseless rivers of throbbing sweat, and I see waters flooding insects and their genetic stench from beneath dark fingernails.

What do these dreams mean, Semicolon?

Love,

Kenny

Journal entry, June, 2011

Here is one thing that we know: beauty often beats the brain, and certainly trounces ugly, over and over again. In this way things, at their essence, always remain the same.

Mr Roper was already fifty years old when he told me that he had never learnt to ride a bike. By then his hair was almost completely gray, and he showed a certain bias towards one foot when he walked. I sometimes watched him walking down the lane as he came to look for my papa. The two of them often stood by the side of the house and smoked. In a way I suspected that they also spoke, but a conversation between them is something I never witnessed.

He still came by to visit after my papa passed away. My sister would see him coming and say, "Look, Mr Acne is coming," because she thought he popped up often and was unwanted. Initially I suspect he came around because he thought it was expected of him, but then I realized that it had become a part of him. They had known each other for more years than I knew, even before I was born, and had built a bond from smoking and drinking together.

One day he told me that there are some things in life that a man should not try to learn when he is already old and his bones are brittle. "Like learning to ride a bike," he said. "Or to cheat," I finished for him in my mind. In his own way he explained to me that when older people learn new things they, like everyone else, will make mistakes, and that they will sometimes get hurt. But when you are already old the hurt will sit in your bones and endure right through to the end of your days.

I was never sure who she was, but I knew that the pain Mr Roper felt long after his wife of thirty plus years, Missus Lorine, left him, was not in any way associated with his bad knee or with falling from a bike. People thought it could not possibly be true, as he claimed, that it was the first time he had cheated on Missus Lorine. But even so, whether it was the first or last, the view was unanimous that she should not have left him for something as stupid as that.

In some parts of Indonesia people call the crawfish a cheating shrimp (*udang selingkuh*) because fable has it that a crab and a shrimp once mated and gave birth to this cross-breed creature that looks like a shrimp but has a crab's claws. The crawfish was born this way they say, and cannot help itself. Like stinging was for the scorpion in the story with the frog, cheating was something that was simply "in our nature."

The sex of my youth was not poetically crafted, or based on

312

knowledge acquired from college classes on literature. It was coarse and crude, and it was frequent and everywhere. You would need a supercomputer to keep track of who was sleeping with whom, as the combinations and permutations were too many. And so we lived in our land of warm crotches and clits, majestic cocks and dicks, firm nipples and tits, honeyed tongues and lips.

A consequence of all of this was the frequent cases of mistaken identity.

There was a form of mistaken identity commonly referred to as a 'jacket'. When a woman gave birth to a child, and her husband or partner was fooled into thinking that the child was his, it was said that the husband received a 'jacket'. At ten years old I knew many husbands and partners who had mistaken the identity of their children. By the way, I should point out that establishing identity was often one of the hardest things to figure out. What could have been more complex? The meaning of life? Nopes! Easy. Just live each day as if it were your last and you had no idea what will happen when you die. Compare to that: "Bwoy, who is your real father?" Try that on for size! Take all the time in the world you need to try and figure it out. No rush.

In some cases these 'jackets' were easy to spot. For example, there was a *blacker than Marassa and Midnight* woman who lived with her pitch-black boyfriend and worked as a housekeeper at the only proper local hotel. She gave birth to a fair-skinned son with curly hair and the soft, blue eyes of angels and demons. It was obvious to all that this was a 'jacket'. What makes this case so interesting, however, is the fact that the woman was able to convince her boyfriend that the child was his. She convinced him that the color of the skin and eyes was due to the traces of Scottish blood that the papa carried in his genes from some distant ancestors. So the papa reminded folks that his surname, Campbell, was Scottish.

It was also easy to spot the 'jackets' when two Indians gave birth to a pitch-black child, or two whites a black. But it wasn't always so easy. For instance, when two blacks had a black child. Unless there was some distinguishing feature, it could sometimes be very hard to tell whether this was a jacket. It was easier when the two blacks were very short and their son turned out to be over 2 meters tall, or when two blacks with cute button noses went strolling around with a son with a monstrous nose spreading like thyme across his face. But, as I have said, you didn't always have such hints and clues. Besides, even if you knew there was a jacket, it was another thing entirely to tell which of the two brothers and the three other men having sex with the same woman at about the same time, was the father of the child.

There were also frequent cases of mistaken intentions. Take Garnet and Taniesha for example.

[By the way, it is perhaps time to do a quick check in on Garnet's son. There he is: eleven years old, walking now with a group of boys behind him, and carrying a bigger 'ratchet' knife and a little artificial gun stuck in his waist. He is black, poor and in the ghetto, so at this point in time his options in life are either prison or sports. But he is coming along fine so far, coming along just fine. Head now full of stories about how his uncle, Tommy, was murdered by some driver who worked for a rich man, and how his papa was brutalized by that same rich man owning the ice factory. Coming along fine.]

As he got older Garnet stopped referring to himself as a 'girls man' and became a 'womanaire', claiming to have been with a million women. But we shall use only one of the million to illustrate. Based on what Garnet said, this is what happened:

He said that she was a virgin. She was in fact a virgin. *So far, nothing to mistake.*

He said he took her to a cheap little brothel because, "Man not supposed to spend too much money on pussy." (I have often felt that if he had the option he would have tallied up everything – brothel, food, taxi, etc. – and tried to split the overall cost of the fuck with her.) *She mistook the identity of the brothel for a cozy little place where they could be alone and have a special time together.*

He said he brought a CD with him that was full of "fuck music", also known as songs to "drop woman panty". *She mistook the identity of the CD for a collection of nice romantic songs that he had personally put together for them.*

He said he only wanted to fuck her because he hadn't fucked a virgin before. Said it looked as if her coochie was so tight it must be squeezing her. He didn't really want a child, just a fuck to loosen up the tightness she was suffering. [We may contrast this with his pursuit of Marsha whose belly, he thought, was just too flat and needed something in it. Which is why he invited her home and gave her a drink and a child. Besides, he thought that at fifteen she needed her own family.] *Taniesha mistook his interest in her for a sense that she was special because of who she was and because she was smart and going to school.*

He said he chiseled into her coochie hard with his tool. *She might have mistaken this for inexperience and excitement.*

He said he told her that she was special to him. He said that he said that because in a way she was, and because she kept whispering all kinds of shit in his ears about how special the moment was for her. *She mistook his words to mean that he loved her.*

He said he never went to see her after that.

I hated him when he told us this story, and not only because I always liked Taniesha, but also because of how easy it was for him to pick up girls. Fat girls, slim girls, Coolie girls, country girls, town girls, girls visiting from foreign, Chinese girls, and more. And he was always telling stories, and they were always crude. Told us he had one against a wall down by the gully, and was giving it to her hard while some ants were biting her and she tried to move, but he held her in 'position'. He would laugh. Standing ovation, round of applause.

Anyway, folks may say that I tell my story in a round-about kind of a way. I hold nothing against these folks, and wouldn't take anything of theirs to the Obeahman to do them any harm. But the truth is, this is how my story unravels as I look back at it and how I try to put the pieces together.

So, I mention these events not to talk about myself and how I discovered who my own real papa was at twenty-seven years old, and how proud he was of his own Scottish surname when I finally met him. These things are scarcely important in the grand scheme of things, and it is pointless to wonder what my life might have been, when I know what it is.

I mention these events instead because of the associations with the things that matter in the end. For instance, for the association with Tommy.

There were times when an alleged father thought, rightly or wrongly, that a child was not his. Such a father would ensure that only the children who looked like him were fed and sent to school. You could tell who the perceived 'jacket' was, as they were the ones that looked least like their father, were the skinniest of his alleged children, and were the ones who stayed home and played in the dirt yard while the others went to school. They were the last to eat dinner and had the least to eat - and this was often only done in secret after the alleged father had gone to sleep. They were the last to come out and play as they had the most cleaning up to do of things they used the least.

Such was the case with Tommy. Good old Uncle Bob also thought, very much like Tommy's alleged father, that Tommy was one of the last remaining 'bastards' in the yard.

"Thou shall love thy neighbor, but do not allow her husband to catch you." It seemed that someone might have loved Tommy's mama at some time before fleeing in the middle of the night while the husband was on his way home. But this was only a rumor.

Tommy was treated like an outcast in his house.

Later it also happened, as it frequently happened, that the first of Garnet's children, his son, was also left with Garnet's mama to be raised. Garnet's papa, who was mostly unemployed, did not like having another mouth in the house to feed, and shunned the boy. Garnet's mama, who had lost a son under a truck and seen another mercilessly mauled by a dog, did not have strong sentiments for a grandchild either. In this way, I am told, Garnet's son essentially lived like an outcast and raised himself, much as Tommy had tried to do.

"The only thing I am sure of"

Guess me this riddle
and perhaps not -
my son loves me,
he loves me not,
perhaps he's not.

My wife loves me,
this love will last,
she loves me,
more than my wives past,
who loved me,
who loved me not.

My papa loved me,
loved me alone,
he loved me,
as though I was his own,
he loved me,
he loved me not.

Disposable People

My father loves me,
though I met him at twenty-five,
he must love me,
mama said so while she was barely alive,
he loves me,
he loves me not.

My mama loved me,
I think that's what she said,
she loved me,
telling me all on her death bed,
she loved me,
she loved me not.

That's the only thing I am sure of.

Undated journal entry

I have learnt that there are, and will be, many things in this life that are beyond my comprehension. Sad, in so many ways, Semicolon, but I have learnt to take it in strides. I think I have lived long enough that dying without understanding no longer concerns me. There are few who understand how a man changes after he has seen certain things, and what he will accept without questions and without answers.

CHAPTER 41

An Unholy Spirit

I will murder you in the broadest of daylight because there is nothing and no one that I fear. I live and breathe evil. I am original sin, pure and undiluted. My weapons are heavy but my conscience is light. My name is legion, for I am many. I drink the blood of the innocent and eat their hearts for breakfast. Behold I walk through the valley of the shadow of death, for I am death. I sleep on the graves of all those that I have murdered. I don't need to know God, I have already murdered my own father, so why would I need another? My name is Al Capone. I am Doctor Doom.

Semicolon, these were lines from songs they started making in the early 1990s. By then I knew that the music sure wasn't so sweet that it would stick between my teeth like candy. Things had changed a lot by then, and the younger generation was already looking very different from ours, and not only in appearance. The hunger in their eyes was also not just for food.

Some were talking about making Duppies, and the baddest ones were known to have made five or more.

In my own childhood Duppies weren't things we made, but just things that existed. And, as I mentioned before, they were real. Let me explain what real means.

This is a story about Calvert. I know it well because I was there when it happened. It was the summer of a year like many other years, but I was young, around nine or ten years old. In those times it was a tradition for us as kids to go and spend the summer holidays with relatives, mainly grandparents, in an even more rural part of the country. My brother and I normally went to stay with one of our grandmas. She had three little pigs and the prospect of pigs proliferating into profits. I found out a pregnant pig was properly referred to as being 'in-piglet'. World without end, what a hell of a thing an education is!

On the day in question, it was Calvert and me, just the two of us and no one else, that were playing. It was about two in the afternoon. The cows and goats had already had their mid-day meals and were lying down relaxing, and avoiding the blazing overhead sun. Calvert and I decided to go to bush to find mangoes, shoot birds, chase other people's cows and goats, climb trees, pick fruits, and perhaps get stung by wasps.

We had everything we needed. Our front pockets were loaded with small, nicely-rounded stones, a few marbles for our slingshots, a few copper coins for an experiment we had always intended to try but never did, and the confidence and courage of youth traveling in a group. In our back pockets we carried our slingshots, a knife my grandpa had given me which was still sharp but rusty from being left out in the rain too often, and a little bit of doubt and fear in case they were needed. In our hands, our sticks to help beat away the bushes as we made our way through charted and uncharted paths. We carried no food with us. Everything we needed was in the bushes waiting for us.

We set off on our journey, starting on the familiar path behind my grandma's house, over the tall barbed-wire fence that had cut every one of us at least twice and past the cashew trees that didn't belong to us but from which we had all eaten more than twice. We crossed the open field where the cows grazed, went past the big mango tree behind which lots of good times were had with girls during the summer, and past the familiar bee hive hanging from the y shaped branch on the wild (good-for-nothing) cherry tree. Then we walked between the two june plum trees that stood like the marble columns at the entrance to an ancient roman ruin. It was there that we saw it. Right there, on the trunk of the june plum tree on our left. The omen. The harbinger of things to come.

It was a lizard that was not just a lizard. A lizard so huge we at first thought it was a new branch growing from the trunk of the tree. It was grass-green, and it was standing guard, ram-rod and vigilant. Like a Roman soldier guarding the tomb of Christ, entrusted with the knowledge that evidence of the body therein would determine the very existence of Christianity. The lizard stood there with a sense of sacred duty. Unyielding.

Something or someone had chopped off a large part of the lizard's tail. Under the circumstances, one might have expected that the memory of whatever had caused the amputation would be so fresh and painful that the lizard would immediately yield when a human sought to pass, but it didn't. We threw stones at it. It did not move. We threw sticks at it. It did not move. We shot at it using our slingshots. One shot struck. It did not move. Then the fear came into our hearts, and with it, all our trembling childish frailties and lack of faith.

It was an omen. Unfortunately, we didn't see the meaning of that lizard until much later.

We retreated to the wild cherry tree, behind which wild things would happen a little later in life, and took a different route into the bushes. A bit of time passed.

We walked for a long while in silence. Neither of us spoke about what had happened. It wasn't shame. It was doubt. Both of us doubted that what we had seen was just an ordinary flesh-and-bone lizard. When we finally spoke we were beneath one of our favorite mango trees and it was time for the usual question, "You going to climb and let me catch, or you want me to climb and you catch?' Sometimes we would both climb - on those days when we had no intention of bringing any mangoes back; we simply stayed in the tree and ate our fill. I said, "Let us both climb." Calvert was a little older and a little stronger than me, and would normally be the one to fill his shirt with mangoes and carry the load over his shoulder, hanging down his back. In that moment when we both decided to climb, the decision was also made that his back would be free from all burdens for the journey back home. Sometimes it is much later that we see how the pieces fall into place.

We both climbed and picked mangoes and ate them. We ate a lot. Much more than we would normally do on the days when we brought some home to share. One of my simple joys was to watch my brother, my cousins and my friends feast like kings on the mangoes I brought them until they were royally stuffed, and then rub their newly-acquired, three-month pregnancies in satisfaction. Full. Content. Happy. But on that day, when Calvin and I had eaten too much, another piece of the omen had fallen into place.

We slowly made our way down from the tree, sat on the ground under the shade and chatted about nothing. We were both full and had little inclination to continue walking. We were feeling tired and sun-dazed, so we lay down. It may have been the combination of the heat, the gluttony and the tension of that confrontation with the green lizard, but, in any event, we both fell asleep. And something else fell into place.

I was the first to wake up. It had gotten late. The sun had furtively escaped and was almost about to disappear from view, but I caught a glimpse of it. It smiled at me, for it knew that I had caught it in the act. I pinched Calvert as this was a highly effective way of waking folks. He woke instantly, with a scream and his fist shooting towards my face. I dodged him, for these were everyday things we knew to expect. He would have done the same to me.

It was now too late to shoot birds. Many generations of relatives before us had learnt the lesson the hard way – never shoot birds at dusk or dawn, for you never know what you may hit. We decided to make our way back home, but by a different route, just in case that creature was still by the june plum tree. Maybe we would walk back along that route another day, when the creature had discovered that the tomb was empty, and the Saviour was gone.

The wind was blowing lightly and in those hot days of summer there were many dry leaves and tree branches which the wind rustled into a whistle. We began to hurry. This wasn't because we feared any Blackheart Men or gunmen, but because it was getting *dark*. The day was when we worked and played; the night was when the *dark* worked and played. The *dark* in deep rural Jamaica was a thing that lived and breathed - an evil birthed in the pits of hell. The *dark* could whisper in your ear and touch your skin to play with you, like a cat plays with a mouse before devouring it. We had to be home before the *dark* came out to play.

It happened on the way home. We went to the grave. Some said it was the grave of an older child, others that it was a baby. Many parents found it cheap and convenient to bury the bodies of young babies beneath a tree somewhere in their yards or fields rather than go through all the formalities of arranging a funeral and purchasing a spot in a cemetery. This grave was in a field beneath a tree, and the roots of the tree had, over time, cracked the grave in many places. The land on which the baby or child had been buried also seemed to have been quite unstable, and the grave had sunk about 1½ ft. There was little we had not seen as young adventurers; we had been to the grave before. In fact, that grave was the reason we always had those two copper coins in our pockets. It was to be the site for an experiment that neither of us had ever been brave enough to undertake before.

It may have been because of the shame we both felt for not having faced that lizard with greater courage, that we decided to do the experiment on that day. It started with a simple question as we were walking past the grave,

"Stephan, you think it's true what they say about throwing the coins in the grave?"

"No, they're just trying to scare us." I said this because at that moment, hurrying to get home before the dark, and to get away from the memory of that lizard, the last thing I wanted to do was sound scared again. If anyone was going to sound scared, it should be Calvert. That way, perhaps, I could later tell jokes about how Calvert was also the one who was really afraid of the lizard.

"Do you think we should try it?" He pushed the ball squarely into my court. Based on how the stars, the darkness and my ego were all aligned, it was not a question that should have been asked.

"Why not?" I said.

I took a quick look at the sun, which was beginning to wave a smug and cheeky goodbye. It was getting darker, but I could not now be the one to point out the obvious: that the *dark* was waking up, and someone was already opening the gates of Hell in preparation for its journey, and it was very hungry.

I tried to catch Calvert's eye to see if there was enough doubt there to make the suggestion of "You think we should do this tomorrow when we have more time?" an immediate reality. But he was already standing by the grave and looking down. And he had two coins in his hand. I could tell that, in that moment, he too wanted to grow out of these childhood fears. He too wanted to go home and tell the older kids that he had done something brave, rather than to confess that he had run from the *dark*, backed away from a lizard, and tried to put his conscience to sleep under a tree.

I took out my coins as well. We both knew the ritual, for it was simple and we had heard it many times before in various Duppy stories told at night. Throw the four copper coins into the grave, one by one, then say the name of the dead person five times. We knew the name was Mildred. This was not from personal knowledge, but based on the reliable word of another older and wiser cousin who knew everything about the bushes and what was in them. He knew the grave and the occupant's name, but what he didn't know was what had killed her. No one else knew either because she had never been taken to the doctor, alive or dead. All that was known was that she had thrown up a lot before she died, and that the liquid that came out of her was darker and more strangely colored than the concoctions they made and poured into her. And that within two days she died, and that was that and no more than that.

Calvert threw the first coin.

Nothing happened.

This was the reason I threw the second.

Nothing happened.

Calvert threw the third.

I threw the fourth.

He said, "Mildred". One. He said it! I couldn't believe he fucking said it! He didn't kick the ball into my court for me to run after it, he brought it to me and placed it at my feet, and went back to his spot to wait on me to kick it.

I said, "Mildred." Two. I said it only because I knew there was time to stop before we got to five, and that he would be the one who would have to say the fifth Mildred. I had processed it in my mind already.

He said, "Mildred." Three.

I said, "Mildred." Four. This time more slowly, and then I looked at him and caught his eye. There was a hint of doubt in those eyes as his mouth formed the name. But before he could say it there was a sudden gush of cold wind as if something was traveling swiftly to block the words from coming out of his mouth. It was enough to stop him. Doubt had become real. It had also grown two legs that were strong enough to run. Which is what we did. We ran from the wind, and kept running until our hearts felt as though they were falling from our mouths. Then we stopped by a tree to catch our breaths, and I turned to Calvert and asked, "Do you think that was her?" And my friend, who was never any use in school, asked, "Who, Mildred?" And said her name for a fifth time. I could see that the bulbs went on right then and there, that he realized what he had just done. And doubt changed into fear, real and palpable. And when the leaves cracked behind us, as though someone was now walking in the darkness behind us, fear grew four legs and two wings and took flight, screaming.

If there is one thing you will learn growing up in rural Jamaica, is that you cannot always run as fast as you wish when running in the bushes. It was Calvert who got caught in a thick overgrowth of vines. Calvert who began to scream louder than anyone might have thought possible for an eleven year old child to scream. Calvert who further entangled himself as he tried frantically to escape. Calvert who issued forth a soul-splitting fifth dimension scream as he felt something had jumped onto his back. His back that was free of mangoes. Calvert who shouted: "STEPHAN!! STEPHAN!!! SHE DEH PON MI BACK!!!! HELP ME!! HELP ME!!!" Calvert who screamed again on a seventh dimension as he felt something bite into the back of his neck. Calvert who looked paralyzed with terror as he shouted, "IS A BABY DUPPY!! SHE ON MI BACK!! SHE SUCKING MI BLOOD!!! OH GOD, STEPHAN HELP ME!!! HELP ME!!!!"

I ran to him and tried to help. One learns in life, however, that if one person who is trying to help another is also in a state of panic, things are unlikely to turn out well. So, we both got entangled, and both screamed in terror, before we managed to get loose and continue flying home. Calvert was still screaming, "SHE PON MI BACK!! SHE PON MI BACK!! SHE SUCKING MI BLOOD!!! STEPHAN HELP!!!" And crying, and wailing, and wailing and running.

There was of course no time for me to stop to check. I kept running, and because I kept running he also kept running. We ran until we made it home. I ran straight into my grandmother's arms. She was not Calvert's grandmother, but she was the only adult he saw, so he too ran straight into her arms.

A few minutes later his mama also came by. His papa was at home but these were not matters meriting a father's attention. They all inspected

Calvert's body. They all told him there was nothing and no one on his back. They all told him that outside of a small scratch which was most likely due to a piece of branch or thorn, there were no signs that anything or anyone had bitten him. They all told him that the things that he had heard about how to bring back a Duppy from the grave were not true, they were just 'Duppy stories'. They all told him that he would be fine.

But he wasn't.

He didn't believe any of them. He said he knew that she was on his back. He said he could still feel her weight. He said it was a Baby Duppy and he could feel her small hands around his neck and her little feet gripping onto his waist. He said she was still biting him and sucking his blood. He said we should believe him.

None of them did.

I did.

The days of summer would pass, and Calvert would begin to get skinny and skinnier. He was hardly eating anything, and was always begging us to believe him, to believe that she was still on his back and sucking his blood.

People say that Calvert weighed about 88 pounds when he went into the bushes with me that day. I would say he came out of those bushes weighing about 91 pounds if we added the weight of the mangoes he ate. They say he weighed 75 pounds two weeks later when they took him to see the first doctor, who found nothing wrong with him and dismissed his chatter about 'Duppies' as ridiculous. He was about 63 pounds when they opted to take him to an Obeahman. Some folks say it was indeed necessary to bring Calvert to that Obeahman four times over the course of six weeks and pay him a total of JA$700 - which was a shitload of money in those days - because they believed him when he said that it was a Duppy unlike any that he had ever seen before, and one that would require 'special skills' to deal with. They felt this was a "Good Obeahman" - much better than the one that could not cure Tiny Tim of what, from all appearances, was the same problem, only a few months before.

I, on the other hand, felt that Calvert was healed from the first minute of the first visit, when the Obeahman said, before anyone had said anything to him, "I can see her, she on you back." Because all Calvert needed was for someone to believe him. And everyone now believed him, because the Obeahman had said that he too had seen the Duppy. Never mind that this was one of the most common opening lines of Obeahmen, who always thought that a Duppy was the source of all ailments.

Calvert survived the ordeal.

I mention this event here, my love, to explain that we all believed, deeply and profoundly, in evil spirits and the Obeahman's charms. And this is the reason, on the first day you said you loved me, Semicolon, I gave you the charm of protection that I have always carried with me from I was a child.

CHAPTER 42

The Holy Spirit

My belief in the unholy spirits was implacable, but I wrestled with whether the Holy Spirit existed, and whether I should believe in Him. Nothing in my childhood could convince me of His existence, and therefore belief was impossible. It was in Business School, well over twenty years later, that I revisited the subject seriously while reading what I thought was a delightful poem: *Bishop Blougram's Apology*. This was a poem about a bishop having a conversation with an atheistic journalist ('literary man') called Mr Gigadibs, who was curious to know why people bothered to believe in the existence of a god. It was a long poem but delightful in many ways. I used the statistics and economics I was learning to summarize the Bishop's argument, which could be presented in the form of a decision tree. The tree would look something like this:

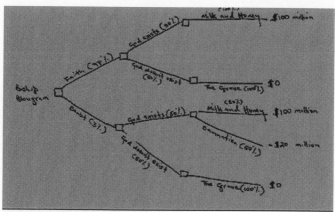

Snapshot of the Original Tree, as drawn in my notebook in business school

I assigned 97% probability to the bishop being repentant at the time of his death, because as he said, the difference between him and Mr Gigadibs was that he had a constant Faith diversified by Doubt, while Gigadibs had a constant Doubt diversified by Faith. There was a small likelihood therefore that he could die at a moment when Doubt prevailed and he would fall into sin (3% probability).

Applying economic theory to this problem I further assumed that the earthly value that the ordinary man would put on going to heaven (the satisfaction or utility he would get from it) would be equivalent to having approximately $100 million in United States dollars. This would be sufficient to purchase an eternity of milk and honey and other niceties, unless, of course, the ordinary man turned out to be a high-stakes gambler or had the IRS on his ass. The earthly value of simply going to a grave forever was US$0. The earthly value of going to hell forever was -US$20 million.

In this model therefore if the bishop chose to be faithful, then he stood to gain, based on the probabilities:

50% x $100 million
+   50% x $0 million
= $50 million

If, however, he chose to doubt and fell into sin, then the potential payoff would be:

50% x $100 million
+   50% x -$20 million
= $40 million x 50% = $20 million

+   50% x $0 million
= $20 million

I assume in this model that the bishop still had a chance of making it into heaven even if he died while doubting, because his God was a merciful God who may recognize that he had been faithful and strong most of his life. So, the choice for Blougram was between a potential payout of $50 million and $20 million. If you continue the calculation you would see that in probability terms his potential payout would be:

97% x $50 million
+   3% x $20 million
= $49.1 million

For the atheistic journalist, the decision tree would look somewhat different, more or less like this:

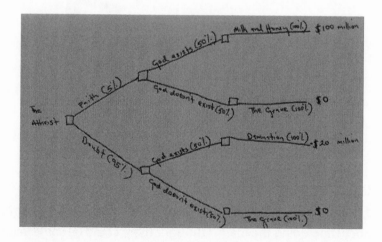

If you were to run the calculations in the same manner you would see that there is a slim 5% chance that if the atheist repents then he stands to gain the same potential payout of $50 million. However, if he doesn't, he stands to lose $10 million. Based on the probabilities, his overall payout can be computed as:

5% x $50 million

+   95% x -$10 million

=   -$7 million

Being a rational man, Blougram chose the option of Faith diversified with Doubt. In other words his conclusion was:

If I believe and there is a God then I win big time

If I believe and there is no God then we are equal

But if you don't believe and there is a God you lose big time

And if you don't believe and there is no God then we are equal.

On average therefore the atheist stands to lose, while on average the bishop stands to gain lots of this:

Questions and doubts were all the atheist had to confront the Bishop's stoic belief. I was, at first, like the atheist, Mr Gigadibs, but after reading the poem and doing the math, I thought there could be some value from believing. But this was only an intellectual and materialistic computation, nothing in my heart had changed.

But then, a few years later, you came, Semicolon, and everything changed.

I think it was because I felt a new kind of love when I met you, and not because you brought me back to church, why I think I found it possible to believe in the love that God has for mankind. For, with you, I felt the spark of life, I felt rebirth, I felt redemption, I felt completeness.

And the day we went to the Shenandoah National Park - the first day you held my hand and told me that you loved me, I believe I felt the love of God. I have never told you this before, but it is true, my love. All of it. I went home and wrote about that moment, because I had finally felt something that Gigadib's never had. I wrote this:

"Diddlysquat and such"

Diddlysquat.
Sums up how much I care about all that
nonsense about 'mysterious ways',
and things being explained at the "end of days" -
as though this were an upcoming conference.

Existentialism I find an abhorrent vexation,
just about as much as that vulgar question
of mortality,
which scarcely interests or amuses me.

I hold no melancholic longing for youth,
the past, or, to tell the truth, home -
which, and you can take my word for it,
is more the hideous transvestite in reality
than the sex-dripping goddess shown in those ads on TV
(and whose apparent horniness may give the misleading suggestion
that she would sleep with anyone, even you.)

For that matter, I am, unabashedly, not nostalgic
about the games I've played with my dick;-

Disposable People

I've grown weary of the hunt for humping delights,
and rather anesthetized to the ins and outs of the lonely night.
I have adapted, and well, to my present condition.
(Or, perhaps, it could be that I am an old man
who is more afraid of the snarling snatch that baits,
than the cold front of eternity which patiently waits.)

So the issue that I face is, plainly, this:
I have little doubts or consternation as such,
that I shall, and soon enough,
be organic, enriching mulch;
but having held together my crumbling container for so long,
I suppose,
that in some way,
and before I decompose,
I am entitled
to a bit more than this mystifying lack of variety
in women, hamburgers and the face of severe poverty.

Entitled,
to a reason for having been kept awake for so long.

Entitled, If not to meet or speak, at least to see,
just a little of
His Majesty,

before becoming nourishment for worms and such,

and for the unspeakably drab journey this has been.

Ezekel Alan

Sure, I have bedded more than the two I've wedded,
but all along, women
have offered me little more than the fleeting scent of summer lilies
(the whores, I would confess, offered a lily less)
and the only thing that lingers are the faint unwanted reminders
of a few jaded lovers
(and those, actually, reek odiously of lavender).

As for sights, I've indeed seen much
of the world and such,
Of course, there was Dalí, Joan Miró, Rembrandt, Van Gogh,
and Gaudi, all with their masterful touch;-
but the 'masters', for all their brilliance and idiosyncrasies
have offered me little more than sketchings
that never etched beneath my flesh -
since our socially stifling sense of decorum would not permit my
endearing their work with terms such as putridity and gaudiness.
(Though I firmly believe that few would disagree
with such a characterization being made of Dalí)

Emotions, yes, I have also felt,
In Anne Frank's home, the Sistine Chapel, the ruins of Rome
and such
but these feelings never dwelt

longer than the Amerindians

gone,
faster than the dope, the marijuana, the hash,
the college education, the trash,
and other cruds of my retreating memory

bygone
not unlike some other things I should have left alone:
like the garish bits of crotches and tits
too easily found in Amsterdam -
the easiness of which, I would have to admit,
rendered such things hard to compare with the pleasure I had in
Lake Atitlan
(a pleasure which, if not sweeter, was certainly deeper)

As for pain, I have been bitten
by both Love and Lust, two wives, mosquitoes and other such insects
that were, I rather suspect, somewhat too impatient of my death.
Or is that I somehow resemble, even before I dissemble, food?
In any event such is the nature of parasites.

As for me, I've bitten and carried only the taste of mangoes.

Now after all
the mountains, safaris, volcanoes, women, music, life, death,
the search for meaning and other things I had hoped never to forget
one thing still perplexes me:
why it should have taken over three scores
and, dignity doesn't permit me to count, but so many whores
and such
for me
to finally see,
in the Valley of the Shenandoah,
my God in His majesty.

I sensed Him then, Semicolon. For the first time, when you touched my hand and we looked to the mountains, I felt His love and protection.

I also thought that if indeed God gives us life but waits decades later to give us a reason for living it, then He did indeed work in mysterious ways.

It was because I felt His presence on that day, that, the day after, I bought you the small cross pendant and necklace to wear around your neck.

CHAPTER 43

The Things They Said

Sometimes when I reminisce, Pain comes along, finds me alone, opens up my mind and implants a humping, haunting melody of the past with maybe a few words of a song. And sometimes I find that I may sing along, and together we may remember an ancient lullaby, and I may rock myself to sleep in his arms.

Sometimes they write and call.

Like the letter I finally read in September 2010. Beyond the death of Uncle Bob they mentioned a few other things as well.

I heard that the shoemaker's shop has been closed, and that some folks I know may be planning to rent the store and open a small hairdressing shop to sell hair products. I heard that artificial hair sells really well in neighborhoods where one's natural hair is not good enough.

They said that the canal was dredged often in the last few months, because elections are approaching soon and this time every vote will matter, even the votes of those who live too close to canals. They said though, that there has not been another flood like the one we lived through that night many years ago. I am happy to hear that no more lives have been swept away to the sea, *but I will not go back to that hateful fucking place to see the canal.*

They said that one of my cousins now has a dog that looks a lot like Ruffy. I was happy to hear this because I now think about Ruffy differently than I did before. *But I will not go back to that hateful fucking place to see this dog.*

338

They said that there haven't been any problems with any Baby or Coolie Duppies in years, and that Calvert is now a grown man with four kids that they believe to be his, for the girl he is with, they said, is a Christian and very kind. They said, however, that there is something about him that no one has been able to put a precise finger on, but everyone knows that it is still there. I do miss Calvert, and would very much like to see his wonderful kids, *but I will not go back to that hateful fucking place to see them.*

They said that my cousin Jimmy (Aunt Josephine's son) was buried, and that the funeral went well. They had sent me a few emails some time ago as the events transpired:

> *hi Kenny,*
> *i got your email and have taken note of the information you have sent. i am bad news, last night auntie josephine son, jimmy, the last one who is jet black, was shot and killed by gunman infront of their yard when he was called by someone. auntie josephine is devastated as courtney is locked up in jail for stealing and she called us on saturday to see if we could help bail him. i am so sorry for her as she is just having a terrible time due to those children i dont know what she is going to do. Simone said jimmy was mixed up in illegal activities he died leaving five children can you believe it. and he was only 19.*
> *i have not called auntie josephine as yet i dont know what to say to her. i knew something bad was going to happen as i dreamt about a funeral but i thought it was one of the old folks who is ill.*
> *i hope you guys are ok.*
> *Love kay*

and

Disposable People

hi Kenny
tamara and i went to ____[that hateful fucking place] yesterday
and came back desprssed. our house roof is rotten and is looking
awful. but thats not even the worst, aunti josephine has no money
to burry jimmy. none of her children are working errol gave her
$2000, thomas sent $23000. mrs adassa gave her $5000 and some
gravel to build the grave and men in the area pitching in to dig the
grave. the funeral was postponed once as she is unable to give the
parlour any money the chepeast funeral plan is $80,000 and they
have taken off $5000 she is planning to postponed it again as she
does not have the money the church alrady changed the date and
may not take too kindly to doing so again.
she has lost a lot of weight she is skin and bone.
i know you dont have any money, but even the smallest amount
will do . after a while the parlour will start charge for extra storage
and she is really going to be in more money trouble. i dont know im
so sorry for the poor lady she looks as if she too soon die
kay

and then

hi Kenny,
we went to the funeral today and the lots of people came. as usual
there was a lot of persons there that we did not know.
auntie josephine remains grateful for your help and she is still
trying to be strong. jimmy had five beautiful chidlren all who look
like him. i am glad it is over. hope you guys are okay and you are
not working too hard.
love kay

I was happy that aunt Josephine was still alive and that my cousin had five beautiful children. Of course, I told them *I will not go back to that hateful fucking place to see them.*

Then some more news came in.

They said that Mr Roper was quite sick, that he fell on the ground and was speaking in tongues and frothing at the mouth, in a similar manner to those revivalist Christians though he never went a day to church.

They also said that the man who owns the barber shop (and who has no other job or business based on all public records) was now driving a brand new BMW 7 series that was really 'stink'! They said that he was also helping to send a lot of kids to school and that many parents did not mind having their daughters, who are still at a tender age, spend time with him because, though not a Christian, he himself was a tender man and very kind.

They said that they have also now heard something about Garnet, the horse-man. This is what my sister said in her email:

i asked William (Billie) about garnet. he said that the last he heard, garnet was in prison and while in there he was in an altercation with someone and was stabbed almost to death in his stomach. thats a few years ago not sure whats happening to him now and if he still is in jail. i think when i go [to that hateful fucking place] next, i will ask his father about him he seemingly has not been there a while as william not sure if he is alive. sorry to bear such sad news i guess when you have parents who are not supportive your days will be full of sorrows poor garnet had a rough life from the get go. i have aplied for my leave so will try and book a flight this month end for first week in august if possible.
love kay

I said to myself:

I will never go back to that hateful fucking place!
I will never go back to that hateful fucking place!
I will never go back to that hateful fucking place!
I will never go back to that hateful fucking place!
I will never go back to that hateful fucking place!

CHAPTER 44

Me and Semicolon

11 p.m.

My dearest Semicolon,

It is late and I need to go to bed. You are already asleep. My heart is aching tonight, Semicolon. And I feel I must tell you about the one other love I have had in my life, beyond mangoes. I am thinking back in time and recalling her face. I recall her lying and giggling playfully on the bed. I remember the way she rolled over on her back, with her hands and feet in the hair saying "I am a cat, come and rub my belly." She made me laugh Semicolon, the same way you made me laugh when we just met.

Last night I had a dream about her, Semicolon. It was a long dream that lasted for a time that was divisible by 3. I have therefore concluded that it lasted for an hour and a half.

In the first thirty minutes of the dream I was on the third floor of Macy's Department Store. I was at the escalator descending, and in front of me there was Kissy Boy, her old boyfriend. He was Puerto Rican, wasn't he? Fell asleep on her sofa on their second date she told me. But he was cute. And she kissed him. I remember she said that she never slept with him. And he wasn't the subject of her

343

experiments: he will therefore most likely go to his grave never knowing what fruits, if eaten for three or more days, will make his cum sweet or bitter, or bitter sweet. Yet he was the one that appeared in my dream, Semicolon. Kissy Boy was the one. He was standing in front of me on the escalator, going down. And though I never met him before, I knew it was him. Which is why I pushed him down the escalator. For thirty minutes. Each time he got up I pushed him down again. So much fun.

For the second thirty minutes of my dream, I was visited by a childhood friend, Mr Tickle. And he tickled me! For thirty minutes! I giggled so much I almost became senseless! And to think I was so afraid of him when I was a child!

Finally, Semicolon, she and I made love. For thirty minutes. The sex lasted for only two minutes or so on account of the fact that I was so very excited. But, for the rest of the time - the other twenty-eight minutes - I was lying there with her; her left breast, Lisa; the right one, Shelly, and her sweet moist spot, which she named Sally. All five of us, like a family. It was right then that I felt love.

I did seen her again, Semicolon. I saw her after her parents sent her away to the US and she went to 'hair school'. When I moved to the US, she came to see me where I was living in Brooklyn. It was in one of those sections where you could never leave anything visible on your car seats overnight, because people would break into your car and steal almost anything. I say "almost" because I learnt there was a difference between some things like a pack of tampons and a book. People would steal the first, as there was a market for it, and it could be converted into a pack of cigarettes or a few bucks. If you accidentally left a book on your car seat, however, and you woke up in the middle of the night remembering this, you could go back to sleep without undue fear, for there was neither a primary nor a secondary market for knowledge in that neighborhood. Those markets were for people peddling dreams in various guises, selling a Prada for nada, and all kinds of instant-win games custom-designed around the ambitions of the poor.

It was one of my cousins who told me where she was. And the good thing about the US is that you can simply pick up the phone book and dial. She was so excited when she heard my voice! She made plans immediately to come and see me.

I was there at the train station the day she came. I was standing waiting, like guys always do in books and movies. It had been many years since I had last seen her, but a month had never passed without me thinking about her a few times.

I had rehearsed what I wanted to say to her for over two weeks, since the day we spoke. It should have been easy enough for me to remember what I wanted to say, for it was all true.

She came off the train and hoisted her knapsack on her back; it was the kind of bag that three people could easily live in. She looked so cute with this big, gigantic bag weighing her down.

And then she turned and looked at me, joy bristling in her eyes. I smiled as she ran to me and threw her arms violently around my neck, sucking my body into hers. With her head behind my neck she screamed her first words in the stifled way that people do when they are still aware of their environment. "God I missed you so much!" Then she quickly kissed me on my lips, and looked straight into my eyes while I searched for the words I had rehearsed. Then I tried to say those words, but nothing came.

What eventually came out instead was a mumble that I must have dropped my keys. And as her eyes went downwards to help me find them, I remember closing my eyes to try and find myself.

"Here, I got it," she said as she bent and picked up the keys and gave them back to me. When I opened my mouth to speak again, all that came out was: "If I saw snot in your nose I would wipe it with my own hands."

My love, she then looked at me puzzled, and her smile temporarily disappeared. But when she looked in my embarrassed eyes she understood my words and what I was trying to tell her. She then placed her lips on mine again, but softly. And this time she slipped her tongue inside my mouth and something inside my heart.

I had felt something with her. Even after ten years.

I believed that I loved her, Semicolon. Like I had never loved anyone until that moment. And if those had been the days when I still wished for things, I would have wished to have everything in the whole world so I could give it to her. The little man in me also said he loved her, for we had conferenced on this, he and I, and had both agreed that what we felt went far beyond nursery rhymes.

She spent two weeks with me in Brooklyn. Then she had to leave. I had asked her if it was because she had to go back to work, but she said no, that she had quit her job and was leaving Detroit. She offered more information than I needed, said she would miss her hairdresser more than her boss. That even though she didn't like her boss, she gave him a kiss. I asked her, jealously, if it was on his lips and she retorted, "What you think I am, a Russian whore?" Also had a sharp tongue. But oh so sweet! She was leaving because that's who she was. Someone without a home. Someone who leaves.

I guess we were never meant to be.

I have not seen her since, my love, but I would like to, for one final time, to tell her thanks for the dreams and the memories.

I wanted to tell you this Semicolon, because I want you to know everything.

I will go to sleep now, my beloved, for the tale which I want to tell cannot be told in darkness.

Kenny
April 25, 2011

My love, the day I met you was also the day I fell in love with you. I knew that you were different from everyone else I'd ever met.

You were not one of those creatures made by God's apprentices while God rested; you were made by God himself. God took you, with his own hands, and gave you His special gift. You were the one He created to connect the idea of Man as he is, to Man as his maker wanted him to be. You were His statement: All my children are this way; but this is how I intended them to be. He used you, Semicolon, to link everything in our existence to His original thought for the universe:

You are the worst of my creation; you are the best of my creation.

You have lived the worst of lives before; you will live the best of lives hereafter.

These are the valleys; these are the mountains.

These are the oceans; these are the land.

This is everything that has been; this is what can be. All connected by you. All my life before; all my life after.

You were His gift to us, to me, Semicolon. You were the connection. And when He sent you to earth this is how you were:

While everyone else thought, mulled over, contemplated and weighed the consequences of their actions; agonized over right and wrong; wondered how to erase their misdeeds and pondered what good deeds they should do to compensate for their shames, you simply acted with His will. You acted with a certainty and clarity of purpose and energy unlike I have ever seen in any other living creature. So comfortable in your own skin.

With your clarity of purpose you conversed with all creatures in the universe with ease and a cosmic understanding. Conversations had no format, no structure, no prelude, no beginning, no end, and words never needed to come from your mouth. But everyone and everything understood you. A conversation with you:

Text message from Kenny: "Hi sweetheart, I mailed letter 4 the IRS 2day."

Text message from Semicolon: "Thanks soupy boy. Have a wonderful day today."

And a wonderful day is all I could possibly have, for everyone and everything understood the clarity and certainty of your purpose.

Another conversation with you:

At 1:43:01 a.m. – as in, very early morning – I get up to use the bathroom (or 'take a leak' as some people say) and I return to bed and lay beside you, and, as I cuddle you, you say, "Soupy boy, on Wednesday we will go to New Orleans." As though this were the natural continuation of a conversation, when, in reality, the issue of going to New Orleans had never been mentioned before. But in the instant you express such a thought, it became *real*, not only to you, but to all living and non-living things. In that moment in time, at 1:43:02 am in the morning, a message would be sent to the Boeing 737 that would take us to New Orleans, and that message would provide clear instructions:

On May 18, 2007 between 2:00 pm and 6:00 pm you will take off from John F Kennedy Airport in New York and land in the Louis Armstrong International Airport in New Orleans. You are permitted a slight delay of no more than half an hour, but you will not, under any circumstance, crash, for I will be onboard. This is my code: Semicolon.

And while we are both drifting back to sleep, the laptop downstairs would be booting itself up to complete the airline, hotel, and car rental reservations. Messages would also be sent to pertinent animals. For instance, the birds would receive their message as regards the appropriate distance they should keep from the airplane's engines. The Taxi company would be instructed which driver should be sent and what speed he should drive at after collecting us from the airport. And lastly, a joint message would be sent to the Sun, the Wind and the Clouds. The Wind would be informed what style your hair would be in and accordingly at what precise time, as you descend the stairs of the airplane, it should gently blow the agreed number of strands of hair from your face. The Clouds would be instructed to give way simultaneously, so that the Sun can shine on you. The Sun, in its turn, would then do its utmost to radiate splendidly, so that as you descend and turn to look at the waiting city, and smile, the world can catch the glint from the spark of life in your eyes. The laptop would then end the messages appropriately:

This is her code: Semicolon.

One thing is for certain. On May 18, 2007 at about 6.30 p.m., we would be in New Orleans.

So too when you loved, there were messages and a flurry of action throughout the universe, as people and things sought to comply with the certainty and clarity of your purpose. For instance, at the moment that you turn to me and smile before loving me, the radio normally terminates whatever crass music it is playing, contemplates whether to take a minute to apologize, thinks better of it, and gently slips into a Peabo Bryson or Lionel Ritchie song. The rain leaves its work unfinished in whatever part of the world it was, hurries to our rooftop, and softly taps a melodious rhythm, being careful not to sound too repetitive or rehearsed. At the same time the coffee-maker downstairs turns itself on to start slowly brewing two cups of Jamaican Blue Mountain coffee, knowing that with Jamaican Blue Mountain it could make no mistake. Knowing also, how much you love the smell of good-quality coffee while it rains, and how we love to sip our cups in bed while we allow the spirits inside of us to catch their breath after we have loved.

Then how I tickled your toes! Then how you laughed and held me close!

And when the morning broke, I would lie in bed and watch you meditate. For everyone else, these would have been routine yoga poses, but with you, it was an approach to life. It was a creative process of constructing the day ahead. The message: this is what I will do today, and this is how the day will be! With bubbles of Champaign in every word.

You changed my mind about that place, Semicolon. You asked me to go back. Back to that place where I was born and spent the worst years of my life. Because only you could. Because only you knew that I could never go forward without going back. You knew that all the remaining days of my life would be Thursdays unless I went back. And because you asked, I went. I went without saying a word, back in time, past the old familiar faces and places - to understand where I was coming from and make peace with my past. I went to places that I had never been before, but I knew exactly where you wanted me to go. For I have always lived with dreams and prophecies and I understand the nature of these things.

I went to the old yard, and you came with me. It wasn't a vacation for we didn't go in search of rest, fun or relaxation. We went in search of peace - my peace. And I sat on the old veranda that I had not sat on for over twenty years. And right there was where they came to see me.

I saw my mama, and she smiled at me with softness in her eyes.

I saw my papa who, as usual, never spoke, but nodded his head to signal that he was proud of me and of what I had become.

I saw my grandpas and my grandmas, my still-born sisters, my friend Tommy, the in-bred boy, the four boys in the car, Ruffy, the other dogs, my cousin Brian, my uncle Thomas, and all the rest. They were all there. Including Millicent, who had her one eye fixed on a spot on the ground until I told her I was sorry for many things, including being the one who made the cricket ball that took her eye. Then she looked at me and I cried, for Millicent was real, Semicolon.

I also saw Old Man Tom for what he was – a person. I told him I deserved being spat on, and that I would have deserved worse for all that I did to him with the other kids. And for how we saw him. And he forgave me.

Finally, I saw The Incredible Hope, saw his skull and bones. Saw the rope still tying his skeletal wrists behind his back. He was long dead, but all I needed to do was touch the smallest particle of his being to bring him back to life. I touched his hair, just as you had asked me to. And then I opened my eyes and I saw you, like I had never seen you before. And the love poured out of my heart like a fountain.

And then we talked. I told you I was now at peace. And you said to me and to the universe:

"Soupy boy, we should now come home, for we are not Americans and we will never be. We should return to the land of our birth, the land from which we came. For though hardships there are, the land is green and the sun shines, and it forever will.

And this is my code: Semicolon"

And I said to you, "Semicolon, my name is Kenny, and I will now go home, though I am still a little afraid of the cemeteries."

CHAPTER 45

The Cemeteries of My Youth No Longer Scare Me

The Deputy Chief of Police, Mark Shields, a top crime-fighter brought in from Scotland Yard, saw the stash and exclaimed, on camera, "These guns amaze me!"

Semicolon, my love, as we grow old the certainties of science slowly displace the darkness of ignorance and superstition. I am no longer a child with a child's understanding of the world. I believe that if Christ died and rose again, He was the only one - all other bodies that have gone to the grave have remained there, and will only rise when He returns, for it is written:

"For the Lord Himself will descend from heaven with a shout, with the voice of an archangel, and with the trumpet of God. And the dead in Christ will rise first. Then we who are alive and remain shall be caught up together with them in the clouds to meet the Lord in the air. And thus we shall always be with the Lord."

Bible, 1st Thessalonians 4:16-17

There are no ghosts walking the land and, as such, I know that the cemeteries of my youth have nothing but dead bodies in them. If challenged to do so, I reckon I would, today, walk into one and perhaps even touch a tombstone. For I am no longer afraid of the cemeteries of my youth.

The cemeteries that I am afraid of though, are those of my adulthood.

And what made me so afraid were the soulless, living beings that moved about inside them.

When I visited Bosnia a few years after the civil war ended, I had, as I told you, a tour guide take me to one of their cemeteries. He was a pleasant man, held a PhD. Before the war he used to be a chemical engineer; drank whiskey with the boys in the pub; went horse-back riding from time to time; loved and ate the tenderest veal, that sort of thing. Now, here he was, a broken man, driving a cab and telling me that even now he still gets nervous when people talk about *bullets* in presentations and *shooting* each other emails. He learned that I was from Jamaica, put on a Bob Marley song and sang along with "One Love".

I was no longer afraid of cemeteries that were filled with only dead bodies. There was, however, something odd about the cemetery he showed me. There were, as expected, hundreds of graves of people who were killed during the civil war. People who were killed by soldiers, college professors, engineers, devoutly religious worshippers, mothers, fathers, former neighbors, and so on. Rows upon rows of tombstones of dead people dated 19___ to somewhere between '92 and '95

What I found to be odd was the number of tombstones for people who had died within two years *after* the war had ended.

I later asked a Bosnian consultant friend of mine *why* this had happened, for *why* is a question you can ask in some places and expect a reasonable response. He told me that *during* the war many people lost everything they had and everyone they loved. Old husbands lost their wives, old wives lost their husbands, mothers lost all their children, lovers lost their beloved, friends lost their friends. Some people lost everything: family, friends, houses, cars, dogs, trust, hope, faith. He said some of these people had nothing to live for, and so they died. Some committed suicide, but many of the older folks simply had no will to live, and died.

Hopelessness and despair are powerful emotions. I remember also reading some sections of Victor Frankel's book on man's search for meaning. In it he wrote about some of the prisoners in the Nazi death camps, and how he observed that the ones who died earliest were often the ones who appeared to have nothing to live for. Nothing to look forward to. No sense of purpose or meaning to their lives. He said you could see it in their eyes as they were marched to the gas chambers.

I have often reflected on what it must be like for a person to find himself in a situation where he feels he truly has nothing to live for. When he becomes hollow inside. When his spirit and his soul have died, and only the flesh still walks.

I mention all this because when I was no longer a boy, there were cemeteries in Kingston and Spanish Town, and near that *hateful* fucking place where dead bodies were removed from their graves and things that were far more evil began to take their place.

I sleep on the graves of those that I have murdered.

It wasn't just the words of songs. There were cemeteries in which gunmen of thirteen and fourteen years old were sleeping on the graves at night. They removed the bodies from the graves and hid their weapons inside. When the police raided their houses in the inner cities, they found neither the gunmen nor their weapons. When the hungry pigs and mongrels scavenged in the cemeteries they dined on dead flesh and bones.

When all of this started in the late 1980s, these kids and their weapons would both rise, like Dracula, at nights in the cemetery, cold as steel, soulless, dead inside. And they would go to work murdering anyone they chose - while some folks can't start their day without a bit of coffee, others seemed unable to finish theirs without a little murder. By the 1990s, they began to rise during broad daylight and went to work in the same way.

I knew one of those boys. You and I saw him when we went back, Semicolon.

This boy lacked decency and politeness, a rare deficiency in kids brought up in rural Jamaica. When I was growing up if you stepped accidentally on someone's toes, you said, "I am sorry, it was an accident". When you went to see someone you said, "Good morning" or "Good afternoon" as the case may be. How important was this? Any stranger could whup your ass if you failed to abide by these common courtesies, and if you went home and told your parents that a stranger hit you and your parents found out the reason, they too would whap your ass. But this boy had no such decency and politeness about him. They say that once, in the middle of the night, he went to someone's gate, called the person outside, and did not say "Good night" before pulling his gun and unloading all his thoughts about the fairness of life in the person's head. Dropping him dead. They say that even when he found out that it was the wrong person he had killed, he refused to apologize to the dead man's family. Not even to this day. Just went about his merry way, hurting and killing other people. No sense of decency and politeness!

He was no longer twelve years old, but about sixteen. Still had his gang of Rude Bwoys and Shottas hanging around him. Still had the old ratchet knife he had gotten from his papa, but now had some amazing guns and other weapons that people say were kept buried in the cemeteries until he went to work with the *dark* at night. Garnet's son. All grown up.

His story began in the early 1980s. His was part of our story, but it was also the beginning of the story of a time when we used to see gunmen and thieves running through the lane after they had finished a job. Sometimes the police would be chasing after them. Sometimes there would be shooting while we ran for cover in our houses. This didn't happen often back in the early 1980s but when it did it provided us with months of conversation: who had seen his face clearly, what type of gun it was, how he managed to escape the police, who in the yard nearly got shot, who had thought about helping the police to catch him, and so on. This would then lead to talk of who was the evilest, baddest, wickedest gunman, and various names would be mentioned in hush voices: first Copper and Sandokan, then later Natty Morgan, Trafficator, and the one who lived in the hills of Mocho and had a gun nobody had ever heard about before. Then who was on the 'most wanted' list; who had escaped to Cuba and was laying low for a while; whose baby mama lied for them, and hid them under a bed. The less fearsome carried names like 'Rude boy' or 'Rudy truants'; they were the early juvenile delinquents carrying out petty thefts and larceny. Only a few of them would mutate and evolve into bloodlusting, murdering gunmen.

In the 1950's Jamaica's murder rate was 5.7 per 100,000 – nothing to write home about and not worth mentioning anywhere outside of the country. But by the early 2000s Jamaica was one of the murder capitals in the world, with newspaper headlines screaming *"Bloodiest year ever: 1,680 murders."* (This is a rate of over 57 per 100,000. I showed you the headline my dear.)

Times had changed. In the early days the notorious gunmen were few and you would never expect to see them. By the late 1990s, you wouldn't expect not to see them: they were holding up supermarkets; robbing schools and forcing the guards to strip naked and touch each other; robbing the church of money, chairs and faith; robbing funeral homes (I showed you that headline as well: *"Even the dead must be alert!"*); following folks and robbing and killing them at the ATM, and following tourists from the airport to rob them. The cat and mouse game had changed, and the mouse was chasing the cat: the police commissioner announced that the criminals were better armed, and the criminals announced that for every one of their members that the police killed, they would kill ten police. Then the criminals started hunting police. This all led the people of the country to ask the Calypsonian to shut his fucking mouth and stop singing his raasclaat songs, because, they said, the music was no longer sweet. On the radio and in the university lecture halls they held debates about whether the music was causing the violence, or just a reflection of reality.

Then everyone started to go home early, close all their windows and doors, lock the burglar bars, turn on the alarms, and peek outside at the slightest sound, wondering if a gunman had followed them home and was out there, waiting in the dark.

Garnet's son was now one of them. He had been following me from my childhood, slinking into the bushes to conceal himself, quickening pace to keep up and not lose sight of me.

The part you already know and should remember, my love: we had gone back to that place for me to make peace with my past, and were visiting the old folks in the yard.

December 18, 2010. After leaving my old house, we went to visit my Aunt Josephine, and we sat on a chair in front of her house. She, who had planted approximately 64 hectares of land with bitterroot sorrow, and had needed hired hands to help her reap the harvest, was still the same as she had always been, just very old.

As I sat there on the chair she had sent one of my younger cousins to fetch, I looked across and saw Georgie's house, and I thought about him. I wondered whether he was somewhere out there, drinking hard liquor and telling his truth to whoever would listen. Sitting on a barstool, opening up his life, dissecting it like a frog, having its blood splash over his face and burn his eyes with childhood memories. I wanted to find out what had happened to Georgie.

While you were still talking with Aunt Josephine, I went inside Cookie's little shack on the side, to talk with her. This part of my conversation with her you never heard:

"I am planning to write a book, you know."

"Really? 'Bout what?"

"About Georgie."

The little room was being gradually surrounded by relatives and folks I didn't know from the other side of the lane. Cookie's door was open so I could see outside while talking to her. The little kids - 5, 6, 7 year olds - were standing close to the door, waving constantly, hoping for recognition from me. Dave, now a grown man, was there too, standing towards the back. Once when we were young he had told me that he had prayed every day for lightning to strike me because of something I had done to him. My cousin Jennifer, older, less cute than before, was also there. When she was young I and a couple other boys sometimes *took the middle page from her book,* same as we did with Cookie. She now had five kids, the last one, a boy, was about four years old. I had said hello to her while she was bathing him in a bucket, her hands moving with the same motion and her face carrying the same expression as if she were washing dishes. When she finished, she came, like the rest, to watch and smile at me, the one who escaped.

Cookie, these days calling herself 'Simone', though she couldn't be anything other than 'Cookie' to me, saw me looking at Jennifer. "She using chicken pill, is that make her batty (bottom) look so fat and round," she told me, chuckling. "She say that her man come from St Mary and love woman with big batty, and she don't want him to cheat on her, so she using the fowl pill. You see her breast dem how dem look like dem have in implant? Same thing. And look on the acne! Nothing she take can get rid of it!"

Cookie did not say these words in subdued tones for me alone to hear. Jennifer's trials and tribulations were common knowledge to everyone. A few of the kids looked at her and laughed. I thought about her going to look for a job and whether people could see beyond her acne, ass and worthlessness. I wondered whether she had considered the option of petitioning some world body to declare an International Acne Free Day to see if she would get some relief. And I remembered my second wife discussing some drug called Accutane. She had said that acne might scar, but Accutane might kill. I am not sure why I remembered those things then.

"You want something to drink?" Cookie offered. I would be expected to pay for such a drink whether I had one or not, because I had come from 'foreign', was her cousin, and, clearly, had cash. I accepted the offer, and she sent her youngest son three houses up the lane to another house to buy two sodas. More specifically, to the house of one of my female cousins, Deborah, who now lived with an older man. Cookie told me that Deborah and her man were both selling the same things, like soda and cigarettes, and would quarrel when people bought from one and not the other. The common-law husband had glaucoma though, and could not see very well when folks were approaching; as such, my cousin would sometimes creep outside the house with a couple of products in her hand to sell to whoever was coming, before her man could hear them coming.

I hadn't seen Cookie in a few years, but it made no difference to the ease between us. We were family. We could pick up on a long-forgotten conversation and continue where we had left off. We could be open. She was abrupt:

"Them use to fuck me hard you know." I knew who she was referring to, but not why she had brought that up. "You know the part I never did like?"

The kids were still hearing the conversation. Was it the fact that people thought she was a whore? The lack of foreplay? The hard drilling deep inside her well?

"The way some of them use to jam them tongue in me throat. I never did like that." I hadn't expected that part. "You did know that Tall Man used to do that to me?" I said no, she said "Yes," with no signs of shame, "from I was about seven."

Tall Man was her papa. Back then Aunt Josephine used to work late helping to take care of an elderly couple. The man was a doctor who had retired after a stroke in his early sixties. It had fallen on his poor wife who herself was in her sixties and feeble, to take care of him. Needing help, she hired my aunt. After that, she was always at work.

Cookie explained that Tall Man used to suck on her chest as if he was trying to suction out her undeveloped breasts. That he would fondle her coochie. She had liked that part. She would play in his hair while he was doing it to her. He used to bring her candies those days. She had felt like a favorite child. I realized it was because I had said that I was planning to write a book, that she was telling me all of that.

She had lost at least two teeth that I could see, and the cavities in a few others didn't need daylight to be visible. She had fraying, fatty, coarse skin. Sweat had darkly stained the armpits of her blouse. The thought had crossed my mind whether if I had known what she would look like at thirty-nine, I would have fucked her when she was eleven.

The house still had the same wooden floor. A plank was missing, and I could see the earth beneath, where a small platoon of ants seemed to be heading. There were two mattresses on the floor, sheets bundled in a corner. Clothes were lying around, hanging from the little table and two chairs.

Outside an offer was made to buy lotto for anyone interested. "I only want 10% of the winnings, or a night with you sister or daughter or goat, but not if it's a ram goat!" Some things had not changed.

There was the sound of a motorbike and someone saying that Vin(cent) come home for him lunch, and they hoped Foo Foo had it ready. If she didn't, perhaps what happened to Georgie would happen to her, I thought.

I could see the house that Georgie lived in through Cookie's window.

The soda was harsher than I expected. Cookie offered a glass with ice, I said no thanks, that this is fine.

"You remember Georgie?" I asked her. Cookie would be one of the few who would remember. My brother Martin was still somewhere in the Bahamas, his mind who-knows-where. Brian, of course, was waiting on the Final Trumpet to call for him to rise again. So too Tommy. Garnet was long gone. Wayne was working in a restaurant in Toronto, and still spitting in people's food. Cudjoe, with his severed toe, was living with his baby mama in Westmoreland. Tiny Tim, though still around, had been too young back then to know much about Georgie, or anything else for that matter. Our inner circle had narrowed.

"Him buddy (penis) did little." She chose to start there for reasons known only to her. "Him puppa used to beat the shit out a him." I had known not to expect organized thought. "You remember that him kill him puppa?"

All these things I had known. I wanted to know what she thought about him and what he was like, and whether she remembered what happened while he was in Juvenile Penitentiary and after he got out. The reference to Georgie's papa brought her attention back to memories of her own papa.

"You know, is because of Tall Man why I start liking sex." She wanted her story to come out. She was aware that her time was drawing nigh, and that when the history of the world is written it may mention her country and Bob Marley, but it was very unlikely that her name would be mentioned. She wanted her own story told. She wanted to be in my book.

The sky had gotten cloudy as though it was getting ready to rain. I looked around and saw one of the trees I used to sometimes shelter underneath. Tiny Tim, who was asthmatic, had told me he could tell when it would rain, as you can smell the rain on the wind. His bronchial passage was conditioned to know when it was time for him to go inside.

The stage was by then fully set. All around us were the stagehands, the props, the stand-ins, the cast. Someone I was told was my second cousin, was standing at the door nursing a baby whose hair was so white it looked oddly as though the child was prematurely aging. I reckoned the child, whose gender I couldn't tell, had perhaps stood at her feet while she made the dough to make dumplings, and the flour had scattered all over its head. Or it could have been dandruff. Another young cousin stood beside them, staring at me with *a sinister old butler in a haunted mansion* creepiness.

I knew there was not much more information I would get from Cookie. After I finished talking with her, I came back around to where you were and we started saying farewell to Aunt Josephine and Carmen. This, as you recall, is when it occurred. We were getting ready to visit another relative and were standing at Aunt Josephine's gate.

I am not sure whether you sensed it too, but I felt his presence before I saw him. It was as though I had a connection to him, and subliminally knew to expect him at that moment.

Cookie had told me that he was 'lying low' as he was being hunted (again) by the police for some crime he had committed (again). It seemed he had now surfaced, was hungry and was roaming the neighborhood like a rabid dog.

I sensed the parting of the crowd and when he came behind me I felt his breath on the back of my neck, foul and rotten like the corpses he slept with. And I heard the dry, cold hollowness in his voice as he said, "Kenny."

Garnet's son and I had never met before, but he had obviously heard about me. I guess everyone had, even the little second and third cousins now growing up. Because I was the famous one that had gotten away. And they had all seen the car and the clothes and smelled the scent of escape. So he came, to see the Kenny that had played with his papa, that had played with Tommy, that had lived in that same *hateful* fucking yard as him, decades ago.

"Gimme two thousand dollars!" It wasn't a question as such. More of a threat in the guise of a statement. You heard it as well, so I guess you know what I mean. Two thousand Jamaican dollars is not a lot of money, less than US$30 dollars; it wasn't the sum of money that was important.

The sudden surge of fear in my cousin Carmen's eyes as she beheld him approaching us from behind, may have helped flick the switch in me. Because in an instant, I knew I no longer ever wanted to be afraid - not of that place, not of anyone nor anything. But it wasn't just that look in her eyes that sparked this feeling.

And it wasn't the shock of his menace. Though the letters I received had rarely mentioned him, the few occasions they did were enough for me to know what manner of a creature he had become.

I have spent months trying to tie that moment to the events of my childhood, looking for connections in all the things that happened to me and the people around me. I find I come back to the same spot. It was simply this: something inside me rebelled at the obvious expectation that things should be given to him. The full thought did not come back to me in that minute, but a shard of it did.

I immediately remembered Karl, one of my friends in college. My mind did not have time to go much beyond that, but it didn't need to, for it was already conditioned. Karl. His hair was already thinning even then, as though his brain could handle neither mental nor physical weight. Karl, who said that he always walked with his hands clasped behind him in stores, because if his hands were free at his sides, store-owners always thought he was going to steal something. Because he had *that look*. Even though he came from a middle-class family and was one of the first to get a telephone. A joker about his life and adventures; a joke in the classroom. He always performed poorly. And then he dropped out.

Unlike Lodenquai, who rarely partied, was always pleasant, always smiling, and always knew the answers to all the questions about everything. Lodenquai. (This was his last name but it was easier to pronounce than his overly-foreign sounding first, so everyone called him by it. Also, I cannot now remember his first). Always worked hard. He had seriously narrow-slit Chinese eyes, such that whenever he smiled, you thought "he's going blind now."

I had dreamt about the two of them once. They were walking in a desert searching for water. In the dream I saw Karl walking for miles under the blazing-hot sun before falling to his knees and then on his face and just lying there, dying. Then I saw Lodenquai, with his yellow skin, less prepared for the heat but walking nonetheless. Walking and walking for miles and miles under the same blazing-hot sun. Then he fell to his knees, but put his hands on the ground and crawled on, for another few miles. Until he fell on his face. But while on his face he rolled on, for a few more yards. And when he could roll no more, I saw him close his eyes to begin transcendental meditation to transport his spirit to the water while his body died. A few weeks after this dream, Karl was no longer in college, but Lodenquai was still there, politely smiling at all the mean Chinese jokes, and *willing* his way to a better life, while others were falling behind, dropping out, dropping down and staying down. That was a turning point for me. I believe it was the moment I understood what it would take to make it in life.

Now, here was Garnet's son making even less of an effort than Karl, stating, "I won't walk in the desert. You go and bring me the water."

I turned to face him. That's when I saw what must have been the famous knife.

I could describe what he looked like, what the houses looked like, what my cousin Carmen looked like and what the day was like. But it is now Thursday and a quarter to midnight, so I must end this story before 12 a.m. Moreover, such descriptive details of things only form the backdrop to our lives. The things that matter are the people - the things they did and the things that happened to them. For all intents and purposes then, each house was just a house; Carmen looked like Carmen, and the day was just a day. They, and the trees, birds and smells all served the same purpose and conducted themselves in the same general manner that they always did. Neither colors, nor scents, nor anything else, had any significance in what happened at that moment or at any other time.

I looked at him. Right in his eyes. And I said, firmly and simply, "No." It was the appropriately timed "No" I had agreed with the devil. And thus, right then the devil took my soul.

That was all it was. It happened, just like that.

My Uncle Bob used to say that Religion will neither cure nor protect us, and neither will Superstition.

I am sorry that I too couldn't protect you my love.

This is everything, all the things that I can recall about what happened before and since. I have copied some of my notes and letters and poems from my journals. I never shared some of these with you, or never had the chance. Some were written while you were awake, others since you've been asleep. They all tell my story.

Perhaps if I were to search long and hard I would find something profound in all of it; something that the world could take note of, be guided by, benefit from. Something more than "We are who we are" and "What will be will be." But the day is escaping, and it is almost midnight now, my love.

$14.95 would have been a really fine price for my book.

I have been with no other woman since I met you.

With you I have known love, and I have loved you more than I have loved my God.

Good night, and I hope to see you soon.

Your Royal Soupyness.

Acknowledgements

I would like to thank my wife for her tremendous support throughout the arduous process of writing this novel. Without her encouragement, I may have given up along the way. The cover design for the novel was done by my ever creative daughter. I worry about her sometimes. Many friends and colleagues have provided helpful comments on various parts of the story that were shared on my blog. I am grateful to them all. Finally, let me thank my editor, Emma Good, for the thorough job she did in cleaning up the draft and also for both the encouraging words and the frank criticisms that helped me to improve the story.

Printed in Great Britain
by Amazon.co.uk, Ltd.,
Marston Gate.